Marc Hammond is the pseudonym of a well-known writer of best-selling thrillers. This is his first Futura Spectacular.

Other Futura Spectaculars:

Marc Hammond

Fathom

Futura Publications Limited
A Futura Book

A Futura Book

First published in Great Britain by
Futura Publications Limited in 1978

Copyright © Marc Hammond 1978

ISBN 0 7088 1423 9

Printed in Canada

Set in V.I.P. Baskerville
on the Pentamatic system

Futura Publications Limited
110 Warner Road,
Camberwell, London SE5

CHAPTER ONE

Brambles in the hedge-rows bore thick black fruit and wasps buzzed everywhere, eating their fill. The stems of the brambles were thick, too, with sharp thorns lying along them, hopelessly intertwined. The grass was lush along the side of the track, and already his boots and the bottoms of his trousers were wet. The sun shone in the tops of the trees, occasionally sending a single shaft of light down into the small clearings below, through which he walked. This path had not been used for a considerable time and few knew of its existence. He had seen it on an old Ordnance Survey map as a meagre dotted line. It did not show on later editions, nor on the military maps, confirmed by aerial photography. One mile to go, through this deserted forgotten glade, deep in these silent woods where only buzzing insects broke an age-old cathedral peace. Acorns on the ground, in their cups, told him not even squirrels lived here; nor had rabbits disturbed the soil of the grassy banks with their tunnels. Here, nature lived in balance with itself, undisturbed by animals; the chestnut thickets sprouted, elm trees were slowly being strangled by lichens growing from the heavy warts on their trunks, oaks bore mistletoe in profusion, assuring their own inevitable death, seeding, and rebirth.

John Libby walked along the path.

At least, he had learned to answer, react, and even think like John Libby. And that was the most difficult part of assuming another identity.

He had learned to fight with his bare hands, a knife, a cord or a short smooth polished rod of wood. He had learned to shoot a pistol with either hand or both, to fire a rifle from his left or his right shoulder, to make a bomb that would crack a railway line, destroy a bridge, blow down a house, or blow up a car. He had learned to walk silently over concrete pavements, up wooden staircases, even across the shingle of a shore, and through dense undergrowth. He had learned how to make saliva when he was thirsty, how to digest grasses, uncooked meats, and blood.

And how to withstand the pain of interrogation.

He was an Englishman, born in Manchester in 1947, nine months to the day after his father returned from the war.

Abraham had two wives, Sarah and Hagar. From Sarah came Israel. From Hagar came Ishmael. The blood-line comes from the mother.

His mother, a descendant of Hagar, worked in a cotton spinning mill. Her identity card said she was British. His father was British; his Army pay-book said so. They conceived and she was delivered of a British child. When the child grew to be twenty, he enlisted in the British Army and volunteered for the Parachute Regiment. When he left the Army, a Captain in the Special Services, his colonel pleaded with him to stay. 'You're just the type we need in the Regular Army,' the Colonel had said. 'Why throw it all away to take some scribbler's job in a grubby office in Civvie Street?'

The Captain did not intend to 'throw it all away'.

John Libby, one of his corporals, had fallen in love with a Chinese prostitute in Hong Kong, deserted the Army, gone to live with her, and disappeared. The Captain had found out, from special sources, that Corporal John Libby had been quietly dropped into Kowloon Bay by friends of the prostitute's pimp. The Army posted him missing, believed killed in action, and forgot about him.

When the Captain left the Army, he travelled to Totnes, in Devon, and obtained an official copy of John Libby's birth certificate. With it, he provided himself with a British passport, and a double identity.

He could become John Libby whenever necessary.

He was six feet tall, with black hair which gleamed naturally without benefit of oil. His dark brown eyes were flecked with green and had a steady, disconcerting stare. Though his shoulders were wide, the rest of his body was thin, almost emaciated, since he carried no fat. Only wiry,

6

immensely strong muscles. For a man of his height, he could move amazingly swiftly, striking like a serpent, his hand or arm, foot or knee, elbow, shoulder or head flashing out with speed and stunning force. At rest, sitting on a chair, squatting on his heels on the ground, even lying along a bed, he had the coiled potential of a cobra.

Half a mile to go through the wood. Now he could hear birds in the tops of the trees, rooks cawing loud above the buzz of the wasps. Yes, they'd be there, within bird-sight. Ready to scavenge among the detritus of human beings.

They'd given the retired Captain a job. 'Just the type we want,' the Managing Director had said. 'Keep your nose clean with us and the top of the tree is yours for the asking. And since we're a brand new industry, the ladder you'd have to climb is not a long one.'

Area Manager had been far enough and he had made that in six months. Selling came easy to a retired Captain; after all, hadn't he needed to sell his men every new situation they had ever gone into? Every new parachute drop they'd made? Every new war they'd helped somebody else to fight? The technological side had been no problem; he had a basic knowledge of electronics, radio, radar, covert and overt surveillance systems. It had seemed almost inevitable that he should become Area Manager of Security Systems Ltd, with more government contracts than they could handle.

These included the ultra top secret Ministry of Defence establishment, the Harwell Centre, buried in the Oxfordshire countryside. Britain's stock-pile of atomic weapons. It was in the woods. A quarter of a mile ahead.

Of course, the employees of Security Systems Ltd, as private citizens, were not supposed to know what the Harwell Centre contained. Ostensibly, it was the headquarters and depot of a company set up by the government for the development and marketing of peaceful products of atomic energy. They explored radiation techniques for medical and scientific purposes, the preservation of food, the cleaning of isotopes for reuse, and the production of harmless helium 7 for weather forecasting.

7

The Captain knew, from the pillow-talk of an infatuated lady scientist employed in the Harwell Centre, that Building B, said to be used for the machinery in which the 'dirty' isotopes were 'cleaned', was also the store for seven atomic warheads. Each one was capable of destroying all life within a mile radius of the point of explosion, and of totally polluting, for at least a year, the ground and structures within a wider circle of thirty miles.

He continued walking down the path through the woods. A wasp settled briefly on his neck. His hand flicked up and he caught it between his finger and thumb, squashing it before it had time to sink its barb into him. He was on schedule. His mind was a blank, deliberately washed clean of all thoughts which did not relate to the job he was going to do. His sixth sense was tuned to the trees of the wood and the undergrowth his eyes constantly probed. His ears were alert for the slightest sound beyond the buzz of the insects, the cries of the birds. From somewhere ahead he heard the hum of the large compressor, outside Building A. As he drew nearer, other sounds could be recognised — the high-pitched whine of the electric trolleys the Centre used, the throb of the dynamo that supplied electricity independent of outside sources. And the rush of air from the giant air-conditioning fans mounted on the roof of Building B.

The tree was young for an oak — about twenty-five years old and not yet grown to its full height or width. The Captain approached it from the south, taking his compass bearing from a hundred yards away. Only a close examination revealed the vertical cuts in the bark, the two horizontals, the two points on which he placed his fingers and pressed. The bark opened on hinges, revealing a slot six inches tall, four inches wide. Inside the slot was a thin metal case with three metal knobs on its side. He pulled on a rubber glove, grasped the centre knob, and turned it clock-wise as far as it would go.

He reached up to the top knob and carefully turned that, too, the equivalent of fifteen minutes on a clock face.

He left the bottom knob untouched.

The side of the black box contained a recess bearing an aluminium printed plate with the insignia of Security Systems Ltd. The black box emitted a beam six feet in height, a quarter of an inch thick. Anyone walking through that beam would set off a silent alarm within one of the four security rooms, one on each corner of the Harwell Centre complex. Sixteen such beams emitted from and received by sixteen such boxes, each concealed within the trunk of a tree, provided the Harwell Centre with its first perimeter warning system.

An electrified fence, eight feet high, offered the second obstacle. He could see the fence about a hundred yards ahead, clear of the line of the trees. At night it would be patrolled by guards with Alsatian dogs. During the day its length could be surveyed from the tinted one-way windows of the security rooms.

He closed the panel in the trunk of the tree. Now he had de-tuned the beam and could walk through the gap between the trees with impunity. He made his way slowly to the edge of the wood and lay down in the undergrowth. He checked his wristwatch. Six o'clock, exactly. He was on schedule, to the minute.

The experimental station had been built on the outer edges of the Arsenal Maritime in the Petite Rade of the vast port of Toulon. On the landward side, entrance could be gained through a steel door set in the face of a two-story building. Above the door was a sign, Institute for Sonar Research and Experiment. Entry Strictly Forbidden.

Inside the door, a small courtyard contained an office with a bullet-proof window manned by two men and another steel door controlled electronically from within the office.

Jacques Morel had entered the outside door; he walked to the window and spoke into the microphone at its side.

'Good afternoon,' he said. 'I am Jacques Morel, number one seven two four five.'

The decoder read his voice, feeding it into the computer, to compare it with a filed recording. Each voice is as individual as a fingerprint. A voice print can be affected, of course, by medical conditions, but it can never be completely disguised. Mimics sound like their originals only to the untutored human ear, and not to a computer. Jacques's voice passed the test and a green light showed on the console below the window. The guard pressed a switch. 'Good afternoon, Monsieur Morel,' he said. 'You can go in.'

As Jacques approached the second steel door, the lock buzzed and the door opened. Jacques went through a short corridor with rooms at each side and into the first room. He opened his locker by dialling the combination, stripped and placed all his clothing, his watch, his car keys, inside. Naked, he walked to the door at the end of the locker room, opened it and passed into the airlock beyond. He pulled a plastic hood from the wall and placed it over his head. He touched a switch with his finger, and stood with legs apart while jets of air washed all over him. The jets of air inside the hood probed deep inside his hair, blowing any slight traces of scurf that might be lying on his scalp.

He inhaled and exhaled deeply, then reached for the glove on the shelf and scrubbed himself all over. The air jets stopped and were replaced by water jets at body temperature. He continued to scrub himself, knowing the water contained a bacteriostatic neutral pH solution of cetrimide that would clean him more completely than any commercial shampoo. The water jet stopped and he put the glove back on the shelf, which tipped it into a concealed disposal unit. The water started again, rinsing him clean, and then, when it stopped again, the jets of air returned, drying his body all over.

He smoothed his hair down. Always, after the cleansing, it felt soft and silky, and his whole body tingled, as if he had just had an exotic massage. Often, when the warm air blew on him, he got an instant erection and felt an almost uncontrollable urge to masturbate, despite the sterility of his surroundings.

Today, there was no erection.

When the air jets switched themselves off, he went through the far door of the lock into a room containing shelves of white clothes, of man-made fibre. The first garment fitted around his legs, his waist, his arms, his neck, effectively sealing in his natural exudations. He put on a skull cap that completely covered his hair, a boiler suit that zipped up the outside and a pair of soft boots.

Now he was ready for work. He went through into the large room beyond. One side of the room was covered with television screens and sonar print-out boxes, with computer output display panels and desks at which half a dozen men could sit. Now there were only four men and a girl in the room. He went round it, shaking hands with each one of them, saying, 'good afternoon,' with cool, scientific detachment. Even the woman seemed dehumanized here, locked within the hygienic sterility of the uniform that hid every trace of her femininity. 'Good afternoon, Sophie. Ça va?'

'Oui, ça va. You ready to go?'

'Yes, quite ready.'

Jacques Morel was thirty, a graduate of the Sorbonne and of the Massachusetts Institute of Technology. He had lived all his life, apart from educational trips abroad, in France. Five feet ten inches tall, weighing one hundred and fifty pounds, he had crinkly hair of a dark red-black hue that women found enchanting. His nose had been broken when he was twenty-five; slightly flattened in the centre and pushed a little off-side, it gave his features a fascinating lack of symmetry, heightened by his slightly crinkled, twisted smile. His mother lived in Paris, in a small alleyway off the Rue de la Mouette.

Five families lived in the house, all once refugees from what is now known as the Gaza Strip.

Jacques's grandfather had been killed by the Haganah, when he was guiding a British patrol.

An old daguerreotype picture of him occupied the place of honour on his mother's wall. Jacques's mother had never ceased to speak of him to her son. 'Your father's father was a good man,' she would say. 'And he died badly. Your father went back in 1950 and became one of the *fedayeen*. He too died badly. Both were brave men and died badly. You must be courageous, but careful.'

'I will be brave. I will not die badly,' Jacques had promised.

Today, he would fulfil the first part of that promise, made so often, and for so long.

The Green Dolphin had grown from a drogue developed originally by the French Institute of Oceanography as an acoustic remote control telemetry system, a listening device that could be towed in the water far from the throb of a boat's engines.

It was a logical development to make the drogue self-propelled, to make it submerge and surface under command from the mother ship, and fully manoeuvrable. It was also logical to equip it with an isotope-decay motor, to screen it and make it sound-absorbent so that it would not interfere with the echo-sounding system being used by the scientists to map the bed of the ocean.

It took a military mind – Jules Lachard of the French Navy – to recognize that the Institute was developing a military weapon of great potency. A submarine that could not be detected by sonar, that could roam anywhere in the Deeps under control from a coded sonar source and carry an explosive warhead. From that moment, the development of the weapon was classified, placed under the control of the French Navy, and transferred to the Institute for Sonar Research and Development. The scientists were screened by the Deuxième Bureau and French Naval Intelligence. Those who passed were conscripted into the French Navy.

Jacques Morel was given the rank of Lieutenant.

Jules Lachard himself was given the rank of Commander, and put in charge of the programme. A scientist by training, but a sailor by breeding and inclination, he was the leading French authority on submarine control and guidance systems, on underwater navigation and sonar.

Jules was sitting in the control room when Jacques arrived. His usual bottle of Beaujolais was by his right hand. Despite the strictly controlled temperature and humidity, he was sweating, and his uniform had enormous damp patches below the arm-pits. He glared at the clock when he saw Jacques's perfunctory salute but Jacques grinned at him, refusing to be intimidated. Today, Lieutenant Jacques Morel could afford to behave like a prima donna. He was the man selected to take the Green Dolphin on her maiden voyage.

'We've checked and double checked,' the Commander said. 'Everything works perfectly. We're ready for the sea trial when you are.'

'I'd like to test it in the tank myself.'

'Jean Luc had it in the tank for fifteen minutes.'

'I'd still like to check it.'

The two men looked at each other in the silence that followed Jacques's flat statement. Of all the scientists present, only Jacques had the nerve consistently to stand up to the senior officer. 'You're wasting time,' Jules said, and turned away. 'Let's get on with the voyage.'

'Do you have another pilot?' Jacques asked quietly, knowing the answer. Claude, aged fifty-five, a brilliant theoretician, couldn't even swim. Sophie knew nothing about the sensing systems since she'd concerned herself exclusively with directional navigation. Pierre Lachasse was a computer expert, Gaspar Delaville a nuts-and-bolts man.

'Okay,' he said grudgingly. 'Ten minutes, in the tank.'

The tank was a large shed built partly below the outside sea-level. One wall of it contained a number of thick plate-glass windows. Half way up the wall, on a gantry approached by a staircase, a platform carried duplicates of the instruments in the main control room. The control team took up their positions. Lights behind plate-glass heat-absorbing panels gave the tank an eerie, phosphorescent glow. Jacques waited at the top of the tank, wearing a mask and flippers, with a small airbottle strapped to his back. He heard the control team going through the necessary pre-launch jargon. Then, when they were ready, he dropped smoothly into the water carrying a torch, a brass dinner gong, and a heating element operated from a battery strapped around his waist below his lead-weight belt.

The far door of the tank slid smoothly open to reveal a totally dark cave, in which nothing moved. Jacques began to tap the gong with the rubber torch. Though nothing could be heard, the sound vibrations went through the water and were heard by the Green Dolphin's sensors. The Dolphin moved forward, slowly, towards the source of the sound.

It was nine metres long, two metres in diameter, with a long blunt snout. Its skin glistened green in the diffused light. Jacques grinned when he saw it. Someone, no doubt Jean Lúc, had painted an evil eye on each side of the snout, and a long row of teeth, copying the advertisement for the film, 'Jaws'.

It came slowly towards the source of the sound.

Jacques stopped beating the gong. It stopped. He kicked his flippers and swam to the right of it. Then he beat the gong again. It turned right, and came towards him. For two minutes it followed him, left and right, up and down, around the interior of the tank, each of its control systems reacting perfectly.

He clipped the gong to his waist and switched on the torch light, aiming in at the Dolphin. Now it reacted to the source of light. Again, by switching the torch on and off, Jacques made it follow him around the tank. Viewed from straight ahead, with that cruel mouth, those teeth and eyes, it was a menacing sight. Even though Jacques knew every part of its construction, even though he was watching its operation with scientific detachment, he still felt a shiver of fear.

He switched off the torch and hung it on his belt. Now it was the turn of the heating coil. The reactions were slower, but still there. The beast still sensed the coil from a distance away and came towards it. This part of the control system would not be of great value in operation. The sea changes temperature the greater the depth, and there are many unexplained heat pockets, some as much as fifteen degrees above the surrounding temperature. The heat sensor function would therefore be tuned down in operation, since it would tend to make the Dolphin rise always to the surface. But in the event of a failure in the other apparatus, Jacques would rely on it to bring the Dolphin safely up into the warmer water near the surface.

He switched off the coil, which cooled rapidly. Then he swam across to the Dolphin, put his arm round its snout and patted it, as if it were truly alive. During the months they had been working with it, the Dolphin had often seemed so. They called it 'la Delfine Verte', and, especially at times of malfunction, had cursed it as a man curses a woman he loves. Even Jules Lachard, cold, domineering, ruthless bully that he was, seemed to soften a little when he spoke of her.

Jacques turned to the control room panel, gave the thumbs up sign, and swam to the surface of the tank. Now, after all these months of preparation and waiting, both he and the Delfine, together, were ready to go.

CHAPTER TWO

The building was tucked behind 11 Downing Street; the men who entered and left it were typical civil servants. Inside the front door a commissionaire who knew every face personally kept the keys of each of the offices locked in a drawer of his desk.

There were twelve rooms in the building.

The offices had all been furnished in uniform manner, with two desks, two leather chairs by a small coffee table, one chair (executive) with a comfortable seat and back, and one chair (secretary) about which the girls had made many unsuccessful protests and complaints. All had tried to solve the problem by bringing in cushions, back rests, or seat pads. None had been entirely successful.

Bill Harrington worked in number 5, which, like the others, bore no name on its door. His secretary, Joan Wells, was thirty, a Cambridge graduate in Modern Languages, pretty, and very married. Her husband was something in the Ministry of Education. They were both vegetarians and took their holidays every year camping in the north of

Scotland. Bill Harrington was forty, with an already receding hairline. He ate meat, but played squash three times a week to keep himself trim. He, too, was a graduate of Cambridge in Modern Languages but, unlike Joan, spent much of his time abroad and was fluent in German, French, Spanish, Italian, Greek and Russian. As a member of the Intelligence Unit of the Counter-Espionage Service he needed to be. His specific job was to receive reports from British agents in the field, from the Intelligence Services which maintained an exchange of information with the British, as well as from the supra-national organizations such as NATO, and to evaluate them for information and possible action.

The machine by his desk was an information terminal through which, by tapping the typewriter keys, he could establish contact with the data base, the memory, on which the Intelligence Unit constantly received information from all sources about every known terrorist, every known foreign agent, every known enemy espionage and counter-espionage unit. No information, however trivial it might seem at the time, was neglected. Each morning the secretaries received a wealth of printed and published matter, all of which was coded and added to the data base. The computer itself could search millions of such digits in a second, could correlate them, sift them, select them, and print them out through any selected terminal at hundreds of words a minute.

The box on the floor by Bill Harrington's left foot was a paper shredder in which most of the computer's prodigious output finished up. Except that which was stored in a safe which formed the right hand side of his desk, or in his powerfully retentive memory.

Harrington was head of the Mediterranean Section; his territory included all the countries which bordered the Mediterranean to the north. It was the busiest section in the Unit.

He was looking at the display panel on his desk, his option to full print-out. By pressing a button he could transfer the information the panel presented onto paper, but at the moment he was reading it, trying to evaluate the information it contained. A meeting had been set up in an apartment on the Rue du Longchamps in Paris. The apartment, occupied by Henri Dupree, a former resident of Marseilles, was under observation by the French Drugs Squad, since Dupree was a suspected dealer. The method of surveillance was by long-range television camera and parabolic microphone. The dialogue had all taken place inside the apartment and had not been recorded; the camera had picked up the faces of five men who, from time to time, came onto the balcony that overlooked the Bois de Boulogne. The features of these men had been recorded and identified. They made an unlikely combination.

Henry Dupree – suspected drug smuggler and round-the-world sailor who had equalled Francis Chichester as a pioneer of modern methods of navigation. It could be said that he started where Chichester left off. A fanatical sailor, said to use his income from drugs to finance his maritime activities.

Kostas Aronakis – a Cretan who had achieved brief international fame after escaping from an island gaol where he had been imprisoned by the Colonels, by sailing a caique single-handed through one of the fiercest storms that part of the Mediterranean had ever known.

Andreas Burgler – suspected of being a member of the Baader-Meinhoff gang and an international liaison officer between them, Black September, the PLA, and the Japanese Shinju Kuji extremists. An expert in radio communications.

Then came two surprising names. The first one was a French naval officer, currently stationed in Toulon, where he was working on Sonar Development. Jacques Morel.

The second was an Englishman. His identification had only been made possible by searching the Ministry of Defence files – a routine procedure for the computer of the Intelligence Unit. He was revealed as a man who had been given clearance to work on secret installations on behalf of the Ministry for a private company, Security Systems Ltd.

He was a former Captain of the Parachute Regiment, attached to Special Services. Joseph Aram.

Bill Harrington punched the button that cleared the visual display screen and transferred its contents to a sheet of printed paper. He tapped the keys of his typewriter terminal, not needing to refer to the coded instruction book. Within seconds, the complete Ministry of Defence dossier on Joseph Aram was spread on the screen. He scanned it quickly, noting the documents it listed. Birth Certificate, Schools, University, Army entrance, Army Commission, Army discharge. Application form for his job with Security Systems Ltd. S.S. Ltd application for security clearance for an employee. His own application. His interview.

He printed that display on a sheet of paper, tore it from the machine, and handed it to Joan. 'Could you process that?' he asked. 'And make up a file, please.'

'Shall I search the police records?' she asked.

'Yes, we might as well, though I don't anticipate finding anything.'

'You never know – he might have got a parking ticket.'

Most of the time, Harrington worked on instinct. A name would leap off the visual display screen at him, a name that for some reason should not be there. Joseph Aram smelled clean to him. Almost too clean. Good school record, good degree; did well in the Paras, good commission, good promotion, got out at the right time, and found a good job. Too clean a record to be marred by any civilian police offence, such as dangerous driving, illegal parking. 'I get the feeling Captain Aram likes being on the right side of things,' he said. 'But it does no harm to look.'

Joan had been studying the dossier Bill had handed her. 'No marriage,' she said. 'We might find something there.'

Again, Bill shook his head, but this time he was smiling. 'All you married girls,' he said, 'take it personally if a man isn't hitched by thirty. It doesn't mean he's queer, you know.'

'And the fact that he's a tough guy from the Paras doesn't mean he's hetero, either.'

Bill had an instinctive feeling. 'On the right side, our

Captain Aram. And that means, if you'll pardon the expression, no encumbrances like a wife and a family.'

She had no answer to that. Bill had been divorced the previous year. Though mutual incompatibility was the reason given, the Intelligence Unit should have been cited as co-respondent. He spent at least six months of every year somewhere in his territory, and no wife could ever cope with that. Enid had been no angel; she'd found herself a man with a good steady law practice, a man who never wanted to move further than his office, his home, his four weeks holiday somewhere in the sun.

'You'll find somebody else, one day, Bill,' she said, then turned and went back to her own desk, avoiding the sardonic look that came to his eye. He looked blankly at the wall for a moment, clearing his mind of the whole panorama Joan had introduced, wiping clean the memory of the hurt, the pain.

He bent down and stared at the list of names again. Five men, meeting in an apartment in the Bois de Boulogne district of Paris. Three men with sea connections, two without. Three men with previous histories, two without. Three older men, two younger. No two from the same country. It was like trying to solve a crossword puzzle backwards, by thinking of all the words that would fit a set of spaces without bothering, as yet, with the clue. Why did they meet? What did they have, what could they possibly have, in common?

He looked at the neat precision of his office, the computer terminal, video screen, paper print-out, magnetic card storage. The functional desk, safe, the paper shredder. No filing cabinets nor pictures on the wall to distract his eye. No pots of flowers nor climbing plants, a comfortable secretary who, though pretty and pleasing, did not disturb his masculinity. Everything efficient, functional. And yet, how much of his activity started from something random, like this, a report of a chance surveillance by another department, a little additional information in which the department itself had no interest.

This one had begun when he had been reading a report

of three known Irishmen who had been apprehended in Athens airport boarding a plane for Germany. Each of them, when searched, had been found to be carrying, concealed in books, a large quantity of US dollars. It is not an offence to take dollars into or out of Greece. Why, then, had the money been concealed? The Greek authorities had asked the British authorities for information about the three Irishmen, whom they were holding in custody.

Bill had supplied the information.

Thinking about the trip to Germany, he had asked himself if they could be going there to buy arms, ammunition, explosives. He had asked the North European man, Jim Stacey, who was currently supplying arms to West Germany, and had received a remembered name, Andreas Burgler. He had tapped the computer to research the data base, at random, for information about Burgler's known movements, and the meeting in Paris, entered in the memory bank three days ago as a piece of knowledge of possible future use, had been printed out. Almost idly, he had asked the computer who else attended the meeting. And the five names had resulted.

Why? he asked himself. Why could they possibly be holding such a meeting in Paris?

CHAPTER THREE

Dutch George was sitting on the side of the Zodiac inflatable, staring moodily out to sea. The water was as still as a sheet of glass; the surface had the oily texture he knew from experience would mean a storm during the night. Dutch George liked storms. He liked the wildness of lightning and electricity in the air, thunder filling your ears and water slashing at your face. He liked the clean taste of it and the sense of danger and excitement it brought. George sucked at excitement the way some people drained a bottle of brandy. A placid life was death to George; an ordered existence provoked wild instincts and the urge to break away. Just now he was feeling the approaching boredom again and knew he would have to do something to break out of the rut. The diving school was going well and every day they had their quota of ten pupils. He had no doubt that when these ten people ended their holiday on Friday and returned to Northern Europe they would be replaced by another ten, already booked for diving instruction.

George's prices were high but the instruction was good and nobody who had taken a diving course ever left Ibiza without feeling confident thirty metres below the surface of the sea. But for Dutch George himself something was lacking, an element of the excitement and danger on which he thrived. He put the glass-bottomed bucket into the water and looked down at the pupils below. The water, made clear by the glass of the bucket bottom, revealed Hans and Elise in their black rubber wetsuits with the vivid yellow dayglow stripes. He could see the ten pupils clustered in a ring around them at a depth of twenty metres, practising the delicate art of bouyancy adjustment, breathing in deeply to cause themselves to rise, exhaling deeply to sink again. They looked like some enormous submarine plant with its fronds undulating in the water. As George watched, Hans made the sign for them to dive deeper and the plant sank another ten metres, each person holding hands with the two people next to him. Now would come the 'buddy breathing exercise' in which each man would share the air supply of his companion. Then they would take off the bottles and put them back on again, resting on the wide ledge they used for training, thirty metres below the surface.

He wet the inside of his face mask, rubbed it with his fingers and put it on his head. With the demand valve in his mouth, he did a backwards flip off the side of the rubber dinghy, plunging in a straight dive to where the school was working. These were the blue-green translucent depths, the only place where he felt truly happy. This was a perfect site for the job, with its broad ledge running out from the cliff face about a mile out of the harbour. Here they could do thirty-metre training in safety. The shelf extended forty metres and then plummeted another hundred or more to the seabed below.

In the crevices of the deeper rock face, lobsters and crayfish abounded. George took a quick look at the school. Everyone seemed happy, enjoying the new experience of this wonderful submarine world. He swam across to Hans and signalled that he was going over the edge. Hans asked if he would like Elise to accompany him, conforming to their school regulation that no man ever dived alone. This time George shook his head, went to the edge and did a head first free fall down into the depths, plunging vertically, parallel with the face of the rock.

Twenty metres down was the first of the many crevices in which he could usually find a lobster or two. The crevice extended deeply back into the vertical rock face. He swam in carefully, his eyes adjusting to the darkness, and switched on the torch that hung at his wrist.

A pair of eyes looked balefully out at him, and a tentacle unwrapped itself from round a rock, waving through the water at him. He was after something more interesting than octopus. A school of pompano, transfixed by the light, hung in the water like guilty schoolboys caught raiding the larder. In the back of the fifty-foot-deep crevice a dozen shrimps walked along the rock face, long antennae probing the waters ahead.

In the full spectrum light from his torch suddenly the true colour values of everything about him were revealed. The golden and silver stripes of the pompano; the blue, red and purple fronds of a variety of sea anemone; the pale translucent pink of the shrimp; the slimy dark green striped, grey-white underbelly of the octopus. George glanced at his elapsed time watch. Here at fifty metres he could not stay long. When he got back near the surface he would need to decompress one minute for every minute of his dive. George did not like decompression time; it irked him having to lie about at six metres depth for five minutes and then again at three metres for another five minutes; but as an experienced diver he knew he had to do it. He returned to the cavern mouth, looked up at the brighter surface of the water shining above him, then arched his body gently, breathed out, and allowed himself to fall, dropping down through the water.

When he reached the sixty metres depth caution over-came him and he stopped by the mouth of a large vaulted hole in the rock. It extended back as far as his torch would shine and appeared to be at least twenty metres wide and about twenty metres high. He worked his fins gently and moved forward into it, like going into a chapel off the main part of a cathedral. Lobsters clung to the underside of the rock in profusion as big as any he had ever seen, along with crayfish that must have measured fifteen inches in length. He reached out gingerly and took two of the largest lobsters he could see, handling them gently to avoid being stung by their barbs.

He was turning to go when suddenly a sharp glint in the rock from which he had plucked the lobster caught his eye. He swam in close and saw that here the surface, absolutely flat, gleamed yellow. He let one of the lobsters go and it swam away gratefully. He took his knife from the sheath on his leg and gently scraped the rock surface, removing soft green moss for about two inches. In the excitement of his discovery he let the other lobster go, dug into the rock with the point of his knife and carved away a long thin sliver about two inches in length, an inch wide, and half an inch deep that felt smooth and heavy in his hand. He tucked it into his wet-suit, grabbed another couple of lob-sters and made his way back to the surface.

Hans and Elise had taken the school up and were prac-tising body movements at the ten-metres depth where they would stay for the rest of the lesson. George checked at six metres; Hans swam over, took the two lobsters from him and carried them to the surface while George began the decompression treatment that would keep him five minutes at six metres and ten minutes at three metres just below the surface, slowly expelling the nitrogen that had dis-solved in his bloodstream.

When he got back on the boat he said nothing about the find he had made.

*

Dutch George went into the narrow house on the Rembrandtsplein. It could have been the house of a physician, dark and quiet, still and hushed. The girl showed him into the front room on the ground floor and the illusion was completed when she said: 'Dr Becker will see you in a moment.'

Dutch George, like so many men possessed of a violent temperament, was able to sit still and silent when required. He waited patiently for ten minutes, without even glancing at the magazines on the side table. When Dr Becker came in he was wearing spectacles and a white laboratory coat. The light in the room glistened on the high dome of his bald head. His fingers were pink and pudgy, as if they had been immersed too long in pickling solution. He was a fluttery little man and Dutch George took an instant dislike to him.

'You have some identification?' Dr Becker said, his voice surprisingly deep and resonant.

George reached into the pocket of the anorak he was wearing and brought out a handkerchief. It was none too clean and Dr Becker winced when he saw it. George spread it on his knee, sensing what the reaction would be were he to put it on any of Dr Becker's immaculate surfaces. He opened it and produced one of the three slivers to be found there. 'Stick that under a microscope,' he said. 'I imagine it will give me all the identification I need.'

Dr Becker produced an eye-glass from his waistcoat pocket, screwed it in and examined the sliver George had given him. 'It will suffice,' he said. He handed it back to George. 'It has a very interesting structure. From a purely scientific point of view, it would be very interesting to know where you found it, and in what sort of quantity.'

George smiled grimly. 'I'll bet,' he said. 'But you can keep your scientific curiosity for the learned journals. All I want to know is what's in it.'

'There is the question of fee, of course,' Dr Becker said. He sat down and made a chapel of his fingers. 'We're in a hard business and no-one should go unrewarded.'

'How about if I let you keep the sample for a fee.'

Dr Becker moistened his lips with his tongue. 'That would depend on what's in the sample, wouldn't it?'

'Five grams. That would make a lot of settings for the diamonds I know you deal in, the ones that don't go through the legal diamond market.'

'Oh dear, it's going to be like that, is it? I don't think we can do business on those terms.' Dr Becker rose from the chair, but not quickly enough. Dutch George had crossed the space between the two chairs in one single leap, and the thumb and fingers that held Dr Becker's windpipe could have been made of steel.

'Get off your high horse, Becker,' Dutch George said. 'I know all about you. Industrial chemist, gold assayist. You lost your job because you had sticky fingers. You've been a pimp on the fringes of the illegal gold and diamond market for years. You'd ship your own mother to Curaçao if it would make you a florin. What's in my sample?' He let go of Dr Becker's windpipe. After all, there was no point in asking a man questions if he could not live to give you the answers.

Becker swallowed hard, flecks of spittle forming on the side of his mouth. 'It's gold,' he said. 'One hundred percent pure. I should say it's outcrop – I haven't seen quality like that for a long time – and I should also guess from the crystalline structure that there's a lot of it. But you'll need help marketing it. You'll need a friend.'

'With all that gold I can afford to rent one,' Dutch George said. 'Rent-a-friend, haven't you heard? It's the latest thing these days. Much less complicated; when you've finished with them, you get rid of them.'' His hand reached out again and grasped Dr Becker's windpipe. His fingers started to close. Suddenly he heard the faint rustle of velvet behind him and turned to see the big Indonesian stepping from behind the velvet curtain which had hidden the communicating door into the next room. The man had a leather cosh held ready to strike. That was his mistake. George went in hard, low and fast, and his hardened knuckles caught the Indonesian just below his chin in a blow that rocked him back on his heels. Before he could recover,

George had turned round, swinging his arm violently from behind him. The point of his elbow finished off the work his knuckles had begun. There was a rattle from the Indonesian's throat which George didn't wait to hear.

He paused on his way out of the house to adjust his anorak, and walked slowly down the road, crossing the street to the intersecting canal, turning right and walking back down its side.

He picked them up within five minutes. A small man wearing a beret and carrying a sheaf of daffodils, a larger man, bare-headed, with the shoulders of a professional wrestler. There was also a Volkswagen car with a French number plate and a girl at the wheel. He made no attempt to shake them off but headed towards the railway station and walked boldly into the Victoria Hotel. There were five people in the lobby and the man behind the desk was checking the passports of a group of American tourists who had just arrived. The small man with the daffodils stayed outside, the large man followed George into the lobby. George picked up a brochure and leafed idly through it for a few moments to give the large man time to come within earshot. George glanced along the row of mailboxes behind the counter and selected one with a key hanging from it.

'Could I have the key to my room please. Number 278.' The clerk, busy with the passports, did not even bother to look at him. George took the key and went across to the bank of elevators. He rode one to the second floor, walked along to room 278, inserted the key, and opened the door an inch. Then he ran quickly along the corridor, found the fire staircase and slid swiftly down it. At the bottom, a door on the left would lead to the main lobby. He ignored it and went right, through a room which contained baskets of laundry and, at the far end, a door out into the street. He smiled as he walked swiftly away, imagining the look on their faces when they burst into room 278 and found it empty.

CHAPTER FOUR

One man who had been at that meeting in Paris had not walked out onto the balcony overlooking the Bois de Boulogne, and had therefore avoided having his picture taken. He would have been recognized instantly, anywhere.

He too was looking at the list of names, though he had written them in a different order. First on his list was the Frenchman, Jacques Morel. Second was the Englishman, though he used the name John Libby, not Captain Joseph Aram. Then came Dupree, Kostas Aronakis, the Cretan, and finally Andreas Burgler.

It was a carefully chosen, hand-picked team. He had done well to find them. Each was a specialist in his own field, but all had extra abilities which would ensure they worked well together. Some were dedicated, some were mercenaries, but all were loyal to him, Yshtak.

He sipped his glass of mint tea, looking down at the bay below the white rail of his balcony and at his motor launch, the *Revenge*.

A rubber dinghy with a sixty-horsepower engine floated aft of the launch and Tony was doing something to the outboard motor. Penny was sunning herself on the concrete jetty which stretched out into the bay. She had taken off the top of her bikini and her full breasts were as brown as the rest of her body. Later, he would take her into San Antonio and park the white Rolls-Royce in the square. Everyone would look at her, at the car, and few would bother with the man sitting beside her, the man who wore dark glasses day or night, the rich tourist with money to burn on girls and cars and motor launches.

When they returned to the house overlooking the bay, he would tell her he was tired and she would slip away gratefully, to spend the night in the arms of the young man, Tony. It was an equitable arrangement and, what was more important, it gave him the perfect cover – a rich, idle

27

playboy doing what so many men of his country were doing, living it up in the fleshpots of Europe.

Marc Chantal drove his black Renault along the Boulevard St Germain and slipped into the parking area just along the pavement from the Restaurant de la Madeleine. He got out and locked the car, then walked along the Boulevard in the direction of the Church of St Germain, turned right into the Croix Rouge district, and stopped outside a door next to a paper shop. The door opened. Inside was a small lobby containing a metal box of bell-pushes fitted with an Ansaphone lock release. He pressed the button on Apartment 3 twice, paused, and then pressed twice more.

'Qui?'

'C'est moi. Chantal. Sorry I'm late.'

The buzzer sounded and he leaned against the door to open it. Inside, the staircase led to the second floor, on which were three apartments.

There was no staircase to the third, fourth, or fifth floors. He rang the bell on the door of Apartment 3. It was opened from inside by a young man wearing black trousers, a black polo-necked sweater and a leather jacket.

Marc shook hands warmly with him. 'Ça va, Phillipe?'

'Qui, ça marche. The Chief's waiting for you. And "sorry I'm late" was the code for yesterday. Today, it's "hope I'm not too early . . .".'

'Bureaucratic horseshit! You can recognize my voice!'

'Call it horseshit all you want. I'm only obeying orders. You'd better get in there to see him.'

'Later? We eat together?'

'If he doesn't give you a job.'

'More horseshit, eh?' Marc punched Phillipe's arm playfully, but still the blow hurt. 'One of these days, you know, I'll tell him where he can shove his jobs and you and me, we'll start a business of our own.'

'As what? Butchers? It's our only qualification.'

'We could be safe-breakers, professional gigolos, teachers of karate and judo . . .'

'Now who's talking horseshit? Go on, get inside.'

The Chief was sitting behind a vast wooden desk whose top was littered with papers, his spectacles case, his pipes, pipe cleaners, boxes of matches, wine glasses, coffee cups. He had been christened Jean Pierre Malhouette, but for the last four years, since he had come out of hospital with the piece of bullet still in his back to take this desk-bound job, they had all called him nothing but the Chief.

'Where the hell have you been?' he growled when he saw Chantal. It would not take much of a psychologist to realize that his perpetually rough tone stemmed from the knowledge that all the men who worked for him were young and still active. He had once been young and active, and was now pinned to a chair; he felt himself to be growing old before his time. Anyone could have told him that what he now lacked in mobility, he made up for in acuity. He had developed the keenest brain, the most extensive memory, and the most perceptive nose in the business.

'I thought you wanted me to find Daudet?'

'That was yesterday. If you'd asked me today, I could have told you. Daudet's gone, pissed off, done a bunk.'

What was exactly what Chantal had been going to tell the Chief. Daudet had left Paris, in a hurry, by car, in the small hours of the morning. It had taken Chantal hours of slow leg work to find that out. How the hell could the Chief know?

The Chief shrugged his shoulders. 'Elementary logic,' he said. 'Daudet came to Paris to negotiate the sale of plastique, right? The people he was going to sell it to were killed in a shoot-out in Lyons, yesterday. It was in the papers this morning, but Daudet would have his own source of information. With no customers, Daudet isn't the sort to hang around looking at the Eiffel Tower . . . Today, he'll be in Holland, talking to the Irish. I've already sent a signal to Amsterdam. Anyway, forget about Daudet. I've received a signal from your friends, the British.'

'They're not my friends . . .'

'You speak the language . . .'

'So did Charles de Gaulle, and a lot of other people.'

'Shut up and listen for once in your life. There's a story

in today's papers about Dupree, sailing in the Liverpool to Limassol Yacht Race. Use that as an introduction and get inside Dupree's place. While you're in there, try to investigate the lay-out. I want to drop a bug in there. Seems he's having meetings with a number of interesting friends, and I'd like to hear what they talk about.'

'Floor and ceiling microphones from the flats above and below?'

'You trying to teach me my business? They won't work. Those are high priced apartments with an acoustic layer – soundproofing – between each. And he owns the entire floor, so we can't stick anything on the wall.'

'A limpet microphone? I could be a window cleaner . . . ?'

'The apartment is fifteen stories up. The windows are cleaned by the Japanese house-boy, from inside. There are balconies on each side of the building, a terrace on one side. Do you think I'd trust *you* to go inside if I could have found another way? Piss off, and let me know what you find there.'

'Charming, Chief, eh?'

'If you want to be charmed, take Philippe out there and start your own business. As a couple of gigolos. You'd both do very well.'

Marc Chantal was on the phone to his contact at *Paris Match* when the Chief left for the night session of physiotherapy. He suffered perpetual pain from the bullet wound; his face was creased as he hobbled across the outer office using both sticks. Any normal man would have allowed himself to be put in a wheel chair, but not the Chief. No wonder he's such a bastard all the time, Marc thought as he watched him go.

A voice squawked in his ear. 'Okay, Marc, what the hell do you want? I bet it's nothing honest . . .'

'Don't *you* start,' Marc said. 'I've had a bad day as it is. When are you going to do a feature on Dupree, the yachtsman. I want to be there . . .'

'You trying to get me fired? If the paper only knew . . .'

CHAPTER FIVE

Each night, immediately after dark, the alarms of the fence around the Harwell Centre were tested.

Tonight the test would take place near the corner of the south-east section.

The Captain was crouched on the edge of the wood to the north west. He crawled slowly forward towards the wire, and glanced at his watch. The grass was wet, and some of the dampness ran up his cuffs as he moved his arms forward, kneeing himself along the ground, flat as a snake. Even now he remembered the words of the sergeant who taught him fieldcraft all those years ago – 'I want you lower than a gnat's knackers when you cross that field.' Well, he had learned to crawl lower than a gnat's knackers in anticipation of this very moment.

He felt as if he had lived all his life for it. He was confident he could make it work. He had to; the whole scheme depended on him. One cog in a small, efficient machine, meshing with the others like the movement of a precision watch, jewelled by training, lubricated by dedication.

The wire mesh in front of him had been made specially of case-hardened steel links, supported on ceramic bobbins. The system they had installed used induction. The mesh did not need to be touched to cause an alert – any solid object brought within a range of six inches would activate it. The outside fence was not electrified and merely served to keep away stray animals, rabbits, cats, inquisitive humans. One tree grew beside the fence, and about nine feet from it. He climbed the tree rapidly, rustling up the trunk and through the branches. All the timber on the side of the tree by the fence had been sawn away so there was no possible overhang. Viewed from the side, the tree had a curious profile, as if waiting for someone to stick it to its other half.

A metal tube, about two inches in diameter and six feet

long, had been bolted along one branch, strapped to it by metal bands two inches wide, a quarter of an inch thick. The Captain knew it was secure; he had attached it himself the previous week when he was testing the perimeter on behalf of the company. Now he reached inside the end of the tube and started to pull out the other tubes, arranged telescopically inside it. The tubes were made of high tensile steel, with very little whip to them. He kept looking at his watch as he worked. By ten minutes past eight, the long tubes extended like a fishing pole across the first fence.

He waited.

At eight fifteen exactly, the lights came on above the south-east sector where one of the guards had activated the induction system by placing his hand near the mesh.

The Captain pushed the fishing rod tubes all the way open and then rapidly slid across the wire.

The act of switching on the lights turned off the induction system, but not the fence electrification.

The pole bent beneath his weight, arching downwards. The strapping on the branch groaned. The branch itself lifted slightly and the leaves shook on the twigs along its length. You had to take a chance, sometimes. Everything else could be plotted, calculated, worked out. The choice of steel, the diameter of the pole, the method of fixing the sections together so they would slide part way but not pull out, the spring loading, everything. Except the strength of the branch of that tree. Certainly, he had been able to calculate its theoretical strength. It was twelve inches in diameter where it left the trunk. But who could tell if it were sound? If, perhaps, the core of it were rotten? Trees are susceptible to diseases, just like any other living thing, and diseases corrupt and weaken even the strongest limb.

He concentrated on keeping his balance, lying along the pole, both arms stretched in front of him, one foot crooked, holding the pole in the bend of his ankle and foot, the other knee hanging down to give him weight counter-balance. Arms forward, he pulled and slid his body. Arms forward again, pull and slide once more.

Now, the fence was directly beneath him. It was six feet

below, well out of reach of the induction effect should the guards happen to go against routine and switch it back on. If he should slip now he would fall across the electrified strands. Four hundred volts, enough to stun him, even if it did not kill him. And enough to blow the whole scheme sky-high.

He inched carefully forward, resisting the impulse to rush. The practice took five minutes: for five minutes all their attention would be directed towards the south-east corner and away from him. For five minutes the guards and the Alsatian dogs would be over there, carrying out the drills that had been designed for them.

Now, he had arrived at the start of the pole's deep incline. No rod could be made rigid enough to take his weight at this distance without sagging. His hands felt moist. Cautiously, he brought his right hand back and wiped it on the serge of his shoulder. Then he brought the left hand back. He had tried this crawl using gloves, fixing the pole along the tree in the garden of the cottage he had rented, but not even a surgeon's rubber gloves had given him the confident contact with the pole he knew he would need. He would leave fingerprints, but only for a short time, until he had a chance to remove the pole, according to plan, the following day.

The bend was steeper now, and he felt himself begin to slide. Now he was using his hands as a brake, but the weight of his body bunched him forward, perilously close to being off-balance. He glanced below him and then backwards; his feet were just clearing the space above the electrified fence. Now he could let himself slide, could let the pole whip and dip.

When he dropped from the end of the pole he was ten feet inside the fence and the pole was only twelve inches above it. He stood and then twisted the end section sharply clock-wise; the spring loading pulled the telescopic sections back into each other, all the way back to the tree. The Captain turned and started a shambling run across the grass towards the silhouette of B Building, a hundred and fifty yards away.

The lights went out. The guards and the dogs started again around the perimeter. But the dew on the grass hid the odour of the intruder.

The British have never been security minded. Most of Security Systems Ltd's time had been spent persuading would-be clients that they needed to protect their premises, their property, their processes. When the systems had been installed, account always had to be taken of the failure of the human element. A factory could be surveyed adequately by closed-circuit television cameras, but if the man supposed to be watching the screens had gone to sleep because he had spent all the afternoon at a football match, the system, however sophisticated, would fail. One of the fail-safe devices Security Systems Ltd employed was a dead man's handle such as were utilized on trains. If the man supposed to be watching the screen fell asleep, the handle would open, and an alarm would sound to waken him again and alert an auxiliary part of the system.

The guards tied down the dead man's handles with string, rubber bands, pieces of wire, despite the threat of instant dismissal if they were caught.

A heat-sensitive panel was substituted for the dead man's handle. The guard had to rest his hand against it. If his hand moved away, the alarms sounded. The guards discovered that a torch shone on the panel generated an equivalent amount of heat. They could then use their hands to make tea, eat sandwiches, fill in football coupons, pick the following day's winners.

The doorman of Building B was supposed to keep the door closed and scrutinize the security badges of everyone coming in and out, on the day and the night shifts. During the night, the door was left unlocked but closed. Anyone could open it. The entrance was covered by an electronic screen which could only be deactivated by the magnetic oxide strip buried in the identity card of anyone with legitimate access to the building. If anyone tried to pass through the doorway without such a card, an alarm would sound.

The Captain had such a card.

He slid open the door, sufficient to allow himself to pass

through. The guard was reading a paper and glanced up when he saw the Captain. He rose to his feet and started to come out of his office, his hand resting on the butt of the Webley in its canvas holster at his belt. His instructions clearly said he should not leave his office, that he should tap one button, that he should speak into the microphone embedded in the bulletproof glass of his office. In the event that the visitor could not provide a satisfactory explanation of his presence, he should kick the lever that would drop a mesh grille, effectively screening off the whole of Building B and locking the outer door. The visitor, who should now be treated as an intruder, would be trapped in a steel cage from which there would be no escape. The main guards would be alerted; it would take them less than one minute to arrive by armoured jeep.

The guards did not like racing round the complex on false alarms. The doorman knew that, and came out of his office to investigate. After all, he had his Webley, had he not, with his hand on the butt?

'What are *you* doing here, sir, this time of night?' he asked, as yet only mildly curious, expecting some suitable explanation.

The Captain glanced quickly inside the building. No one was in sight on this floor, which was mainly a store for gas cylinders, pipe-work on racks, sheet metal stacked against the wall, the offices of the day-time staff.

He twisted and kicked up his foot, angled sideways. The blow took the guard across his throat and snapped his neck instantly. The man fell over backwards, sliding across the guard room, ending with his shoulders against the back wall, his head bent at an awkward angle.

There should have been two guards, according to the System. One always covered for the other in the evenings. The second guard would be down in the rest room, one floor below, reading, cooking his supper. Security Systems Ltd had wanted to abolish the rest rooms, but the Union, all powerful, had threatened a strike. If the management wanted two guards on duty, they argued, the management should employ three men so that one of the three could, to

35

quote the Union negotiator, 'exercise his natural functions'.

Sometimes both men left the door together, especially when one of them had cooked a hot dish, but even the Union frowned on that.

The Captain pressed the button that would sound the buzzer in the rest room. Then he dragged the dead guard across the floor and hid him behind the desk, stuffing him into the knee-hole. He was standing behind the rest room door when it opened and the second guard appeared.

'What the hell are you buzzing me for?' he swore. 'I've only been down there five minutes . . .' Those were the last words he uttered. The Captain stepped from behind the door and, with both hands clenched together, chopped the base of the guard's skull, at the top of his spine. As the guard fell, the Captain caught him, dragged him back through the rest room door, down a short flight of steps, and into the rest room itself. There was a smell of cooking, and a pan of eggs, bacon, sausages, tomatoes on the two-ring gas burner, which had been switched off. The guard had set a table for himself with a knife and fork, a pot of tea, even a book. The Captain laid him along the sofa.

'Sleep tight,' he said. He opened the book and draped it across the guard's face. The cover of the book was plain, the contents lurid. 'Sleep tight,' the Captain said again, and closed the door as he went out.

The atomic warheads were contained in a vault about fifteen feet cubic, two stories below him. Each was in a lead-lined wooden box twelve inches by twelve, six inches deep, a hundred pounds in weight. The room in which the vault was contained was forty feet by forty feet, and also fifteen feet high. Two guards were locked inside that room and the main patrol checked them every hour. In addition, the room was bugged by open microphones and closed-circuit television cameras, controlled from the main guard room by the gate of the complex. The door into the vault could not be opened except by two men, each using a key, and a third man with a combination known only to the Minister of Defence and the Director of the Harwell Centre.

The walls of the vault itself were eight feet thick, of concrete, steel, and lead. The floor and ceiling were of similar construction.

When the Captain first learned this, his immediate impression had been that the vault was impregnable, that the only way to get into it would be by using the Director of the Harwell Centre, under duress. That would be a messy operation, needing a number of men with weapons. It would alert the nearby Army camp and bring all the might of the military into play.

The alternative solution was ludicrously simple.

The vault was air conditioned and the extracted air passed through a duct to a chamber where it was tested continuously for any sign of a radiation leak. The radiation testing chamber was on the floor above where he was now standing. The duct came out of the top of the vault, built into the wall behind the racks holding the spare lengths of pipe. The duct itself was constructed of ceramic lined steel plates, sealed with lead. He crouched behind the pipe-rack and slowly eased one of the plates of the duct away from the wall, breaking the lead seal with a chisel. With the plate removed, he was able to secure a length of rope to the pipe-rack, and drop down it into the vault below.

The vault was pitch-black and he switched on his torch. Each of the boxes containing a warhead was standing on a separate shelf of a stack. He took one of the boxes, tied it with a length of cord through the handle so that it hung on his back, round his neck, and quickly climbed the rope back up behind the pipe-rack. It took him one minute to push the plate of the duct back into position, working the lead seal with the handle of the chisel to push it back into place again.

When he left Building B, he had been inside only five minutes and forty-five seconds.

The Security Systems Ltd Bedford van was where he had left it earlier in the day. The box fitted neatly into the space in the floor. He drove the truck to the main gate, and signed himself out. After a perfunctory look inside the back of the Bedford, the guard opened the main gate and motioned him to pass. Why should he not? This was the third night in succession the Captain had worked late in the plant, installing a new type of radar scanner on the top of Building B to give an alert of any approaching low-flying aircraft or helicopters.

'Still clocking up the overtime, Captain?' the guard said as the Bedford came level with him.

'This evening should see it finished.'

'Ah well, you can't win 'em all. Good night!'

'Good night, sergeant.'

'Drive carefully. It looks like rain coming up . . .'

'I shall. Thank you, and good night again.'

'Good night, Captain.'

Jules Lachard was seated at the master console, a ground glass screen in front of him about three feet round glowing with a pale green light. One bright pinprick of light moved slowly across the screen. A microphone was suspended above Jules's head and about fifteen centimetres in front of his forehead. On the console before him a number of dials flickered, showing the pressure inside the Green Dolphin, the temperature, the engine speed, composition of the oxygen/helium air mix.

The Dolphin was heading east south-east. 'Keep her steady at that,' he said, his voice unusually low and tense, 'for one thousand metres.'

The instruction was unnecessary; the track the Dolphin would follow on its test run had been plotted exactly. So far it had performed impeccably to the commands they were feeding, by sonar, into its computer brain. In the comparatively shallow water of the shelf outside Toulon, they had anticipated trouble with extraneous noise. Close to the surface and the coastline, the sea contains a tumult of sound: they were using a piezo-electric pulser of their own design, hanging in the water at fifty fathoms. It appeared to be transmitting and receiving perfectly. In operation, they would be able to drop it below a naval vessel into the deeps. From there they would be able to

38

control the Dolphin from anything up to fifty thousand metres away.

The blip gradually grew nearer the edge of the screen.

Jules read the coordinates; in forty metres the Dolphin would turn sharp right, then sharp right again, and head back home, the rest over.

Now it was approaching the farthest point of its run.

'Okay, Jacques?' he asked.

The voice of Jacques Morel boomed hollowly back from the loudspeaker. 'Okay, everything fine.'

They had run the Dolphin on automatic and on manual, with Jacques himself taking the controls. Now the Dolphin was back on manual, and Jacques himself would make the first right turn, before flicking to automatic for them to make the second one via sonar.

The blip hovered over the turn point. 'Okay, Jacques, turn now,' Jules instructed.

The blip carried straight on.

'Turn right, Jacques, turn right now!' Jules said.

The blip continued its straight line. Now it was almost at the edge of the screen. Jules pushed forward a switch. 'Control,' he said, coldly, efficiently. 'Over-ride to automatic, now. Complete the programme as arranged.'

He let go of the switch. 'Do you hear me, Jacques? We're switching to automatic. We'll take you over from here. What's gone wrong your end, over?'

Silence.

'Do you hear me, Jacques?'

The voice of the radio controller came over the speaker, 'We've lost radio contact, Commander.'

The blip was now at the edge of the screen.

The voice of Sophie came on the loudspeaker. 'Not responding to navigation. Not responding.'

As her words sounded, all the needles in front of the Commander suddenly went dead.

The blip disappeared off the edge of the screen.

'All contact lost,' Sophie said.

There was a moment of shocked silence, then Jules

reacted quickly. 'Alternative transponder,' he said. There was a rapid flurry of activity and then another silence.

'No reaction from the alternate,' Sophie said. 'We've lost him!'

Jules pushed the switch that connected the sonar sender to the loudspeakers. They could all hear the ping as the coded sound signal was projected into the hissing torrent of the ocean. They all heard the ping as the sound came back from the bed of the ocean, fainter and distorted by the valleys and hills on the bed of the ocean itself.

Ping. Pause. Ping. It was a lonely sound, like a shout from the mountains that produces only its own mocking echo.

'We can't locate him,' Sophie said.

'I know we can't, woman,' Jules shouted in frustration. 'That's how we designed the damned thing – so that nobody, *nobody* can find it . . .'

CHAPTER SIX

The gleaming black Rolls-Royce stopped outside the door of Number 10 Downing Street, and the Minister hurried inside. The Prime Minister, waiting just inside the door, led him up the stairs and along the top corridor to his own small den. He waved the Minister to a chair, sat down himself and stared at his hands before speaking.

'I don't need to tell you how bad this is, Frank,' he said. 'Quite apart from the human element of two men killed.' The Prime Minister was a great one for stressing the human element. He had come to power not only through his parliamentary wheeler-dealing, but on his promise to bring the human element back into government. 'I thought we'd have a talk about it in here first, and then decide how much we're going to tell the Cabinet.'

Frank Moody was a political politician; he had fought his way slowly but surely from the back benches to his present Ministerial position by covering all his options, with an instinct for self-preservation that was surpassed only by the PM's. He had avoided either siding with, or opposing overtly, any of the factions within the party. Though he could not know it, his own lack of commitment would go against him in the future. Minister he could certainly be, but never Leader of the Party, never Prime Minister. Politicians find it hard to forgive anyone who never makes mistakes.

'We're going to have to tell them something, I would think,' he said. 'Apart from anything else, something this big can't be kept from the press. We've already had local reporters saying they've heard there have been deaths at the Harwell Centre, and would the Press Officer explain.'

'Nothing – you understand, Frank? Nothing must come out.'

'Somebody's going to have to talk to the families of the two men. They won't go on believing that the men are on a job of national importance that has taken them away for a few days. We were lucky the Guard Commander locked the door of that guard room and called the Director personally.'

'I don't believe in luck, Frank,' the Prime Minister said. 'Whenever you most need it, the luck runs out.'

'Like certain parliamentary supporters one could name?'

'But won't. Look, Frank, we need absolute silence on this affair. For you, and for me, personally, this could be a disaster. You know without me telling you, I'm sure, just what the Shadow Defence Minister would make of you . . . And the Leader of the Opposition would, quite rightly, make mince-meat out of me.'

'But it's bound to come out, Prime Minister. We tried to keep our Special Services team a secret, and look how they were blown after Mogadishu . . .'

'You can't blame Schmidt. He badly needed a public relations coup. It happens to all of us, Frank.'

'This chap from Security Systems Ltd was in the Special Services – it won't be easy to catch him. I'll get on to Special Branch right away . . .'

'No Special Branch, Frank,' the Prime Minister said

hurriedly. 'They work as a team; once we brief one of them, they'll all know about it. And we don't want too many people sniffing around the Harwell Centre.'

Frank Moody had rarely, if ever, seen the Prime Minister so – yes, afraid. That was the word. Of course, the storage of those atomic devices was a political time-bomb; Frank could remember the Cabinet meeting in which the whole matter had been debated, the fight from the Left to have them destroyed, and the Right of Centre group the Prime Minister had been wooing so arduously at that time, insisting they should be retained, that without them Britain really did become a third-rate Power. The Prime Minister had double-crossed the left, it would seem. Frank had assumed the PM must have told them his decision to retain the atomic warheads privately, using his well-known in-fighting skill to win them over.

'You *did* tell Richard and Barbara and Bob we were keeping the stock-pile, Prime Minister?' he asked quietly. He had no need of an answer. It was an open secret that the Prime Minister depended on those three, to stay in office. If they should learn how he had deceived them . . .

'What do you want me to do, Prime Minister?' he asked.

'Find me one man, on a personal authorization from me, put him in charge of the whole business. One man. Not anybody from the Special Branch, the Met, the Flying Squad. No one from MI6 – I don't want a James Bond. I want one skilled trained investigator, and I want him to find Captain Aram, preferably while he still has possession of that box.'

'It'll be hard to find somebody qualified who isn't already employed. We could try the Forces.'

'No. I don't want a soldier, with loyalties to the Regiment and all that nonsense. I want somebody who'll be answerable only to me. Look around the research boffins.'

The call had not included all members of the Cabinet, only the select few who, unknown to the press and even the rest of their colleagues, advised the Prime Minister on matters of national security. Frank Moody, of course, as Minister of Defence. Mary Twywell, who advised the Prime

Minister on just about everything. Dick Feather, blunt North Country campaigner and now Leader of the House. Lastly, Clyde Farriman, leader of the Opposition.

They were grouped at one end of the long Cabinet table. 'I won't take too much of your time,' the Prime Minister said breezily. 'We've had a tragedy down at the Harwell Centre. Two guards have been murdered. We think the man responsible might be a Captain, retired, called Joseph Aram, who has now disappeared. We've got everybody out looking for him. The usual people are handling it, with full assistance from airport police, Scotland Yard, and the appropriate crime squads.'

No one spoke. They knew he would not have called them just to report two murders.

'What is it, Prime Minister?' Clyde Farriman finally said, emphasizing the title as if to stress the other man's responsibility.

'I think you can all probably guess. This Captain Joseph Aram has taken one of the boxes with him.'

Mary Twywell shuddered. 'How many times have I said, Prime Minister, that those boxes should have been destroyed. If the Americans or the Russians should ever get an inkling of the contents of that vault . .'

'It's no good crying over spilt milk, Mary,' Dick Feather said. 'We've now got to think of the political implications, both nationally and internationally. You're going to tell the President, are you, Prime Minister?'

'Not yet. We're exerting all our efforts to find this Captain Aram. It's not a thing he'd likely take out through Customs, is it?'

'I think I'd like to go on record, Prime Minister,' Clyde Farriman said instantly, 'that I think the President of the USA ought to be informed at once. Also the Russians, the French and the West Germans. I think this is too big a matter, too dangerous for the world, to be left to the whims and vagaries of any one Party faction.'

The Prime Minister permitted himself the first smile since he came into the room. 'I knew we'd have to listen to that little speech, Clyde,' he said. 'Now you've got it off your chest let me say that I don't believe there's any purpose to be served by starting to trot around the world telling all our friends of our misfortune. I've been giving this matter much thought since Frank reported it. I've been asking myself why Captain Aram could possibly want to steal one of those boxes. He can arrange somehow to launch and explode it, I imagine. Provided he knows how to prime it, he could drop it out of an aeroplane. But I don't believe he has any such intention. I believe he means to sell it back to us. For a considerable sum of money. I think that's what he intends, gentlemen. And lady, of course . . .'

Jules Lachard mounted an immediate search for the lost Dolphin, using frogmen and the bathyscope from his own unit. It was a vain search, and he knew it.

The tapes of the voyage were re-run while they scanned the instrumentation for any sign of what could have gone wrong. Everything technical had worked perfectly; the instruments revealed no malfunction whatsoever. The recordings of the sonar were computer analysed, and they found nothing, absolutely nothing, to indicate any reason for the Dolphin to disappear.

Georges Portier and Sophie were sitting side by side, watching the last moments of the voyage, hearing again the Commander's question, and Jacques's answer. Why had Jacques not been able to make that right turn? On the panel in front of where Jacques would be sitting was a system of buttons. All he would need to do would be to press buttons to dial the new compass bearing required, then to press another to tell the computer to act. The computer had all the power it needed; the isotope engine had been registering full power at the time. The computer would have worked out the necessary manoeuvres to turn the Dolphin to the desired compass bearing, would have activated the servo system that would actually make the manoeuvre, would have monitored the vessel round the turn. It had the power to do all that. And Jacques had the necessary instruction printed on the screen before him. So why, why, had the turn not been made? 'If I didn't know such thing was totally impossible,' Georges said, 'I would say that Jacques must have stepped on a plug.' Such an accident was impossible, and both knew it.

'A heart attack . . . ?' Sophie suggested. Georges did not even bother to reply. Jacques's medical condition had been monitored throughout the entire voyage and the results transmitted.

'Narcosis?' When air was first used for diving, many men had suffered a form of craziness, anoxia, caused by the nitrogen content of the air they breathed.

The Dolphin used a mixture of helium and oxygen for that very reason. No adverse effects had been recorded from anyone breathing that mixture.

'It's as if someone, or something, just switched off the Dolphin,' Georges said.

'And to do that, they'd have to switch Jacques off, too,' Sophie said. Tears ran down her face. Georges patted the back of her hand, embarrassed by the emotion. But even he felt infinitely saddened by the loss of Jacques. In his bones, a distinctly unscientific inner feeling told him they would never see Jacques alive again.

Jules reported the loss to the Strategic Weapons Committee at the French Naval Command, Toulon, in the Arsenal du Mourillon. One Rear Admiral, one Naval Commander, one Captain. The Rear Admiral had served out his career with conventional naval vessels. He was a naval strategist, a student of warfare at sea. To him, the submarine was an undesirable weapon, typical of the way the Boches made war. Under the surface of the sea was the place for fishes and drowned heroes, for the suitably shrouded remains of Rear Admirals.

'Tell us again, Commander, exactly what this thing is, and what it does.' He liked to pretend to be a simple, untechnical man; it was a trick that had caught out innumerable junior officers seeking to confuse the old man with scientific jargon.

'It's a submarine,' Jules said patiently. 'It has a self-powered engine that will allow it to travel underwater for a considerable length of time. It has a life support system that regenerates oxygen from the sea. It can operate either manned or unmanned. Since it has been constructed of a sound-absorbent material, it does not reflect sound waves and therefore cannot be located by sonar. However, it will *absorb* sonar waves, therefore those waves, suitably coded, can be used to give the submarine's brain instructions.'

'You tell it to turn right and it turns, eh? Tell it to turn left and it turns left?'

'Exactly so, Admiral.'

'But right now, it's not doing as it's told?'

'We can get no reaction from it.'

'And there's a chap inside it, this Naval lieutenant, Morel?'

'Yes.'

'And he could be steering it, bringing it back home?'

'Yes.'

'Only one thing I don't understand. You said you'd made this damned thing of sound-absorbing material, so that it wouldn't reflect these sonar waves, and yet you were tracking it, presumably by sonar. How does that come about?'

'The Dolphin has a retractable sheet; the sheet is not absorbent. The sheet reflects sonar. Obviously, if we don't want anyone to see the Dolphin on their sonar, we retract the sheet beneath the absorbent covering.'

'It all sounds a bit gimcrack to me, Commander. I'll have to talk to Paris again about this sort of thing. Especially now you appear to have a lost a man in one of them. When I think of the budget you get for messing about with this — what do you call it, a Dolphin? When I think what I could do with even a fraction of that budget . . . You say you're down there, looking for it? A damned lot of ocean if you've no idea of where the thing might be . . .'

Jules Lachard was a courageous, straightforward man who believed in accepting his responsibilities totally. 'I have to report, Admiral, that I have no hope of finding it. I am searching as a matter of form, nothing else. I believe something has gone wrong with the apparatus. And I also have to say – I've no idea, as yet, what that could be.'

'In other words, to quote the lower mess deck, a complete cock-up, Commander? Right. Carry on with the search. In twenty-four hours, notify the next of kin – you know the drill. Missing in Action, it had better be. Presumed Killed. Just one other thing. Get on to the chaps at Naval Intelligence. All this Dolphin tarradiddle carries a top-secret stamp. You said the sonar reflector was retractable, and that it had life support systems and fuel for a considerable time. One thing apparently hasn't occurred to you, but then, you're too close to it. Your Lieutenant Jacques Morel might just have taken it upon himself to steal the damned thing. I imagine the Russkies would pay well for that sort of gimmick. In roubles, of course. Personally, I wouldn't give a sou for the whole damned crack-pot idea.'

The Head of Naval Intelligence at Toulon was a career diplomat who hoped, one day, to get onto the French Navy Board, with a house outside Paris and a glittering social life that befitted a man married to a noblewoman. The life of Toulon was too provincial for her, too rooted in Service procedure. She craved the more sophisticated life of the Elysée, the charm and the gaiety of the capital. He told her, over dinner, of the conversation he had had with Jules Lachard.

'That oaf,' she said, disparagingly. 'So he's lost one of his little toys and killed a man in the process. What can you expect of a peasant from the Auvergne? I warn you, Hector, not to get yourself involved with such a matter. If a man is dead, there could be a scandal. Give it to someone to handle, someone preferably not of your office. You don't want to touch anything at the moment that might be, how shall I say it, questionable.'

'Heloise, as usual, you are right. Tomorrow, I'll talk with Paris. Ask *them* to find someone.'

47

CHAPTER SEVEN

Bill Harrington lived alone in a second floor flat in Crawford Street, off Baker Street, with his collection of classical music, his 'wine-cellar' tucked into a cool cupboard under the stairs, a rented colour television that he seldom watched, an Akai stereo tape system, and a couple of thousand books, all of which he had read. He had two telephones. One, the white one, also had an extension in his bedroom, next to his bed, and a box screwed to the wall that effectively scrambled all conversations incoming and outgoing.

He looked at Sally Price sitting in his wing chair, a glass of armagnac in her hand. The Vivaldi Oboe Concerto had just come to an end. Sally was looking at him, and the meaning in her eyes was clear. To both of them. Okay, what next? He had cooked supper for her – nothing special; a sliced tomato to start, with oil and vinegar dressing. A pork chop to follow, with frozen brussels sprouts he had brought to life in the French way by braising them in butter; a cheese to follow – dolce latte from the grocer's shop round the corner. Nothing special. But a Montrachet to start with, and a Grands Echezaux, had lifted the simple food to the realm of a memorable meal. Coffee and armagnac did nothing to spoil the taste.

Another girl, another meal, another evening, another brief love affair? Another entanglement for the sake of sex?

Damned silly, really, to have invited her – the first girl he had ever brought home 'from the office'. What did they say about not fouling your own doorstep? The words of the invitation had come out almost of their own volition. He had not meant to say them. They had worked late together on one of her cases. An Icelander had penetrated the fishing fleets' code systems and was relaying the information back to the Icelanders. No wonder a gun-boat turned up whenever they tried to drop a net, even in the still legal limit. Gudrun Olaffson. He had put her onto the Norwegian

48

Office of Information in Bergen; she had talked via the computer with Sverre Bull – a descendant of Ole Bull, it was said, who quickly turned up a list of names and aliases. Gudrun had been a pain in the arse to the Norwegians before they had deported him.

They fed the aliases to Special Branch, who sent them to Stormont; the answer came back in three minutes. Only two people had access to the codes being used, apart from the trawler skippers. Two naval ratings. Back to the Admiralty, check the men's records. Both were naturalized Icelanders, who arrived in Britain in 1944 as child refugees. Both were nearing the end of a thirty-year Navy stint, and Gudrun had no doubt promised them a pension. In Rekjavik . . .

It was seven o'clock when Sally rubbed her eyes, strained from looking at the computer read-out screen. 'I would never have got there,' she said. 'This job was like solving a crossword puzzle without having all the clues.'

'You'll learn,' he said. 'How long have you been in the office?'

'Five months, now, but I've been working the Middle East. The PLA, the Arab-Israel axis, the Libyans, Moroccans, recently Somalia. My father was a civil servant; I travelled all round there as a young girl and in my teens. I took Oriental languages for my degree.'

'What are you doing for supper?' he asked.

'Nothing in particular. I was going home to bacon and egg. I hate cooking for myself.'

'So do I. Why don't we see what I have in my fridge.'

During the meal they had talked, much to his surprise, about his life, his marriage, the wife who had left him, the messiness of his divorce.

'I suppose that would make you reluctant to try it again?' she said.

'Not with the right person. I shall look more carefully next time.' But would there be a next time? Did he really want to take on the responsibility for another person. Which was more selfish – to live alone and avoid any sort of responsibility for anyone else, making do with a succession of brief encounters, or to be so afraid of being alone that you grasp at anyone compatible? It was a question he had often asked himself, since his wife had left. He could see, now, that he had clung to his wife for the latter reason. Not because he still had any true affection for her, but he was, in a sense, afraid of living the rest of his life without her. She had become someone to come home to, someone to anticipate. The reality had been so much less satisfying than the anticipation.

'We've had the meal – wonderful; the wines – wonderful; the music – wonderful; the dialogue – fascinating. Where do we go from here, Bill?' Sally asked. She raised her glass in a toast, looking at him over the rim as she sipped the last of the armagnac. At thirty, she had few pretences left. She had never been married, though she had come very close to it a few times. But there had always been an alternative. Do I marry this man, or take that scholarship to Damascus for a year? Do I improve my knowledge of Farsi, or trot behind this lad to the altar? Now there were no alternatives. Now she had the job she knew best suited her – now she could use her knowledge of the vast labyrinth of the Middle East with political commitment. And she needed to be committed.

For a long time she had thought of a purely academic life, either teaching languages in England, of only slight interest to her, or of following any one of the many branches of knowledge open to her. For a while she had flirted with the idea of archaeology, but that would have been too dead, too dry. Perhaps she could translate some of the wealth of Middle Eastern writings? But that, again, failed to interest her. Then, a year ago, she had been approached one day in a restaurant near Victoria Station which sold passable Greek food. The man, she immediately thought, was far too old still to be trying to pick up girls eating alone in restaurants.

'Before you tell me to go away,' he had said, 'listen to me for five minutes.' He was speaking Farsi and obviously had a command of the intricate language, though he looked as British as Robert Morley. And had a similar shape.

'This is not the way we normally do things, usually we write to people, asking them to call at an office. But, since you're leaving the day after tomorrow to go to Athens, I thought I'd take a chance on having a quick word.' He had held out a card. 'Don't worry, Miss Price,' he had said. 'I'm not part of the white slave traffic, recruiting on behalf of some oil rich sheikh.'

'You know my name, you know I'm booked on the BA flight to Athens tomorrow, you knew I was eating here tonight, though I didn't know that myself until five minutes ago. So you can cut out the preliminaries. Who are you, who do you work for, and what do you want?'

'My name is Rhodes, I work for the British government, and I want to offer you a job as a civil servant that, after training, will make use of your Middle Eastern education and interests. The job would be fully pensioned, super-annuated; you'd get the usual paid holidays each year, according to the grade you achieve, and we could give help in finding accommodation here in London until you find something suitable yourself. The job would entail a certain amount of travel, and, from time to time, a certain amount of physical danger.'

He had handed her a card. 'If you would care to come to my office tomorrow, we could go into details.' The address on the card could not have been more respectable.

11, Downing Street, London.

'I'm a lousy typist,' she had said, 'and I can't take short-hand.'

'I know that,' he had said. 'I also know you're not married. You've had your appendix removed, and are undecided as to what to do with your life.' He had risen to his feet. 'Try the chicken here,' he had said. 'It's delicious.'

'Sit down a minute,' she had said. 'That's if you don't mind my asking a few questions for a change.'

He had sat down again, chuckling. 'I was expecting a few.'

The waiter had come to their table. 'I think I'll have the chicken,' she had said. 'I'm told it's quite delicious.'

'I should be angry.' She had turned to Rhodes, if that

were his real name. 'I don't like the fact that someone can probe so deeply into my life without me being aware of it.'

'Big Brother?'

'A nightmare to Orwell. A reality to us, it would seem.'

'But you're not angry?'

'Not really. I suppose I'm amused. Some people might say your approach has been, how can I put it, a little crude . . .'

'Finesse is a luxury we reserve for our enemies, Miss Price. For those we hope will be our friends, we prefer a direct approach, even at the risk of seeming a little – what did you call it? – crude.'

'Of course, I'm flattered that you should find me significant enough to be considered for such surveillance. It's nice in a way to learn you've been sitting an examination you knew nothing about, and that you've passed . . .'

'With flying colours, I believe the expression is.'

'So we come to the sixty-four dollar question. Why *me*?'

He had chuckled again. 'Look, Miss Price, I'm not dissimulating when I counter your question with another question. Why *not* you? Nor do I mean to flatter you when I say that out of a number of new people we have – shall I say, examined – you come closest to what we think we want. We're a very small team, Miss Price. All what you might call hand-picked. I happen to think you will fit in with that team.'

'And its always done like this. Across a restaurant table?'

He had shaken his head. 'Time and place are not important in the overall scheme of things, Miss Price. Wasn't it Omar Khayyám who required simply "thou beside me in the wilderness"? He could hardly have been less specific about place. Somehow it didn't seem to matter too much to him.'

Sally had known instinctively that she would get no more out of him.

She went to the formal part of the interview the following day, and came away from No. 11 a graded civil servant. She extended her stay in the hotel, and promptly cancelled her flight to Athens.

Now she was working her way through the sections of the Intelligence Unit. The Icelandic job had been her first one on the North European desk.

'Where *do* we go from here, Bill?' she asked. 'Perhaps I should get up, say something dreary like: "well it's been a wonderful evening and thank you very much for the meal, and where's the nearest taxi rank, or shall I call a minicab." But you've been sitting there, listening to the Vivaldi, and having an argument with yourself. As my mother, who was a most diplomatic Diplomatic wife, used to say of amorous equerries, you've got a touch of the moodies. There are three stages, you know. Moodies, stage one, are followed by fancies, stage two, which, if not instantly quelled, lead to intentions! I know I'm talking too much, and most of it is probably a lot of nonsense . . .'

He was bending over her chair, reached in and kissed her. 'Yes,' he said. 'You are talking too much. But we can soon put a stop to that!'

He put his arms round her and lifted her from the chair. Her glass fell to the carpet and rolled. But neither tried to stop it.

'I want to take you to bed,' he said.

'And I want you to . . .'

He smiled.

'But I want to go to the bathroom first. It's been a long tiring day. I could use a shower! Is that my age showing?'

'Neither one of us is eighteen . . .'

'Thank God for that.'

He was on his way to the bathroom with a second towel for her when the white telephone rang. He took the call in the bedroom, instinctively closing the door and checking the scrambler was in position. 'Bill, this is John Rhodes. Were you having dinner?'

'Just finished. What's up?'

'You okay? I know how you like wine with your meals.'

'I'm okay, John.'

'Good. I've got a job for you. I might as well tell you straight away, it's messy and I don't like it. If I were you, I'd tell me to stick it.'

53

'But still, you're on the telephone . . .'

'Yes.'

'To me. Not to Joe, or Percival, or Sally Price . . .'

'No, Bill, to you.'

'Why? Damn it, John, don't make me pull teeth to get it.'

'Because you were in the Parachute Regiment, once. When can I see you?'

'My car's in the garage near Marble Arch.'

'I know. That's why I've sent one. It should be arriving at your door any moment.'

'You were so sure I'd take it?'

'No, I wasn't. But I'd rather waste some chauffeur's time than yours or mine. If it's any consolation, Bill, I'm calling everybody in. But you're the one who gets lumbered with the job.'

'Don't bother calling Sally Price. She's been having dinner with me. I'll bring her in my car.'

'Good. That'll save me time. And Bill, I'm glad you didn't pick up the phone straightaway.'

'Why not, John?'

'Because I know you keep it by your bed. I'd have it on my conscience if I made that girl a widow . . . before she was even married.'

John Rhodes briefed Bill Harrington in the conference room. 'Simple facts, Bill, first, and then we'll get into the rest. An ex-Army officer, Captain Joseph Aram of Special Services, ex-Paras, retired from the Army, found himself a job with a company, Security Services Ltd. He used that job to get inside a building in the Harwell Centre which, as you know, is top of the pile for Security. While he paid a clandestine visit there last night, he killed two guards, we think, and stole an atomic device. I can't tell you any more about the atomic device except that it's in a box. There'll be a complete specification on that box, but not its contents, in your dossier, which is now being prepared. Your job . . .'

'Save it, John. Don't say any more. You know I can't take a job on that basis.'

John Rhodes sighed. He had hoped to get that one through but, knowing Bill, never thought he would have a cat-in-hell's chance, and had told the Minister of Defence so. 'He'll want to know exactly what's in the box, Minister,' he had said, 'or he won't take the job. I know him. With respect, Sir, I myself wouldn't take the job without knowing.'

'Okay, Bill, you can't blame me for trying. This is Alpha Zero Plus, if you know what I mean. I'm not even supposed to say it out loud. The contents of the box are listed on a sheet of paper which I personally will put in your dossier. The sheet is to be memorized by you and then returned to me, understood?'

'Understood. Now tell me, John, without the scientific data – what is it?'

'It's dirty – in every sense of the word. An atomic bomb. Captain Aram has stolen it. You have to find it. If you find him along the way, so much the better. But we want to find that bomb before anybody else knows we have lousy stinking politicos who'll authorize a bunch of scientific idiots to manufacture such a thing so that the bloody turds in the War Office can hold them against possible future use. Sorry about the language, but I said this was a lousy mess and I meant it. Give me a cigarette.'

'You gave up smoking a year ago, John.'

'Tonight, Bill, I smoke.'

'One more question, John. You said Captain Aram did all this last night. Tonight is tonight, you know what I mean? What have they been doing all day?'

'Looking for somebody with an asbestos orifice up which they could stick this hot potato. Finally, they got around to us. By my reckoning, about twenty-three hours too late. Bill, it's a lousy bloody job. You'd be insane even to contemplate it.'

'But you're asking me to take it, all the same?'

'I'm not asking, Bill. I'm pleading . . .'

The meeting of the Intelligence Unit was a no-nonsense

affair. John Rhodes had successfully let off his anger; he let Bill read the dossier and then brief the others.

'There seems little doubt,' Bill said, 'that ex-Captain Joseph Aram killed the two guards. Classic side-kick for one, neck chop for the other, such as Special Services are taught. I don't, therefore, propose to waste any time on a conventional murder investigation. The local boys are doing that, with the brief that they're not to stir up any mud. We must concentrate our efforts on finding Aram, and that box.'

'Any clues?' a man from North European section asked.

'Two theories only. One, the box has been stolen, as pictures in Italy and German industrialists are taken, to be offered back for ransom. Straight theft for gain, with no political overtones or undertones.'

'You don't seem very enthusiastic about that one,' an operative from the North American desk said laconically.

Bill shook his head. 'I'm not,' he said. 'I have a feeling somewhere in the pit of my stomach that it's political. In that case, it can be one of two things. For a start, it could relate to the UK, and that includes Northern Ireland. Remember, Aram was there, in Belfast. He could have been turned.'

Sally looked around the room tentatively, conscious of her status as the new girl, the junior. 'Could I say something?'

'Please do, Sally.'

'It seems unlikely to me that they would actually use a device from Harwell – I know you haven't said what it is but I think we've all guessed what it must be – except as a threat. No doubt they'd try to force the government to bring home all the troops, release all prisoners, grant Northern Ireland Home Rule, that sort of thing?'

'It could be European political,' someone cut in. 'Release all the Red Army faction being held in Germany and elsewhere, the two in Turkey . . .'

'One thing we all learned from Baader-Meinhoff, Martin Schleyer, and Mogadishu,' Sally said, more confident now that she was on her own territory, 'is that these demands

56

are international. Just because this device has been stolen in England, we shouldn't limit our thinking necessarily to UK and or Northern Ireland.'

'That's why I wanted all of you at this meeting,' Bill said. 'I want each one of you to go into the computer and ask it the kind of questions you best know. Aram didn't plan this theft entirely on his own. Who was responsible for him getting his job with Security Systems Ltd? What kind of an outfit is that? Does it have overseas connections that could give it the opportunity for involvement elsewhere? Have they done any other government contracts abroad? Especially in the Middle East, in Germany, in any place that is politically sensitive.'

'You have the dossier on Aram as a starting point,' John Rhodes pointed out. 'The UK Section will take that apart, and feed each of you any appropriate material it may find.'

'I can give you one thing already,' Bill said. 'We have a report of a meeting in an apartment in Paris. Captain Aram was there. Come to think of it, a Baader-Meinhoff man was there, too, and a Greek – no, a Cretan. You can start with this one, Sally. The despatch was C144, and either 1268 or 1269.'

No one marvelled at his prodigious memory; he had shamed them with it too often in the past.

John Rhodes was watching him, reassuring himself he had been right to pick Bill for this assignment. He knew Bill was quiet, methodical, painstaking. But somehow, John had always felt in Bill's presence an untapped potential. Of course, for years Bill had been dragged down, held back, by the tragedy that so often happens to either a man or a woman who marries the wrong partner. John had respected Enid, Bill's ex-wife, but she was not the sort to sit quietly at home while her man went gallivanting round the world. She had needed someone by her side the whole time. Many people did. Others did not. Bill was one of them. He could either operate in the closely knit team John had built at the Intelligence Unit, or he could work alone in the field as a self-contained, self-motivated unit.

'You indicated two theories, Bill?' Sally Price asked. She

was all business now, though she knew, as he did, that the scene they had been about to play in the bedroom had merely been postponed, not cancelled.

'So far we've been assuming that Captain Joseph Aram is a sane man with a purpose, a cause . . .'

'Even if that "cause" is to raise a lot of money, quickly?' Sally asked. 'Or to get his murderous colleagues out of gaol?'

'Yes. But we also have to face the fact that he may be an *insane* man with a cause . . .'

'And that cause . . .'

'To use the bomb not as a means of blackmail, but as a bomb. To use it to start World War Three. The one none of us will walk away from.'

CHAPTER EIGHT

Marc Chantal and Phillipe were eating supper at a small restaurant in the Rue du Bac where the menu was cyclo-styled in purple ink, the table cloths red and white check, and the prices terrestrial rather than astronomical. A salade de tomates, a cotelette de porc, a slice of Brie to finish. A carafe of house wine. Phillipe was laughing at Marc, who did not enjoy it too much. 'Look, Marc,' he said. 'You always say the same thing. Give you one month, one week, one day even, of inactivity and you start talking about our resigning from the Service and opening a place of our own. At first I took you seriously. Remember when I spent all that time looking into that restaurant near the Place Maubert. We could have earned a fortune there. Then they gave you that assignment in Agadir, and the whole subject fell splash into the Seine. D'accord! I understand! But don't keep on giving me all this merde every time you're desk bound for a day. And don't pull such a long face when I tell you about it. What shall we do? Walk down the Boul' Mich, find ourselves a couple of foreign students?'

'Fuck the foreign students.'

'Now you're getting the general idea, Marc. Come on, my turn to pay for supper. You can pay for the students . . .'

They did not get to the Boulevard Mich.

Jean Pierre Malhouette was sitting in the back of a car illegally parked half way across the pavement when they came out of the restaurant. 'Get in,' he said, without pre-liminaries.

Marc felt a stirring in his blood; it must be something important for the Chief to come hunting them. Something a damn sight more important than chasing a couple of skirts half way down some side street.

'What's on, Chief?' he asked, twisting in the front seat to look back. Phillipe was sitting with the Chief, whose two legs stuck out stiffly in front of him. The car was an old Alvis, specially chosen so the Chief could get into the back without bending his knees.

'You'll find out soon enough. How much wine did you both have back there in that merde of a restaurant?'

'One carafe between the two of us.'

'Good.'

The car went swiftly down the Rue des St Pères, despite the number of pedestrians. At the bottom, they turned and drove alongside the Seine turned onto the Ile de la Cité, then pulled up outside a large wooden door which rattled open on two wheels. The courtyard in front of them rose three stories only; the rooms on each side had long windows indicating high ceilings. When the car stopped, the driver got out and opened the back door. The Chief swung himself out, ignoring the driver's proffered hand, took his two sticks and hobbled across to the concierge's lodge.

'He's expecting you, M. Malhouette,' the concierge said. 'I've brought the lift down for you.'

'You two walk,' the Chief said. 'Second floor. Do your legs good.'

He got into the lift. It was barely big enough to carry a man of his bulk. They looked at each other, without speak-ing, and started up the wide stone stairs.

'What kept you?' the Chief said. 'Hopelessly out of con-dition both of you must be. Follow me.'

'One of these days,' Marc whispered to Phillipe. 'I'm going to take both those sticks and ram them right up his arse, see if I don't!'

'They wouldn't fit,' the Chief said drily.

The Minister who awaited them was in white shorts and a white Lacoste shirt with the distinctive green crocodile on its chest and a monogram under the pocket. He was wearing tennis shoes and a terry cloth sweat-band round his wrist; it seemed as if the proceedings bored him unutterably, when he could be at the Racquets Club.

'Voilà, so there you are,' was his only greeting. He did not invite them to sit down, but the Chief lowered his bulk slowly onto a banquette, his legs stretched out before him, sweat on his forehead. The Minister eyed him with distaste. He was himself, doubtless along with all his family and friends, one of 'the beautiful people'. Wealth and leisured exercise kept him in trim.

'There's no point in wasting time,' he said. He meant *his* time, without a doubt. 'The Navy have, or think they might have, a small problem. They want it looked into, quite discreetly, of course. Above all, you are to report anything you find to the Head of Naval Intelligence, at Toulon. You needn't bother me with it; he will attend to the details.'

'This small problem, Monsieur le Ministre,' Marc Chantal said, his laconic manner matching the Minister's. 'I presume someone is going to tell us what it is? Or do we get that information too from the Head of Naval Intelligence at Toulon. And while you seem to be permitting me these few moments of speech, may I remind you that anything, anything, we discover as a result of *any* investigation we make is automatically given, not to minor heads of intelligence, Naval or otherwise, in the provinces, but taken directly to the President? Correct me if I'm wrong, but our office was established by the President, to be above politics. Do you have authorization to change that arrangement?'

The Minister was speechless. He looked at the Chief as if to ask who was this impertinent idiot he had brought into his office. The Chief was grinning, and shrugged his shoulders. He knew exactly why he had brought Marc

Chantal along, why he had picked him up outside the restaurant and shown Marc the rough edge of his tongue.

The Chief was just as good a politician as the next man. Why, he had asked himself, had he been summoned to the Minister's town house, and not his office? Why had the Minister asked *him*, and not someone from Deuxième Bureau? Why was an enquiry to be handled outside the Navy? The answer, knowing the parliamentary bureaucracy, was simple. Because the enquiry was a sensitive one. And, in that graphic Americanism Frenchmen are no longer supposed to use if they respect the purity of the Gallic tongue, because the shit was likely to hit the fan.

Whatever else it seemed Marc Chantal may have been, he was an undisciplined renegade who had no respect for authority. Especially not for someone who treated them, as the Chief had known the Minister would, like a bunch of hired servants. Marc was quite right; the Minister had no authority to order them to report to the Head of Naval Intelligence in Toulon.

'You can go,' the Minister said, his face white with anger. 'You can all go. I'm already quite late enough as it is for my game!'

Marc was shaking his head slowly and deliberately from side to side. 'The Navy has a problem at Toulon. You've suggested as much. It's an Intelligence matter. We don't have to get any *departmental* authority to investigate *any* Intelligence problem we might uncover. You know that, Monsieur le Ministre. So, thanks to your tip off, we shall be looking into matters at Toulon. *With* or *without* your authority . . .'

The Minister, deflated, sat down. He was astute enough to know when to compromise, when to run for cover, when to try to turn an enemy into a friend. 'Please take a seat,' he said. 'I pray you will forgive my apparent rudeness. It's been a difficult day. Let me tell you what I know of the Toulon affair. After you have heard me, perhaps you will decide if you consider an investigation is justified. If so, I know you will pursue it with all vigour, since that is the reputation of your Unit. Of course, you will report directly to the President himself. If, at the time, you care to do so, you can discuss your findings with me, acting, of course, in a purely advisory capacity. Does that clear the air a little?' His smile was warm and he beamed at all three of them.

Marc and Phillipe sat down. The Chief introduced them by name. Neither offered to shake hands, nor did the Minister.

'Good,' he said. 'And you, Monsieur Chantal, will be leading the investigation?'

'Yes.'

'Good. Now here is the story. The Navy has been developing a midget submarine in an experimental dock in Toulon. The dock is run by Commander Jules Lachard, a very fine scientific naval officer, a brilliant man. This midget submarine had its test run yesterday. Unfortunately, as can happen, something went wrong and the submarine was lost. It carried a crew of one, and he, too, has been lost. I don't know anything of the technicalities but, apparently, they cannot look for this lost submarine by conventional methods. They cannot find it, using ordinary techniques. Or, come to think of it, extraordinary techniques.'

'We aren't usually called out on salvage jobs, Minister,' the Chief said. 'This submarine – is it nuclear?'

'Good Lord, no. It's only a tiny thing. It runs, apparently, off what they call – you'll have to forgive me, I know nothing about these things – an isotope engine.'

'That's nuclear,' Marc Chantal said. 'But not sensitive. They're becoming as common as long life batteries. They wouldn't call us out for an isotope engine, unless it was very special.'

'There has been a *suggestion*,' the Minister said. 'And it is only the merest suggestion. But the Naval Officer piloting the submarine might in some way be responsible for their failure to find it . . .'

'They think he might have done a bunk with it?'

A pained expression crossed the Minister's face. Really, political life was getting too much. He had had a harassing

conversation with that crusty old devil down in Toulon, he
had talked with Head of Intelligence down there – and
what a slimy devil he was. Now he had this lout of an
investigator bandying words with him. 'I didn't say he'd
done any such thing, Monsieur Chantal. I merely said it
has been suggested that possibly, only possibly, he might
in some way be responsible for their failure to find it.'

'And so you want us to check him out, is that it?'

'Yes, I suppose that's it. I want you to find out if he had
any reasons, any reasons whatever, for removing that submarine from our control.'

'Then, presumably, delivering it into someone else's
hands. And you'd like to know who those hands belong
to?'

'Yes. That's what I, for one, would dearly like to know.'

How did you track a man's life? How do you use his everyday effects to gain some sort of knowledge of him? Marc
Chantal had flown to Toulon by a French Air Force jet.
He spent the night partly at the experimental station looking at procedures, partly at the Hotel des Bains, partly in
Jacques Morel's apartment overlooking the Darse Vieille.
The rooms of the apartment yielded little at first sight, but
for the moment Marc was interested in superficial impressions. Jacques was obviously meticulous in his personal
affairs. All his papers were in an escritoire in his living
room, all his clothes were in cupboards and drawers, except
for one pair of slips, one vest, one pair of socks and one
handkerchief in a laundry basket.

Jacques obviously liked to cook, and his kitchen contained all the ingredients, the herbs, the equipment. But
the fridge was empty of fresh food, and all the pots had
been washed and put away. The vegetable rack was also
empty, along with the bread basket.

The bedroom contained one double bed with two pillows
stacked one on top of the other. There was one reading
light above the bed, one ash-tray beside the bed, but no
sign of any cigarettes or matches. The bed was overlooked
by no mirrors; the drawers contained no stimulants, no

devices, no contraceptives. There were no long blonde hairs intertwined in the blankets. Marc reached his hand below the bed and the inevitable fluff contained no hairs, no bobby pins.

The medicine chest in the bathroom held two bottles of medicated shampoo, a tube of aspirins, a bottle of digestive tablets. Tooth-paste, tooth-brush, antiseptic gargle. Medicated talcum powder, under-arm deodorant. A metal comb, and an electric razor.

Marc went back into the living room and sat on the metal-and-leather reading chair. He swung round – near his right hand was a collection of *Time* magazine and *Newsweek*, in English. Each issue was carefully, chronologically piled. The bottom ones were six months old. When he swung to his left he found *l'Express* and *Der Spiegel*, the latter in German.

There were no other books in the apartment, no other printed news matter. No newspapers, no magazines, nothing.

Marc was free-wheeling, his mind merely receiving impressions without trying to evaluate them. It was the method he preferred. Later, he knew, certain conclusions would rise from his subconscious; later, certain of the facts he was observing would emerge again, each with its own particular significance. Later, he knew, a whole impression would form. A person chooses where he wants to live, and the objects with which he surrounds his daily life, according to some inner principle of conduct. This apartment, he already knew, had been rented unfurnished. If everything within it had been chosen by Jacques Morel, that choice would certainly reflect the man's taste, his characteristics, his preferences.

He went back to the escritoire and looked again at the papers, grouping them in a few small piles. Bank statements, cheque book, cancelled cheques, credit transfer slip carbons. Jacques had earned a good salary as a scientist and naval officer. The salary had been deposited in the bank each month and the bills regularly paid. Any balance had been taken from the bank, in cash, at the beginning of each new month. Marc looked at the cheque book and saw each entry was clearly marked on the stub, each new balance correctly calculated. Four days earlier, Jacques had cashed a cheque marked 'personal'. Marc added the balance from the bank statement, worked out the cheque book stubs and the credit transfer slips. The balance in the bank, assuming all the transactions had gone through, was exactly zero.

The escritoire contained no personal letters.

Jacques Morel's life had been insured for half a million francs. The beneficiary was his mother, with a Paris address. Marc quickly skimmed through the policy still contained in the letter from the company. Acts of God, and war, were the only exclusions. Suicide was included after two years from the date of the acceptance. The policy, taken out three years before, contained a complicated clause about the Legal Presumption of Death after a Fixed Period, but Marc did not bother with it. The lawyers could argue that one out between them.

If Jacques Morel could be presumed dead, his mother had become a comparatively wealthy woman, which was no doubt what Jacques had intended.

There was a mess of papers to do with Jacques's formal education, in France and America. Certificates of Competence in scuba diving. His driving licences, French, American, International. A Navigation Certificate, a Letter of Assessment of Achievement from the School of Computer Sciences, Lyon, which awarded him a grade of Class Two Programmer (All Systems).

Marc remembered the kitchen cabinet's contents, found a bottle of wine and another of cognac, took the latter and a glass and went back to sit in the chair. 'Cheers, Jacques,' he said. 'Wherever you are. And whoever you may be, you bastard. You don't fool me for one moment.' As he rocked gently backwards and forwards in the chair, the reflection of the light in the mirror seemed to be winking at him.

Marc left the apartment, and walked through the quiet streets that bordered the Darse, gazing out at the ocean.

The moon was low on the horizon; the water glittered silver at him. Boats moved in, and out, their lights flickering green, red, white, as they rode the gentle Atlantic swell. Somewhere under the glistening water, he felt, as strongly as ever he had felt anything, that Jacques Morel was alive. That he was sitting at the controls of that hand-crafted mini-submarine, with its contoured chair, its coffee-making machine, its dehydrated food containers, tasteless but protein packed. He must be down there, urinating into the garbage disposal unit, his sweat being drawn from him and absorbed by the air cleansing system, thumbing his nose at the whole of France.

'I'll get you, you bastard,' Marc said. His voice held no rancour, only the willing acceptance of a challenge worthy of him, a touch of admiration for a powerful rival, but a quiet determination not to be beaten.

He dialled Paris direct from the first public telephone he saw, tucked in the corner of a bar still full of sailors. The noise they were making, teasing the three prostitutes seated on the bar stools, effectively masked anything Marc might have said. He dictated instructions for almost ten minutes, knowing Phillipe would have the tape machine running. First thing next morning, the leg men would arrive, drawn from all the nearby offices, the tentacles of the Bureau in Paris. They would be knocking on doors asking the usual questions. 'Do you know this man, have you seen him recently, where does he eat and drink, who does he eat and drink with?' Another team would take that apartment inch by inch and search it with forensic skill. By the end of the day, they would have a dossier of fingerprints, hairs, hidden weapons, explosives, letters, notes. Anything that would give them a clue to who Jacques Morel really was.

The following morning, at seven o'clock, Bill Harrington in Oxford, and Marc Chantal in Toulon, received virtually the same message from their aides.

'Marc, I think you'd better come quickly back to Paris,' Phillipe said, staring at the computer print-out in their office in the Croix Rouge.

66

Sally was in the office in 11 Downing Street. She had her information on the visual display panel, prior to punching the button that would print it out. 'Bill,' she said, 'I think you'd better come to London.'

The computer had recalled the meeting in the apartment of Henri Dupree. Both Jacques Morel and Captain Joseph Aram had been there. Both London and Paris had asked the same question, and each had put an Alpha Zero Plus priority on the name of their own suspect. Two Alpha Zero Plus names, together, spelled bad news.

A Mirage jet fighter brought Marc to Paris in time for Bill Harrington's call at noon.

'Can you tell me why you've coded this name, Jacques Morel, as Alpha Zero Plus . . . ?' Bill asked.

There was a silence on the line, then finally, 'I was going to ask you the same question about a certain Captain Joseph Aram. By the way, isn't that a strange name for an Englishman?'

'Yes, it is. His grandparents came from the Middle East a long time ago.'

'Interesting. The parents of Jacques Morel came from the Middle East also, a long time ago. His father is dead. Why did you say you had coded Aram Alpha Zero Plus?'

'I didn't. I don't have the authority.'

'Who does have it?'

'The Prime Minister.'

'Also interesting. The only person who has the authority to de-code Jacques Morel for you is our President. I may call you Bill, do you think?'

'Yes, of course.'

'Bill, I think we have something very interesting here. I think I should talk with my President, and you with your Prime Minister. Then we should meet.'

'To further the Entente Cordiale? I thought that was dead, killed by Charles de Gaulle?'

'Even Charles de Gaulle was prepared to bend a little, sometimes, in the cause of mutual security.'

'I'll try, Marc, but I don't think I'll get very far. The

French have not exactly been cooperative over the last few years, especially over Middle Eastern matters.'

'Try, Bill. It could be very important.'

Bill went immediately to see the Minister. Frank Moody looked aghast at Bill's suggestion, but took him to see the Prime Minister. The Prime Minister listened to Bill's request in stony silence, then shook his head.

'Strictly off the record,' he said, 'I'd rather trust the West Germans than the French. I'm not doubting the sincerity of this man, Chantal, but the French bureaucracy doesn't work the way ours does. If we tell Chantal, we tell the President of France. If we tell him, we tell everyone in his office. We might just as well ring Reuters or the Press Association.'

He sat back in his chair, pinching the corners of his eyes between his thumb and finger, a nervous habit that had endeared him to cartoonists and television impersonators, who had looked in vain for any other lampoonable feature. 'Surely the fact that these two men have met, and that now we separately give each one a top priority, doesn't necessarily mean a collusion in the matter of the missing box?'

The Prime Minister had never referred to it as an atomic warhead, had never called it anything other than the box. Almost as if his mind were refusing to accept the enormity of the loss.

'Jacques Morel is listed in the preliminary enquiry as a naval officer working out of Toulon . . .'

'And this chap, Aram, was presumably listed as an ex-Army Officer? I can't quite see the point you are trying to make. This was part of the PM's parliamentary technique. Get the Opposition to explain what they meant over and over again, and often they would lose the original point of the question. It worked well with his parliamentary colleagues and opponents, his wife, his stubborn twenty-one-year-old son. It did not work with Bill Harrington.

'I mean this, Prime Minister. The potential in possessing an atomic warhead is enormous. The potential in also possessing a means of transporting it is cataclysmic! Our man

68

Aram has stolen a device. What if this man Jacques Morel has stolen a vessel, the means of transporting it. Even a submarine, perhaps.'

Bill was on thin ice and knew it. So did the PM. 'That's pure speculation, Mr Harrington,' he said. 'And you must think me very naive to believe I would confide in the French with nothing better than a speculation to guide me. No, I'm afraid I can't declassify the Alpha Zero Plus rating of this matter. Especially not to the French. Now, if that's all . . . ? I shall tell them that enquiries are being prosecuted with the utmost vigour. You won't let me down, will you?'

Frank Moody and Bill Harrington left the PM together. 'I told you you didn't stand a cat-in-hell's chance,' Moody said. 'If you knew how touchy the PM can be on the subject of the French . . .'

'I think the Prime Minister may be given reason to change his mind,' Bill said quietly. 'And quite soon. You'll let me know the minute you hear anything, any ransom demand, any offer to return the atomic warhead on conditions . . .'

'I will that, lad. It's all too much of a hot potato for me. You're welcome to have it, every bit of it.'

Bill called Paris and spoke to Marc. 'Are you recording?' he asked.

'Not yet.'

'Would you care to keep it switched off?'

'Okay. I'll tell you when I intend to switch on, d'accord?'

'D'accord. I drew a blank with you-know-who.'

'I thought you would. Don't worry, so did I.'

'I wondered if we could meet. Somewhere quiet?'

'For an exchange of mutual points of view?'

'Off the record?'

'Hang on a moment, will you?'

'Not switching on, are you, Marc?'

'Don't be so suspicious! I'm punching out the airline schedule on my magic roundabout. There it is. Paris to London. I could be in Heathrow at four o'clock. You could be at Orly at 1615 hrs. Which do you prefer?'

'London. Landings are more likely to be on time than take-offs these days.'

'The English disease, eh? We have our share. How will I know you, Bill? A red rose in your button-hole? A copy of *Private Eye* under your arm?'

'I'll be sitting in the car at the bottom of the steps when you get off the plane.'

'I thought the plane went straight to the unloading bay?'

'It will, Marc. After I've had you taken off at the end of the touch-down runway. Don't forget, this is Alpha Zero Plus, and there are a lot of eyes watching people arrive at airports these days.'

The Air France flight came in on time, touched down on the runway, rolled to the end, turned for its taxi to the terminal and stopped. A mobile staircase was driven to the side of the plane; the door opened, a man came out, the door closed again, and he came quickly down the steps. Bill Harrington was waiting in the black VIP Humber of the British Airports Authority. There was no driver. Marc opened the car door and got in, and Bill drove, without speaking, to the side of the arrivals door of Terminal Two. He stopped the car under an arch where they could not be seen switched off the engine and held out his hand.

'Bill Harrington.'

'Marc Chantal.'

'I suppose we should exchange cards?'

'I suppose we should.'

'But I left mine behind, in my office.'

'So did I!'

Both laughed. 'I always feel like a berk when I go through an identification routine, even after this length of time.'

'If it's any consolation, so do I, Bill. That's a rotten picture of you they pushed through the computer.'

'But identifiable?'

'A computer picture tells you less than nothing about a person. I hate them. At least a photograph captures some of the essence.'

'Who's going to end the small talk first?'

'You are, Bill. The duties of a host, remember?'

How can you assess a man in two minutes? Marc Chantal, dressed in a black leather jacket, a polo-necked cashmere sweater, black trousers neatly creased, black shoes with a small gold chain across the tongue. Black hair, bushy eyebrows. Aged thirty, ten years younger than Bill. But that is only the physical description, Bill thought. What about the rest? Is he reliable, trustworthy? Is he ambitious in his job, prepared to screw anybody to further his own career? Is he a Frenchman first, an investigator second? If Bill were to trust him, would he go straight back to the Elysée and break any agreement he and Bill might have reached, for the glory of France and the advancement of Marc Chantal? How the hell can you tell a thing like that, at two minutes meeting.

'Marc, I'm flying on instinct at the moment.'

'Often, in your situation, that must be necessary.'

'Not in your situation?'

'That, too, but the French are masters of self-preservation. The British are the quixotic of Europe. And look where it's got you – in comparison to the French and the Germans, I mean. And the Dutch and the Flemish. Look, Bill. I can't give you any reason to trust me. I can't give you any promises, any evidence. I have an Alpha Zero Plus, so have you. I'll tell you quite frankly, I don't believe my Alpha Zero Plus. Not yet. I think it's been coded as high as that so that some self-seeking professional politician can get rid of it. That's what happens in France, you know. Eh bien, they say, this is too big for me to handle. Either make me big enough to handle it, or give it to someone else. Have you ever tried to apply for *anything* official in France? So, I think that my problem will turn out to be Beta One. You, on the other hand, are British. Yours is a British problem. The British traditionally *under*play things. Look at the way your Queen went to Ireland and as good as told the terrorists to go shove themselves. That could never have happened on the continent of Europe. Right now, the West Germans have barricaded themselves in to Bonn because of this Hans-Martin Schleyer affair. What

I'm trying to say is symptomatic of the trouble we have understanding each other. *You*, I believe, have a problem. A real honest-to-God Alpha Zero Plus problem. Mine is not so big. So, I've decided, on the plane coming over, that I'm going to tell you about it, trusting your British sense of fair play, and all that crap, to see me through. D'accord?'

Bill felt an immediate rapport with the Frenchman. 'D'accord!' he said. 'You're on!'

Marc told him, missing nothing. The known history of Jacques Morel. The apparent dedication to education and to his job. The fact that Marc saw it as being too 'copy-book'.

'As if he were a sleeper, if you see what I mean.'

'Yes I do. Nobody goes through life as blamelessly, as pointedly, as that.'

'Unless they've dedicated themselves to some sort of ideal. Well, Jacques found his ideal. He's stolen a sub-marine, I believe. A rather special kind of submarine.'

He told Bill all about the Green Dolphin, about the test voyage. 'Look, that bastard never intended to come back. Okay, a guy about to do something like that might believe that something could go wrong. In that event, he would write a note and leave it on his dresser. If anything should happen to me on this flight, please tell my mother I love her, pay the phone bill, and see the cat gets a good home. None of that. No sign of a note. But – no fresh food in the fridge, no vegetables, no money in the bank, no trace of any cash about the place. That bugger *knew* he *wasn't* com-ing back. He's out there, somewhere, in the Atlantic. Sail-ing that submarine to a rendezvous somewhere. Where that rendezvous might be will depend on what you can tell me.

'I'm afraid you've reached decision time, Bill. Either you have to say my Alpha Zero Plus has nothing to do with that missing sub, *could not conceivably* have anything to do with it, or you've got to come clean. Which, Bill?' Marc glanced at his watch. 'There's a BEA flight for Paris in ten minutes. I guess with your pull you could still get me on it. The Air France flight leaves in half an hour. Which one am I catching, Bill?'

How could he adequately balance the one thing against the other? The international standing, the international honour of a country against the need to be effective quickly. If news of the dirty bomb were to leak out, the good name of every Englishman around the world would be destroyed. If the bomb were used, the international repercussions would be too immense to contemplate.

'I think Joseph Aram has an atomic bomb,' he said quietly. 'I think the meeting in Marcel Dupree's apartment may have been to coordinate his theft with that of Jacques Morel. I think Jacques Morel has a rendezvous, yes, with Aram and his warhead. I think they mean to put the two together, and aim them . . .'

'Target?'

Bill shook his head. 'Target unknown,' he said. 'But it could be anywhere that submarine can reach. And that, presumably, means any city with a waterfront. New York, London, Paris . . .'

'Stockholm, Oslo, Copenhagen?'

'Tokyo, Singapore, Hong Kong?'

'Athens, Tel Aviv, Cairo . . .'

'Target, unknown. We've got to find them, Marc. Both of them. Before they can join those two damned things together and launch them.'

CHAPTER NINE

The *Marie Cinq* was fifty feet overall, a long boat to carry a Bermuda rig without staysail, a long boat to handle alone. Henri Dupree had no fear of the *Marie Cinq*. He had taken her across the Atlantic to Newport, single-handed, arriving fifth in 1977. He brought her home on his own, via Bermuda. His only companion on board, on each occasion, was Marie, the steering vane of his own invention and design that fitted aft with its outstretched arms. During his long voyages, he talked to *Marie Cinq*, the fifth and final modification on his original design.

'How are we doing, Marie? Are we still on course? Not letting us wander, are you, Marie?' The questions were rhetorical. Henri Dupree carried a compass in his head day and night, awake and asleep. A shift of one degree would register itself on his inner mind.

The hull of *Marie Cinq* had been built to his own design in Toulon; the masts and spars were wood, the rigging stainless steel, the sails manufactured to his specification in England of lightweight dacron.

The inside of the boat was sparse, as befitted a working vessel; she had six berths, used only when being sent from one mooring to another under a crew of six. When Henri sailed, he slept in a special chair in the aftermost cabin, ready at any moment to scamper topside and make some adjustment to steering or to sails. The crew who had brought *Marie Cinq* from Toulon had berthed her in the Mersey alongside the other competitors, twenty in all. The race was being sponsored by the Cyprus Tourist Board, anxious to attract more tourists to Cyprus, especially from the industrial north of England. The winner of each class, of which there were three, would receive a prize of £10,000.

Henri did not care about the prize.

He knew this was one race he would not finish.

He sat on the bench at the side of the cockpit watching the last of the pre-race preparations. Few other boats seemed ready for the start, which would take place at noon the following day.

Vans were still arriving with provisions; last minute adjustments were being made to rigging, to stowage below decks. Every boat seemed to contain some kind of committee. Of course, most of the boats were commercially sponsored and the PROs swarmed on and off the gangplanks quick as dockside rats with yet another photographer, yet another interviewer.

Henri had winched himself out on his anchors, lifted his gangplank inboard, and a distance of fifteen feet separated him from the dock-side. His supply cables had been disconnected. The other boats were ablaze with lights, humming with last minute cocktail parties and the arrival of goodwill messages and flowers. Henri took no notice of anyone who came to the edge of the dock to summon him. His administration was complete; the boat was ready to sail, trimmed and tuned.

With the arrival of dusk the activity aboard the other boats rapidly increased in volume and noise. Someone fell overboard from the boat further up the line, the Dutch 45 footer, *Amsterdam Avenue*, and had to be fished out of the water with a boat-hook.

The noise finally quietened down around four-o'clock in the morning and the last parties sang their drunken Auld Lang Synes. Regulations said that all boats must be single-handed from 0800 hrs, four hours before the start of the race. The boats themselves would leave from the dockside. The finishing post was the dockside at Limassol, the route taken, optional. No one was permitted to dock anywhere en route; if they did so, they would automatically be suspended from the race.

The lights were out along the line of moored boats, as, one by one, the cars drove away and the dock was clear.

At four thirty, a black van drove along the quay and parked opposite the stern of the *Marie Cinq*. At the same moment, two boats floated silently to the bows, using boat hooks to hold themselves alongside while black-dressed figures jumped over the gunwhales. Ten men went aboard, silent as wharfies, and stalked the decks towards the stern and the cockpit hatch.

At the same time, four frogmen slipped off the two boats, and dived under the *Marie Cinq*, their powerful torches cutting through the murk of the Mersey water.

Henri was standing on the steps leading up from the after cabin. In his hand he held a Verey signalling pistol, that would fire a blazing explosive charge.

'Who are you,' he exclaimed. 'And what the hell are you doing on my boat?'

He heard the clatter as the anchor winch was knocked

free, and saw the two men pulling his stern lines to bring *Marie Cinq* to the dock.

One of the black-clad men came forward. Another shone a torch on the identity card the first man held in his hand.

'We're the police,' he said. 'We have a warrant to search this boat. I'd be very grateful, Mr Dupree, if you'd put down that signalling pistol; we don't want to have an accident, do we? And would you please step on shore, where I'll be glad to show you my credentials and the warrant.'

Henri shrugged his shoulders, put the signalling pistol back into its holster clipped to the bulkhead and came up the steps. One of the policemen had already lowered the gangplank; Henri walked across it, turned, and waited. The policeman beckoned.

'If you'd care to sit in the van, Mr Dupree . . . ?' he said.

Henri walked across to the back of the van which contained padded seats along each side. He got in and sat down. The policeman opened a briefcase that had been lying on the bench seat, and showed Henri the search warrant. He beckoned two policemen forward. They stood each side of the back of the van, the dim light of the interior revealing only their expressionless features and the dark blue coveralls they wore.

'I am Chief Superintendent Wilton of the Special Branch,' the policeman who had first addressed Henri said. 'This is Inspector James, and Sergeant Bullock, also of the Special Branch. In accordance with the powers granted to me by warrant of the Justice of the Peace, which warrant has been handed to you in the presence of these officers, I am hereby instructing my men to make a search of the premises mentioned in the warrant, specifically, one boat named the *Marie Cinq*. You understand that the warrant permits me or my men to remove any object that may impede our search, to investigate the contents of locked or sealed receptacles, to open any bedding cushions or other sewn materials . . .'

'If you mean you can take my boat apart, I understand. I protest, of course, but I know it's no use. The *Marie Cinq* is my boat, registered in France, and so far as I'm concerned nobody has a right on board it without my permission.'

'We could argue legal points all night, Mr Dupree . . .'

'We won't bother. Look, Chief Superintendent, I'm tired. Tomorrow I'm sailing in a race. I want to get as much sleep as I can. Tell your men not to mess the boat about too much, eh? Though I imagine you've picked lads who know about boats, and know where to look. There's nothing on board, I know that. You think there is, or the Magistrate wouldn't have given you your warrant . . .'

'Justice of the Peace, Mr Dupree. And I should warn you that anything . . .'

'Look, Chief Superintendent, don't bother. Just do what you came to do, as quickly as you can, and then, fut le camp, eh? You know what that means, eh?'

'Every schoolboy knows what that means, Mr Dupree.'

It took them five hours to find nothing, inside or outside the boat, that should not have been there.

They had brought a ship's carpenter with them, a ship's engineer, a ship's bosun. The carpenter, the engineer, and the bosun supervised the reinstatement of everything they had taken apart. They even resewed the mattresses and the cushions, filled the engine with new oil, the cans with fresh water and diesel fuel, the batteries with fresh acid.

When the town hall clock sounded mid-day, and the cannon they had brought for the starting ceremony boomed, Henri Dupree was third off the mooring.

The Committee had waived the 'alone since 0800 hrs' rule after the Chief Superintendent had had a word with them.

Henri Dupree was the only competitor to take his boat off the mooring under sail. It seemed like thumbing his nose to the Chief Superintendent. And anyone else who might have been watching . . .

By common consent, all the competitors had chosen to sail down through the Irish Straits on their way south on the first leg of the journey that would take them to the far end of the Mediterranean. Near every port on the way, enthusiastic locals, stirred by the publicity, came out in their small boats to watch the progress. Companies that were financially interested in the race's outcome had chartered light planes and helicopters that flew over the fleet of boats, staying more or less together at the start. The real competition would come during the first night and across the Bay of Biscay, when the men would be separated from the boys. The *Marie Cinq* was lying comfortably in the centre, heeling slightly under a strong westerly that promised to increase as night fell. For the time being, most of the competitors were happy to be doing six knots or so, many with heads still aching from the previous night's goodbyes. With the automatic steering vanes active, most of the men were scrambling topside, still adjusting rigging, still bringing their boats to the final stage of tuning and pitch that would mean all the difference at the race's end.

Marie Cinq needed no such titivation; Henri knew she was as perfect as she would ever be. He could have set the sails a fraction tighter, perhaps, might even have chanced heeling a little more with the next size up in jibs. But, for the moment, he was content with his position.

A whole fleet of small boats awaited them off Anglesey, and a light plane flew a streamer overhead saying 'Morgan's Boatyard salutes the sailors'. The *Marie Cinq* was riding further to port than the rest of the fleet, closer inshore.

A British Navy vessel was steaming ahead of the fleet; someone from the bridge was using a loud-hailer to tell the scattered small boats to keep out of the path of the competitors.

One speed-boat in particular was whirring in and out of the fleet of sailing boats, a sixty-horsepower Evinrude engine sending it scurrying across the water. The boat was painted a vivid yellow; the man driving it, standing behind the spray-hood, waved at each boat as he passed. Most of the sailors, men who despised engines, power-boats, and especially speed-boats, ignored him completely. Suddenly, when he was about four hundred yards in front of the starboard bow of *Marie Cinq*, his engine stalled. The speed-boat came to a stand-still while the driver investigated the propellor, hanging over the back of the stern. He went back to the steering position, pressed the self starter, and the engine fired. He shot ahead, only fifty yards in front of the *Marie Cinq*. Henri Dupree, standing in the bows, shook his fist angrily. The driver ignored the anger and waved back. When he was fifty yards to the port side of *Marie Cinq* his engine stalled again. The *Marie Cinq* continued on her way, past him. After a couple of minutes of wrestling with his engine, the speed-boat driver got it started again, and headed back to the shore. No doubt he had had enough for one day.

Henri was sitting on the stern counter. No helicopters over-head, no private planes. Some of them, he guessed, had not been so private. Slowly and inconspicuously he worked the lever of the winch on the stern, bringing inboard the line that had been streaming out behind the boat. On the end of the line a three-point grapple hook had been hanging below him in the water since before their arrival off Angle-sey. He admired the performance of Joseph Aram in the speed-boat, behaving like a typical English berk. The first time the speed-boat stopped, Joseph had dropped a buoy that hung just below the water. As he sped across in front of *Marie Cinq*'s bow, he had paid out a line, to which a waterproofed box was lashed. The box, heavy with lead, had sunk instantly. The end of the line was attached to the speedboat, and Joseph was holding it in his hands. When the grapple hook hanging below the *Marie Cinq* caught the line, Joseph Aram allowed it to be jerked from his hand.

The box was now attached to the grapple hooks hanging below the *Marie Cinq*.

And the police had searched the *Marie Cinq* before it left port, pronouncing it clean.

Henri carried on winching. The three-pronged grapple came on board. He wound the line it had snagged around the winch drum, and slowly it came on board.

He looked over the stern. Soon he could see the outlines of a box, hanging just beneath the surface of the water, bobbing in his wake. He left it there. Soon, it would be dark. Ample time to bring it on board, when no one could see him. The drag of the box in the water had brought him towards the back of the competing fleet. He tightened his jib, hauled in his mainsheet a fraction, feeling the sails begin to throb and the rigging to hum. He altered the course on the vane. 'Vas-y, Marie,' he said. 'Vas-y!'

As if to answer him, the *Maire Cinq* took her new bearing, slipping through the wind and the seas, surging ahead, the slip waves rippling along her sleek sides and spuming at her wake in phosphorescent foam.

The elderly man with the greying hair, slightly stooped shoulders, and pot belly ill-concealed beneath his water-proof suit, moored the speed-boat at Morgan's Boatyard, some fifteen miles down the North Wales coast from Caernarvon.

'Had a nice run, Mr Belling?' Gwynneth asked him when he went into the office, to return the key and collect the balance of his deposit. 'What a beautiful sight! All of them sailing boats. Quite a picture, it was. It must have been marvellous, out there among them. I quite envy you, Mr Belling.'

She paid him the balance of his money. It was not every day you got somebody prepared to pay a day's hire charge for the use of the boat for an hour or so. 'Still got your suitcase, I see. Not got it wet, have you? You could have left it by here in the office you know!'

He smiled at her. 'At my age,' he said, 'you become a bit overcautious. I'm going down the coast to take a bit of a holiday. I don't want to lose sight of my stuff, do I?'

'No, I reckon you don't,' Gwynneth said. Really, for an old boy, he still had plenty of vigour about him. She watched him walk out of the office and across the yard, his suitcase in his hand. The trip to sea must have done him good. When he left, it was as much as he could do to carry his suitcase; now he was throwing it about like a two-year-old. Ah, well, takes all sorts, doesn't it. He turned at the gate and waved to her. Such a nice old boy, really. She watched him place himself by the bus stop. The 273 would be along in five minutes. She could buy three pairs of tights with the pound he had left her.

The old man rode half a mile down the road, then walked up a lane opposite the bus stop. The car was parked at the side of the lane, in a small lay-by.

He started it, and drove back down the lane after making a U-turn in a field gate. At the bottom, he turned right and along the road, checking the mirror.

Nobody followed him.

Once on the M6 he pulled into the first motorway cafe and took his suitcase with him into the lavatories. At that time of night, they were deserted. Once inside the cubicle he opened the case and balanced it on the pan. He took off his grey wig, revealing black hair beneath. He took off his jacket and then the pad on his shoulders that had given him a slightly humped back. He folded the pad and put it into the suitcase together with the jacket and trousers of his grey suit. He unbelted the pad he had worn around his waist to give him increased girth, and put that into the suitcase too. From the case he had taken a pair of jeans and a denim shirt which he now put on. Finally, he exchanged the sneakers he had worn for a pair of well scuffed brown loafers.

He glanced at himself in the mirror as he went out of the washroom. There was no way Gwynneth, or any of the people he had met since he left Oxford, could have recognized in this athletic looking thirty-year-old the rather seedy travelling salesman who had refused to be parted from his case of samples. He dumped the case, weighted, into the water tank at the back of the car park. Nobody saw him.

He made Elmdon Airport on schedule at 0100 hrs and went straight to the check-in counter. The airport was a milling throng of people, all carrying suitcases with Guaranteed Travel stickers. He waited in the queue until his turn came, then dumped his plain blue canvas bag on the weighing scales.

'You haven't put on your sticker, Mr . . . ?' the check-in

girl said reprovingly. He took the ticket from his breast pocket and placed it on the counter. The girl looked at the young man with his crew-cut hair, his rimless steel spectacles. Really, some of these young fellows did like to make themselves look American. Still, he was tall, and attractive . . .

'That all the luggage you've got, Mr Libby?'

'Yes. I like to travel light.'

Nice voice, too. At least he didn't try to talk American. She checked his ticket. Everything in order. Looked down the list, yes, John Libby, travelling alone. Well, he would not be alone long. She could swear to that. What a pity she wasn't flying. 'We don't anticipate the flight will be delayed, Mr Libby. We'll be calling it at about a quarter to two. Have a nice holiday, and thank you for booking with Guaranteed Travel. Next please . . . ?'

He walked across the crowded room through the families trailing children, passed excited kids for whom this was a first time flight, the first real adventure. A young girl collided with him, said sorry shyly, then turned and dashed away.

The sign read This Way for Embarkation. He followed its direction. He had stuck his boarding card into his top pocket; now he took it out and slipped it into his passport. The first control desk was manned by a woman of about forty-five and a younger man. They glanced at his boarding card and his passport, then waved him through.

There was a queue at the immigration desk. Two men were standing behind each of the three immigration officers on duty. He walked forward, slowly, keeping in line. Before him a woman, a man, their two sons. The woman had a prunes and custard voice and had not stopped issuing a stream of instructions to her husband and sons all the time he had been standing behind them. He waited until her husband pushed their passports forward for the immigration officer. Then, as if exasperated, he said in a voice loud enough for the immigration officer to hear – 'Missis, why don't you stop nagging your 'usband. What kind of an 'oliday is 'e goin' to 'ave, if you nag 'im all the time?'

82

She turned to him, gasping. 'What did you say to me?'

'You 'eard, missie. You get on the plane first, so's I can pick a seat a long way away from you . . .'

'Did you hear that, Arthur?' she said to her husband. 'Are you going to let this lout get away with that . . . ?'

'Come on, Letty,' her husband said, looking anxiously at her and the two boys. 'Come along, Percy and Thomas.'

'Are you going to let him get away with insulting me? At the very start of my holiday . . .'

'Now, we don't want any fuss,' he said. 'We don't want to make a spectacle of ourselves . . .' He put his arm round them and swept them forward, away from the immigration desk.

The immigration officer was smiling behind his glasses. 'Mr Libby, is it?' he said. He opened the passport, checked the date of issue, the issuing office.

One of the plain-clothed policemen looked at the other. Height right, shape of face right. Hair wrong. Glasses. Didn't stand like an Army officer. Certainly didn't sound like one. And Army officers are polite to women, aren't they? He reached over and took the passport from the immigration officer. John Libby. Issued over a year ago. A new passport would have been suspicious. He handed the passport back without saying anything. The immigration officer closed it and gave it back. 'Have a nice trip, Mr Libby, if Madam will permit it! Somehow, I don't think you, or anybody else for that matter, will hear too much from her!'

Aram smiled at him, said nothing, and passed through the immigration control. First obstacle. Had he made it? Impossible to tell. Hardly likely they would stop him then and there. More likely to make some sort of signal that would expose him to colleagues waiting elsewhere. They would want the box more than they would want him.

He walked through the door into the next section and found a scene of pandemonium. Instead of the luggage being shipped out to the plane as it had been checked in, it had all been stacked in this room. People were moving about, looking for their cases and bags. A desk had been thrown across the far side of the room, manned by six Security men. They were unlike any other security men he had ever seen. These were serving coppers, from one of the heavy mobs. And they were using highly sophisticated apparatus.

A stewardess was waiting just inside the door, repeating the same message to all the travellers. 'Will you find your luggage and take it through the security check with you.'

Porters were waiting at the far side of the security counter with trolleys which extended in a long line out of the shed to an electric tractor.

Aram saw his blue canvas hold-all. It was by Letty's foot. He went to the pile on the other side of the room and pretended to look through it. By the time he had appeared to have realized it was not there, Letty's suitcase was open on the bench and the security men were emptying it. The case had made a bleep on their machine. Radiation. Apart from one brief exclamation, Letty was speechless as they examined her clothes. She had the external appearance of the matron in a hospital for retired gentlewomen. The contents of her case, however, were far from matronly. Underwear – pink, blue with black lace frills. Black leather briefs. A black leather bra with holes from which, doubtless, her nipples would protrude. A many thonged short black leather whip, with a shaped handle.

Her husband had taken his suitcase, with those of the boys, to the other end of the counter.

The radiation came from a garment, shaped like a body stocking, on which the 'manufacturer' had painted, in thick luminous paint, a heavy drawing they would not have permitted in an Indian temple. When the security officer held it up, the machine on the desk clicked, furiously, as if in the last throes of orgiastic excitement.

'All that luminous paint, madam. It radiates, you see,' the security officer said impassively. He folded the garment and put it back in the case. 'Perhaps madam would prefer to repack it herself,' he said, and beckoned Aram forward. He unzipped the blue bag. Two shirts, two pairs of underpants, two pairs of socks, six handkerchiefs. A spare pair of jeans.

He zipped the case shut again and marked it with chalk. 'If you'd just walk through that gate, sir,' he said.

The Special Branch officer was telephoning to London, dialling the number he had been given. A woman answered.

'Sally Price. The tape is running. Go ahead.'

'Elmdon, Birmingham, Miss. I think we have your man. He's travelling under passport number 9076412, name of John Libby. At the present, he's going through baggage control.'

'You're certain?'

'As certain as anyone can be.'

'Have you anyone standing by?'

'Yes. He's already booked through onto the plane. We've been doing that as a precaution all day, booking a man on early, and then yanking him off at the last minute if we don't have anyone.'

'Just one man?'

'No, a pair.'

'Look, we want the man, but we want something he's stolen even more. A heavy wooden box. Tell your people to do nothing overt. Just to watch him. Where is the flight going. Give me the details.'

He gave her the flight number, the destination, the ETA.

'Right, we'll pick him up at Tunis. Tell your man to be careful. He's already killed at least twice.'

'Very good, Miss.'

He walked back through the terminal into the departure lounge, briefly glimpsed Joseph Aram standing in line for the baggage check entrance. He went back to the booking desk, and leafed through the pile of tickets of those who had checked in, finding John Libby's seat number.

He walked through the terminal again, through the crowds of holidaymakers waiting for check-in for flights to all the holiday spots. No one took any notice of him, just another airline official. He stood next to the Special Branch man. Nobody saw the ticket stub change hands.

'Have a nice trip,' he whispered from the side of his mouth. 'But watch it, he's a killer.'

'Thanks a lot, Superintendent . . .'

Aram walked through a steel doorway to which wires and machines were connected. 'You wearing a watch?' the man reading the dials asked. Aram pulled back the wrist of his denim shirt and showed it to him. 'Stick your arm back through,' the man said. He did. 'That's all right, sir,' the man said.

Aram walked out of the security check, across the departure lounge to the bar, and ordered a whisky and water.

'You don't close at eleven, then?' he asked.

'Special licence.'

'When do you close?'

'At four, when the last plane takes off.'

'It must be a long night?'

'It is. But the pay's good.'

'It'd need to be . . .' Aram had been looking through the mirror while he had been chatting. Impossible to tell, at first, who was the watched, who the watcher. He had trained with Special Services and knew the tricks. Stay in one place long enough, and you would see eyes flick in your direction, flick away when they had verified you had not moved. Make a sudden move, turn back as if you had forgotten something, and often you would catch the eye-line. Best way to hide the eye-line was to read a book, a paper, holding it at an angle, keeping your subject at the extreme edge of the page. Then, if he moved, you could follow him with the book and it looked natural. Trouble is, if you held a book in your hand, you were a sitting duck if it turned out the man you were watching had a friend.

Nobody was holding a book, with Joseph Aram, alias John Libby, at its edge.

Still, this was a closed room. No way out, except through the door onto the tarmac, or back through Security.

He watched Letty come into the departure lounge. Saw the defiant tilt of her head as she realized the few people who had seen the contents of her case were either smiling at her, or trying hard not to smile. Chin up, chest out, she walked through the crowd to where her husband and the boys were sitting.

'Atta girl!' Aram said silently. The Dunkirk spirit. The days of the wives of the officers of the Raj. And, apparently, the nights . . . The great unflappables.

He was relying on that, wasn't he? All of them, including Jacques Morel, and Henri Dupree, were relying very much on that.

The flight was called on time and they went aboard the buses to the chartered Tri-Star. The plane was filled to capacity. Letty and her family, he noticed, had been allocated seats in the front section. Travelling alone, he had been given a seat at the extreme rear of the plane, on the port side.

He felt under the seat and located the Colt ·45 tucked between the seat and the life-jacket. Although he knew it should be loaded, he touched the bottom of the butt, verifying it contained a clip.

'Fasten your seat belt, please,' the steward said.

He looked up. 'Thank you,' he said.

The steward nodded. He had wiped his fingerprints off the gun before he had hidden it under the seat. He glanced up at the locker above the seat, and Joseph Aram followed the direction of his eyes. The steward nodded, then went on his way.

It was an easy flight, a milk-run. Jimmy Wilberforce liked the Tri-Star, liked his crew, liked flying charters. Sure, it was hard work in the peak seasons, and few lay overs, but who needs to lie over in some stinking airport hotel on the other side of the world? He was happy working out of Elmdon, with his house just a few miles down the M45, his wife, his kids. Most nights he slept at home, and that was the way he liked it. As a senior captain he could more or less pick his flights. He had chosen this one, to Tunis, because it gave him a four-hour stop at the far end. Time to go into town, pick up the brassware he wanted for his daughter's wedding present when the soùk opened just after six o'clock, and be back in England by eleven, home by noon. She wanted one of those inlaid brass, copper and silver water jugs, on a tray. Should be able to pick one up for ten quid at the most. Couldn't stand the stuff himself, but if that was what Polly wanted . . .

He picked up the internal phone, seeing the wink on the console. Barcelona just behind them, a straight run down across the Med now, flying the western alternate. 'Captain,' he said.

'Jimmy, Captain. I have a passenger with a VIP logbook. Wants to know if he can come on to the flight deck to have you sign it for him . . .?'

'Sure.' The auto was flying the plane. Some airlines gave kids a book and the skipper of each aeroplane signed a page and added some kind of comment. It was a public relations gimmick, but Captain Wilberforce was PR minded, and often took press men on flights as Guaranteed opened new holiday routes.

He beckoned to Harry to watch the auto. Planes flew themselves these days. Dial-a-destination.

The door from the stewards' galley opened and the steward came in followed by a young fellow, about thirty, crew cut hair. Probably had the book since the early days of the New York flights, when they stopped at Keflavik. Be interesting to flip through it. 'Wilberforce,' he said, holding out his hand.

The damned kid was pointing a gun at him.

He looked up at the steward, as if he ought to have known. But, of course, how could he?

He saw that Harry had not noticed the gun. Not yet.

Nobody had seen it, except him. The kid was shielding it with his hand and the blue, leather-bound book.

The book was thrust forward. 'Open it,' Joseph Aram said.

The Captain opened it. On the last page it said, in neat, easy to read printing: 'I am hijacking your plane. Take me to the following bearing. Do not communicate with the ground. Do not activate the automatic hijack warning. Take the plane down to nine thousand feet and depressurize the cabin. Do as I say, and no one will get hurt. Fail, and I will kill the steward.

Captain Wilberforce unclipped the pen from his shirt pocket and wrote on the same page of the book. 'Okay. I'll do as you say.' He showed the page to the man with the gun, who nodded. The Captain reached up, switched the radio to flight deck local. 'Okay fellahs,' he said. 'Listen to me. We've been hijacked. Don't anybody do anything. He's got a pistol and I, for one, am not yet bored with life. He's given me a location, and wants us down at nine thousand feet, depressurized. So I guess he means to jump. Fawcett, plot us a route to this location.' He read the numbers off the book.

The navigator ran his two slides across the face of the map. The position was more or less ahead, off the island of Mallorca in the Baleares.

'ETA five minutes,' he said. The skipper spoke again. 'Harry, take us out of auto and start descent. They'll go crazy in Barcelona but that's their worry. Joe, start progressive depressurization.' He flicked the radio switch, pushed the microphone away from his face.

'Which door are you going out of?' he asked.

'The back one.'

'You know the speed I'll be travelling?'

'Yes.'

'I take it you have your own pack on board?'

'Yes.'

'You know we have a security man on board?'

'Yes. And I know you have a code to call him.'

'Look, buster, whatever your name is. I'm a happy man. I don't want any trouble. I'm not interested in politics or any of that. All I want to do, my sole responsibility at this moment, is to get this planeload of passengers to their destination safely, to get my crew on the ground in one piece, and then home to their wives and families. Get me?'

'And all I want to do is get off this plane.'

'Okay. I understand. I have two ways of calling the security man. If I ask the Assistant Chief Steward to go to the galley, he'll know I'm in trouble. If I say the Chief

Assistant Steward, he'll know it's all right and I want to see him about something routine. But I'm damned if I'll bring him here for you to knock about. Understand?'

'I won't touch him unless he moves first.'

The Captain reached up, switched the intercom to the extreme right. 'This is your Captain speaking,' he said. 'I have two announcements for you so would you please listen carefully.' He looked at Aram, who pushed the gun harder into the steward's stomach. 'Would the Chief Assistant Steward please come to the galley? The second announcement concerns all of you. Due to a slight technical difficulty, I'm going to take the plane down to nine thousand feet. The passenger cabin will be depressurized for a short while at that altitude. Any of you who feel the slightest discomfort should put on the light, when the stewards will come to advise you. I repeat that this is a brief and unavoidable manoeuvre, which we will complete as rapidly as possible. Needless to say, we shall resume normal flight as rapidly as possible. I estimate we shall be at our destination on the ground about six minutes ahead of schedule. At the completion of the manoeuvre, the stewardesses will bring out the trolleys and I'd like to offer each of you a complimentary drink. Thank you.'

The door opened and Letty's husband came in.

'What's the matter, Jimmy?' he asked. 'Forgotten how to fly this damned thing?'

Joseph Aram reached his right arm out, his fingers straight, heading for his shoulders. At the last moment he flicked his wrist and his hand went into the security man's inside pocket, closing on the gun. He pulled the gun out of the man's pocket.

'Joseph Aram?' the man said. 'I had my doubts about you.' His eyes licked around the cockpit, taking in the scene. The plane was descending rapidly and his ears were popping. He saw the switch by the navigator's hand that would have sent the automatic 'we have been hijacked' signal. It had not been pushed down.

'Sit on the floor,' Aram said.

He did as he was told. You don't mess around at that

height, when a man has a Colt ·45 in somebody else's belly, and a planeload of passengers depends on the skipper to get the plane down. John Libby, eh? He'd tipped himself as Joseph Aram in the departure lounge. Sitting at the bar, chatting with the barman, his eyes following the pattern of surveillance he obviously knew so well. That ploy with Letty. Too much. Reverse psychology. Nobody takes any notice of the man who's making enough noise to get himself noticed. You're supposed to look for the guy who skulks in corners. People aren't that rude to people in Birmingham airport at night waiting for a holiday charter. Sure, they grumble. But they don't make waves. The wave-makers are the arrogant bastards going out of Heathrow on a Full Fare ticket supplied by some company. Not the 'how cheap can I do it' charter holiday makers. And the accent had been wrong. Still, Jimmy Wilberforce was in charge, and he'd obviously decided to play it safe.

'Now I want you all to listen to me,' Aram said. The radio operator handed him a pair of head-phones and a microphone which he held to his head with his right hand. His left hand still held the Colt ·45, unwavering, in the steward's stomach. He looked up at the communications rack, turned the switch to Flight Deck only, then spoke. 'I'm going out of the flight deck when we level off short of the location I have given you. I'll walk behind the steward to the back of the plane, take my parachute and the steward behind the curtain so as not to panic the passengers. When we are flying level and the pressure is down to atmospheric, I want you, Captain, to make an announcement telling everyone to sit down and fasten their seat belts. As soon as that has been done, the steward will open the back door and I shall go out. Once I'm gone, I see no reason why you shouldn't resume normal flight. Just one more thing. Radio operator, I want you to take the transistor clip out of the first stage amplifier . . .'

The radio operator glanced at the skipper. The bastard obviously knew about ground to air, air to ground communications. With the transistor clip out of the amplifier, the radio was useless. The Captain pulled his microphone to his mouth.

'Do as he says,' he ordered.

The radio operator unclipped the panel, about four inches by five, with its printed circuit on which the transistors were mounted. He gave it to Aram, who had hung the head-set round his neck, liberating his right hand. He threw the transistor panel to the deck, and ground it under his heel. The circuits shattered.

'Now the two spares,' he said.

'I only carry one spare.'

'Captain,' Aram said. 'Tell your radio operator not to mess about with me. I know he has *two*.'

'Give them both to him,' the Captain ordered. What the hell, he could fly blind into Tunis. They were expecting him; they would read his flight number from the transponder beneath the plane, realize he could not talk to them, and light a runway. He would get down all right. For a moment he thought of turning back, but they would not be expecting him in Barcelona, and the chance of emergency procedures working was that much more slender. At least, in Tunis, they had a flight path for him, an ETA. Runway six, the long one, would be clear in anticipation. He would turn a triangle over the airport to tell them he had radio difficulty, and give them time to clear Runway Six. Then he would make his own approach. Jesus, he had been flying Tri-Stars before they even went into service, and landing in Tunis when the runways were made of ground up coconut shells. At least, that's what they had felt like in those old Britannias.

The radio operator made one last try. 'Look,' he said. 'I don't know how technical you are, but you don't need to destroy those transistor clips. If you knock out two of the transistors, these two here, you can prevent us sending a message to the ground, but we'd be able to receive landing instructions . . .'

Aram held out his hand, carefully put the two extra clips down, and smashed them with his heel. 'You could repair them in two minutes flat,' he said, 'for W/T transmission.'

Harry had been watching the altimeter. 'How are we doing for position?' he asked the navigator.

'ETA two minutes.'

'Okay by you if I circle your location?' the skipper asked.

'Good.'

'Radius two miles?'

'Good.' Joseph Aram checked his wrist watch. 'Okay,' he said to the steward. 'You first.'

The passenger cabin was deathly still as if, somehow, the drama of the scene in the flight deck had conveyed itself through the bulk-head. Several passengers were using the yellow oxygen masks the stewardesses had provided for them, pulling them down out of the bulkhead. Acting on her own initiative, the chief stewardess had switched on the 'Fasten Seat Belts' sign, and the 'No Smoking'. Everyone looked at the two men as they walked purposefully down the port side aisle to the back of the plane.

Aram checked his watch. Thirty seconds to ETA.

He beckoned the steward to open the lockers above the seat he had been occupying. From there he took two green canvas bags, approximately fifteen inches by twenty by twelve, closed by one long zipper.

Both felt the plane bank at the start of its slow, two miles radius turn.

Aram looked down the plane and saw the woman, Letty, get up from her seat and start down the aisle of the plane towards him. The steward saw her. 'Go back to your seat, Missis,' he called. 'Go back to your seat!'

She kept on coming down the aisle towards them.

The Captain's voice boomed over the loudspeaker system.

'Will all passengers please observe the Seat Belts sign, and remain seated until I make another announcement.'

One of the stewardesses came out of her emergency seat forward, and half skipped, half ran down the plane after Letty.

Letty was holding her hands forward, partly raised. Joseph Aram recognized the stance from his own training. He cursed himself. He ought to have guessed there would be two operatives on board, not just one. But who would have thought of a man and woman team. And all that business with the underwear was just to distract anyone who might be watching.

A collective murmur in the plane rose in pitch as the passengers looked at Letty, then twisted backwards to look at the man facing her. His mind was racing. Shoot her and he ran the risk of the heavy slug penetrating the skin of the plane, causing a panic that would prevent him getting to the emergency door to open it.

One woman, sensing the tension, gasped loudly and started to moan.

Letty came nearer, her eyes locked on Aram's as if defying him to raise the pistol she guessed he carried, and shoot her.

The noise began to rise to a crescendo above the sound of the engines. 'What the hell's going on?' a man said.

Another man threw off his seat belt when Letty had passed and started to climb into the gangway. His wife grabbed his arm. 'Sit down,' she hissed. 'For God's sake, sit down.'

Letty came on. Ten paces to go.

Someone shouted. 'What the hell is happening? We have a right to know, we have a right to know.' The rumble of panic started, and rolled down the plane like fog. Four paces to go. Letty paused, her body weaving like the trunk of a cobra ready to strike.

'They'll find you, Joseph Aram, wherever you try to go.'

She turned her body slightly to the left. Not much room for manoeuvre. The men sitting in the few remaining seats by the aisle unbelted themselves, climbed over the seat rests where they could, in the centre of the plane. The ones near the skin cowered left, crowding their neighbours.

She was fast, damned fast. Feinted straight, wove, and ducked down under his arm. He felt her stiffened knuckles strike the breastbone just below his heart. Then sideways, slamming with the blade of her hand against his muscle. The gun dropped from his grip, but he managed to kick it back between his legs. The stab had exposed the side of her head. He slammed his elbow sideways, and inwards, hard gristle slamming into her jaw. Then the other elbow in sideways against her other side. Knee up, into her breasts. Women have the disadvantage; their breasts hurt badly when you bang them hard, as he had just done.

She was not going to give in easily. Dropping her head to go in and down and get under his centre of balance, she would try to throw him over her back, the only thing she could do in that confined space.

He broke, sagged, then jumped upwards, lifting both knees together under her chin. She flipped over backwards, her neck broken before she hit the deck. Women and children were screaming, men were shouting. But the gun in the steward's hand, waving sideways, backwards and forwards like a hosepipe, stopped any of them playing the hero. A woman came out of her seat defiantly and crouched over Letty.

The Chief Stewardess had raced to the back. 'Everybody sit down,' she shouted through the loud-hailer she had brought with her. 'Everybody sit down and face the front. Or do you want to get us all killed? Sit down, and face the front.'

She turned to Aram, a look on her face that would have cracked a steel plate. She took the loud-hailer from her lips.

'Get out,' she said. 'Get out, both of you. And I hope you both break your damned necks when you land.'

Aram pushed the steward behind the curtain. He put the Colt ·45 in the waist-band of his trousers where he could easily reach it.

The steward opened the two canvas bags, drew out two packs with straps that went round their shoulders and up between their legs. The pack Joseph Aram wore had rings under each arm; the steward's had only one ring.

The steward turned the wheel that unlocked the rear escape hatch, then opened both retaining catches. When he pushed, the hatch sprang upwards and outwards, exposing a gap at their feet. The air rushed in waving the curtain madly behind them. Several people in the plane began to scream. They heard the Chief Stewardess use the bull horn in a vain attempt to quieten them down.

'There's no danger,' she shouted. 'The cabin isn't pressurized. There's no danger.'

The steward sat at the lip of the gap, looked back at Aram. His face was green with fear. Aram pressed his back, prepared to push him out if necessary, but the steward gulped, shrugged his shoulder to get rid of Aram's hand, gave a finger-and-thumb circle 'okay' sign, and allowed himself to be swept away into the two hundred miles an hour slip-stream.

Aram let his legs dangle. The wind velocity whipped them out straight. He felt as if he had stuck them into a tearing waterfall, as if all the weight of a Niagara was pushing behind his knees. The wind clutched at his clothing, eddy currents lapping over his body, rushing into the plane.

He put his hands beside him, and pressed down with them, taking the weight from his buttocks.

Immediately, the slipstream grabbed him and tore him from the plane. He saw the underbelly flash past him before the slipstream hammered into his eyes, rammed into his nostrils, spun him round and round like a cork in a maelstrom.

Within seconds he had fallen through the slipstream and had started his parabolic downwards fall. He spread his arms and legs cautiously, arresting the spinning movement. The steward was about two hundred yards away. To his right. He brought his knees up to his chest, then, slowly projecting his shoulders forward, he lay flat across the fall-path. He felt himself slipping at a vector to his downwards path, drawing himself, flying his body, nearer and nearer to his companion.

Time is deceptive during free fall and he knew they were both losing height more rapidly than they seemed to be. The blue waters shone beneath them. To the east he could see the hilltops of the island of Mallorca. To his left was the single peak of Mount Atalaya. No cloud between them and the ocean below.

Several boats – specks of white on the ocean.

The steward, fifty yards away, had gathered control of his descent though this was his first free-fall drop. There had been no opportunity to practice.

Aram reached under his arm and pulled the ring on the left side of his pack. The catch snapped open. He felt the rush of silk past his ear, the jerk of the strap in his crotch. The parachute spread out above him, blue as the sky.

The steward, watching him closely, pulled the ring on his own 'chute when he saw the other start to flake upwards.

Aram looked to the south. The Tri-Star was climbing again. No doubt the skipper had seen them go and had closed the rear escape hatch. Now he was doubtless explaining it all to his passengers, giving them the thrill of a lifetime. The stewardesses would be pushing out the trolley and many a non-drinking man would be reaching for a brandy.

The clear ocean was rushing towards them. 'Just when you hit,' Aram had told the steward, 'make certain you have your legs firmly clamped together, your heels up, your feet slightly forward. And, whatever you do, hold onto your nostrils, pinching them tight, or the rush of water up them will seem as if it's blowing the top of your head off.'

Heels up, toes forward, legs stiff, right hand clenched over his nose, head back, and in. Down through the water, like a warm bath, strike out immediately with both arms, paddling back up again. He came back to the surface with the lines of his parachute twisted round his shoulders, unbuckled the belt passing between his legs, snapped open the shoulder straps. Felt himself clear of the lines and the pack. Reached out for the pack, found the ring and the cord, and pulled. The right hand side of the pack began to hiss and swell. From it burst a day-glow orange sausage growing larger and larger as more compressed gas was fed into it. It heaved and twisted on the water. Aram steadied it, drawing it from the parachute lines.

Fully inflated, it became a dinghy, just big enough for the two of them. He reached into the pack, found the two flat boards that had held it rigid and now would become paddles in their hands. He lifted himself over the side of the dinghy in one long heave, collapsed into the bottom, and righted himself.

The steward was heading towards him, swimming strongly. He had kicked off his airline shoes, trousers and shirt, beneath them he wore a tee shirt and swimming trunks.

'Salaam!' he said as he hung on the dinghy's side.

'Salaam, Akhtar.'

Akhtar the steward grinned up at Captain Joseph Aram. 'I've just realized something,' he said. 'Today is the ending of Ramadan. Tonight, we can eat . . .'

The *Revenge* found them in thirty minutes from splash-down. On board were Kostas Aronakis, and Andreas Burgler. Kostas was at the wheel, handling the powerful boat as if he were moulded to it. They pulled the parachutes and their lines inboard, wrapped them with the green canvas bags and the deflated dinghy into a parcel weighted with a piece of pig iron, and dropped them to the bed of the ocean. They each used the hot salt water shower on board, finished with the cold fresh water, and put on white cotton shorts, white cotton shirts with REVENGE stencilled across the chest, and white canvas gym shoes.

'It's madness to drop here,' Akhtar said. 'The minute that plane arrives in Tunis they're going to start looking for us right here. We've told them where to look . . .'

Joseph Aram smiled at him. He was sitting at the back of the boat, a glass of orange juice in his hand, to wash out the salt taste of the sea. 'You must learn to relax, Akhtar,' he said. 'From here, this boat could take us to Barcelona, to Valencia or Alicante. From any one of those places we could get a bus, a train, a plane, to anywhere. We could use the boat to go further. Corsica, Sardinia, the south of France, the mainland of Italy. Believe me, they won't know where to look for us. And, don't forget, they can't throw a net round an ocean the way they could round an airport . . .'

'So, of all these places, where are we going?' Akhtar asked.

'To none of them. We're going to the island of Ibiza. It's

98

so close to where we dropped, they'll never think of looking for us there . . .'

CHAPTER TEN

Bill Harrington was in his office when the message came through.

'The Guaranteed Travel flight is overhead. We can't make contact with it by radio. The pilot has triangulated twice and now is coming to land on Runway 6, along which flares have been set.' Sally Price was sitting opposite him, and heard the call on Bill's speaker.

'We've lost him,' Bill said. He did not know how, or when, or where, but he had an undeniable feeling that Joseph Aram had escaped them.

At least, for the time being.

'Ought I to have held him at Elmdon?' Sally asked anxiously. 'Perhaps I should have told them to yank him . . .'

Bill shook his head. 'I don't pretend to be wise,' he said. 'But there's an old saying. If you want to catch the fox, let the chickens run.'

'I never heard that . . .'

'I know. I just made it up . . . Joseph Aram is a chicken. Jacques Morel is a *poulet*. Somewhere behind them is a fox. Okay. For the moment, we've lost the chickens. But we'll find them again, and with them, this time, the fox.'

The Green Dolphin was performing beautifully. Jacques was proud of their invention. He was sitting comfortably, with no sign of fatigue. The short-range sonar probes were working, scanning the seas ahead and to the side of his position, reading the deeps like a map and projecting them on the screen in front of his driving position. Not that he needed to do any actual driving. The isotope engine was working silently, driving the man-made carbon fibre propellor, pushing the boat at a steady ten knots through the water. He had given the details of the course to the computer, had streamed out a short-distance log. From Toulon he had headed on a course that would take him past the northern tip of the Iberian Peninsula, had turned south, keeping well off the coast of Portugal until he could eventually turn east through the Straits of Gibraltar and into the Mediterranean.

He had plotted the Dolphin's destination, had keyed in the coordinates. Now, if he wished, he could lie back and go to sleep. At each turn, the computer would change their bearing. The sonar would check they did not ram anything, turning them to port or starboard round the object, then bringing them back on course again. He checked the oxygen content of the helium air – even that was computer controlled, to adjust automatically to his rate of breathing.

The Green Dolphin was sliding along at fifty fathoms, all systems go.

He pressed one of the buttons on the panel that lay at a slight angle to his finger-tips. The display screen cleared.

All the systems continued functioning without need for him to watch them constantly.

He tapped 997.

Thirty dots appeared on the screen in a set pattern. Two dots at the top left hand corner, four spaces and then five much larger dots. One space and then three large dots, three spaces and then five small dots, all along the top of the screen but extending downwards into it. The pattern of dots along the bottom was a mirror image of the pattern along the top. Any games enthusiast would have recognized the outlines and placing of a board, ready for play. The data base of the computer held one hundred games played by experts in its memory, and could pick, at will, any of a hundred alternatives.

Jacques Morel settled back, munching a high protein, high sugar, dehydrated peanut crisp bar. And there, fifty fathoms below the surface of the Atlantic Ocean, somewhere off the coast of Portugal, he began to play the computer at backgammon, one of the oldest games of them all.

Bill Harrington looked at the dossier the computer had

prepared for him. A complete account of the life and career of Joseph Aram, also known as John Libby. It had not been hard to discover the source of the second identity; the files of the War Office had yielded complete information.

'One of these days,' Bill said to Sally, sitting opposite him, 'we'll have all birth certificates and all death certificates on a matched data base, and it will be impossible for anyone to get a false passport by this method.'

'Another axe for the Civil Liberties people to grind?'

Bill had accepted the intrusive nature of the job they had to do. Sally, newer in the job, still had hang-ups about the invasion of privacy inherent in their kind of investigation.

He read the transcript of the interview she had had with Joseph Aram's parents. Tape recorded, of course, but with their permission. Later, he would listen to the tapes, hear the voice inflections that often told him if a subject was lying.

The interview had yielded little they did not already know. Sally had skilfully guided them through the boy's history, stressing his personal tastes, his expressed opinions, rather than the factual matter they already had from documentation. What kind of a boy was he? Did he have many friends? Did he have any hobbies, any interests? Did he read a lot? What kind of books? Was he interested in history? In geography? Had they seen him with any maps? What were his politics? Did he attend any meetings? Any rallies? Did he receive any phone calls at home – he'd paid for them to have a telephone installed, hadn't he? Did anyone ring him on that line and leave any messages. Did he have a girl friend? What did he believe in? What sort of subject excited him? Did he speak German? French? Arabic? What did he think about Jews? What did he say about the Palestine Liberation Movement, if anything?

Two confused old people. 'He was always a good boy to me,' his mother said, while his father nodded agreement to most of what she was saying. 'He wasn't interested in any of the things you are talking about. He was a great source of pride to us; the son of two poor immigrants, making it as an officer in the British Army. We were so proud. And then he decided for himself to leave the Army and go into business. Fancy, our son, a successful business man! He never said a word out of place in our house. He respected the house, respected his parents. We lived a British life. We are British subjects. They won't take that away from us, will they?'

'No,' Sally said, 'they won't do that.'

'You understand, we had no control over what he did. When he was away from this house. And now you say he's gone. And done a bad thing . . .'

'I didn't say he'd done a bad thing. I simply said that we wanted to find him.'

The father spoke. 'In our experience, whenever the authorities come looking, it means a bad thing has been done. If our son has done a bad thing, you can take my hand to pay for it, my right eye.' The old man stood upright with a solemn dignity. 'But that will not undo the damage, this I know.'

'I wish to hell I'd been able to get something out of them,' Sally Price said, biting her lip in frustration.

'You did a good interview. I couldn't have done a better one myself . . .'

'There's praise for you . . .'

'I didn't mean it like that. I simply meant, no one could have got any more out of the two old folks because they don't *know* any more. Joseph Aram obviously was a loner; he played everything close to his chest. I don't believe the "blackmail for money" theory. Aram was doing very nicely in his job; he had the rent of a cottage, drove a modest car, didn't seem to spend a lot of money, had a very very modest social life. Don't forget, we haven't turned up one girl friend, one steady boy friend. He appeared to travel a lot, but that's normal in his job.'

'If not "blackmail for money", then what?'

Bill got up from behind his desk and walked to the window which looked out across the park towards the Palace. He turned after a few moments. Sally could see the concern on his face. 'Aram was dead set,' he said. 'On an ideal. Some sort of burning passion. Look, at his age, he should have had a string of girls, and we can't find one. Not one steady. And there's absolutely no suggestion of his being queer. Okay, so he was sexually neutral. In that case, he should have had outside interests, hobbies.'

'Racing cars? Playing golf? Surely, all that sort of thing is twentieth-century sublimation, the substitute for the real thing – whatever that may be? The ra-ra rugger club. Pinching your secretary's bottom . . . ? The *cogito ergo sum* of the modern plastic man . . . ?'

'Aram wasn't, isn't, a modern plastic man, Sally. He's the last of the line of a chain of peasants, who made it in competition with all the others. Suddenly, this peasant boy is a caliph with the right-to-die-or-kill decision in his own hands. What more natural than that he should use his intellect for a cause. It doesn't have to be the right cause. Not even a good cause. Just so that it's something in which he, personally, can believe.'

'The modern world is full of causes, Bill. Take your pick. Right now, the focus is on Germany. The Red Army Force. Soldiers of the Revolution, the Berlin Undogmatic Group. Yesterday it was the USA. He fought in Northern Ireland – perhaps that's where he's going. The Middle East? You can take your pick.'

'We know he jumped into the Mediterranean . . .'

'Don't let us be confused by that, Bill. I'm not trying to split hairs, but he didn't jump *into* anywhere. He jumped *out of* a plane. I think he guessed we had a man on the plane, and would have a team waiting for him in Tunis.'

'He'd put a sleeper on the plane. A sleeper who smuggled a gun and two parachutes on board.'

'Okay, so he dropped in the water from a charter plane. Presumably he knew what he was doing. If they're as well organized as they seem, a boat would be waiting for him. Right now he could be in Palma de Mallorca, Barcelona, Valencia, anywhere along the south coast of France. But there are other charters, Bill, to all those places, *from all over Europe*. What easier way, if you have the organization – and we know he had – to charter yourself out of England to a holiday resort, carrying in your pocket the return half of a charter holiday from, say, Hamburg. When I travelled about the Middle East it was often quicker to hop on a plane to London. Try going from Heraklion to Barcelona. It takes for ever by the so-called direct route. But Heraklion/London, London/Barcelona can be done in half a day. You remember what happened on Mallorca with the Beauty Queen flight? They wound up in Mogadishu, right? They rarely check those charters. Have you ever seen a Spanish holiday airport in the summer? They're chaos enough at the best of times, but with charters arriving every ten minutes . . . You could walk through Customs with a SAM missile in your arms, if you could carry it . . .'

He walked round her desk, saw the scribbles she had been making on her pad, dots and arrows, swirling around a sketch of Europe and the Middle East. He put his arm round her shoulders, and she leaned into him. 'Bill,' she said, 'it's like looking for a haystack. Knowing that even when you find it, you'll have to search for the needle somewhere inside it . . .'

'You're tired, Sally.'

'I know I am. Bone tired, eyes popping out.'

He kissed her forehead lightly, just below the hairline.

'That helps,' she said.

He took the pencil from her fingers and put it next to the pad. 'I think it's time we went home.'

'That's the best suggestion you've made today, boss!' she said.

The box was on the deck of the *Marie Cinq*.

Henri Dupree had hauled it aboard during the night.

The moon was half way on the wane, and a sea-mist had rolled towards the shore, hiding the mast lights of the competing boats, dousing their running lights in a dark grey blanket. From somewhere, miles distant, a fog horn sounded a melancholy note. The night had turned cold and the wind had dropped. The sails were covered in fine spray; the sheets and shrouds were clammy to the touch.

He broke open the plastic lid of the lifeboat container. It was a short thick cylinder three feet long, two feet six in diameter, banded with nylon clips sealed with wax and lashed to the deck with short break-cords and rubber toggles. In an emergency, the whole container could be thrown overboard. The act of throwing it would snap the manufacturer's seals, and cause the life-boat to inflate itself. The Special Branch had broken the seals when they had searched the boat, but had switched off the air bottle before the lifeboat could inflate. Henri took the lifeboat out of its container, replaced it with the box, and then stuffed the lifeboat back in on top of it. He snapped the rubber toggles closed, disconnected the break-cords, lashed the life-boat cylinder securely to the deck.

He went back to the counter, checking the compass on his way. Marie was holding them dead on course. It would be dawn in an hour. Already, he guessed, he would be about six miles ahead of the rest of the competitors. The only vessel that could catch him was the *Amsterdam Avenue*. The skipper, Henk Kool, was the only other sailor of merit in the entire race. The rest were a bunch of amateurs, Henri thought. He went below and brewed a cup of coffee on his gimballed stainless steel stove. 0330 hrs, GMT. He checked his position by radio beam, reading each of the three positions clearly, triangulating them across his chart with pinpoint accuracy. The winds would return at dawn, and then he would show them all a clean pair of heels. Then he plugged in his tape recorder, set it to record and spoke into its microphone.

'One two three four five, one two three four five, this is the carrier, I have it safe, this is the carrier, I have it safe, one two three four five and out.'

He took the cassette from the machine, plugged in another machine, and played the cassette on it. The words came out at three times the normal speed, a fast jumble of sound.

He connected the output of the tape with the radio transmitter.

0335 GMT. He turned his transmitter frequency to Ultra Long Wave, fine-tuned it when he could hear the incoming signal with the beat frequency oscillator.

The distant operator started to broadcast. 'One two three four five, one two three four five.'

In the pause that followed, Henri pressed his transmission switch and fed the brief message out over the air, from his accelerated tape recorder.

The distant station acknowledged. 'One two three four five.'

Henri switched everything off, threw the cassette over the side of the boat, settled in his bunk, and went to sleep.

The *Marie Cinq* lolled on the water, slowly moving forward, waiting for the dawn wind that would speed her to her destination.

Marc Chantal did not like to admit defeat. He had set himself the task of answering a number of questions. Some of them were easy to answer. For example, if Jacques Morel had led a double life, where was his other base of operations?

The net Marc had cast widened rapidly throughout Toulon. Do you know this man? Does he live hereabouts? Have you ever seen him going into any nearby building, eating in any local restaurants, talking with any local people?

Jacques had made few attempts to hide his tracks for the determined interrogator. He had occupied a top floor apartment near the Boulevard d'Emile in the district of Toulon known as Fort Rouge. Yes, he had been away frequently. No, he never had any visitors. Yes, he sometimes had mail addressed to Jean Vaubert – why, was that not his real name? Fancy M. Vaubert using an assumed identity. Not a criminal, was he?

The concierge of the apartment block was taciturn. The rest of the apartment dwellers were well-to-do. Mon Dieu, the rents of these apartments . . . Yes, of course, she had a spare key, but what about showing her some kind of authority, hein?

The apartment was one-bedroomed and contained the sort of furniture an absentee landlord would buy from a catalogue, to honour his rental obligations. The bed looked as if it had never been made up, never been slept in. None of the dishes had been used; the kitchen contained no food. The bathroom had the bare look of an exhibition stand in a plumber's showroom, with no detergents, no shampoos, no deodorants, no towels except those folded in the cupboard. The water in the lavatory bowl carried a thin iridescent film.

A safe address; a drop for mail; a place to be used only in an emergency. A place in which to concentrate on one's alternate being. Here, Jacques Morel could be Mr Hyde. The man who intended to steal the Green Dolphin. In his other apartment, he could hope to remain Dr Jekyll. The team took the place apart and found nothing. Apart from a few letters there had been nothing to find.

Still, Marc Chantal felt happier now they had located Jacques Morel's alternative hideout.

'You knew him as well as anyone, I'm told,' he said to Sophie.

'As well as anyone, but that's not saying very much. I never had what you might call a *personal* relationship. He came to my apartment a couple of times. Once I cooked him a meal. But we talked about the job, nothing else, unfortunately.'

'Your interest in him was not shared . . . ?'

'He was a man. The most interesting, the most handsome man in the whole team. We worked together a lot. It would have been, how shall I put it, a bonus, to have had a stronger relationship with him. Anyway, why ask? We didn't, and that's that.'

'But, if you had this *interest* in him, I imagine you would notice little things about him that others might not see . . .'

'Like what?'

'Do you think he had any other girlfriend? Could that have been the reason for his, shall we say, lack of enthusiasm?'

'No, it wasn't that. A girl knows if a man has another girlfriend. How many men think they are deceiving their wives when, all the time, their wives can read the whole story in them? If he had had a girlfriend, I would have known it.'

'So, what were his interests?'

'His work. The perfection of the Green Dolphin. Nothing else. Why, he hardly ever noticed the food he was eating . . .'

'What were his political opinions?'

Sophie laughed. 'I have never seen any man with less political interest than Jacques. You know, several of us have left wing leanings. We wanted to compose a letter for Mitterand to use. Jacques could have supported us, but he didn't.'

'Perhaps, as a Naval Officer he felt . . .'

'A Naval Officer? That's a joke. We only joined the Navy because the Navy took over our work. Nobody was less interested in the Navy than Jacques Morel.'

Always Marc had found these negatives. No outside interests, no traceable contacts, no indiscretions. A blameless life; that was the word, blameless. Deliberately, carefully, calculatedly, blameless. And dedicated to only one thing; the perfection of the Green Dolphin, so that he could sail it away.

Marc had a crusty interview with Jules Lachard. 'Look, I don't know why you buggers have bothered to come down from Paris to turn this place upside down. What happened was a technical error. We're investigating that. We're completing the second structure, exactly similar to the original, and this time we're going to test it to destruction, both in the tank and on the bed of the ocean, but with a bleeper on it so that this time we won't lose it. You're wasting my time, and that of my staff. Jacques Morel, Lieutenant Morel, went down with his ship in the best Naval tradition. His next of kin have been informed. The search for the vessel has been discontinued. Somewhere, somehow, we permitted an error in that vessel, and Lieutenant Morel paid for it with his life. I intend to see that error forms no part of our future programme.'

'You've been able to prove it was an error, a malfunction?'

Marc had talked with a group of the scientists engaged

on the project. They had done the normal thing. They had programmed their work into the computer and had asked the computer to tell them, of all the millions of possibilities, what set of circumstances could have caused *all* the symptoms they had observed – the retraction of the echo plate, the loss of radio contact, the loss of sonar contact and control.

The computer had looked at a million times a million possibilities.

The answer had been negative.

And, to scientists, negative meant *human factor*.

Whatever had happened to the Green Dolphin, its pilot, Jacques Morel, had been totally responsible.

'We've told the Commander,' Sophie said, acting as the spokesman for the group. 'But he refuses to accept what we say. He's still in the old way of thinking. A Naval Officer, even a temporary, acting Naval Officer such as we all are, can do no wrong!'

'So, what's your collective opinion?'

'We think that Jacques decided to tinker with something. We don't know what. In order to tinker, he retracted the echo plate and then did something that blew the main engine out of action. Hence the loss of reactions, the loss of radio and sonar, the loss of control from this end. Look, none of us is perfect, right? We all make small mistakes, we all behave like human beings. A good scientist builds a checking element into everything he does, to overcome what you might call the human error factor. Jacques was a perfectionist. For that reason, he sometimes wasn't too popular with the rest of the team. He'd insist on doing things his way, a lot of the time, and he'd check and double check the work the others were doing. It was as if he couldn't trust anybody, couldn't work with the *team*. Sometimes, you would think the whole Green Dolphin programme was his sole responsibility. A lot of the chaps resented that. And he'd push, push, all the time! The rest of the team are human beings, with homes and wives and kids. I remember when Hubert wanted to take a day off when it was his kid's birthday party, and Jacques really made a stink about it.

Said the programme came first, *no matter what*. As if he was working to some kind of a personal deadline all the time. Well, I guess what happened in there was that he discovered something he thought wasn't quite one hundred percent and, instead of noting it so that we could correct it when he came back, he tried to correct it himself. In his own impetuous way. And that's when it all went wrong. You understand that I'm only guessing . . .'

'But, if you're right, what would happen inside the Dolphin?'

Her eyes had filled with tears. For a brief moment the woman replaced the scientist. 'Poor Jacques. He'd suffocate. The oxygen regeneration plant would fail, and he'd suffocate.'

'In how long?'

'Assuming the plant failed when we lost contact, in four hours. The interior has a low volume . . .' Her voice tailed away almost, as if she were talking to herself. 'Poor bastard. Let's hope he pulled open the hatch and drowned himself.'

CHAPTER ELEVEN

The story had built rapidly. On September 19th, in a red bordered box covering pages 26 and 27, *Newsweek* showed a photograph of the Israeli Foreign Minister with his Prime Minister. The caption read:

'Israeli Foreign Minister arrives in Washington next week to begin the third stage in the New Administration's attempt to move towards peace in the Middle East.'

On September 26th, *Time* magazine said on page 18:

'MIDDLE EAST
WARNING FROM WASHINGTON
The U.S. wants the Palestinians at Geneva.'

The *Time* magazine photograph showed Israeli folk-dancing at the new para-military settlement on the West Bank.

On September 26th also the British *Daily Telegraph*, which 'went to bed' later than the *Time* Magazine published the same day, was able to up-date the story:

'ISRAEL AGREES TO PALESTINIAN ROLE IN TALKS

In a diplomatic breakthrough yesterday the Israeli government accepted an American plan for the participation of Palestinians at the opening of the Geneva peace conference on the Middle East.'

'Which only goes to show,' Joseph Aram said, throwing the copy of the *Telegraph* on the table top, 'that we can coerce some of the people some of the time, but the American Big Brother can coerce *all* of the people *all* of the time.'

He turned in his chair and looked out over the small bay, to where the *Revenge* was riding at anchor. The bay was no more than a hundred feet long, seventy feet wide. Its sides of volcanic rock rose sheer for fifty feet. From where he was sitting he could see that the end of the bay turned round the corner in a dog-leg, with a small lagoon almost completely enclosed by a rocky overhang.

The house had been built at the start of the boom on Ibiza in the 1960s. Yshtak had bought it in 1964, and spent the next years making certain alterations to it. Now it had the appearance of a rich man's 'get away from it all' holiday retreat. Yshtak had cultivated that aspect of his life on the island over the years and was well known in Ibiza harbour, along the waterfront of San Antonio, and in the bars of Santa Eulalia. His white Rolls Royce was seen everywhere. His light plane flew regularly between Ibiza and the mainland. Yshtak could often be seen at the 'in' restaurants, the tables pulled together to accommodate a large party with everybody who was anybody on the island of instant reputations.

Yshtak never entertained at home, except for his one

special girlfriend of the time. And never went to other people's houses. It was a small foible that everyone accepted. As was the wire rope stretched across the mouth of the bay on which he lived.

Ahktar put down the book he was reading. 'You know, Joseph,' he said. 'I'm still getting cold shivers thinking about that free fall jump! You'll never get me to do that again, never, as long as I live.'

Joseph laughed. 'If all goes well,' he said, 'you'll never need to!'

The room in which they were sitting was shaped like a letter D. The curve faced south; the high windows, which could be rolled completely aside, took advantage of the sun. The room was constantly flooded with light, though the overhanging projection kept out the sun's direct rays in summer and let them in in winter.

Yshtak came into the room, nodded to them, and sat in his easy chair. The fingers of his hands were pressed together. Both Joseph and Ahktar had felt an urge to rise when he came into the room. Yshtak was that kind of man, with that kind of commanding presence, that aura of leadership.

'I see you've read the newspaper,' he said.

Joseph nodded.

'It tells us nothing we had not anticipated,' Yshtak said, speaking quietly in English. 'Of course, Israel will attend the Geneva peace conference. There will be the farce of an opening ceremony, in the presence of the mayors of the towns on the West Bank of the Jordan. Meanwhile, the Israelis will continue their meetings with King Hussein, and with Sadat, pretending to work towards some sort of compromise.'

His quiet voice carried a deep assurance. He was a man who had spent all his life in a position of command, of responsibility. 'The Israelis will continue to thrust deeper into the territory around them, establishing new kibbutzim, taking over new territory. There is nothing new in all of this.' He stood up, towering six feet high. His dark eyes glittered beneath his still black eyebrows, though the hair on his head had long been grey.

He pressed his fingers together again, thinking back over the years to Palestine, to the wars when the Israelis had bombed and shelled his village, killed his wife and children and most of the villagers. He had been wounded so badly in the leg and the chest that he could not move, and they had left him for dead.

He could still hear the Israeli bombers and the exploding mortar shells and the screams of the women and children at night when he tried to sleep.

The Israelis had called it 'aggressive self-protection' – taking the war into the enemy camp. When had he, Yshtak, made war? When had he ever pointed a weapon at the Israelis? He acknowledged that some of the men of his village had become *fedayeen*, but he had banned them from the village. Why make the entire village responsible for what a few men had done?

He remembered the Israeli tanks and the machine guns slaughtering the few remaining villagers they could find. Covered by corpses, he alone had survived when the Israeli advance swept on.

He remembered crawling across the mountainside at night, hanging to a sheep part of the way, drawing warmth from its fleece for his body, wracked with cold and loss of blood.

He remembered the pain in his chest and his legs where the bullets had torn his flesh, the way he had fallen into delirium, the curses he had called against the sons of Isaac, the vows he had made to avenge his tribe.

'All this terrorist activity helps us. Foolish destructive people kidnapping industrialists, hijacking planes, demanding the release of prisoners and ransom money; it forms an effective smoke screen for the reality of what we will do. These people are concerned with protest only as a means of working out their own frustrations. They will embrace any anarchic cause because they have not yet matured sufficiently to live within their own societies and communities. The ideals to which they dedicate themselves and their destructive abilities have no relevance for them. But they help us by clouding the real issues. These meetings are unreal. Israel will not honour any pledges because the Israeli believes, with reason, that the extremists on the other side will not honour their words. We shall honour our words. Tonight we have reached the conclusion of the first phase of the active part of our plan. We have waited for this moment for many years. We have been patient. You, Joseph, and you, Ahktar, Jacques and Henri, have all been most efficient, most patient. Soon we shall begin the second part of our plan. Now we are moving forward, and nothing will stop us.'

Joseph Aram pointed to the newspapers. 'And if Arafat achieves a settlement?'

'Arafat will compromise. The Israelis will compromise. The Russians and the Americans are running things between them, forcing these compromises. But that will not be our way. Our way can only be the way without compromise. The way of justice for our people . . .' He sank back in his chair, and the memories came flooding back again.

The first sound he had heard was one he could not identify. The cool wind blowing across his face was not from the north, from thyme and sage laden slopes that carried the odour of clean dung, lemons and oleander.

This wind carried with it the sick smell of chemicals, like one of the trucks the World Health Organization sent to spray the wells.

He opened his eyes when he felt a hand on his brow and a cold wet stick thrust into his arm-pit.

A *girl* was bending over him!

He struggled to resist her when she put a hand on his shoulder and, to his shame, was able to hold him to the bed.

How had he become so weak? How had this *girl* taken away his strength? He turned his head from her, from the foul smell of her breath and her body, the sight of her unveiled face, female features, reddened lips. He had heard of these girls in the towns who sold their caresses for money, gave their bodies to any stranger, daubed themselves with colour, sprayed themselves with false odours to attract men.

'Allah, where hast thou brought me?' he cried.

He saw the fine cotton sheets on the bed and knew then that he had been shamed.

His mind was in turmoil, his memory absent.

The girl spoke to him. Just like that. She spoke words to him, Yshtak, to whom no-one spoke without first seeking permission. He was too weak even to shut his ears.

'You're going to be all right,' she said. 'Today is the third day you've been here. We've taken the bullets out of you, and cleaned your wounds. You're going to be all right.'

Without turning his head he asked, 'Where am I?'

'In hospital. In Beirut.'

They cared for him, treated him with medicines, made him well again. Yshtak learned to adapt to their ways, to permit girls to speak to him first, to eat their food, to permit them to cleanse his body with water and soap, to carry away his water and dung when he could not leave the bed, even to cleanse his manhood.

The physical part of his new life came easily to him. Less easy was the masculine side. One day, when he was well enough to take a walk in the garden, he felt the swelling beneath the nightgown they had given him. He touched the arm of a passing nurse. 'Lie down quickly, girl,' he said. 'Yshtak will take you now.'

The girl ran laughing away.

The doctor came later to his bed and patiently explained the ways of the modern westernized world of Beirut. 'Here,' he said, 'you ask the girl. If she is willing, you go away to some quiet place together.'

'Willing? How would she not be willing? She would pleasure me and I would give her my seed!'

'That's what they're afraid of, Yshtak,' the doctor said, smiling. Patiently he explained something of the strange ways of the western world. Independence, marriage, monogamy.

It all sounded the wierdest heresy to Yshtak but he

determined to learn. The fuel of a burning ambition for revenge was already banked deep inside him, though, as yet, it had no real heat, no flames.

When he left the hospital he had learned the western ways, and had come to accept he was no longer a village leader, able to command at will. He went to live in the doctor's house in the American quarter of Beirut. There, he taught the doctor's wife and the doctor's children to speak Arabic, while they taught him to speak English. He would hold up an object; they would say its name in English, and he would say it in Arabic.

His chief difficulty was that most of the objects they held up had no word in Arabic – many of them he had never seen before. And many of the ideas they expressed were completely strange to him. 'I like you,' the doctor's wife said one day.

'You *like* me? What is like?'

'Oh, gosh, I don't know how to explain . . . It's kind of, well, sort of love, but not quite so much, I guess.'

Later, when he spoke with others in his native tongue, they explained to him how much more direct is the Western way of speech, and that what the woman had said was: 'you please me.'

The small group of people he taught grew larger. Soon he had a class of six that included an American broker working in a Lebanese bank. By now he had no problem with words such as 'like' and could even study the Western system of stocks and shares. The doctor had been paying him a wage in food, lodging and money. The broker paid him in information. Soon the small pile of money began to grow larger as the American invested it for him.

When the formal classes ended, Yshtak had the equivalent of a thousand US dollars. Now he started to walk around the old city, listening, always listening. What he heard he was able to pass to the American broker who paid him for the information by investing his money for him. Beirut was the financial capital of the Middle East. The American left his job with the bank and set up on his own, taking Yshtak as a partner. Yshtak now wore Western clothing, lived in the Western manner. Now, the people with whom he talked in the coffee-shops were still Arabic, but more influential and knew more of the flow of money into and out of this volatile but lucrative market. Yshtak and his partner prospered, sold out, prospered again.

Shortly after the ending of the Six Day War, Yshtak's partner decided to return to America. Yshtak's share of the business came to four million US dollars.

Yshtak could see the end of the bonanza days in the Lebanon. In the bazaar, there was talk of impending war. He sold out the business, transferred his assets to London and there went into the oldest business of all, money-lending. In London, however, they called it by the respectable title of merchant banking. Here, once again, his background in the Middle East helped him. When the price of oil shot through the ceiling, he was holding, through a client company, four million pounds sterling worth of crude oil. He held on to it, sold it to an oil hungry world after only six months for a total of twenty million pounds, and took the money, tax-free, in Switzerland.

He bought a small house on Lake Geneva, near the dull but central location of Lausanne. There he perfected the French and German languages he had already begun to learn in Beirut and London and began to work out his plan.

He met Henri Dupree while he was in Toulon looking at yachts for sale. To Yshtak, a yacht represented not luxury but Mediterranean mobility. Henri advised him on the purchase of the forty foot diesel-powered motor launch which he later christened the *Revenge*. Something in the way Henri spoke, the way he pronounced some of his words, made Yshtak wonder about his origins. Henri had been born just outside Gaza. Both of his parents had died in a refugee camp.

He also met Jacques Morel in Toulon. Henri knew Jacques's parents and introduced Yshtak to their son. The liking was mutual. Without knowing it, Jacques had lived his life away looking for a cause. When he began work on the Green Dolphin, he told Yshtak. 'Work at it,' Yshtak advised him. 'Perfect your knowledge of it. Someday, we will discover a use for it.'

Yshtak was in Hong-Kong, where he still retained an interest in the gold market that yielded him an annual six figure sum, when he met Captain Joseph Aram. The name interested him, and he struck up an acquaintance with the taciturn officer. One of his merchant banking clients was doing very well in England with a company Yshtak had financed – Security Systems Ltd. When his client began to obtain Government contracts Yshtak, acting primarily on impulse, suggested to Aram that, if he was looking for something useful to do with his life, a job with Security Systems Ltd could be arranged. It was Yshtak who suggested to Joseph Aram that he take the precaution of securing the identity of John Libby.

Slowly he built his team of men. All were former Palestinians, all had left the country because of the Israelis, all had deep blood ties.

The only exceptions were Kostas Aronakis, the Cretan, and Andreas Burgler. Both were mercenaries. He had to buy their loyalty, and their knowledge.

Yshtak was a slow but methodical planner. The final details of his simple scheme came to him when Joseph Aram told him that one of the government installations for which he was designing and installing part of the security system had a stock-pile of atomic warheads.

All this time Yshtak had been quietly and politically active through a number of fronts. He had invested money in the various Palestine Liberation Organizations, hoping they would achieve his purpose for him. One by one, they had either been destroyed from outside by Israeli Intelligence, or from inside by internecine rivalries. His best hope had been Arafat.

That hope was quenched when Arafat made it obvious he was open to compromise, that he was prepared to divide Palestine with the Israelis, to accept an Israeli presence in the country all Palestinians knew to be theirs. Yshtak was not prepared to accept such a compromise.

He was not prepared to accept one Israeli foot on the soil of his native land. Not one.

And in this, there could be no compromise.

Yshtak could still hear the explosions of the mortars and the shells all those years ago, the screams of the women and children of his village, the pain of those bullets ripping apart his chest and his leg, the nightmare delirium. But the will to survive had taken him across those mountains. Now he would return to take his revenge.

Not an eye for an eye, a tooth for a tooth. But a life for an eye, a body for a tooth, and a nation for a village.

And there could be no compromise. It was the will of Allah . . .

The Green Dolphin arrived on schedule at half past four in the morning, coming into the mouth of the bay at ten fathoms, the sonar and the computer lifting it off the bed of the ocean and guiding it between the rock faces with pin point accuracy. At the far end of the bay, it turned left into the dog-leg and there, according to its own pre-set instructions, it stopped, six feet from the natural dock wall.

At four twenty-five, the sub-surface lights had been switched on. The water was clear as glass as Yshtak, Joseph, and Akhtar watched it arrive.

A crane arm swung out over the cove and a wire rope dropped down, carrying a canvas net.

Two men dived into the water, pulled the net below the Dolphin, hooked it to the cradle and signalled upwards. Slowly the electric winch brought the Dolphin out of the water and deposited it carefully onto a wooden platform at the dock-side. The green monster streamed with water for a few seconds and then stood glistening under the lights. Yshtak went down the rock staircase and stood beside it. It was just as Jacques Morel had described it, even down to the evil eye and the jagged teeth painted on its snout. He was grinning with pleasure when the hatch on the side opened and Jacques squirmed out. The two men embraced, kissing each other's cheeks and pounding each other's back. Then it was the turn of Aram and Akhtar.

'It swam along like a fish,' Jacques said. 'Do you know, I never had to do a single thing. I just told it where to go, and it went . . .'

He patted the soft, sound absorbent skin, as if the Dolphin were truly alive. 'It will work, Yshtak,' he said exuberantly. 'I tell you, it will work.'

He closed the hatch tight. 'Now we can drop her back into the water,' he said. 'I think she's happier there.'

At five o'clock that same morning, Gibraltar radio, keeping a listening watch on the assigned frequency for the contestants of the Liverpool–Limassol Yacht race, received the following message from the yacht *Marie Cinq*:

'MY MAST HAS SNAPPED AND I AM RETIRING FROM THE RACE. WILL MAKE FOR THE NEAREST PORT WHICH I CALCULATE TO BE IBIZA HARBOUR.'

The radio officer plotted the position *Marie Cinq* had given him. Yes, the nearest port was Ibiza.

'UNDERSTAND, MARIE CINQ. ROTTEN LUCK. DO YOU REQUIRE ESCORT OR ASSISTANCE?'

The reply came back immediately:

'NO THANKS. HAVE AMPLE FUEL AND BRITISH ENGINE. MAST LASHED TO DECKS SATISFACTORILY. OVER AND OUT.'

By the time the message sent from Gibraltar was broadcast by the BBC, the box was lying on the bottom of the continental shelf off Espalmador, its position marked by a fisherman's buoy.

Joseph Aram put on a wet suit and a pair of bottles and went down to secure an extra line to it. It was more fun than taking a swim in Yshtak's bay.

They winched it on board the *Revenge*. When they opened

the packing Joseph Aram had used, the box was not even wet.

Henri moored the *Marie Cinq* in Ibiza's tatty yacht harbour. The news had been broadcast by the Overseas Service of the BBC and the crowd that had gathered to see his arrival included the Ibiza correspondent of Reuters.

'What are your plans now, Monsieur Dupree?' he asked.

'I'm going back to France to shove the remains of that mast up somebody's arsehole, and then I'm going to have a new mast made. But not in France. Quant à moi, I'm going to check into the quietest hotel I can find, and sleep until I waken again.'

A taxi took him to San Antonio. Another to San Jose. Only when he was certain he was not being followed did he signal the jeep that took him to the house of Yshtak, over two kilometres up a rocky cliff path that would have broken the springs of any normal vehicle.

Yshtak clasped his arm when he arrived. 'All these years, Henri, leading to this moment . . .'

Henri grinned. 'You owe me a new mast,' he said. 'I had a hell of a job to break that one and make it look convincing. And not capsize the *Marie Cinq* while I was doing it!'

When Andreas Burgler returned later that day, the team was complete and work began, installing the contents of the box inside the nose of the Green Dolphin. Now those monstrous painted teeth could really bite.

CHAPTER TWELVE

Bill Harrington walked along the passage that led from 11 Downing Street to Number 10. Frank Moody was waiting for him by the door at the end. He did not speak as they hurried up the staircase and along the corridor to the Cabinet Room. The Prime Minister was sitting at one end of the long table. Next to him, Mary Twywell was already doodling on her pad. Clyde Farriman had smoked three cigarettes, though the PM did not normally approve of the Cabinet smoking during meetings. Dick Feather was sitting to the PM's left, holding an unlit pipe in his hand. They all looked up as Frank Moody came in.

'This is Bill Harrington,' he said. 'From the Intelligence Unit. I imagine you know everybody, Bill.'

'Yes, of course.'

'Sit next to Mr Feather,' the PM instructed. When Bill and Frank Moody were seated, he opened the red leather book in front of him. Bill could see a new sheet between two of the normal pages of blotting paper.

'An hour ago,' the Prime Minister said, 'I received this cable from Switzerland. It came to me in code. I gave it to the Head of Telegrams, who arranged for it to be decoded under a provisional Alpha Zero Plus grading. It was fortunate we took that precaution. The code used is one known to any Army officer who has served in Special Services, but I needn't bother you with its details. The message, when decoded – I suppose I should say, deciphered – reads as follows:

'WE ARE IN POSSESSION OF A DEVICE RECENTLY REMOVED FROM THE HARWELL CENTRE STOP WE ARE IN POSSESSION OF A VESSEL RECENTLY REMOVED FROM TOULON STOP YOU WILL IMMEDIATELY ARRANGE A MEETING BETWEEN THE PRESIDENT OF THE UNITED STATES, THE PRESIDENT OF FRANCE, THE PRIME MINISTER OF THE COUNTRY CALLING ITSELF ISRAEL AND YOURSELF STOP THIS MEETING WILL TAKE PLACE IN LONDON TEN DAYS FROM NOW 1ST OCTOBER STOP YOU WILL RECEIVE FURTHER INSTRUCTIONS.'

'The message, gentlemen, and lady, of course, is not signed. But then, you would hardly expect it to be. I have spoken on the telephone with the President of France who, though somewhat reluctantly, agreed that he had received a similar message. In his case, the message was in Navy Cipher. He further admitted to me that the vessel referred to in the cable is an experimental submarine, capable of travelling long distances underwater under its own power, and under a pre-set guidance system. The submarine does not require a crew. And cannot be detected.'

The significance of what he was saying sank swiftly into each one of them. Mary Twywell's doodle had taken on the shape of a submarine. She drew a series of sharp arrows, radiating from its nose, stabbing the paper as she did so. 'So they can deliver what is, in effect, a sea-borne atom bomb . . .'

'That's right, Mary. And what's more, once they've launched it, there's nothing we can do to stop it.'

The PM looked at Clyde Farriman. 'Okay, Clyde, let's have your party political broadcast and then we can get down to the real business of speculating about what we can do. I think we'll come to the swift conclusion that the answer to that question lies in the hands of Mr Harrington here.'

'No party politicals, Prime Minister,' Clyde said. 'So long as we don't get any left wing Union crap from Dick. I think we're all agreed, this is no time for striking attitudes.'

The nightmare had come to pass. Every prime minister must live with it. Schmidt lived with it at Mogadishu. The Italians over Moro. It had sent Neville Chamberlain scurrying to Munich; it had pushed Edward Heath out of office. The political crisis without solution. The irresistible force, and the immovable object.

'On the one hand,' the Prime Minister said, his voice firmly held free of any emotion, 'we have an atomic warhead that can be delivered on the shoreline of Israel by a group efficient enough, ruthless enough, to have stolen the component parts and without a doubt skilled enough to put them together. On the other hand, we have an aggressive nation that has amply demonstrated its willingness to go to war as a means of resisting territorial invasion of any kind. We have no way of knowing who is holding the submarine bomb, except that we know the names of the two men who stole the component parts, and we have traced a Palestinian origin to one of them. We don't even . . .'

'Two of them,' Bill said quietly, interrupting the Prime Minister firmly. 'I've been working with my opposite number in France.'

'Despite my specific instruction . . . ?'

'Your instruction, Prime Minister, if you will forgive me reminding you, was that I did not inform the French President.'

'Point taken, Mr Harrington. I hope you had good cooperation from your opposite number.'

'I did. I knew the President of France had received his telegram *before* I was told you had received yours.'

No one could mistake the irony in his dry voice, nor the anger in the Prime Minister's when he said: 'There are political considerations, Mr Harrington, in all of this. Perhaps the British government operates more democratically than the French . . .'

Bill's voice took on a pointed edge as he addressed the whole table. 'With due respect to all "politicians",' he said, 'this is no time for democracy. No time for shades of *political opinion*. We're up against a strong organization, containing skilled and ruthless men, patient planners who, when they strike, are totally effective. One man went straight into the Harwell Centre and walked out with one of our most carefully guarded secrets. He was able to get in there because we made mistakes and he took advantage of them. If I take on his investigation, I intend to limit my mistakes as far as possible, by ignoring *political* matters. I will want permission, authority, to proceed uninterrupted. I shall require authority to co-opt any help I might need from any of the Services, including our attachés in Embassies abroad, and any Forces we might have in the field. And I want to be answerable to one man, *not* to a committee.'

They were all silent. All remembering what could happen when one man asks for, and is given, absolute authority. Good and bad. Hitler and the Third Reich counterbalanced by Churchill. Montgomery and the fiasco at

Arnhem. The good from the bad, or the bad from the good. Lenin created Stalin, Eve came from Adam's rib.

Clyde Farriman cleared his throat. 'We're not very good at giving *absolute* authority, Mr Harrington,' he said. 'History, I think you will agree, is against it. Even our modern history, which contains the growth of the unions, represented by our colleague Mr Feather here.' He held up his hand. 'No, Prime Minister, I'm not making a party political broadcast. I'm merely explaining to Mr Harrington why it will be difficult for us to give him what he wants. Though I, for one, am certain we *must* do so, if he is to succeed.'

'The vital question,' Feather said, 'has nowt to do with history, nor with trade unions. It has to do with Mr Harrington's fitness for the job. That's what we're talking about, really.'

'And that's something none of us can assess,' Mary Twywell said. She had been Minister of Education long enough to know the difficulties of assessing ability of any kind. 'We can only accept it or reject it. So, you see, Mr Harrington, at the onset you are dependent on a committee, on that most democratic of all procedures, a majority vote. I propose, gentlemen, that we put an end to this meeting and give Mr Harrington the authority he requires and our urgent instructions to find that bomb . . .'

'I second that,' Clyde Farriman said.

Only Dick Feather voted against, his left wing suspicions too deep-rooted within him.

The Prime Minister looked round the table. 'I think we can proceed on that clear majority,' he said. He stood up. 'Good luck, Mr Harrington,' he said. 'You will be kept informed of where you can reach me, night and day. I shall arrange the meeting as demanded, for ten days from now. But let's all pray it never has to take place.'

'I need you. I need you badly,' Bill said when he returned to his office.

'That's the best offer I've had all day,' Sally Price said. 'In fact, it's the *only* offer I've had all day.'

He put his hand on her shoulder. 'Sorry, I don't mean it that way. I want you to talk to me, about the Israeli situation vis-à-vis the Palestinians.'

She made a moué of disappointment, thought for a few moments and then started to give him a run-down on the history of Israel, going from highlight to historical highlight. 'The problem is an old one, but the modern aspect of it began when the Jews made a unilateral declaration of the formation of the State of Israel, a state they were prepared to defend with all the force at their disposal. Immediately,' Sally said, 'many people who had been born and bred in that territory found themselves aliens in their own land. Many found themselves actual refugees and are still, effectively, refugees, living in camps without proper homes of their own. Of course, many of them could have been assimilated elsewhere but the various Palestine for the Palestinian factions over the years have used these people in the camps, keeping them there often in dreadful conditions, as pawns in some game of their own. They don't want the people in those camps to be assimilated – they want them to remain as evidence of the monstrous inhumanity of the Israelis.

'There have been many proposals: the latest is that these people be allowed to live throughout Israel as a minority. But subject to the laws of Israel. The line is softening, bit by bit. Once, the Arab world, and that included the Palestinians, swore to drive the Israelis into the sea. Now, some sort of compromise seems to be reachable. The Israelis will be permitted an enclave inside what is now Israel. But that means pulling back out of all the territory they've invaded, the Occupied Territories, as they are called. Arafat was one of the most virulent in his opposition to any Jewish, i.e. Israeli presence anywhere in what he calls Palestine. But now Arafat seems to have softened his tone. The Israelis, of course, have always refused to accept the existence of the Palestine Liberation Organization, Arafat's outfit. But now it looks as if the Americans under Carter have forced them at least to accept that some people have the right to be called Palestinians, and a right to be heard. Some people don't agree with Arafat's new "softline", but not many.'

'If you were a Palestinian, and you had a sea-borne bomb, what would you do with it?'

'I'd point it at Jaffa, or Haifa, and give the Israelis an ultimatum. The contents of that ultimatum would depend on which faction I supported. Arafat would say – withdraw completely from the Occupied Territories, from Jerusalem, Bethlehem, Beersheba, the Golan Heights, the Gaza Strip, into a stretch of land north of Tel Aviv. If I belonged to the TAIO – the Total Annihilation of the Israelis Organization – I would have shouted like a union organizer, "Everybody out". Interesting, isn't it, that one of the alternatives to Palestine was Uganda . . . When you think what happened there recently . . .'

'Who commands this TAIO?'

'Nobody. It's been scattered. The Israelis killed most of its leaders when they raided Orik from the Golan Heights; the rest of them seem to have dispersed. One of them is in gaol in Brixton. She tried to hijack a TWA plane. She was going to kamikaze it onto the Knesset with all its passengers. The security man on board disarmed her before the plane had left British air space. They brought her back here, to Heathrow, and she's in Brixton, on remand, while they decide what to do with her.'

'Khaylia Patin – I read the papers. Right, give me your opinion. Who sent the telegram, and where from? Switzerland is obviously a cover.'

'Not Arafat, nor anyone to do with him, that's certain. Right now, he's concentrating on getting to Geneva. Not anyone connected with Hussein; he wants to retain his Hashimite empire as long as he can – he's even negotiating with Dayan. Not the Egyptians. Anwar Sadat is negotiating – he's on very bad economic ground and is likely to be kicked out if he doesn't negotiate a peace settlement soon. And not any other Arab nation. It could, I suppose, be Libya – Gaddafi's a nut anyway. Come to think of it, it could be Amin wanting revenge for Entebbe. Somehow I don't think so. It's all too cool for either Gaddafi or Amin.

My guess is that someone unknown has picked up the pieces of the old TAIO. It has all the hallmarks – the leader has been patient over the years, and smart enough to build his team quietly, with ruthless, deadly efficiency. He achieved the first part of his plan exposing only two operatives, only *two*, Bill. I think he's the man we have to look for. Someone from the Middle East, someone with a blood-lust for revenge against the Israelis, someone with enough money to finance and enough initiative to organize a large-scale clandestine operation. But can we start looking for him after lunch, Bill. You look as bushed as I feel!'

Marc Chantal had been confirmed in his job by the office of the President.

Like Bill, he turned his thoughts to Israel and the Palestinians, and that meant the Mediterranean. The Green Dolphin would need docking facilities in secret. Three dozen men were recruited from the Deuxième Bureau throughout France. Each was given a stretch of coastline, an island, and told to circle it, looking for a place that would provide the appropriate facilities, preferably with quarters for a number of men in a nearby house. Possibly with a radio mast. They were to start at the extreme east of the Mediterranean and work their way west. A number of light planes were commandeered from private owners, mostly to give negative reports for unoccupied stretches of coast-line.

It was Phillipe who threw the first spanner into the works. 'They don't need to store the Dolphin by the shore-line,' he said. 'They could pull it out of the water at some quiet cove at night, mount it on a trailer, and take it inland, during the hours of darkness. That gives you at least a fifty miles bandspread.'

'And if they could hide it during the day,' Chantal said, 'or stow it in one of the big trans-continental wine lorries, for example, they could take the damned thing all the way across Europe if they wanted. But somehow, I don't think so, Phillipe. They are good planners and patient people – you notice the way they've given us ten days in which to set up the meeting. They're holding it fully prepared somewhere on a coastline. They will want to be able to drop it into the water at a moment's notice and aim it where they want it to go.'

Phillipe shivered. 'God help mankind when it arrives, eh, Marc? Israel retaliates against the Arabs with a nuclear bomb, the USA joins in, Russia joins in, Red China next, and the whole world ends in cataclysm. I don't hear you now talking so much about setting up our own business? Perhaps we should form a company to build nuclear-blast-proof shelters.'

'We *must* find it, Phillipe. We must somehow cover every inch of the coastline. And while we're doing that, you must track back along the life of Jacques Morel He's been very patient over the years, training himself for this moment. But somebody is behind him, someone is motivating him. And that's the someone we must discover.'

'And we have only ten days in which to do it?'

'Yes, only ten days . . .'

When the Prime Minister had put down the telephone to the President of the United States, he hurried along the corridor to the room in the Cabinet Office he used for larger meetings. His PPS, Gordon Winter, was waiting in the corridor, nervously chewing the end of his spectacles, when he saw the PM arrive. 'They're all in there, Prime Minister,' he said, 'with the Minister of Defence.'

'Good.'

'Will you need me in there, Prime Minister?' Winter asked, even though the PM had told him he wouldn't be required. Winter didn't like being 'excluded' from such an important meeting – it was a negation of the position of privilege he occupied as personal private secretary. It could signal the thin edge of the political wedge. And Gordon Winter was very sensitive to political wedges.

The Prime Minister patted his arm. 'Gordon, I don't need you in there. I just thought it was time I met them all again, personally, off the record. It can't be off the record if you're there, can it?'

'But the Minister of Defence will be there.'

'They all know old Frank. He'll give it the right touch of informality. Now stop fretting, Gordon. I've something much more important for you to handle. The US President will be coming here in ten days' time. Lunch with the Queen at Buckingham Palace, honorary degree at Oxford, dinner in the Guildhall and the Freedom of the City. I'm putting you in charge of all the arrangements. That's more your style, Gordon. Do a good job on it, and there's an OBE in it for you . . .'

'But I get the OBE anyway, Prime Minister, when I retire as your PPS.'

'This way, you'll be the first to get it *before* you retire!'

Gordon Winter's eyes lit up. A personal, instead of a routine, OBE. That *would* be something. He scurried away down the corridor like a hamster smelling cheese.

The Prime Minister opened the door and went into the room. All of them rose to their feet when he appeared. He waved for them to sit down, walked to the lectern at one end, and rested his arms on it, as if grateful for its support.

The PM was beginning to look old, the editor of the *Daily Express* thought, making a mental note to ask the features department to look into the possibility of an article on the aging effect of high office.

The PM looked around at the assembled editors of the British press. Young and old. Conservative or brash. Gullible or shrewd. Amateurs or professionals. Each was a mixture of each of these qualities.

He saw Frank Moody seated next to the editor of *The Times*. He noticed the editors of the weeklies were there, without exception a donnish-looking lot who cultivated a holier than thou attitude that asserted they had time to think about what they were doing. Gordon Winter had done well; not a single face was missing. The editor of the P.A., the editor of Reuters. Even the news editors of the BBC and ITN. *Yorkshire Post*, *Birmingham Post*, *Liverpool Echo*. *The Scotsman*. *The Glasgow Herald* – he must have flown them down by RAF plane.

'Good morning, gentlemen,' he said.

They murmured a polite 'good morning' back.

'Let me start by thanking you all for attending this hasty and somewhat impromptu meeting,' he said. 'As you'll see, I thought the matters I am about to place before you should be delivered personally, by me, man to man. I'm aware that some of you have come long distances for this meeting,' he said, nodding at the Scotsmen. 'I'm also very conscious of the fact that I can give you nothing to take back for your pages to justify your journey. What I am going to tell you is subject to a D-notice of the utmost rigour, the reason for which you will shortly learn.'

A loud groan echoed across the room. They had all feared a D-notice when they had seen it was a general editors' meeting – the D-notice effectively prevented them publishing anything of what the PM told them, on pain of prosecution for breaking the Official Secrets Act. They knew they could not complain. A body of editors, consulting with the government information agencies, had originally invented the D-notice system under which they could be kept informed of high security stories for background information only.

The Prime Minister sensed the moment was ripe for him to come out from behind the lectern, to show them he had no notes, and was speaking off the cuff. He hoped that he would get the facts right.

'As all of you know,' he began, 'the government is constantly aware of the need to create alternative sources of energy, and is constantly probing the possible uses of atomic matter for peaceful purposes . . .'

'Charlie,' he had said to the Director of the Harwell Centre on the telephone, three hours ago. 'I've got to tell the editors *something*. The minute I mention the word "atomic", their ears are going to prick up. These lads have photographic memories – you need one to be an editor. You've got to give me a name for that warhead, and a description of its function, that gets me off a hook. *I'm* not the one who allowed them to be made and stock-piled. It's yet another mess I took over when I took office from that smooth talking bastard – my much respected predecessor.

So, I need a description of the damned things that makes them sound like God's gift to Progress. And I want it when I go into that meeting. Peaceful uses of atomic energy – okay. Alternate sources of energy, okay. Something about the ecology would go down very nicely. But, for Christ's sake, give me *something*. And make it something I can talk about without notes . . .'

'A short while ago, gentlemen, we thought we had achieved something in the nature of a breakthrough. A breakthrough with enormous consequences in our constant struggle for the preservation of the ecology of our much-loved countryside . . .'

In the dramatic pause that followed, one suggestion could be heard quietly at the back of the room. 'A motor car powered by chicken-shit?' Fortunately, the rumble of muted laughter did not reach the Prime Minister. Damn it, he had had a momentary mental black-out. What the hell had Charlie called it? Ah yes.

'Our atomic scientists, working in secret – you know I can't say exactly where, gentlemen – have invented what, at the present time, we are calling an atomic energy converter . . .'

This time the Prime Minister did hear the reaction of his audience. A hand shot up.

'Yes, Mr Grantham?'

'Sorry to interrupt you, Prime Minister, but what's the position with regard to taking notes? I'm sure some of us aren't too good at remembering scientific matter. Or are you going to distribute a paper afterwards – with the D-notice on it, of course?'

'I'm very much afraid there can be no note-taking. Sorry chaps.'

'A paper afterwards, Prime Minister?'

'And no paper, either, I'm afraid.'

Now the grumbles were definitely audible. The Prime Minister was enough of a politician to realize that, if he did not act soon, the whole climate of the meeting was going to go against him.

'Gentlemen, this is not a Rutherford Lecture. I'm not

going to talk about atomics. I am going to talk about a *crime*, gentlemen! A crime involving the murder of two loyal, humble, government employees . . .'

Now he knew he had them. Crime, not atomics, not governments, not politicians, is closest to the heart of every living journalist.

Not one of them interrupted until the story of Joseph Aram, the 'atomic energy converter that *could* be adapted for non-peaceful purposes', the murder of the two guards, the telegram, the intended meeting with the heads of governments, had been completed. All heard him out in hushed silence.

'We are doing everything in our power, gentlemen, to apprehend the men responsible for this crime. Obviously, I can go into no details about that, but we are optimistic, that much I can say. Very optimistic.'

It was obvious that none of the editors present shared that optimism. Nor did Frank Moody. The Prime Minister regretted not having brought Bill Harrington to the meeting. So far, in all his dealings with Harrington, he had been aware of a strength that seemed to emanate from him. He could have used some of that strength now.

The first question was a full toss. From the editor of the *Daily Telegraph*: 'Would the Prime Minister please tell us what action he plans in the likely event he does not succeed in recovering this device, or finding this man, in the allotted time? And has the Prime Minister considered what demands the group responsible for the theft is likely to make? Does the Prime Minister intend to yield to those demands? Or is he prepared to risk a nuclear holocaust?'

'A good question,' he said. 'I have, in truth, given those three questions a *considerable* amount of thought.'

'Then, presumably, Prime Minister, you have a ready answer . . . ?'

'I have an answer ready. It's not a *ready* answer. In a situation such as this, fluidity and mobility are of paramount importance. It would be foolish to adopt fixed attitudes in advance of the information I know I will receive from my investigating team. I intend to await the outcome of those investigations, and to act accordingly.'

'In other words, Prime Minister, you haven't yet made up your mind just *what* you intend to do. Do you intend to consult the leaders of the other two political parties in the country?'

'I am in constant communication with them on all matters of national importance.'

'Do you intend to give them a decision-making role to play in this specific matter?'

'Rest assured, we shall continue to adopt those same democratic procedures that have served us so well in the past.'

'Do you intend to place this matter before the Security Council of the United Nations? Surely a supra-national problem such as this could not be handled chauvinistically from Downing Street or from the Elysée . . . ?'

'I intend to clean out our own stable . . .'

'To mix metaphors, Prime Minister, after the horse was bolted . . . ?'

That one drew a strained laugh, but by now the Prime Minister was back in his stride. The questions came thick and fast, but it was a game he adored, drawing on his full repertoire of political strokes, stone-walling many, sneaking some through the slips, and slamming the others over the boundary.

When the ordeal was over, his head was buzzing, but at least he had achieved his purpose. The visit of the American President would get a favourable press. Nobody, in print anyway, would ask any awkward and potentially unanswerable questions about *why* exactly he was there.

Bill and Sally had made their preparations carefully. The documentation was impeccable. 'Luckily, you can use your own identity,' Bill had said. 'That will stand any scrutiny. The last year is what we must take care of.'

'And the phoney documentation. The stuff I got for myself . . . ?'

'Good enough to stand normal investigation, but it will all fall apart when people really start to probe.'

They were in his apartment. All day they had worked together. She was the one to suggest he cook her a meal.

Now the remains of the meal stood on the plates in the kitchen. Neither had had a big appetite.

They were sitting together on the sofa, listening to the ending of the Beethoven Violin Concerto, that wonderfully soft and evocative recording made by Oistrakh.

'I repeat, Sally, this is strictly a volunteer assignment,' Bill said, looking down at her head cradled in his arm.

'I know that, Bill. I want to do it. I know I can do it.'

'I wish there had been time to train you more. Weapons, self-defence, all that stuff.'

'Don't you realize that my lack of training will be an asset? I'm going to go in there, strictly an amateur. Screwing up my courage for something in which I believe. If I were trained in kung-fu, it would show. If I knew the procedures, that would show. As it is, I know nothing. I'm a normal healthy girl, who's kept herself fit. I can give a normal account of myself – and no more. I've had my training. I've read Grahame Greene, Eric Ambler, John le Carré, Len Deighton. What more can an amateur need?'

'Only luck, Sally. A great deal of luck.'

The recording came to an end; the cassette switched itself off.

'I shan't see you for a while, Bill.' Sally said.

'I'll miss you.'

'Will you really? I've been over in my mind a dozen times the things I said when I was last here. All that talk about my Mum being a diplomatic diplomat's wife. I must have seemed a cold calculating bitch to you.'

'No, you didn't. You seemed to be someone who knew what she wanted, and was afraid no one was going to offer it to her. Like a kid at a party who asks "please may I have some of that coconut cake?" before he's finished the fish-paste sandwiches.'

'And you, Bill, do you want the coconut cake?'

He bent down and kissed the top of her head. 'More than anything else in the world . . .'

'Apart from catching Joseph Aram, with that box . . .'

'We'll decide that in the morning.'

Their lovemaking was slow, gentle and deeply passionate. She felt all the years of longing that had built up in him explode into a fully satisfying completion, leaving her saturated with wonder. She had never known such contentment. Her few brief relationships, she now knew, had been superficial on all levels, an urgent release of a developed tension, a palliative for some deep-felt ache. Now she knew what had been lacking in her life all those years, why nothing she had done so far had made her feel fulfilled.

She lay on her back beside him. 'All this independence crap people talk,' she said into the black velvet silence of a room that contained only the sounds of their breathing. 'All this women's lib, and being your own creature . . . Take your book of verse, take your bough, your piece of bread and your wine. Without a "thou" it is one hell of a wilderness. But you know that, too, don't you, Bill?'

'I guess I do. Especially when you think you have it all in balance, and you watch the "thou" walk away from it. And suddenly realize the "thou" walking away is yourself.'

'You're not a man who normally walks away, Bill. I've learned that already. Perhaps you ought to ask yourself why you did walk away from the situation with your wife. Perhaps, if you could explain that situation to yourself, you'd stop blaming yourself for it. Because you *are* blaming yourself. I know that. And I wish you wouldn't. That wasn't just a quick ride, Bill. I meant the things I said to you while we were making love. I *do* want you, with me, part of me, deep inside me. And I think that you want me the same way.'

Bill had been lying beside her, listening to her breathing in the dark, thinking exactly the same thing. But what kind of a bastard was he? Tonight they had made wonderful love. Tomorrow, he was going to launch her into a position of terrible danger. True, when she had heard the plan, she had volunteered. But the whole thing would never, could never, have been conceived without her participation. In a sense, the plan had been born around her and the fact of her existence. Plus, perhaps, the certainty that she would agree to carry it out.

'You're lovely and brave, strong and loyal,' he said, whispering the words into the hair which covered her ear.

And he felt like an absolute bastard as he did so.

CHAPTER THIRTEEN

The Prime Minister listened to him in silence, then exploded with exasperated anger. 'I can't possibly sanction such a thing, Harrington. My God, man, if news of that ever leaked out, I'd be finished, totally finished both politically and professionally. Quite apart from what I think, personally, about the dangers involved. Especially for that young lady.'

Bill allowed the explosion to subside before he spoke, then quietly said: 'You misunderstand my motive in coming to see you, Prime Minister. I didn't come to ask you to "sanction" it. I came to inform you about what we are doing. There's no question of my asking permission to do it. I already asked that, in the meeting of the Security Cabinet. You will remember that, on that occasion, I was given carte blanche. Now I'm exercising that carte blanche. But I'm informing you that, if the plan goes wrong, a girl may be killed and I myself might be in some disgrace.'

'You're not asking my permission?'

'Certainly not, Prime Minister. I wouldn't expose you to that responsibility.'

'And you're prepared to carry the can . . .'

'Yes, I am. But, more importantly, Sally Price is prepared to risk her life.'

'She's a brave woman. If she succeeds, that fact will not be forgotten.'

'And if she fails . . . ?'

'She won't care, will she, one way or the other. My

responsibility, Bill, is to the living. I leave the dead to the historian and the poet.'

Renée Lebegue eyed the contents of her wardrobe with the disparagement that always accompanied the end of autumn. Thank God the new collections would be out next week, and she could get a few more interesting things for the start of the next season. Next week, thank God, Bruxelles, leaving Henri to cope with the dreary round of pre-Christmas functions.

Henri was sitting on the bed. Really, he looked so funny wearing her bathrobe, her pom-pom mules, his hair all bed-tousled. Still, better sex before the party than a drunken brawl after it. And it did make her arrive at these embassy functions feeling a certain sparkle in her flesh. Le pauvre Henri. Nearly past it. They would have a few more years, and then she would need to find someone a little younger to satisfy her needs. But not yet awhile.

'Vas-y, Henri,' she said. 'I must get dressed. And so must you if we're not to be late.'

'Yet another damn party. All the same people.'

'But much more interesting. I'm quite looking forward to meeting all those ballet dancers from Los Angeles. All those lovely American men . . .'

'And all those heavy footed American ballerinas. Merde!'

'You always say ballerinas are heavy footed. Just because you fell hopelessly in love with Furtzievna as a young student . . . Anyway, go and get dressed. And don't say "merde" in my bedroom. C'est pas gentil, tu sais!'

'I don't feel very gentil! I want to spend one evening, one delicious long evening, at home. Alone with you.'

'Then, Henri, you ought to resign as Ambassador, and we ought to go back home to Belgium, to the chateau, where you can spend your declining years watching the grass sprout, the herds grow fat, the mines spew out their coal. And you could spend your evenings, your oh-so-long evenings, alone at home with me!' She kissed the silver hair on the top of his head, that distinguished halo of hair that elongated his fine patrician features. 'D'accord, cheri? Now, vas-y, and get changed.'

The Chef de Protocol, as Sir Maurice Winfield preferred to call himself – Chief of Protocol sounded such a non-U title – had wondered where he might hold his farewell party. Just a few friends, the ambassadors with whom he had established such a rapport during his term of office. At first, he thought of somewhere steeped in privilege, like the dining room of the House of Lords, Londonderry House, the Government Dining Rooms on Carlton House Terrace. But that was all a bit second rate. His mind wandered through London's dining clubs and restaurants. Perhaps he should take over Quo Vadis for the evening, or any one of the clubs of which he was a member. That, also, did not seem right. Then the answer came to him. Why not be vulgar, and take the roof-top restaurant at the London Hilton. Deliciously vulgar, of course, and invite some stage people to be his guests. Assuredly, a few would add a certain piquancy to the normal ambassadorial pudding.

Eh bien, Sir Maurice had manfully coped with the problematic ingredients of that pudding for four years. Now he could retire with dignity from government service, accept the job of Warden of Angel College, Oxford, and develop his quite promising television career. Who else could have *fifteen* ambassadors and their wives to say farewell to him? And none of the lesser countries for padding, either. French, German, Belgian and Dutch, Italian and Spanish, Norwegian, Danish, Finnish and Swedish, the American *and* the Russian Ambassadors, the Japanese, the Brazilian and Argentinian. Plus twenty really delightful young people, boys and girls, from the Santa Monica Modern Ballet Company. It should be a simply *lovely* party. Too bad Walter could not be there, but then, he could keep Walter by his side once they got to Oxford. And Walter would only misbehave himself horribly, once he saw all those nimble, muscular male ballet dancers.

What a bore he had had to invite the two Special Branch

officers and their wives. He did so hope they would not behave like PC 49s.

And what a bore about this chap Harrington, and his girl friend. Really, some of the people who crawled out of the back corridors of Whitehall were quite unacceptable. Inviting oneself to a private party, even with a letter from the PM giving full authority to do *anything* on goverment business, was just *not on*.

Still, all in all, it could be a jolly party. A jolly goodbye to governmental responsibilities, and all that. He did hope the Faisan Farci would be cooked properly.

'Any idea what we're getting to eat, Tom?' the American Ambassador asked.

Tom put his arm round his wife's waist. 'I called 'em. We're getting pheasant.'

She shuddered. 'Not again! That's the second time this week. I can't bear to think of those poor birds, and all you overweight men banging away at them. Red faces, tweed suits, funny hats, boots too big for you – it makes me feel quite nauseous.'

He nibbled her ear. 'And we're drinking Clos de Vougeot.'

'Now you're talking.'

'You sybarite, you.'

'Just because I like this European habit of drinking wine with meals instead of getting stoned to the eyeballs on martinis and then drinking water. This dress all right?' She slipped from his grasp and pirouetted in front of him. His eyes sparkled at her.

'I don't know how you do it all the time,' he said. 'You'll be the belle of the ball! And you with a brand new grand-daughter. I called 'em today, by the way, while you were looking round that block of flats in Pimlico.'

'Flats? Tom, it's time I took you back to the U.S. of A. You're beginning to talk like a Britisher, even. Next thing we know, you'll be kissing the backs of hands . . .'

The telephone rang. 'That'll be the car,' she said.

He picked up the instrument. 'Thanks,' he said. 'We'll

be right there.' He turned in time to help her into her mink coat. 'You look like a million dollars,' he said. 'Mrs Ambassador!'

'Not tonight,' she said. 'Tonight, Tom, it's just you and me. Stepping out to dine and dance with an old friend, okay?'

'Okay, lady,' he said. 'Just puttin' on the style . . .'

'Tom,' she said, pausing at the door. 'Every time I step out of a door, I chide myself for something I haven't done. Every time I walk out of the safety and comfort of just being with you!'

'Something you haven't done, Mary?'

'I don't always have time to remember. But this time, I do. Tom, I love you. Never forget that, will you?'

He touched her cheek lightly. 'I never will,' he said.

One by one the guests started to arrive for Sir Maurice Winfield's party. He had booked the entire restaurant at the Hilton, with the adjoining bar, both with their panoramic views over the rooftops of London.

The first two to arrive were the Special Branch officers, Superintendent Jones and Sergeant Mottram both immaculate in black dinner jackets.

'Kind of you to invite our wives,' the Superintendent said. 'But we've taken the liberty of bringing along a couple of police women. They'll be arriving later among the throng. We'll just have a quick look round before anybody comes.'

'You don't anticipate any trouble, do you?' Sir Maurice winced.

'None at all, Sir Maurice, but with so many important people in a public place – it's wisest to take care.'

'With your permission, I shall introduce you respectively as Mister Jones and Mister Mottram. And give your occupations, if anyone should ask, as civil servants.'

'That's all right by us, Sir Maurice. We're well aware this is a private function. We've no wish to intrude. We're quite experienced at keeping out of the limelight.'

Two by two the guests arrived. They had been screened by the security men at the front door – it would be a long time before the Hilton management forgot the bomb blast that had wrecked part of the entrance lobby – and an elevator had been reserved for them at the end of the bank. The Russian Ambassador's chauffeur rode with him as far as the restaurant, got out of the elevator first and looked around suspiciously before beckoning the Ambassador out. Sergei Lutrov was a small man with a thatch of snowy white hair that made him look a little like Albert Einstein. He did not like being compared to the Jewish scientist. His wife was equally small, but exquisitely formed, a Tartar with the delicate features of the East. That she had trained in a Moscow Ballet Academy was obvious from the way she walked. She looked forward to talking shop with the dancers of the American Ballet Company.

'You wait, down below, in the lobby,' the Ambassador said to his chauffeur,' who looked suspiciously round the entrance to the bar and the restaurant, before getting back into the elevator for the descent. The Ambassador knew he would spend all evening with his eyes fixed on the elevator door, his hand near the Tokarev pistol he carried. It had taken special dispensation from the management to allow him through the security screen with it in his pocket.

The German Ambassador and his wife were accompanied by two 'chauffeurs'. Baader-Meinhoff was still not far from *their* minds. Both the men were heavily built, from the south of Germany. Both, too, had required special dispensations from the management. One carried a Mauser, the other a Walther PPK. The head waiter, standing at the entrance to the lift on the restaurant floor to direct the guests to his right, towards the bar, was swept back between both pairs of broad shoulders.

'Excuse me, *please*,' he said in vain.

The West German Ambassador, Herr Gunther Broeckel, and his wife, stepped out, turned, and marched along the short corridor. Only when they had gone did the two chauffeurs permit the head waiter to step away from the wall, to dust himself and straighten his tie, trying, as best he could, to recover his composure.

The restaurant manager was standing with the hotel

under-manager by the door into the bar. Both bowed as each guest arrived, like marionettes pulled by the same string. The hotel under-manager directed the ladies to the cloakroom; the restaurant manager looked after the Gents.

The American Ambassador's car stopped outside in the forecourt. The man sitting beside the chauffeur spoke into the microphone. 'Outside now, Al.'

The reply was a soft murmur from the speaker below the dashboard.

'Okay, Will. Joe and Frank are in the lobby. It's clean, except the Russian goon is sitting watching the door of the elevator like it was trap three, and the two West Germans are trying unsuccessfully to hide behind a palm shrub. We've had a word with Security. Just hold up your arms and they'll give you a quick once-over, okay?'

'Roger and out.'

Mary and Tom looked at each other. Such procedures were a tedious concomitant of everyday political life around the world.

Mary knew they were designed as much as to save her life as to preserve the prestige of the United States. A history major at college, she had learned quickly that the conduct of young people is cyclic, one phase following the other with an inevitability revealed throughout time. Okay, today it was urban revolution. Yesterday, campus protest, flower power, the crazy drugs scene. Her favourite game, one she always used to play in moments of tension, was to ask whatever happened to . . . ? And then name some headliner of yesterday. Whatever happened to Patty Hearst? Whatever happened to Aldrich Cleaver? Whatever happened to Jack Kerouac? Whatever happened to the Tupamaros? How long would it be before she was asking whatever happened to Baader-Meinhoff? She hoped, not long.

'Okay, Ma'am,' Will said. 'Let's go!'

Driver out and right. Will out and left. Both round to the inner back door. Tom opens the back door from inside, but *does not get out*. Poor Tom, with his old-style New England courtesy; that had truly hurt him, not to be permitted to get out and offer *his* wife *his* hand. Why, Tom could show the British a thing or two in the matter of courtesy towards a lady . . . Mary had to climb over Tom's feet and get behind and between the two men. Tom slipped behind her and slammed the door shut, the signal for the wedge, with Mary, the Ambassador of the United States of America, in the middle, to speed its way across the sidewalk and into the lobby of the hotel.

Al saw them come in, tapped the arm of the security man who, against instructions, waved them straight through to the bank of elevators.

The Belgian Ambassador and his wife were waiting there.

Mary looked at Renée round Will's wide shoulders. 'See you upstairs,' she whispered. Renée smiled, the elevator door opened, and all six went inside. At the last minute, the Japanese Ambassador and his wife arrived. He bowed and managed to get in by a quick undignified scramble, just as the door was closing. Will hit the OPEN DOORS button; the doors opened again and the Japanese Ambassador's wife, wearing a full kimono, glided in as if running on small wheels. Her head was down-cast. The Japanese Ambassador looked around, a smile lacquered to his teapot face. 'Good evening, everybody,' he said. He did not get all the consonants right, but they all understood him. Then he caught sight of the Belgian. 'Bon soir, Monsieur,' he said, and clicked his mouth open and closed like a camera shutter.

The wedge came apart on the restaurant floor. 'Have a nice evening, Ma'am,' Will said, happy that two of the waiters were his men.

Bill and Sally arrived in her car. The commissionaire parked it for her in the bay to the right of the front door. 'Nervous?' Bill asked as they went in.

'Yes. But I'll manage.' She held up her arms for the Security Services matron to quickly frisk her. She opened her handbag and the woman took a quick look inside, a wallet, a lipstick, a comb, a handkerchief lying in the bottom. 'Okay, Miss,' she said, with a professionally detached smile. Sally walked a couple of paces then stopped. 'Oh,' she said, 'I've forgotten my glasses . . .'

The matron smiled at her. 'I'm like that,' she said. 'Forget my head if it was loose!'

Bill looked annoyed. 'You'd better go and get them,' he said. 'And hurry it up. We're late enough as it is . . .'

The matron flashed a look of sympathy at Sally that said 'Men!' with considerable contempt. Sally hurried out, and back to her car.

When she came back through the front door holding the spectacle case the matron waved her through.

Sally and Bill did not speak as they made their way across the Arab-strewn lobby to the elevator bank. She held his forearm, pressing it reassuringly.

They rode to the top floor with the Spanish and Brazilian Ambassadors and their wives, both of whom talked all the way up.

Sir Maurice Winfield was waiting inside the bar. 'So pleased you could come,' he said to Bill and Sally, then turned and addressed himself volubly in Spanish to the Spanish Ambassador.

Bill and Sally walked to the window and looked down across the park. From that height, they could see the whole of West London spread before them, St George's Hospital a tiny doll's house in the distance. The night was miraculously clear and Sally had never seen such a glitter of street lights, house lights, car headlights, blending into the exquisite ceiling of the stars themselves. She held Bill's arm compulsively. Such a short time she had known him, but such a tempestuous time within her.

He turned his back to the window, standing half a pace away, looking behind her at the crowd within the room, the waiters hovering with trays of champagne, the plates of canapés. Everyone seemed to have arrived. Sir Maurice had left his station by the door and was now talking with the American, French, and Russian Ambassadors.

'One Special Branch chap sitting at the end of the bar with a girl who looks like a copper,' Bill commented, so quietly that only she could hear. 'The other one is along here to my left, standing by the window. He's with the girl wearing a powder blue — I think you call it — dress and a gold band round her throat. That's a mistake. Anybody could grab that and use it against her. I would guess the waiter who gave us the champagne is American. Probably CIA. Waiters don't wear big cuff-links. From the look of the studs on his shirt, I'd say he has a transmitter in his pocket, with the aerial down his trouser leg. But I could be wrong. Maybe the stud is its own transmitter, radius a mile. Anyway, whichever it is, the magnet I gave you this evening will disable it.'

'I may decide to use it. It would be a good means of communication.'

'That's up to you, Sally. Damn it, once we go, so much of it, all of it, is up to you.'

The Special Branch man who had been standing in the window to Bill's left walked along slowly, apparently looking at the view.

'Good evening,' he said, as he came level with Bill. 'I don't think we've met? My name's Mottram.'

'Mine's Harrington.'

'Ah yes, Mr Harrington. We were told you'd be here.'

'Were you told about the waiter? The one with the champagne?'

'No, we weren't. I've been watching him.'

'Left hand side of his jacket. Low down.'

'Thank you. I'll have a word with the Super.'

'I would, if I were you.'

'Otherwise, looks like a quiet night?'

'That's the way it looks.'

'I'll mingle, Mr Harrington. Nice meeting you.'

'Enjoy the pheasant.'

They both watched him go. 'Now we'd better circulate,' Bill said. The minute they broke apart, Renée Lebegue accosted him. 'I don't think we've met, Mr . . .'

'Harrington. Bill Harrington.'

'Renée Lebegue. What rugby team do you play for, Mr Harrington? You see, I know all about you strong silent Englishmen.' She seized his arm and dragged him, like a trophy, into a group of three wives. As he sank beneath their chattering smiles, he saw that Sally had got herself a couple of ambassadors. He spent the next thirty minutes going from group to group, talking French to the Danish and Finnish Ambassador's wives, both of whom had recently been stationed in Paris, and Italian to the Japanese, who had recently been posted from Rome. As the champagne flowed, the chatter grew louder, though it never surpassed the bounds of diplomatic good taste. Sir Maurice beamed on the assembly with a happy smile. He knew when a party was going well. This one certainly had all the elements. He had been so right to pick the Hilton. Here, away from the stilted diplomatic trappings of embassies and government hospitality suites, everyone could relax. They could feel themselves, if only for one brief, fleeing evening, to be on holiday. Alors. If he, Maurice, couldn't throw a good party with all his years of training, then who could?

He glanced at his watch. The ballet company would be arriving en masse in ten minutes. Fifteen minutes to circulate, and then next door. The table had been a problem. How should he seat everybody. All together, or at separate tables, each carrying a mixture of six people each? Should he adopt the excruciating modern habit of changing tables between courses, so that everyone could sit with everyone? So many alternatives. Finally, he had decided to be quite revolutionary, and quite bourgeois at the same time. He chose a hexagonal table. And, at Tom's urgent pleading, he had arranged to let husbands sit with wives. In some cases, he knew that had not been a popular move. Señor Joaio was not speaking with his wife Arabelle more than was necessary these days, and Jean-Pierre Audon, the French Ambassador, treated his wife as if he could not bear to be in the same room with her.

Mais, comme Chef de Protocol, that sort of friction was meat and drink to him. He gave Arabelle the Norwegian Ambassador on her right hand – and he would bore the pants off anybody. He seated the Japanese Ambassador next to the French Ambassador's wife. Kurata would talk all through the meal, and Poupette – what a silly name for a grown woman – could sulk all she wanted.

Sally was standing next to the American Ambassador.

'Excuse me,' she whispered confidentially into Mary Foster's ear. 'The clasp has come undone on your necklace, I think.'

Mary's hands flew to her throat. 'Oh heavens,' she said. 'It's been loose for days. I've been meaning to have it fixed.'

'Shall I clasp it for you?'

'If you wouldn't mind.' She sat on a nearby chair.

Sally stepped behind her, put her hands either side of Mary's neck and drew the necklace up. Tom saw the movement from a couple of groups away, but Mary called to him. 'It's my clasp again, Tom. Miss Price is fixing it for me.' He turned his head away.

The first Special Branch officer was by the window. The second again by the bar. Both police women were with them. The waiter – behind the bar, pouring champagne into glasses. And Bill standing beside the American Ambassador's husband.

Mary felt the cold chain go round her neck.

'What the . . .'

Then she felt the heavy object pressed into her throat. At the same moment the chain drew tight, though not enough to strangle her, locked around her neck.

She looked down, all sound choked within her.

She recognized the object hanging around her throat instantly. Sally's hand came up behind her, then to the right. Mary saw the movement as if in slow motion. Her finger, firmly inside the ring at the top of the grenade, withdrew a pin about three quarters of an inch long.

Sally's other hand was clasped around the bomb, holding a lever which went from top to bottom of the squat cylinder.

'Don't move,' Sally said. 'It's a grenade, and if I let go it will explode in exactly four seconds. The chain is locked at the back of your neck, and I don't have the key with me.'

'Tom!' Mary screamed.

All sound stopped within the room. All eyes turned to the American Ambassador.

The Superintendent of the Special Branch was the first to speak. His voice was loud enough for everyone to hear him quite plainly.

'Don't anybody move,' he said. 'That girl's holding a primed hand grenade. I am Superintendent Jones of the Special Branch of the British Police. Don't anybody try anything. I suggest you all sit down, exactly where you are.'

Sally beckoned to the Ambassador's husband. 'Bring a seat, Mr Foster, and come here beside your wife. Facing forward. You can hold her hand.'

Tom Foster quickly grasped one of the light-weight chairs and dragged it across. He placed it next to his wife's chair, and they clasped both hands together. 'You're going to be all right, Mary,' he said.

Sally looked coolly at the Special Branch Superintendent. 'Explain to them about grenades, Superintendent,' she said mockingly.

He looked at her for a long moment. 'You're a cool one, Miss,' he said. 'What organization are you?'

'Explain about grenades, before someone behind me decides to play hero and give me a rabbit chop.'

He cleared his throat and turned. 'Would you all please listen to me most carefully,' he said. 'The object round the American Ambassador's throat is a grenade with, I imagine, a four-second fuse. That grenade will not fire so long as the lever is depressed. This young lady is holding the lever. It is normally kept in position with a pin. The young lady has pulled out that pin. If anything happens to cause the young lady to let go of that lever, it will fly from the grenade quicker than anyone can stop it, and the grenade will explode.'

Mary Foster gave an enormous gulp, seeming to have understandable difficulty in breathing. 'Hold on, Mary,' Tom said, squeezing her hands tightly.

'I *am* holding on, Tom. This is some kind of nightmare I'm having, isn't it? Tell me it's a nightmare, Tom?'

'Yes, Mary, it's a nightmare. But I'm afraid we're all horribly awake. I'll stay by your side, Mary, by your side . . .'

*

Will was relaxing in the front seat of the car, smoking a cigarette, listening to the muted chatter of the party with only the back of his mind. Then he heard the American Ambassador scream. He sat bolt upright, ground his cigarette into the ashtray. The microphone Al was wearing could pick up anything within that room and transmit the sound a mile. They were picking it up by aerial on the roof of the Bentley, feeding it into a receiver, with a looped cassette. His fingers hit the button that stabbed the loop onto full tape. He leaned forward, heard the silence that followed the scream, then Al's urgent whisper.

'Snowball, Will. Snowball.' *The Ambassador's life was in danger, and he could do nothing about it.*

Will listened to the next voice, that of the Special Branch Superintendent. Now he realized why Al could do nothing about it. Why nobody could do anything about it. He picked up the phone, waited until the Embassy operator came on the line, via radio.

'We have a Snowball,' he said. 'Pick up on line 7 for a direct feed. Keep all other lines free. Now hear this – we have a Code A for Alpha alert, repeat Code A for Alpha. Go to it.'

Code A for Alpha:

1. Inform the President.
2. Alert Bob Wilkinson, Head of Security.
3. Inform all units FBI and CIA in London.
4. Activate radio net at scene of incident.
5. Inform Assistant Commissioner (Crime), Scotland Yard.

Across the bottom of the plastic card listing the A (Alpha) instructions, someone had scrawled 'Then get down on your knees, and start to pray.'

The operator picked up a phone and dialled. When a voice answered he said, 'Patsy, I'm gonna be kinda late. We've got a kinda crisis here. I'll call ya. You better put the kids to bed, uh? May take a little while.'

The Assistant Commissioner (Crime) was being very patient on the telephone in his car. He had been on his way to dinner with his son and daughter-in-law in Lincoln's

Inn when he had received the first call. He turned the car round and waited patiently for the second call to come. 'How is it, Bob?' he said to the second caller, Chief Superintendent Bradshaw of the Special Branch. 'And why the hell do the Americans always beat us to the punch? Especially here, on our own patch? I got this from the Embassy two minutes and sixteen seconds ago. Needless to say, I'm on my way to the Hilton now. I shall see you there, no doubt.'

Sally had instructed all of them to drag chairs to the far wall, which did not have a window or a panoramic view, and sit facing it. All had done exactly as she said. Now she beckoned to the waiter. He came and stood in front of the Ambassador's chair.

'Take it easy, Ma'am,' he said. 'This can't last for ever!'

She smiled weakly at him, reached out her hand and touched his wrist. 'Thank you, she said, 'I know I'm going to be all right, so long as no one does anything foolish. Give me your gun,' Sally said.

He reached reluctantly into the inside pocket, low down on the left side of his jacket, and produced a heavy Colt ·45. 'Put it into my handbag,' she said, holding the bag forward with her left hand. He opened it, laid the gun carefully inside, and closed it again. She reached forward and grasped the stud of his shirt, one of a seemingly identical set of four, jet black, about three eighths of an inch in diameter.

His mind worked fast. If he could just crowd in, use his left hand to hold her right clenched tight around the grenade, chop her below her ear with his other hand, grip the lever . . .

Sally read it in his eyes. So did the Ambassador. 'Don't try it,' Mary Foster said. 'We have a room full of innocent people. We must be patient. We must learn to be patient and negotiate.'

She knew every word she uttered was being fed over the microphone the girl was now holding, that eventually it would find its way onto the American radio and TV networks. There would be growls within the Republican Party from the right wingers, accusing her of being soft on Commies and terrorists, but she no longer cared. It *was* time to be patient. It *was* time to wait, and negotiate. Suddenly, she felt a thrill of pride. This had been, was, her greatest testing time. And she was not afraid. She squeezed Tom's hands again, and turned to the girl. Miss Price. Wasn't that her name? Something in the Civil Service?

'Miss Price,' she asked, her voice steady, firm. 'I have one request to make. I am the Ambassador of the United States of America. Appointed by the President to represent my people here in your country. No doubt that is why you have chosen me as your hostage. My husband holds no official position within the government, though he is the head of our house. Would you please send my husband to the farthest corner of the room? We have grandchildren who have not yet learned what a fine man he is . . .

Sally felt a lump come to her throat, a most un-terrorist-like lump, at the bravery of this quiet women. 'Certainly, Mrs Foster,' she said.

'I won't go,' Tom said firmly, but his wife looked at him.

'Not for my sake, Tom. Not even for your sake. But for the kids' sake. Remember?'

They had made a quiet pact. Never travel together in the same airplane, whenever possible. Never drive an auto when they had had more than two drinks. Take an annual medical check-up.

'Okay, Mary. I remember.' He stood up. 'I don't know who in God's name you are, lady, or which crack-pot outfit you think you represent, but I'll make you one promise. If you harm my Mary in any way, in *any* way, you understand me, I'll come looking for you. I'll track you down like the bitch you are. I'll hunt you, and I'll kill you. And you hear that, lady, loud and clear!'

He turned, squared his shoulders, and walked to the wall. He drew a chair, turned it, and sat looking across the room at the group.

Sally glanced at her watch. Already her arm was beginning to feel heavy, holding the grenade to Mrs Foster's throat.

'Give them five minutes,' Bill had said. 'The first ones will be in position, but they won't yet have had time to organize fully.'

'Right,' she said crisply. 'Let's get on with it. This is a microphone, right.'

Al nodded.

'Broadcasting to a car somewhere outside?'

'Yes. And the reception is perfect. We tested it.'

'I'll bet you did. Right. My name is Sally Price. Until five minutes ago, I was a British civil servant. I have been disgusted for a long while with the handling of the situation in Israel and am now determined to do something about it. Personally, I will not stop until every last Israeli has been driven out of Palestine. I demand two things. Firstly, that Khaylia Patin be released from Brixton Prison and brought here. You have a deadline of exactly thirty minutes in which to do that. Then I want a British Airways plane, fully fuelled and capable of flying three thousand miles non-stop. Flight crew only, and one cabin staff. Take-off from Heathrow must be in ninety minutes from now.'

The output from that microphone, amplified by the powerful receivers on the roof of the US Embassy in Grosvenor Square, was being fed directly to the White House in Washington, to the Prime Minister at Number 10 Downing Street, and to Scotland Yard.

Other wires were buzzing like swarming bees. Who the hell was this 'Sally Price'? What were her affiliations? More importantly, what was her mental stability? Was she likely to blow her stack, let the lever fly out of that grenade?

The Prime Minister was on the telephone immediately to the Commissioner of Police at New Scotland Yard who, luckily, was still in his office.

'Get that girl, Khaylia Patin, out of Brixton and down to the Hilton Hotel.'

'I'm clearing the lobby, Prime Minister, and keeping everyone away from the elevators.'

'Good.'

'I have snipers in the park, but it's a long shot.'

'Don't even think of it.'

'But Prime Minister, with respect, we must do something . . .'

'Commissioner, we will and can do *nothing* for the moment.'

'But, Prime Minister, no politician will be safe . . .'

'I haven't the time to indulge in polemics, Commissioner. I take full responsibility for my actions. The girl will be brought from Brixton within the deadline. The plane will be prepared for take-off. And as soon as possible, we must establish two-way contact with this Sally Price. There must be telephones up there. I suggest we try them. All of them.'

CHAPTER FOURTEEN

Bill was sitting facing the wall, in the second of the two rows of chairs. Sir Maurice Winfield was sitting in front of him, to his right, his head buried in his hands. He was weeping softly, but pitying only himself.

The Special Branch Sergeant was in front of Bill and to his left. He had worked the pistol out of his inner pocket and was holding it in his lap. A police Webley Special, ·38.

'Put that damned thing away,' Bill whispered urgently.

The Sergeant looked over his shoulder resentfully, then tucked the pistol defiantly into the waist-band of his trousers.

Renée Lebegue was looking back into the room, openly curious. There was a film of excitement on her upper lip. Embassy parties had never been like this . . . ! 'Whatever else they'll say, Sir Maurice,' she said flippantly, 'at least no-one can say your party was dull!'

'Tais-toi!' her husband said.

Bill looked back and Sally caught his eye, but quickly looked away.

'You brought her!' Sir Maurice suddenly said, his voice full of venom. 'You brought that *renegade* to *my* party! I'll have you for this, you see if I don't.'

Yes, Bill thought, I brought her. Exposed her to this great danger. The old argument. Do the ends justify the means?

Especially when the ends are so chancy, so doubtful. Okay, if they could succeed, everyone would say that what they were doing was justified. If not, if it was all wasted endeavour, then how would they justify the risks they were taking?

But what else could they have done? There had been no viable alternative.

There was a telephone within twelve feet of Sally Price.

Its ring sounded clamorous in the silence. 'Answer it,' Sally said to the Special Branch Superintendent. The CIA man had dropped to his knees and was holding Mary Foster's hands. She was lost in the world of her youth, thinking yet again, as she always did in times of stress, about her girlhood in New England, filling her mind with the fall tones of the woods of Vermont and Massachusetts; trips to Providence, Rhode Island: the sailboat they used to take to Martha's Vineyard.

The Commissioner of Police was on the line.

The Superintendent gave him a quick word picture of the scene, then carried the telephone on its long extension across to Sally Price. 'The Commissioner of Police,' he said.

Sally took the instrument in one hand and held it to her ear.

'Sally Price.'

He identified himself again. 'Now, Miss Price,' he said. 'You must stop this nonsense, stop it at once, do you hear!'

She laughed out loud. 'Yes, father,' she said. 'Right away.'

She handed the telephone back to the Superintendent. He too had been assessing the situation. Should he have a go, or not? She had seen the CIA man shake his head, warning him. She had also noticed the CIA man edging himself closer, slowly sliding his hand up Mary Foster's

155

arm, ready for a quick grab. Quickly she brought her own hand up and round. The grenade came to the back of Mary Foster's neck, at the top of her spine. The brass lock that held the chain ends together was in front of the CIA man's face. She opened her bag one handed, felt inside for the magnet, and slipped the transmitting microphone on to it. Those listening heard the click, then the airwaves went dead.

The Special Branch Superintendent was talking into the microphone, explaining the situation in detail. She did not care. She and Bill had been through this thing, over and over again. It had to be something fool-proof. Some way she could hold one person. The grenade and chain had been her own idea. Something everyone could see, and know could not be removed quickly. Something that did not require skill or an aim. A grenade strikes more terror than a rifle or a pistol. It is indiscriminating. Especially a high-fragmentation grenade, such as the Mills bomb.

The danger would come if any one of the many forces they would pile up around the Hilton had not understood the message. And decided to take a shot at her.

Or, of course, if she should stumble . . .

The Superintendent came across the room. 'Khaylia Patin is on her way,' he said. 'She left Brixton a short while ago in a fast police car. They'll bring her to the lobby downstairs and wait for your instructions. It's still not too late to give it up, Miss,' he added kindly. 'That Khaylia Patin. I was one of the men who interrogated her – well, questioned her, I should say. She's definitely round the bend, I wouldn't trust my daughter to go five yards with her.'

'I'm not the Commissioner's daughter, Superintendent, and I'm not yours either. Bring that telephone over here, sit down, and shut up.'

BBC radio got the first tip-off and raced a radio reporter to the Hilton. He found a scene of chaos. No one knew anything; everybody knew everything. The lobby had been emptied except for the night manager. He was standing nervously at the bottom of the lift shaft. There was a line of uniformed London policemen across the front door. The whole area outside the hotel was occupied by police cars, a police emergency truck, a radio command post, and several ambulances. The Assistant Commissioner (Crime) was standing with the Commissioner on the pavement.

A milling throng of five thousand or more were gathered around the outside of a perimeter of policemen which extended all round the hotel. Nobody was going in, nobody was going out. Hyde Park carried many of the people. The police had made a large D-barrier in there when they blocked off Park Lane to the north and south. Vehicles were being routed back through the park exits, and two-way traffic ran, for the moment, down the carriageway in the Park itself. The radio reporter, Graham Manson, identified himself. He showed the Commissioner his Uher tape-recorder hopefully. For once, the Commissioner was cooperative. 'Right, Mr Manson, I'll give you a short statement and that will have to do. I shall look to you to pool it, so that I am not bothered by other people. A private party, taking place in this hotel, was recently interrupted by an unidentified person. A hostage has been taken. That person is making certain demands in exchange for the return of the hostage. At the moment, we are concentrating our efforts on making contact with the person concerned, and evaluating the situation. As a normal security measure we have evacuated the lobby of the hotel and traffic is being re-routed. The general public would greatly assist the police by staying away from this vicinity.'

'Has there been any blood-shed, Commissioner? Any loss of life?'

'No, there has not.'

'Any violence?'

'Police officers are at the scene of the incident which, at the moment, is being contained.'

As a matter of course, the BBC newsroom received lists of all the important functions taking place in all the big hotels each evening. Graham had read the list for the Hilton.

'This private function – is it Sir Maurice Winfield's ambassadors' party? His farewell dinner for fifteen ambassadors and their wives? Including the Russian and the American?'

Tape recorders do not record smiles, but Graham Manson knew he had scored a bull's eye and knew the Commissioner would not admit it.

'Several private functions are taking place at this hotel tonight, Mr Manson,' he said. 'And we have no wish to spread alarm.'

'Then you admit there is cause for alarm, Commissioner?'

'There is always cause for alarm, Mr Manson, when private citizens ignore the existence of our own excellent police forces and decide to take matters into their own hands. As I have repeatedly said . . .'

Graham knew he was in for the standard police patter. 'Thank you very much, Commissioner,' he said. 'This is Graham Manson at the Hilton Hotel, London, returning you now to the studio.'

He put the tape on to rapid rewind and pushed his way through the police cordon to where he could see the masts of the BBC radio van. He handed the Uher to the driver. 'A load of cods on that,' he said. 'But you'd better play it back to the newsroom right away. I'm going to have a sniff around . . .'

The loudspeaker crackled in the back of the van. Both recognized the voice of the duty news editor. Graham picked up a microphone.

'We're just getting a feed for you,' the news editor said. 'The New York networks have just interrupted normal programming. They were broadcasting a tape taken from the roof of the Hilton. Some civil servant girl, Sally Price, holding the American Ambassador with a grenade round her throat. She's demanding the release of Khaylia Patin, and a plane out of Heathrow. Get cracking, Graham, would you old boy? We don't like having the shit beaten out of us by the Yanks. Especially not on our own doorstep.'

*

Scotland Yard set up a special information room, the telephones of which were almost immediately jammed by the rush of incoming calls, once the re-recording of the US broadcasts was fed out by the BBC. Television programmes on both BBC and ITV were interrupted. Remote cameras were quickly on the spot, their long lenses, normally used for sports events, highlighting the roof-top restaurant dramatically against the sky.

One of the first shots they got, repeated over and over again in the absence of other 'hard' news, was that of a plain car arriving, being surrounded instantly by policemen. A figure emerging and being rushed into the hotel lobby. With a journalist's licence, the figure was positively identified as being that of Khaylia Patin.

It was not, in fact. While the decoy had been arriving at the front door, Khaylia had been slipped in the back.

She was now waiting in the lobby.

The Commissioner telephoned to the roof, spoke to the Special Branch Superintendent, Jones. He relayed the message to Sally Price. At that moment, a helicopter appeared, skimming low across the park. The enterprising news reporter in it trained his field glasses on the window. The cameraman beside him was looking through the view-finder. 'Got it,' he said. 'Hold the son of a bitch steady.' The news reporter picked up his microphone and held it to his lips while he peered through the glasses. The helicopter was bouncing wildly in the turbulence.

'I can't get any closer,' the pilot yelled.

The reporter pressed his microphone button.

'This is Larry Bernstein of NBC,' he said, 'talking to you from a helicopter hovering outside the rooftop restaurant of the Hilton Hotel, London, England, where I can see the United States Ambassador to England, Mary Foster, being held close by a young girl, aged about thirty. There appears to be some sort of constriction around the neck of our Ambassador, who is sitting in a chair. The girl is standing behind her. Near to them is a large man wearing a tuxedo, holding a telephone in his hand; I guess he must be Superintendent Jones of the Special Branch of the London

Metropolitan Police Force, who is in constant contact with the British Commissioner of Police in the lobby below. The other guests are . . .'

An updraught caught the helicopter at that moment and it soared thirty feet above the roof tops. The pilot pointed, stabbed his arm. Coming towards them across the city were two other helicopters, both with searchlights on top. The searchlights were pointed directly at the news helicopter.

'Time to go, chaps,' the helicopter pilot said. He put the chopper into a whirling bank, and headed westwards, over the park. 'Did you get what you wanted?' he asked.

'We sure as hell did, we sure as hell did,' the reporter said, forgetting for the moment that his microphone was still live.

Sally Price had added a helicopter to the list of her demands. When she saw the two arrive, she bent over Mary Foster. 'Right, Mrs Foster, I want you to get up, carefully and slowly. We'll walk out of here and take the lift down to the lobby. The police will clear a path for us to the helicopter, we shall get into it and be taken to London Airport. If you wish, we'll take your husband with you.'

'No,' she whispered, 'Not Tom. Anybody else but Tom.'

He had heard the interchange. He left his chair and rushed across the room. 'Yes, Mary,' he said. 'This time, I overrule you. I'm coming with you, and there's nothing you, or anybody else, can do to prevent it.'

The Superintendent was speaking into the telephone. Mary slowly came out of the chair on Tom's arm. They walked towards the elevator. The terrified cloakroom attendant was still there, and gave their coats to the Superintendent.

The lift was empty. Sally turned and slowly backed in. Mary Foster backed in with her, feeling the tension in the chain around her neck increase. Tom Foster came next, and then the Superintendent, who touched the lobby button. The doors closed and the lift dropped down its controlled path, riding smooth on its hydraulic system. No one had thought to turn off the Musak; the tune, Mary remembered, was from 'Oklahoma'. She and Tom had taken Phyllis to see it. When? Where? She was having trouble concentrating on the events of the moment. It all seemed such a terrible nightmare.

They walked out into the lobby.

The night manager was hurrying forward towards them but Superintendent Jones waved him back. The chairs in the centre of the lobby, the shop to their left, the desks, the booths, were all empty. No one behind the porter's desk, no one at reception, no one visible in accounts.

Sally caught a movement at her side. A man in plain clothes, by the lift shaft. 'Stop, Mrs Foster,' she whispered. Mary Foster stood still. Tom halted. The Superintendent halted. 'That man,' Sally said. 'Tell him to come over here.'

The Superintendent waved the man forward. He was carrying a rifle. 'Who the hell are you?' the Superintendent said harshly.

'Sergeant Pritchard, D-Division.'

'You were told . . .'

'I thought I could get near enough to come up behind. She'd have sung a different tune, perhaps, with a rifle in her back . . .'

'You damn fool,' the Superintendent said, almost speechless with rage. 'You were told. All units were told . . .'

'Give me his radio,' Sally said. The Superintendent walked across and snatched it from the sergeant. 'Get outside,' he said. 'Report to your Superintendent.'

Khaylia Patin was standing in a group to the right of the front door, handcuffed to two officers, one each side of her.

'Take off the handcuffs,' Sally said. Though she had cleared her mind of all thoughts except those necessary to carry out her mission, she could not help feeling a thrill of power, at the same time despising the fact that it came only from a threatened use of force.

Khaylia Patin was about twenty-five, dark skinned, with black hair, wearing the ubiquitous blue jeans and denim shirt. Her eyes burned with a fierce intensity as she looked from one to the other, not comprehending the situation, though she could understand quite clearly the international message of the grenade.

'I am Sally Price,' Sally said to her. 'I made them release you from prison. We have a plane waiting at London Airport, and a helicopter to take us there.' She spoke in Farsi. Khaylia came to life when she heard the familiar language.

'Why are you helping me? she asked. 'Though you speak our language perfectly, you are not of us. You are English.'

Sally quickly explained what she had done, her great regret at the compromises the nations were about to make in Geneva, her hatred of what the Israelis had done and were still doing to the people she had come to love and understand through her studies of the language and their country. Khaylia laughed, happy as a child. 'Come then,' she said. 'We will go together!'

The radio broadcasts of the kidnapping of the American Ambassador were transmitted throughout the world. Many countries interrupted their evening programmes on radio and television to give them coverage, especially those with an ambassador at the party.

Joseph Aram had been listening to a concert on Spanish Radio Two when the news broke.

'Listen to this, Yshtak,' he said, turning up the volume. Yshtak listened for a few minutes then tuned his powerful receiver to the BBC Overseas Service. There, the coverage was more complete. Yshtak and Joseph Aram both showed great interest when the girl's first statement was re-broadcast, the account of her aims.

'Damned amateur,' Joseph said. 'She believes as we do, but so does Khaylia Patin and look what happened to her. They'll never get away with it: both will end up in Brixton Prison . . .'

'Yes, she believes as we do,' Yshtak said. 'She speaks from the heart, as we do!' It was obvious that he was fascinated by the girl and her exploits. 'We are *too* professional,' he said. We could use such an amateur, to put fire into us when we need it!'

Then he heard them broadcast the fact that Sally Price

was a defected civil servant. Though the government spokesman had obviously played it down, the reporter had probed deeply and was able to say, on the air, that Sally's employment in the government had been 'of a sensitive, information-gathering, nature'. He likened her to Kim Philby, Burgess and Maclean, calling her, without equivocation, a 'defector'.

Yshtak had made up his mind. He went to his desk, picked up the telephone, and dialled. 'We have to move quickly,' he said, his mind clicking like a computer.

Sally and Mary Foster went slowly up the ramp steps leading to the Boeing 707. A four-ring captain was waiting for her, with a crew of three men, and a steward. 'I've been given instructions, Miss, to cooperate fully with you. This is my crew. Mr Plenham here is the steward. We are carrying a full load of fuel and I estimate we can fly 3,500 miles at 35,000 feet. You have nothing to fear from us. We will carry out your instructions implicitly, and none of us is armed. I hope that is satisfactory? We are cleared with the tower for take-off at any time.'

'Do you mind if I sit down?' Mary Foster said. 'I guess I'm feeling a little faint.'

Sally allowed her to sit, standing behind the seat. Tom had wound his handkerchief round the chain to prevent it chafing his wife's neck. He sat on the seat next to her, rubbing her wrists. The Special Branch Superintendent, Jones, who had accompanied them all the way so far, looked around the plane, out of the windows, and saw the heads lining the roof. He knew that all the airport police, Special Branch and Flying Squad officers had surrounded the zone in which the plane had been parked, away from the terminal.

A car came across the runway and a tall, thin man got out. He was wearing a dark suit and carrying a brief-case. He walked unhurriedly up the ramp steps and into the plane.

'Miss Price?' he said in English. He then spoke to her in Farsi. 'My name is Fairclough. I'm with the Foreign Office, Middle East Section. I've been asked to come here to speak to you, and Miss Patin, in Farsi, since you seem to prefer that language, and to ask you your plans. If necessary, I'm prepared to travel with you to your destination, wherever that may be.'

Sally smiled. Fairclough was a type she had come to know well during her government service – the great unflappable, the breed of men who have carried the British flag and the British Empire all over the world. Now, in this context, he seemed a terrible anachronism.

Superintendent Jones left the plane.

The pilot and his crew went through to the flight deck and started pre-flight procedures.

'Who has the grenade pin?' Fairclough asked suddenly, in Farsi.

'I have,' Sally said.

'Let Mrs Foster hold the grenade lever herself. Make her husband move one seat away, but tell them to go further up the plane.'

Sally did as he told her. Mary and Tom Foster walked slowly up the plane and sat in the centre about half way along, Mary Foster holding the lever of the grenade at her throat, sweat glistening on her forehead.

Fairclough watched them settle, then whispered fiercely at the two girls. 'Listen to what I have to say,' he said, speaking in an urgent tone of voice. 'And don't interrupt me. You're a couple of amateurs. You've done very well to get as far as you have, but from here on, you have no chance. The minute this plane takes off, another will take off, following it. And on board that one will not be a bunch of amateurs, but a group of the most highly trained commandos in the world, the British Special Service, who've been trained for situations exactly like this one. Remember Mogadishu? They went in with the Germans, as well as supplying them with special equipment. What chance do you think you two will have against them?'

Khaylia and Sally looked at him in astonishment. Gone was the quiet, deferential, civil servant. Fairclough's features had hardened; he spoke with an authority that had nothing to do with his civil service rank.

'Who are you?' Khaylia asked.

'That doesn't matter. What does matter is that I'm on your side, and we don't have much time.'

Sally's mind was racing. She knew he would not have been allowed past the police cordon unless he had had high authorization, backed by impeccable credentials. She reached into her bag and drew out the Colt ·45 she had taken from the CIA man at the Hilton.

Fairclough looked down at it. 'Put that away, you silly girl,' he said. Holding it in her hand she did, indeed, feel like a silly girl. Khaylia reached across quickly and took it from her. There was no doubt that she felt anything but silly.

He sat down in one of the seats, folded his hands across his lap patiently. 'Search his pockets,' Khaylia said to Sally. 'But keep out of the way of this gun.'

Sally stood in the seats behind him, reached over and took out his wallet. It contained a cheque book and a banker's card, an American Express card, a Diner's Club card, a Hertz Rent-a-Car card. About thirty pounds in notes. A card which carried his photograph behind laminated plastic. Foreign Office. Category Two. Which made him a fairly senior officer.

'Okay, Mr Foreign Office,' Khaylia said, 'tell us what this is all about.' She was puzzled and uncertain. Only a short while ago she had been sitting in a cell in Brixton, waiting, for people didn't want to hold on to a political prisoner these days. It merely increased the risk of another hijacking, another terrorist action demanding the prisoner's release. Most countries try to ship the politicals somewhere abroad, as fast as they can. The difficulty is that nobody else wants them either.

'There are many ways to work for something you believe in,' he said. 'Many ways to help a cause.' He might have been explaining the facts of life to a backward child. 'We don't all need a gun in our hands . . .'

'We . . . ?' Sally said.

'Yes, *we*! Look, I've spent a long time building a cover for myself at the Foreign Office. I'm not going to compromise that cover any more than I already have by talking to you. It's up to you now to make a decision. Kill me, try to go it alone, and you're both already dead. Listen to me, and there may be a way, just one way, you can both stay alive . . .'

'Why should you help us?' Khaylia said, still truculent, still unwilling to trust anyone.

'Give me back my wallet,' he said. Sally handed it over. 'Didn't I say you were a couple of amateurs,' he said. 'You missed this . . .' He was rubbing the silk lining of the wallet and it came apart from the backing. Between it and the leather was a photograph. There was no mistaking the nationality of the girl it showed posed somewhat stiffly on a parapet. A Palestinian.

'I was going to marry her,' Fairclough said. 'Then the Israelis killed her. She was a courier . . . The Israelis tortured her before she died.' Written on the back of the photograph it said, '*To Denny*, the only man I have ever loved . . .'

'Tell us,' Sally said, 'what do you want us to do . . .'

CHAPTER FIFTEEN

The voice of the Prime Minister was steady and composed as he answered, the cradle of the telephone relaxed in his hand. He was not feeling at all relaxed but, particularly on the hot line, one had to keep up appearances.

'Yes, Mr President,' he said. 'You *did* hear me correctly. I have let them go. The plane has already taken off and is no longer over British air space.'

There was a long silence on the telephone, though the Prime Minister imagined he could hear the President breathing deeply, as if fighting for control. 'I couldn't believe it,' the President finally said, 'when I received the message from our people that the plane was airborne.'

'A decision had to be taken, Mr President. I took it. The

future will tell if it was the right decision, or the wrong one.'

Again the silence. Then again that angry but carefully modulated voice. 'You took a decision. Just like that? No consultation, no reference, no phone-calls, nothing. You took a decision?'

'I need hardly remind you, Mr President, that one of the more difficult aspects of the job we both do is the taking and implementing of decisions . . .'

'Oh come on, Prime Minister! I don't need a lesson in political philosophy, not right at this moment. And if I did, I have a dozen guys here on the pay-roll who could give me one with all the trimmings. I asked you to hold off on that decision. Mary Foster and her husband, Tom, are personal friends of mine. I personally gave them London. And now you tell me you made a *decision*, and let some chit of a girl take off with them from Heathrow, destination unknown. Prime Minister, the Vice President has already left Andrews Air Force Base. He's coming at my instructions to England by military jet, specifically to ask you, officially, why you have permitted the abduction of two American citizens from your country despite my explicit and strongest representations that the plane be held at Heathrow until we could have time to evaluate the situation.'

'With respect, time was the one commodity we had none of. I chose not to endanger the life of your Ambassador and her husband. I'll hold myself responsible for that choice to *my* Parliament. I'll meet your Vice President and give him copies of any reports I may make, to that Parliament. I'm certain that, on your behalf, he will realize that, tragic though these events have already been, the tragedy would have been infinitely greater had there been any loss of life. That might, almost certainly would have occurred if I'd made the slightest attempt to keep that plane on the ground.'

The two US Air Force jets had the plane well in sight as it flew across France. They were in constant touch with the base in Germany, from which signals were being flashed to Washington. On direct instructions from the White House, via the Pentagon, they made no attempt to draw near the Boeing or to intercept it in any way.

They tracked it over the Pyrenees and saw it head for Barcelona.

Barcelona accepted it into its air space, asking if the skipper wanted landing facilities.

The skipper declined the invitation.

Barcelona asked for his destination.

He did not reply.

Air Traffic Control at Palma de Mallorca accepted the Boeing into its air space, and made the same enquiry. Again the skipper did not respond. But when the plane was overhead it suddenly made a turn and began to lose height.

The control tower plotted it, reported the height and position to the plane. Normal procedure.

The plane continued its long, wide turn, losing height all the time. It had reached six thousand feet when the skipper came on the air, requesting emergency landing facilities.

Air Traffic Control flashed back a message, refusing permission to land.

The skipper came back on the radio, repeating his request.

The airport refused again.

The skipper called their bluff. 'This is Baker Tommy Oboe,' he said, his voice calm and unhurried. 'I am coming in to land, on instructions, at Palma de Mallorca. I have no alternative. Please give me a runway, and bring me in on normal procedures or I shall find one for myself and land on it without your assistance. I am turning now onto final approach. I repeat, I am turning now onto final approach.'

Air Control had no alternative, either. They had to accept him.

The news caught the Police Chief of Palma unawares in his office in the Castello overlooking the harbour. He waddled along to the radio room, seized the microphone, and ordered all cars to converge on the airport. Three were dealing with a traffic accident on the new motorway, above Palma Nova. He screamed to them to get to the airport as fast as possible.

'Ready for final approach,' the skipper quietly said.

'We have you, Baker Tommy Oboe,' Control said. 'You're on the flight path. Come in as you are.'

'Roger. One last message from our passengers. No cars on the runway. I repeat, no cars.'

The plane came in to land on Runway Two, specially built for tourist jumbo jets. Perfect touch-down with no bounce. It rolled along the runway, flaps up, engines on reverse thrust to brake. The only two police cars that had managed to get to the airport in time were waiting by the terminal. As the plane landed, they disobeyed instructions and set off down the runway after it. The plane halted without turning.

An emergency chute fluttered out of the side exit, and two figures slid down it.

A grey Fiat raced towards the plane from the campo to the east of the airport. It slewed to a stop by the two running figures, who jumped in, then it turned in a tight arc, its tyres squealing, and left the airport the way it had come. The police cars chased after it, their engines screaming. The Fiat turned left, heading north towards the main road. The police driver radioed instructions. The squad car coming out of Palma switched direction at the airport turn and carried on straight ahead.

The Fiat, carrying the two terrorists, gradually pulled away from the heavier police cars. One of the pursuers leaned out of a window, levelled his pistol and began to shoot. The Fiat turned a corner on two wheels, grazing a wall that surrounded a grove of thyme. The first police car made the turn after it, and ran straight back into the back of a container lorry. The second slammed into the back of the first before he could apply his brakes.

The terrorist's car turned right, and disappeared along a track, then deep into a grove of pine-trees.

The co-driver of the second squad car, dazed, picked up

his microphone where it had been flung to the floor. The radio still worked.

'Bad news, Capitano,' he said. 'I'm afraid we've lost them.'

Mary Foster reached into her pocket and drew out a key which she handed to Tom. He used it to open the lock and took the chain thankfully from around her neck.

He reached into her pocket again, took out the pin Sally Price had left there, and carefully re-inserted it into the grenade. Just to be safe, he bent back the end of the pin so that it could not slip out.

Then Mary let go of the lever.

The pin held it, safe.

They both heard the screaming whine of the US Air Force jets landing, one by one.

The skipper of the Boeing came from the flight deck. 'Are you all right?' he asked, his forehead glistening with perspiration.

'Fine. How do I say it, Captain? Thank you for a wonderful flight.'

He grinned, and turned unsteadily back to the flight deck. They looked out of the window and saw the cars approaching the plane, US Air Force men running from their machines. For one brief moment, they were alone together, before the diplomatic fuss began once more.

'Bill Harrington ought to give you an Oscar for that,' Tom said, and then he kissed her tenderly.

The jet containing the British Special Services team landed at the far side of the airport, quietly. Its doors stayed closed. In the operations cubicle behind the captain's flight deck, the Army major sat with headphones glued to his ears, listening to the traffic between the tower and the Boeing, and the two US Air Force jets.

His men, wearing their grey coveralls, sat quietly in their seats, patient, waiting. Each man had been hand-picked over months of rigorous selection training, then tempered by fire and moulded into one efficient unit that could operate, anywhere, at lightning speed. Looking out of the windows they could see the deployment of the Americans on the ground as they approached the jet.

Hijackers very often leave bombs.

They had seen the girls picked up by the car and setting off with the Spanish police in pursuit.

They saw the skipper of the plane appear in the doorway, watching as the Americans threw themselves to the ground in firing positions. The Captain waved his arms.

They saw the woman appear beside him – no doubt the US Ambassador. A truck was being driven from the terminal, pushing a set of steps. The Captain of the plane beckoned it forward.

The Americans got up, walked towards the plane, carrying their rifles across their chests.

The steps were clipped to the side of the plane and then the swirl of official cars began to pour from the airport buildings and sheds.

The Major switched his intercommunications set to 'Skipper'.

'I think that's about all,' he said. 'I would suggest we head for home?'

'Roger, Major,' the Skipper said, and called the Tower.

Yshtak was alone when Sally and Khaylia Patin were brought to his house on Ibiza, standing by the door as the Land Rover drew to a halt on the concrete car park. They came from the vehicle still in a whirl. They had switched from car to fast boat and from boat to car, always moving, from one island to the other. It had been, as Fairclough had promised, a truly professional operation that far exceeded in efficiency anything they might have done for themselves.

As they had travelled, Khaylia Patin had kept up a non-stop interrogation of Sally Price. She could not understand why an English girl should take such an interest in the Palestinian cause, and how she could turn out to be more ruthless, and apparently more efficient, than Khaylia herself. She was full of admiration for the English girl. 'That was a beautiful stunt you pulled with the US Ambassador bitch,' she said. 'I wish I'd thought of that. I would never have been taken.'

For her part, Sally had asked few questions but had listened. It became apparent that the TAIO was a broken force. It had been full of extremists and individuals, without cohesion, who never learned to work together. The Israeli Secret Police had penetrated them easily and had killed most of them in one raid.

In answer to the question of where they were going, Khaylia appeared to have as little information as Sally herself.

'I am Yshtak,' their host said, speaking to them in English. 'Welcome to my house. For as long as you wish, this house is yours.'

He had given them a double room facing south with its own terrace, its own bathroom suite. Laid out on the bed were a collection of garments, long loose dresses, underwear, shirts, all obviously purchased recently. There was a veritable chemist's shop of toilet articles in the bathroom, including a hair-dryer. Sally noticed with amusement how feminine Khaylia suddenly became, ripping off the jeans and plunging beneath the hot shower, shampooing her hair, rubbing the body creams and oils into her exquisite dark skin. Her hair had obviously been slashed by an amateur. She begged Sally to trim the rough hewn ends to make it look decent.

It was two o'clock in the morning before both were ready for bed.

Sally fell immediately into a deep, exhausted sleep, without dreams. During the night, she was aware of voices, but they were not loud enough to cause her alarm.

When she woke the next morning, the bag she had left on the table beside her bed had been moved to the other side of the room. The Colt ·45 she had taken from the CIA man had gone.

The lining of the inside of the bag had been slashed.

But the metal clasp was still intact.

Yshtak was waiting in the large lounge, sitting at a table on which were placed yogurt and cucumber, coffee, local bread. He rose when she came into the room. 'Ah, Miss Price,' he said. 'I trust you slept well?'

'Completely dead! And Khaylia is still out like a light.'

'I'm afraid you'll have to help yourself to breakfast,' he said. 'My staff, a Spanish family from Estremadura, have gone back to the mainland for a month's vacation.'

'I'll share your bread and coffee, if I may?'

'Please help yourself.'

He studied her with polite interest as she brought herself a plate and a cup from the sideboard, settled down and started to eat. She watched him in return, waiting for him to speak.

'You realize, Miss Price, that you are an enigma? A young English woman who, if the radio is to be believed, has suddenly turned renegade, despite a good education, and a good position in the government service? You were very daring in the Hilton Hotel. Daring and, apparently, quite ruthless.'

'And you, Mr Yshtak, were quite daring last night, when you took my handbag from beside my bed and cut the lining, stealing my gun.'

He laughed. 'You are bold, Miss Price.'

'Bold enough to get Khaylia Patin released. Bold enough to embarrass the British and the American governments. Bold enough to get the Palestine question raised once again throughout the world! What I am, Yshtak, is not important. What I may do, what I may be able to do in the cause of true Palestinian Liberation, is what counts.'

'That was well said. I beg your pardon.'

She looked at this haughty, silver-haired man sitting across the table from her. She felt like a school-girl who had been invited to tea by the head-mistress. If he could have known how little courage she possessed at that moment. This man was born to rule, to command, with an organization and a strength to reach out across the sea. If Fairclough, the man from the British Foreign Office, was in his pocket, how many other people around Europe could he call upon at a moment's notice? There had not been time for more than one phone call to Fairclough and one to Mallorca setting up the whole scheme.

She felt a sinking feeling in her stomach as she realized how foolish Bill and she had been, to think that one amateur with none of the training that had gone, for example, into making Khaylia a terrorist, could penetrate the organization of such a man.

It appeared there were no other people in the house but Yshtak and the two girls. The man who had brought them the final leg of their journey by Land-Rover had turned around and driven the vehicle away.

She got up, walked through the open windows to the balcony and looked down. A boat, the *Revenge*, was riding at anchor. It looked a powerful enough vessel to have picked up Joseph Aram and Ahktar, as they now knew them, at the end of their parachute drop.

Yshtak had the look of a gentleman pirate about him. He would take a delight in well-planned exploits. His lean, hawk face rested easy in repose, but she could imagine it transformed by anger or passion, could feel the way those deep, dark eyes would flash.

She walked back inside. 'And you, Yshtak,' she asked. 'Who are you? Obviously a wealthy man who can afford to indulge himself. Do you make a practice of rescuing damsels in distress?'

He laughed. 'Lord no,' he said, urbane, sophisticated. 'I listened to the radio, admired your pluck, guessed you could use a little help, made a few phone calls, and had you brought here. You're free to leave, of course, any time you choose. Though you'd obviously have to think carefully about where you chose to go. I wouldn't suggest anywhere within reach of the CIA.'

'Which eliminates a lot of territory. If it's okay by you, Sir Galahad, I think I'll accept your invitation and stay.'

'You would be very wise. Your exploits of last night are bound to cause an enormous stir. All sorts of people are going to make political capital out of it. There'll be crises in the British and the American governments. Many editorials will be written and your features and biography published all over the world. And then, when the next crisis comes along, your face will disappear from the front pages, and from people's minds. You'll change the colour of your hair, the style of your dress, and no-one will ever know you.'

'In the meanwhile, they're going to be swarming all over the Baleares, looking for me and Khaylia Patin.'

'What if they are? Mallorca is a large island. And close to the mainland of Spain. I can predict what will happen. Later today, a sergeant and a soldier of the Guardia Civil will walk up that stony road along which you came. When they arrive, they'll be hot and thirsty. I shall give them a glass of beer, each. German beer – they seem to prefer that. I shall give them a cognac each, French cognac, of course. We'll talk about the weather, the fishing, the crops, the garden. After half an hour they will ask me if I have seen two girls. No one could possibly recognize the two of you from the description they will give. I will make a joke, say, 'No, I haven't, but if you find two and they turn out to be blondes, bring them up here for me'. They will laugh and go away. Despite the death of Franco, Spain is still the land of the privileged, Miss Price. And it is my particular privilege not to have my house and grounds searched.'

There was a hard edge beneath his voice. She took his words as a warning, a hint of the ruthless side of his nature.

'I'll remember that,' she said lightly. 'Only one more thing. Thank you for bringing us here so efficiently.'

He smiled at her. 'It was the wish of Allah,' he said.

Unlike Sally, Bill had not slept at all that night. He had raced back to his office as soon as the helicopter had taken off for London Airport and the ambassadors had been released. By unspoken but common consent, no one had suggested continuing Sir Maurice Winfield's party. And he had been too distraught even to wish them a proper goodbye.

Bill was waiting in his office when the call came, informing him that Denford Fairclough of the Foreign Office had gone aboard the Boeing. He punched the name on his com-

puter terminal, tapped the FO code, and within micro-
seconds had Fairclough's official biography on the screen
in front of him. He read the Middle East connections. Two
years in Jerusalem before the Six Day War. Before that,
four years in Amman. He had served in Damascus, then
back to Amman. Spoke fluent Arabic and Farsi, even Per-
sian. Now an Under Undersecretary. Middle East specialist. Heavily involved in the arrangements for the Conference
in Geneva. Had been in Morocco at the time of Yasser
Arafat's emergence. Had met Arafat several times. Twice,
clandestinely, in Damascus.

Had applied to return to Jerusalem.

Application refused.

Bill felt a twinge of interest. He reached into his safe for
a red leather-bound book, opened it and scanned the
addresses and telephone numbers it contained. He picked
one and dialled.

A sleepy voice answered. 'Broadbent?'

'Bill Harrington, Sir Henry. Sorry to disturb you.'

'You're not only disturbing me, Bill, you're awakening
me. What time is it, for God's sake.'

Bill had known Sir Henry's habit of shifting the span of
his effective day. He always went to bed immediately after
an early supper, but rose at 4.30 each morning. By the time
he arrived at his Foreign Office desk at eight o'clock, he
had already done the equivalent of a day's work. Bill also
knew and respected Sir Henry's encyclopaedic knowledge
of internal Foreign Office matters. 'Denford Fairclough
applied to go back to Jerusalem after he'd been in Amman
the second time. His application was refused. I wondered
why?'

He heard Sir Henry chuckle. 'Trust you to sniff out the
anomalies, eh, Bill? Why indeed? Blameless career. Lots
of good quiet negotiation between parties. Acted what I
think of as the true Foreign Office role, operating quietly
behind the scenes, making friends, influencing governments. I'm afraid I can't help you too much, Bill. His
application was refused because that old war-horse, Golda
Meir, didn't want him. As simple as that! We sniffed around,

of course. Tried to discover why she'd made him 'persona non grata'. It happens, you know. Fellah's face doesn't quite fit and the local people black-ball him.'

'You never found out why?'

'Bill, you know Golda Meir. Who could ever find out "why" when she said "no". She didn't want him, so he couldn't go. As I remember we sent him to Morocco for a while instead, and gave him a small promotion. Sort of consolation prize.'

Bill thanked him and put down the telephone.

For Golda Meir read the Israeli Secret Service, a branch of the Mossad. The Mossad had always been a law unto itself.

He opened his red book again, and placed another call. To the Talbieh suburb of Jerusalem, on Oliphant Street.

CHAPTER SIXTEEN

Marc Chantal read through the reports of his men in the field, scouring the coastlines of the eastern Mediterranean by boat, by light plane, following up individual leads on foot and by car. By now he had more than a hundred men active on the search. All had the same brief. Look for an isolated house on the water's edge from which you could launch a vessel on a negotiable route to Israel.

He got up and stood before the large-scale map of the Mediterranean he had pinned across one wall of his office in the Croix Rouge.

He looked along the south coast of the extensive island of Crete. Merde, that would be the ideal place, but his men had sailed all along it without noticing any signs of anything strange. They had put in everywhere from Nisos Elesa on the north-east tip, round Alatsomouri, Ierapetra, Tsoutsouros, Lentas, Aghia Galini, Plakias, Chora Sfakion, Paleochora, to the island off the south-west tip, Elafonisos. One or two place were 'possibles' – Tris Ekklistes, a forgotten fishing village at the bottom of a remote track below the mountain of Asterousia; the ancient port of Phoenix, nestling behind the fishing village of Leutron. Both had been investigated by land, after the sea-borne reconnaissance. There had been some recent activity, but in both cases it turned out to be caused by groups of prospective property developers.

No one had found any trace of Jacques Morel.

They had toured the off-shore islands, Nisos Gavdon, Gavdopoula, Paximadia, Gaidouronisi, Koufonisi.

Merde! The Green Dolphin had to be there, somewhere.

He had approached the problem with Gallic logic. The reason for the proposed meeting could only be that *they*, whoever they were, intended to offer an ultimatum. Either do as we say, or we will launch the Green Dolphin, at Israel. It *had* to be Israel.

And this time, Jacques Morel would not be driving it. They would set the computer, batten down the hatches, and let the computer do the work. They would de-activate the heat, noise, and light sensitive mechanisms, arm the British atomic warhead, and let the Dolphin take care of itself. Obviously, to do that, they would need to start the launch as near Israel as possible. So it had to be from either Cyprus or Crete. And so far his men had drawn a complete blank on both islands.

Merde!

'All right,' he said to Phillipe. 'Switch the major part of the search. From the East of the Mediterranean to the West. Let's start by taking an intensive look at the Baleares. Formentera, Ibiza, Mallorca, and then Menorca. Perhaps that Sally Price *did* have a rendezvous in the Baleares, after all.'

The Prime Minister of Israel was an old kibbutznik, a follower of Ben Gurion and Golda Meir, far removed from the intellectualism of Rabin and Allon. He had worked with his hands, as Gurion had, in the south, in the hot, hard lands. He had cleared stones from arid fields, planted agave, manhandled the huge water-pipes that brought refreshment to the desert. He had stood night after night, by the perimeter fence, on guard against the *fedayeen* marauders. He had killed to support his idea of Israel. A non-religious man, he practised all the Jewish observances only for outward show. He had no time for the readings of the Torah, the endless arguments over the meanings of the Scrolls. When in a dispute, he would bend down, pick up a handful of soil, and say: 'This, and this alone, is our justification. And our destiny.'

And, like all other *sabras*, he was a natural born fighter, a rough and ready soldier who loved the life of the army camp. He was never happier than when he rolled over the ground, his ground, in a tank, or a jeep, at the head of a column of men, fighting Arabs, killing Arabs, to hold a claim on the territory they had conquered. Because Israel was theirs, by right. Possession is ten tenths of the law!

He had come to politics in disgust at the vacillation of the weak intellectuals, the men who tried to please all the factions of the Israeli people and therefore satisfied none. Somehow, his blunt aggression had touched a nerve and he was swept to political power on a promise that never again would he permit the larger powers in the world to push them around. His creed was naive and simplistic – as naive and simplistic as the *sabras* of Israel themselves who believed that any fight, any disagreement, could be solved by the man who punched hardest, and first.

Rolf Mueller was such a man. Hit hard, hit first, and trust no one.

When he received the message, hand-delivered by the British Ambassador to Israel, calling him to London for a secret and urgent meeting with the President of the USA, the Premier of France, and the British Prime Minister, he was immediately suspicious. He had three separate deals going. One with the British for atomic breeder fuel. One with the Americans for a whole range of offensive weapons. And one with the French for a secret supply of motor torpedo boats.

Were the three powers thinking of ganging up on him?

No weapons, no breeder fuel, no torpedo boats unless you toe the line on the Occupied Territories, unless you agree to a Palestine Representation at the Geneva talks? He had already agreed to a partial representation, but he knew, they all knew, that was only window dressing.

Were they now going to try to put real pressure on him?

Both America and the United Kingdom had suffered a diplomatic kick-in-the-balls over this Sally Price/Khaylia Patin affair. The French Ambassador had also been involved. Were they trying to arrange a diplomatic coup, to paper over the wounds? To show the world there was at least one person in the world who could not kick them around?

It would be a challenge. And Rolf Mueller loved a challenge.

'Tell your Prime Minister I will be pleased to accept his gracious invitation to meet with him in London, to discuss matters of mutual interest.' That was the way the message read in London. In Israel, Rolf Mueller had said 'Okay, tell him I'll come. Fifteen rounds, all in, no holds barred. And sod the Marquess of Queensbury!'

At half past ten, Sally went down the rock staircase wearing the bikini she had found in their bedroom. Khaylia was still asleep and she did not disturb her. On the large concrete platform at the edge of the ocean she found a wooden cupboard against the wall. Inside were a number of flippers, masks, snorkel tubes, all perfectly clean, washed free from salt water. She found a set that fitted her and slipped over the edge of the platform into the deep, clear water.

She took off the mask and rubbed the inside so that it would not film over before she put it back again. Then she did a powerful flip that sent her straight down to the rocks, about fifteen feet below at the edge of the concrete platform, considerably deeper just a couple of metres out. She swam with powerful strokes round the rocky sides of the narrow bay. Soon she discovered the dog-leg and swam in. Here, the concrete had been carried below the surface, and formed a wide underwater ledge about two metres deep. At the back of the ledge were heavy mooring rings in galvanized iron, set solid into the concrete. Though she swam around for about an hour, alternately on the surface and then plunging as deep as she could go without bottles, she could find nothing else that should not be there.

When she swam around the *Revenge*, she discovered that what she had taken for anchors were mooring buoys, with galvanized chains reaching down forty feet to large concrete blocks on the rock bed below. She pulled herself down one of the chains as deep as she could go, but was in no condition to reach the bottom. When she reached the top again and flipped her way back to the concrete landing stage, she found Yshtak looking down at her. 'Are you enjoying your swim, Miss Price,' he asked solicitously. She took off her mask and spat the end of the tube from her mouth. 'I haven't done this in a long time,' she said. 'It's absolutely gorgeous!'

'Enjoy yourself,' he said. 'There are no sharks in these waters to disturb you. Human or otherwise . . .'

'You have a super boat,' she said. 'Do you take it out often?'

'Not as often as I'd like,' he said. 'If you feel like going aboard at any time, please do. The key to the cabin is under the seat in the stern, and there's a plentiful supply of drinks aboard. Only soft drinks, of course.'

'Of course. Thank you. If I get tired of dry land, I'll stretch out on the sun-deck.'

'Any time. Perhaps when I am less busy, we might take a trip together.'

He turned abruptly and effortlessly climbed the stairs back to the house almost sheer above them. She came out of the water, washed the equipment she had used in the tap beside the cupboard, and left it in the sun to dry. She lay down on the concrete, and let the still warm rays of the sun soak into her.

This was too large a house for one man. Even with a Spanish family to look after him. And what about the driver of the Land-Rover? Who had chosen the clothing that lay on their beds waiting for them? Feminine instinct told her it was not a man. Certainly no man could have been relied upon to choose such a simple but comprehensive set of toilet articles. What man would remember to buy a hair-dryer? Or hair conditioner?

Look for a wooden box, Bill had said. Look for the lead lining of a wooden box. And, of course, look for a short stubby submarine which will look like a shark or a dolphin, with eyes and teeth painted on it.

But, whatever you find, do not touch it.

The sun was hot and she had no desire to burn herself. She sat on the concrete and dangled her legs in the water. She glanced idly up. Here, she could not be seen from the house above. She looked down through the water. In the shade, with no sun's rays bouncing off its surface, she could see clear down to the depths.

It was no more than a silver glint, such as a fish might make, turning rapidly. She went back quickly across the landing and took the mask again. She dipped it in the water and put it back on. Then she dived. It was much harder to descend without flippers to thrust her; she dragged the water with her arms, pulling herself down. Four metres below the surface, a long silver line ran like a scar along the edge of a sharp rock's tooth. She kept away from the rock face, turned in the water and swam vigorously upwards and outwards towards the moored *Revenge*. Only when she was near the anchor chain did she come to the surface. She held on to the bottom of the ladder that hung over the stern, turned and looked up at the verandah.

Yshtak was standing there, looking down.

Khaylia Patin was standing beside him, training a pair of binoculars on her.

Sally waved then did a powerful crawl stroke back to the concrete, up and out.

She stood beneath the shower, washing the salt water from her hair and her body.

Then she climbed the rock stairway.

With Khaylia Patin and Yshtak was a man with the muscles of a boxer. He was wearing white trousers and a white T-shirt. His hands were huge. His eyes were small, and cruel.

'Would you come inside, Miss Price,' Yshtak asked courteously. 'I think it's about time we asked you a few questions.'

CHAPTER SEVENTEEN

Professor Smithers looked at the assembly before him. Cathode ray oscilloscopes, radar screens, flat, dark computer print-out panels. A large speaker in the corner of the room was emitting an intermittent warbling note through which, every three seconds or so, would come a sharp blip.

He picked up the telephone and dialled. When the distant station answered, he asked for Professor Challenger.

Challenger came on the line.

'I'm on to the Orbis satellite,' Smithers said. 'Are you reading it?'

'What band and wavelength?'

'Band F. Two thousand.'

'No. We've been looking at weather, low wavelength.'

'You wouldn't like to tune up, would you?'

'It'll take twenty minutes or so . . .'

'Would you do it and call me back?'

The use of satellites in geography had advanced considerably in the last few years. In particular, the use of orbiting satellites to plot the direction and velocity of ocean currents, the movements of sea masses, tidal variations.

A group of radiating objects could be dropped into the sea, for example, off South America, and the orbiting satellite would trace their movement up the coast of South and North America, across the Atlantic Ocean. In this way the limits of the known water-flows such as the Gulf Stream could be more clearly delineated than ever before. Two such installations, in constant touch with satellites for general weather as well as specialist geographic and oceanographic studies, were located at Goonhilly Down in the south-west of England, and at Manchester, gateway to the industrial North.

The radiating devices dropped into the sea were tiny, no

larger than plastic thimbles. They contained relatively small amounts of decaying atomic matter. The satellite traced that decay as a fixed frequency signal that could be made to appear on a display panel as a light, or on a loudspeaker as a blip.

Professor Smithers had found a blip.

When Professor Challenger came back on the telephone from Manchester, he, too, had found a blip. He gave the coordinates to Professor Smithers. Both men agreed.

It was emanating from the coast of an island in the Mediterranean. An island called Ibiza.

Challenger wanted to chat, but Smithers cut him short. 'I'll see you at the British Association dinner tomorrow evening,' he said. 'Why don't you turn up early, and we can have a yarn in the bar together.'

Smithers dialled London. 'I think I've found what you're looking for,' he said to Bill Harrington. 'I've got a definite confirmed reading. You know we can't be accurate to more than half a mile, but it's coming from the coastline of Ibiza. Here's the map reference.'

Major Roger Masters looked around the hangar at his thirty men as they sat quietly relaxing, reading, dozing, playing chess, drinking tea at the improvised canteen.

All were wearing plain grey jackets, boots, denim trousers.

They were ready to go.

The RAF plane was outside, fully fuelled, and ready to go. Through the hangar door he could see the air-crew sitting in the cockpit, running yet again through a pre-flight check.

Odd sort of job, really. No target, no destination, no hint of what they were going to do, if anything, when they arrived.

And all those questions about Captain Aram. Yes, of course he remembered Aram. He himself had been a Captain in those days, before he got his crown. Always wondered what had happened to Joseph Aram. Good officer, but the quiet type. Hard to get to know, really. Ruthlessly efficient, men either loved or hated him. He worked them like a bastard slave driver. The slackers detested it, even the good ones found it tough going.

The telephone rang. 'Major Masters?' a voice asked.

'Present and correct.'

'Bill Harrington. Kangaroo in thirty minutes?'

'Wilco. Thank God. The chaps were getting stale.'

'I'm coming with you.'

'I say, Bill, is that wise? How long has it been . . . ?'

'I'm coming.'

'Well, if you say so. After all, it's your show.'

The word had come from the Colonel to take thirty of his best men to Northolt and have them ready on thirty minutes' notice. To go anywhere. 'This is an odd one, Major,' the Colonel had said. 'The authorization has come through from the War Office like a streak of greased lightning. Remember that chap Harrington who was with us in the old days?'

'Harrington? Bill Harrington? He and I were at OCTU together . . . I heard he'd gone into something dreadfully hush hush in Whitehall . . .'

'He must have climbed the ladder. He's signed the TMO himself.'

'What about weaponry, sir?'

'Stens, grenades, pistols.'

'Other equipment?'

'Small pack, and haversack rations.'

'Quick in and out, eh?'

'Looks that way, Major.'

He put the whistle to his mouth and blew two short blasts. Everyone in the hangar heard him. All games stopped. Boards were folded away silently, books were closed and placed on the floor. The thirty men rose to their feet, picked up their parachute packs and formed in three ranks in the centre of the hangar. The two lieutenants and the sergeant-major were at the extreme right, one to each rank. At the other end were a sergeant and two corporals.

Major Masters gathered up his parachute and his small pack. His sten gun was slung over his shoulder, his pistol in its holster by his left side. He marched to the front of the three ranks, which came to attention as he approached.

'Operation Kangaroo will begin in thirty minutes,' he said. 'We shall have an old colleague jumping with us. Some of you may remember him as Lieutenant Harrington. We shall receive a briefing on board the plane. At least, I hope we shall . . .' He smiled, and they smiled back at him. There was no tension; these men had soldiered together for too long and Major Masters had brought no untried troops with him. 'I'm not even going to speculate,' he said. 'We shall be boarding the plane in fifteen minutes from now. I suggest you take care of any little details you might have forgotten. Fall out!'

The men were aboard the plane when the motor-cycle carrying Bill Harrington arrived at the airport. The traffic had been jammed solid on the motorway, and not even the police escort could get his car through. He had had to abandon the vehicle and jump on the back of his escort's powerful Harley-Davidson. There were five minutes still to go before his half-hour deadline. He went into the hangar, where Major Masters handed him a parachute pack, a pair of boots, a sten and a pistol. 'Take care of that lot, Bill,' he said. 'I've had to sign for them.'

There was little time for greeting. They both hurried on board the forty-seater jet. The steps were removed, the door was closed, and the plane swung away from its stand.

Major Masters and Bill Harrington sat together in the front seat. The plane had a wider corridor than usual down one side, floored with non-slip aluminium. A rail ran the length of the corridor, about one and a half inches in diameter, ending by the door to the port side at the rear, beneath the high tailplane.

'Are you going to be all right, jumping out of this thing?' Masters asked quietly. 'It's not like going out of a forward door. You have to twist yourself through a half-circle as you go – grab the rail with your right hand and kind of spin yourself out. Can you manage it?'

Bill nodded. 'I'll manage,' he said lightly. 'It'll all come back to me.'

'Like riding a bicycle, eh? Never forget? So, Bill, this Kangaroo. What's it all about?'

'We're going to jump into Ibiza. Low level. Near a house. In that house I hope to find two girls, one ex-Captain Aram, one Frenchman Jacques Morel.'

'What if we find them?'

'We snatch the British girl out, and try to take the other three alive. That may not be possible . . .'

Masters whistled. 'One of those, eh? Presumably there'll be guards?'

'I guess so. I hope there will also be a small submarine, and a box. Once we've located the English girl, I'll concentrate on looking for them. You secure the house.'

'This girl,' Masters said. 'Might her name be Sally Price, and the other one Khyalia Patin?'

'You've been reading the newspapers,' Bill said.

'And listening to the radio and watching television. And seeing the name, Bill Harrington, turn up with alarming frequency. This girl Sally Price was your assistant. You took her to a party. She walked out with one of the guests . . .'

'Things are never what they seem, Roger. I'll be passing round a set of photographs.'

Masters looked at Bill steadily. The whine of the jet engine seemed momentarily silenced as they hurtled southwards through the sky. 'Bill, *you* signed the Troop Movement Order yourself. This exercise is okay, is it? You've gone a long way since we were at OCTU together, Bill. I'm not one much for patriotic flag-waving. I'm a simple soldier, obeying orders, but I hope the orders are genuine. Not just some private stunt of yours!'

'The plane has a radio,' Bill said quietly. 'If you have any doubts, use it to call anyone you like . . .'

Roger thought for a moment. 'Okay, Bill, I'm sorry to have doubted you. But you'll understand my feelings. You chaps down in Whitehall move in some pretty mysterious ways. Like I said, me, I'm just a simple soldier. I could ask you a hundred questions, but I won't. I'm not convinced you'd give me the true answers anyway!'

He gave Bill a crooked smile that removed any suggestion of offensiveness from his words. 'Let me have the photographs, and I'll brief the chaps. They'll be happy to know we're not going chasing Micks again.'

The flight path took them south and east, out into the Mediterranean, mid-way between the islands of Corsica and Mallorca. They they turned sharp west, gradually losing height.

The RAF transport roared over the coastline of the island of Ibiza at 1200 feet, still descending. By now the pilot had throttled back and their speed had dropped to two hundred miles an hour. Bill was standing at the cock-pit entrance. 'I'll bank left,' the pilot said, 'and you go out when I level. At the speed I'll be travelling, if you all go out fast, you should straddle approximately a mile. At this height, there won't be much time for manoeuvre on the way down. With luck, the stick will fall within half a mile on the ground. Okay?'

'Okay,' Bill said.

'There's a slight wind from the sea. You'll have to correct for it on your way down. But, I repeat, you won't have much time.'

The men were in line down the aisle to the port side of the plane, all hooked onto the rail, holding the rings with their hands to make certain they would slide when the men began to run.

'Remember,' Roger said. 'Grab that rail with your right hand and swing. Go clean: you'll only have one second before the next man comes out. That'll be me, and I don't want to wind up with my feet in the small of your back.'

The plane banked, turned, held.

The door was yanked open, sliding along the side of the plane. Wind whipped in, then it steadied.

'Go!' the pilot shouted, and switched the blinker to 'steady'.

The stick moved as one, each man shuffling rapidly along the aisle of the plane, grabbing the rail, swinging, dropping. Bill and Roger were in the centre of the stick. Bill saw the rail approach his hand, felt its cold, smooth surface, grabbed it, swung, dropped. Into a thousand feet of nothingness.

He felt the old familiar sensation in the pit of his belly, the upward lift of his heart, the air in his nostrils. He gulped rapidly, swallowing air, expelling it. The static line snapped and he felt the judder in his limbs as he momentarily checked. Then the descent smoothed out. He looked up, saw the unfamiliar holes in the parachute canopy. He corrected right for the force of the wind. Looked down and saw the rocky landscape, the low scrub, the few pine trees, the cliff edge. Then the house with its dazzling white walls and flat roofs, the small bay, the boat moored there, the breathtaking blue-green water. And then the ground was rushing towards him; stony earth, scattered with small grey-green shrubs. He braced himself for the landing, eased himself up in the shrouds of the parachute, holding steady in the direction of travel. It did all come back. Thank God. Just like riding a bicycle. Knees slightly bent to release the stiffness from his legs. Toes pointing downwards to break his fall.

He landed in the middle of a bush about three feet high, with sharp prickly branches. As he hit, he was aware of an overpowering odour of crushed thyme from the bladelike leaves and purple flowers all about him. He lurched forwards, unable to do the full roll. He twisted his feet free of the small twigs, aware of the figures rising from the ground around him, the parachutes billowing along the ground. He snapped his harness, hooked it into the bush, and ran, cocking his Sten gun.

He took a swift look about him. The stick had landed neatly in a tight bunch. Now they were running, taking up an arrowhead position, Roger Masters at the point, Bill beside him. The house was about four hundred yards away, its large metal filigree gates open. Inside he could see the twisting drive, edged with trees and pots in which geranium grew profusely, their petals a gash of red running along the edge of the grey concrete.

The house was surrounded by a seven foot wall, topped with a twelve inch high triple strand of barbed wire, stretched tautly. They could not see the house from where they were running.

Roger was beckoning in the sign language they all knew so well. Inside the gate, right flank right, left flank left, centre up the drive.

Getting through the gate would be the problem.

Roger Masters signalled again, peeling off the extreme ends of the flanks to go round the outside of the walls. Just in case there was a back door.

A hundred yards to go to the gate.

Roger shouted. 'Lieutenant Brown, take three men, ignore the house and go down to the dock. Take command of the boat, if you find one there.'

There was only one way to go through a gateway, a doorway. Fast and low, then spin left and right alternately.

If they were expected, a machine gun could be trained on the entrance, spraying left and right across the twelve foot gap, at waist-height. A moving curtain of death.

Don't think. Go!

Roger Masters first. No chatter of machine gun.

Bill second, left towards a fig tree, running up through the grove that flanked the drive. No machine gun. No pause, up through the trees. The drive bent like an S. At the top, a concrete car park, with the sea at the far side beyond a verandah. Main door of the house to the left, open.

Roger looked round. His men were all in position, tight but not bunched. Windows at the first floor level, all covered by green mesh fly-screens.

Flat roof with a fifteen inch parapet.

He jerked his arm back and down. The cover men dropped to the ground, their Stens trained on the edge of the roof parapet and the fly screen windows.

Roger glanced at Bill as if to ask, 'Inside?'. Bill nodded, leaped for the doorway, went through it in one long roll and finished to the left, below a window. Roger, rolling right, fetched up against a cupboard, jarring his elbow. No one in the room. Nothing. Three men in and past them, to the far door, into other rooms. This was an entrance lobby, filled with plants in pots, a profusion of green leaves and red flowers, walls built of colourful stone, cacti with long spiny stems. One man ran to the window, crouched, looked out, then made the sign that told Roger, negative, again.

They found Sally in a downstairs bedroom, with a verandah and terrace that overlooked the ocean. Her arms were tied to the head of the bed, her legs to its foot. She appeared to be asleep.

Bill was about to rush across the room to her when Roger stopped him. 'They've learned a few tricks since you resigned your commission, Bill,' he whispered.

He beckoned up the stairs and Sgt Willoughby came down quickly, treading with his feet at each side of the steps. He walked slowly and silently into the bedroom, eyeing the girl on the bed who lay beneath an ordinary bathing towel. The bed was made of heavy wood, carried a chunky mattress beneath a tight-stretched sheet.

There was a red leather suitcase beneath the bed.

The floor was of marble tiles.

There was no pillow beneath her head.

Bill suddenly remembered Sally asking him if he had another pillow for her. That one night they had spent together.

She was breathing steadily, rhythmically.

Sgt Willoughby went out of the room and took off his boots and socks. He returned in bare feet, without any of his equipment, and slowly walked round the bed, examining the floor with each step before putting down his foot. Only when he had examined everything did he draw near to the bed. He bent over, touching nothing, looked at the girl's arm. He turned and nodded. Bill had known Sally had been drugged; her sleep was too deep, her breathing too regular.

The Sergeant squatted down and looked at the red leather suitcase. It filled the gap between the floor and the slats of the bed.

He straightened himself and bent over the girl, taking the two top corners of the towel in his fingertips. Gently he began to peel the towel down over her body.

She appeared to be naked beneath it. As it came down,

Bill could see the bruises on her chest, though none showed on her face. The towel checked.

The Sergeant beckoned Bill to come forward. He made a sign for Bill to hold the towel exactly as he himself now had it. Bill bent over Sally, found himself looking into her face, sad in repose. Her eyes were closed; her mouth had a pinched look of considerable pain. Her skin appeared to be tinged with yellow and grey, as if she had known some inner hurt. The Sergeant slowly put his hand beneath the towel, feeling for the obstruction. He appeared to find it and held it while he signalled for Bill with his head to draw the towel downwards.

The bruises on Sally's belly were burning red, already turning a vicious purple.

A plastic-covered steel cord was looped tightly around her waist. The towel had caught in the lock. The Sergeant reached into the breast pocket of his shirt, drew out a pair of wire side-cutters, and snipped through the cloth. When that had been done, they were able to remove the towel completely.

Sally was quite naked. There were vivid cigarette burns at the top of her legs, on her inner thighs. Bill felt a terrible revulsion and shame, too, that he had exposed the girl to this kind of treatment. A fierce hatred welled up in him for the men, or the woman, who could have done this. But his deepest feeling was one of remorse at his own inability to protect this girl.

The Sergeant looked up and saw the agony on his face. 'I know how you feel, Sir,' he said quietly. 'You can imagine the way we do, when we put a couple of lads into the Falls Road, and drag 'em out again with their balls cut off and stuffed in their mouths. And them, sometimes, still alive to know the full horror of it. Your young lady will live, Sir. The burns and the bruises will heal. If we can get her out of this damned harness.'

He explained the situation to them, in a natural speaking voice now he knew that the apparatus was not sound activated. 'I guess the suitcase beneath the bed is full of explosive,' he said. 'And the harness around Miss Price here is connected to the detonator through the mattress. It'd be a natural instinct, wouldn't it, when we came in, to cut her hands and feet free and lift her off the bed. And consideration for the girl's modesty would prevent us lifting that towel off her. The minute she saw us, she'd yank the harness, and the suitcase would explode. Now, I suggest you all get out of the house, and leave this little lot to me. No point in us all catching it if I make a mistake, is there?'

'I'm staying,' Bill said. 'But the others must go.'

Nobody argued with him. They filed out of the house. The sergeant reached inside his shirt pocket, drew out a flat key with slides along its length. He examined the lock of the cord, grunted, pushed in a couple of slides, inserted the key. The lock snapped open, the end came free of its socket.

'Now you can cut the young lady loose,' he said, handing Bill his side cutters. Bill snipped through each of the nylon cords and gently lowered Sally's arms by her sides.

'I'm going to hold the lock open,' the Sergeant said. 'I want you to draw the lady up, ever so gently, towards the top of the bed. Whatever you do, don't put *any* weight on the bed.'

He opened the lock and Bill put his arm under Sally's back, lifting her gently and sliding her higher up the bed. Now the sergeant could see the wire that passed through the mattress and was attached to the lock. He held it in his fingers, gauged the pressure. Then he took out a knife and carefully started to carve out the sheet and the mattress around the wire, slicing it away piece by piece. Soon he had cut a hole through the stiff foam rubber of which the mattress was made and they could see the red leather of the case through two of the wooden bed-slats. The wire carried on into the case.

'I hope you're feeling strong, Sir,' the Sergeant said. 'Now you've got to pick up the bed, slowly, from the bottom end, while I feed the bicycle lock through this hole. Think you can do it?'

Bill could have lifted a mountain at that moment.

He grasped the foot of the bed and tested the weight. No

problem. Acting on the Sergeant's instructions, he slowly lifted it, and held it while the sergeant fed the bicycle lock down through the hole, inch by inch.

The blood was pounding in his forehead by the time the sergeant had finished.

'Now, Sir, you can let it down again, slowly, ever so slowly.' Bill did as the Sergeant had told him. 'Now, Sir, we're going to pick up the bed between us and lift it off the suitcase. We'll take it over there, and put it beneath the window, nicely out of the way.'

With two of them lifting, the strain seemed less. They hoisted the bed, keeping it steady, lifted it clear of the suit-case, and carried it to the wall.

The Sergeant went back, snipped through the wire level with the suitcase top, then gently opened the case.

It had been packed with sufficient gelignite to blow the entire house sky-high.

By the gelignite was a clock mechanism. The Sergeant reached in and snipped the wires.

Bill stared incredulously at the contents of the case.

'That's right, Sir,' the Sergeant said cheerfully. 'It was also on a time clock. Stands to reason they wouldn't just leave the girl there until somebody found her. It would have blown us to kingdom come in one more minute . . .'

'You knew . . . ?'

'No, Sir, but I guessed.'

'And didn't say anything . . . ?'

'No point in spreading alarm and despondency, is there, Sir?'

The Prime Minister was on the telephone to Señor Antonio Clapes, the President of the Council of the Baleares in Palma de Mallorca, and not enjoying himself.

'Señor Clapes,' he said, 'I have to report to you that, due to a malfunction of the aircraft carrying them, a group of thirty British para-troopers, on a training flight over the Mediterranean, has been compelled to bail out over the island of Ibiza. I shall be sending you a diplomatic tele-gram about this unfortunate incident and will, of course, be notifying our Ambassador in Madrid, who will make the appropriate representations to the government.'

The President of the Council spoke and understood English perfectly, but needed time to digest this information. A second voice came on the line. 'This is the President's Secretary,' the voice said in English. 'The President present his compliments and ask that you repeat the message in Spanish, please?'

The Prime Minister had been prepared for such a contingency. He motioned to the man from the Foreign Office to pick up the telephone. While he covered his mouth-piece he said, 'They want it in Spanish.' The man from the Foreign Office nodded. 'Speaking on behalf of the Prime Minister of the United Kingdom,' he said, his Castillian Spanish quite flawless, 'we would like to announce our regret at an incident which has just taken place over the Sovereign Territory of Spain . . .'

The President of the Council had recovered his second wind. Speaking English, he interrupted the man from the Foreign Office.

'When did these para-troopers land?' he asked.

The Prime Minister looked at his watch. 'Five minutes ago,' he said. 'They will go immediately to Ibiza Airport and be picked up by British military jet . . .'

'If we permit it to land . . .'

'I am assuming, Señor Clapes, that following my explanation of the incident to you *in person*, there will be no cause for *diplomatic* representations?'

'The big stick, eh, Prime Minister. They landed five minutes ago, you said? Communication between the air space over Ibiza and 10 Downing Street must be pretty quick these days. Quicker, for instance, than when we want to talk to you about sponsoring our membership of NATO and the EEC. Anyway, you know I can't give permission for a military jet to land on Ibiza; for that you have to apply to Madrid. Someday you must get the people on your foreign desks to explain to you exactly how little the autonomy of the Balearic Islands really means. You'll have to ask Madrid. They'll check with me. I'll tell them what I think . . .'

'Or rather, what you want them to think you think?'

'Perhaps you don't need that foreign desk after all, Prime Minister. Send in your military jet. I'll talk to Madrid about it, after it has taken off again. And, next time in London, perhaps we could meet and you could tell me the true story of the plane's malfunction . . .'

Sally woke between cool sheets in the bedroom she had occupied when she first arrived. As her senses returned, so did the excruciating pain of the cigarette burns. She reached down her hand, found the wounds covered with gauze and sticking plaster. A young man wearing a military uniform was leaning over the bed. 'You're going to be all right,' he said.

He turned aside and Bill, who had been standing behind him, came to the side of the bed. She took her hands from beneath the sheet and he held them. He reached forward and kissed her forehead. She was still only partially conscious, but felt a wave of relief flood over her at the sight of him.

'The clasp on the bag worked then?'

'It worked. We were watching on that frequency by satellite. We picked it up immediately, and I had the lads standing by, with a jet. But we didn't arrive soon enough, it seems.'

The young man was watching her. He reached out, disengaged her hand from Bill's and read her pulse rate. 'You'll be all right, Miss,' he repeated. 'They put you to sleep with a strong dose of chloral. In a while, you'll feel sleepy again, but just let yourself drift. When you wake up the second time, you'll be quite all right. Those burns will take about a week, no more.'

He turned to Bill. 'If you want to talk, Sir, you've got about ten minutes, I would say.'

'Thanks.'

The young man closed his satchel and left them alone together. Bill sat on the side of the bed, looking down at her. 'Feel up to telling me what happened?' he asked gently. 'When we arrived, you were the only one in the house.'

'They were here, Bill. At least, I think they were.' The words came spilling out of her as she told him about discovering the lead smear on the rock face; the mooring rings on the concrete underwater platforms; coming back up; Yshtak starting to ask her questions to establish her knowledge of Palestinian affairs.

'He was trying to find out how much I knew, Bill. If I knew enough to have hated the Israelis sufficiently to become a terrorist. He was gentle, and kind. As you instructed me, I told him all about my job, held nothing back. I told him we knew about the meeting in Paris, gave him the list of names of the people there. But I didn't tell him that kidnapping Mary Foster was a stunt.'

'You said he was kind,' Bill probed gently. 'So who gave you your wounds?'

'He had a telephone call,' Sally said. 'He seemed to have been waiting for it. His bags were packed and everything. I heard the jeep come back, and they carried out his stuff and he left. Is the boat still here?'

'The *Revenge*? Yes.'

She seemed reluctant to go on. 'And then, Sally? I have to know, I really have to know. Believe me, I wouldn't make you suffer any more. I reproach myself enough, as it is . . .'

She showed the first spark of her former self, half sat up in bed but fell back exhausted. 'You mustn't reproach yourself,' she said. 'I knew there was danger. I volunteered. I just pray I did some good. That man Andreas Burgler was there. I recognized him from the computer print-out picture. Yshtak left me alone with Khaylia Patin and Burgler. They weren't satisfied with the answers I'd given Yshtak. Burgler's a big, strong man. He beat me, Bill. He hurt me. And then, Khaylia started on me, with the cigarettes.'

'Don't say any more,' Bill said.

'I must tell you. Burgler told her about picking up Joseph Aram and the man called Akhtar, in the *Revenge*, after they parachuted. He told about them waiting there for the submarine. Bill, the submarine was here. And they've put the atomic warhead on it. That was Burgler's job. He's a specialist in explosives, so he said.'

Bill remembered the way Sally had been wired to the suitcase full of gelignite. But it was apparent she knew nothing about that.

'I didn't tell them any more than I'd told Yshtak,' she said, her voice becoming quieter as she slowly began to sink back into sleep. 'Thank God I never trained to withstand pain. Every time Khaylia touched me with a cigarette, I just fainted away, Bill. Just fainted.' Her head lolled on the pillow. She was nearly asleep.

'That phone call to Yshtak, Sally,' Bill said urgently. 'Do you know where or why he went?'

'No, Bill, I don't.'

'Do you have any idea where Joseph Aram, Jacques Morel, and the submarine now are?'

'No, Bill, I don't. But I know that Burgler and Khaylia have gone to join the others for what they called the last phase.' Now she was struggling to keep awake. 'One thing I do remember, Bill.'

'Yes, Sally. What do you remember?'

'That phone call was from somebody called Phillipe . . .'

Her head rolled sideways and her eyes closed. Her breathing became heavy and rhythmic as she slept again. He stroked her forehead tenderly, tucked her arms beneath the sheets, drew the curtains, and went out, closing the door behind him.

An ambulance took Sally from the airport to the military jet, which the authorities permitted to land without fuss. A tourist bus had taken the para-troopers and they were all on board, chatting happily. They were silent, however, when Sally Price was brought up. News of her torture had spread throughout the ranks.

'Too bad we couldn't have caught the buggers who did it, Sir,' the Sergeant-Major said. 'After all this time, it's still beyond me that anybody can do that sort of thing to a girl.'

Still sleeping soundly, Sally was put into a private ward at the London Clinic, with a policemen on the door night and day.

They had draped a sheet over her face when they carried her in on the stretcher from the airport ambulance; the policeman was from Special Branch and knew how to hold his tongue. The nurses were used to preserving a diplomatic silence at the clinic; they had performed too many quiet operations on heads of governments and royal families to be a chatty lot.

Bill saw Sally safely to bed and then went to his office, despite the lateness of the hour. Now he had two names. Yshtak, and Phillipe. The world contained a million Phillipes, but, presumably, only one Yshtak. The computer located him within micro seconds. The financier. The man behind Security Systems Ltd. Once they had a full name – in the United Kingdom he had operated as Ishmael Y. (presumably for Yshtak) Mohamed – they were able to trace his apparent history. Place of Birth, Palestine. Age now fifty-eight. Wealth estimated at around £40 million. Homes in New York, London, Ibiza, Beirut. Heavy supporter, at one time, of the PLO. Offered the post of Treasurer to the *de facto* PLO after Morocco but refused it and, seemingly, severed all connection with Arafat and others. Concentrated on his International Bank for Industrial and Commercial Finance – a sort of unofficial National Development Council, able, because of the lack of government accountability, to take more commercial risks. The IBICF had prospered with its interests all over the world and offices in many of the major capitals. Now Bill could see it for what it was, a front organization, able to move funds around, to make arrangements to suborn people of the right political inclinations.

Joseph Aram had been one. Doubtless Denford Fairclough was another. And Jacques Morel. And Phillipe.

He called Paris. 'You alone?' he asked Marc Chantal.

'Yes. Why? Do you want to tell me why my men arriving on Ibiza should just be in time to see a British military jet landing? And who really owns the house overlooking the bay at Cala Minor? The Ibicencan authorities, I've just learned, say it's owned by a company called – would you believe it, Cala Minor Properties S.A. Two Spanish lawyers own the company. If you believe that, you'll believe anything.'

'The house is owned by a man who calls himself, in England at least, Ishmael Y. Mohamed. The Y stands for Yshtak. That's what he prefers to be known as on Ibiza. I'm putting a full report about him onto the computer terminal for transmission to your office. But that's not why I'm ringing. Does the name Phillipe mean anything to you?'

'Yes. It was my father's . . .'

'I don't mean that. I mean, anyone special. In the game?'

At times, it did seem like a game, a game played with computers, data bases, international finance companies moving men and money to achieve their own personal aims. A game that took no account of individuals, that was prepared, in the last extreme, to use cigarette ends between a girl's legs, to wire them to explosives that would distribute their mortal self to the winds, as if they had never existed.

'Why do you ask?' Gone was the banter, the relaxed Gallic insouciance.

'You do know someone . . . ?'

'I might. Why do you ask?'

Warning signals were flashing in Bill's mind. So far, he and Marc had got on very well together since their first meeting at London Airport. Now he could hear the old suspicions raised in Marc's voice. 'I ask,' he said, 'for the same reason I've just pushed all the information we have on Yshtak onto the computer for transmission to you. I asked because I thought we were supposed to be cooperating. Now, who is Phillipe?'

'The only Phillipe I know, in the game, as you call it, means two things to me. He is my friend. And he is also my assistant.'

'Then I'll leave you to ask him,' Bill said, 'if it was he who made a call to Yshtak, to tell him you were switching your search from the East of the Mediterranean to the West, and to get the hell out of Cala Minor as fast as he could. Yshtak took his clothes with him, and nothing else. He even left the boat on its mooring, in the bay in front of his house. Somebody made that call, Marc, somebody who knew exactly what you were planning to do.'

'This is my business. D'accord, Bill? Mine.'

'D'accord. But whoever made that call incidentally put *my* assistant, and *my* friend, on the rack. So you had better deal with it, Marc, or by God, I will . . .'

CHAPTER EIGHTEEN

Jacques Morel was bored, crouched at the controls of the Green Dolphin. Though few people had ever known it, fighting boredom was one of Jacques's major problems. He enjoyed the challenge of something new, something difficult, but once the problems were solved, he quickly lost interest. The whole of his career to date had offered him new challenges, new things to learn. The Green Dolphin had been the culmination of those challenges. Its technology had been so demanding that, for the first time in his life, Jacques had been able to combine all his interests in achieving perfection. The rest of the team working on it had been make-weight, mere technicians, and Jacques had despised them. Not an ounce of truly creative scientific ability among them. Oddly enough, only Sophie had approached his ideal. Only with Sophie had he been able to express his enthusiasm, his complete dedication to the project.

The Dolphin had been completed, and he had achieved his other overwhelming ambition. He had stolen it.

Now he could use it to satiate his burning desire to see the recreation of a Palestinian homeland, and the total expulsion of the Jews from the state called Israel.

Fitting the atomic warhead beneath the Dolphin's skin had been simple – he had not needed that fool, Burgler, though Yshtak seemed to place a lot of confidence in him. Yshtak was wrong to trust a mercenary, to trust two of them, in fact. Kostas Aronakis was an idiot of a man, a shambling Cretan full of mouth-wisdom, a Zorba-like character, who treated their whole enterprise as a game, a joke.

Now all Jacques Morel had to do was to deliver the Green Dolphin to its final launching place. It could have sailed there on its own, given a map reference and coded instructions for its data base. And Jacques had already programmed it to the final target, with the switch ready to throw at a moment's notice, in case they ran out of time at the last moment.

If they did, of course, they could blame Yshtak, and his quixotic impulse to rescue those two girls, Sally Price and Khaylia Patin, from the stupid dilemma in which they had placed themselves.

For the first time, Jacques Morel, doubting the wisdom of something Yshtak had decided, had argued with him. It seemed foolish to undergo any risk, any risk at all, when they were so close to success.

Yshtak had listened to the declaration the girl had made, each time it was broadcast on the radio. 'She's one of us,' Yshtak had said. 'It cannot be the will of Allah that we who are able to help her should leave her alone. The atomic warhead has been mounted successfully?' he had continued, looking at Burgler.

Burgler had shrugged. 'Ask Jacques,' he said sullenly. 'He's the expert. He wouldn't let me get near his precious baby.'

Yshtak had looked first at one and then the other. The friction between them had been apparent from the time of their first meeting. Was it just the normal Frenchman's chauvinistic contempt for Germans, the dedicated man's hatred of the mercenary, or the scientist's mistrust of an uneducated technician?

'I have done it,' Jacques had said. 'It will work perfectly, as the Dolphin herself will work. Perfectly.'

Yshtak had made quick plans. Burgler to stay behind.

Joseph Aram to go to the final rendezvous, which Kostas Aronakis had arrived at already. Jacques to take the Green Dolphin.

'She will take herself,' Jacques had said petulantly. 'She's been designed and constructed to take herself.'

'And, what if she doesn't get there?' Yshtak had demanded. Of course, he knew nothing about such matters. He had the layman's distrust of scientifically inspired and controlled devices. How many people had said it was inconceivable that one could aim at the moon, and actually land a man there? 'No, Jacques, I prefer to take no risks at this juncture . . . I am sending Khaylia out of harm's way to Libya.'

'But you were taking a risk, in bringing those girls here . . .'

'That,' Yshtak had said, 'was not my doing. It was the will of Allah.'

Now Jacques was bored, chauffeuring the Dolphin round the ocean.

He checked the data base yet again – yes, there was the final target, a mass of numbers. He checked the programme, the system of instructions that would be activated by what it found on the data base. Yes, the programme was simple and clear.

One by one, he checked the functions of the Dolphin, the engine, the generator, the rudder control mechanisms, the vertical trim, the servo systems. All were working perfectly.

He checked the life support systems, the helium/oxygen mixture – perfect. The air conditioning, the oxygen replacement apparatus, the waste disposal.

He punched up a game of backgammon, but playing it bored him even further.

When the light bulb fused above the control panel, he welcomed it as something to occupy himself with. He threw the trip switch that cut off the generated electricity supply from the instrumentation, turned on the emergency light by which he could work.

He remembered they had had trouble with that light back in the docks. He had even designed a new fitting that would not overheat in prolonged use. He opened the thumb screws that permitted him to drop the panel. Damn it; a long human hair had wrapped itself round the shaft of the micro-fan he had installed to cool the bulb in action. A long blonde hair. One of Sophie's no doubt. So, the bitch had taken off her skull cap while she was working in the cock-pit. 'I'll roust her for that,' he said, 'when I get back!' But then he chuckled. He was not going back. His life in France was over. He could look forward to his new life in a re-born Palestine, using his knowledge to build a scientific community, to jerk the Palestinian peasants into the twentieth century. Slowly, carefully, he unwound the hair from the shaft of the micro-fan. He took a meter and checked the fan's motor. No, it had not burned out, but merely been stalled by the hair. If he had not spotted it so quickly, it would have wrecked itself, and he would have needed to replace it with one of the spares the Dolphin carried. He replaced the bulb, screwed the panel back in position, and switched on the main power.

But Jacques did not know, would never know, that one of the engineers doing routine work on the Green Dolphin had had the same problem with the lamp. Too lazy to reconnect the emergency supply system that had been disconnected while he worked, he had replaced the mercury switch in the trip connector with a piece of aluminium foil.

When he had finished work, he had forgotten to take out the foil.

The motor of the micro-fan had overheated. The insulation had melted from some of its coils. The current shorted to earth.

The trip should have been thrown, alerting Jacques.

The aluminium foil prevented it from being so.

The excessive current down the circuit sparked across two adjacent wires, isolating the life support system, but *bypassing the indicator*, which continued to glow.

The oxygen regeneration plant failed.

The helium content of the helium/oxygen system slowly increased.

And still the indicator continued to glow.

Jacques could not understand why he was beginning to feel uncomfortable. Why breathing seemed to be more difficult.

He could see the life support indicator button glowing, telling him everything was functioning all right.

He began to sweat, and his vision seemed to be blurring.

He punched the button that would turn the life support system onto emergency. The system button continued to glow but the fused wires prevented the emergency supply from operating.

His forehead was damp with sweat. He was gasping for breath. Already he could see tiny nebulae, the classic 'spots before the eyes'.

He reached across to punch the oxygen access button, but it seemed a mile away and he could not focus on it.

He gulped deeply, trying to fill his chest, but the supply seemed useless to him. He half rose in his seat, his arm extending towards the oxygen access button, but seemed incapable of reaching it. It danced before his distorted vision like an octopus tentacle.

And then his vision blurred completely, exploding into a red tumult. He jerked forward as if electrified, his limbs totally out of control.

His elbow jabbed the computer access button.

Then his face smashed onto the panel in front of him, his forehead re-arming the sensing devices for heat, light, and sound.

As he died, the nose of the Dolphin slowly turned through fifteen degrees, reacting to a sonar wave which came at it across the ocean, a sharp, repeated percussion.

The light sensing device also received a signal from the same source.

Slowly, the Green Dolphin began to nose forward, homing in on its new and unknown target.

Hans glanced at his watch. Five minutes to go before the end of the shift. He took the hammer in his hands, put the chisel against the rock face, and slowly chipped away the hard stone.

It is a mistake to assume that sound does not travel underwater. Once the ears have adjusted to depth, they can hear perfectly well. The sound of the hammer striking the chisel reverberated through the lofty underwater cave. Hans directed his lamp towards the rock face, scraping the slime of algae that hid the metal streak. Ten inches remained until the streak turned suddenly into the rock, but the slice of yellow metal ran deep.

He glanced at his diver's watch again, checking the time, confirming he had only five minutes left. Routine air check; well over a thousand p.s.i. in his bottles, plenty to finish the shift and return through the decompression levels. The tips of his flippers rested against a small ledge; he pressed his elbows back to ease the tension in his muscles.

His thoughts wandered as he worked. This *was* a well paid job. Where else could he earn two hundred deutsch-marks a day with his record? The work was nowhere as hard, for example, as on the North Sea rigs, where he had been earning well – before he had a fight with the boss from Texas and had been fired. When this job was finished, he would take his money and do as Dutch George had done, finding himself a little business somewhere here in the Med – a diving school perhaps. And this time, he would keep his fists and his temper to himself, knock off the heavy brandy drinking, and keep out of trouble. If he completed the contract, Dutch George had promised him a bonus large enough to set himself up somewhere.

He cut free a large chunk of the heavy yellow metal, and dropped it into the bag hanging round his waist. That would do for this shift. He hung the hammer and the cold chisel from their nylon thongs on the nail he had hammered into the rock face.

Suddenly, he felt the premonition that often comes to a diver underwater, the feeling that something is hovering outside the narrow tunnel of vision the mask permits.

He turned his head, slowly.

Last time Hans had felt it was when a moray eel emerged from a hole in a rock-face. Moray eels are the fiercest bastards of the underwater jungle, with razor-sharp teeth that could take off a man's hand.

He looked towards the entrance of the cave, illuminated by the high power lamps hanging from the rock face where he was working.

He saw the bared teeth, the eyes, the grey-green skin, the snout aiming directly towards him.

It moved silently, slowly, inexorably forward.

Hans backed off towards the depth of the cavern, moving slowly. He reached down his leg and drew the knife from its sheath.

It appeared not to have noticed, and continued its glide towards the rock-face where he had been.

Now he could see along its sleek flank. Jesus, it was at least twelve metres long and unlike any other man-eating fish he had ever seen. It did not seem to have a proper tail, but two dorsal fins that controlled its movement.

There seemed to be a hole at the front end of its belly, and another just beneath its tail.

He dropped slowly down in the water until he was fifteen feet lower than the monster. He swam slowly along the line until he was underneath it. It seemed to have stopped, fascinated by the light on the rock-wall. He knew that fishermen used lights at night to hypnotize octopus. He unclasped the leather lead-weight belt, then, with a powerful scissor kick, sped up through the water, the knife in his hand aiming straight for its belly.

CHAPTER NINETEEN

One of the several offices of the Mossad, the Israeli Secret Police, was in the district of Jerusalem known as Talbieh.

The Talbieh office specialized in investigating threats against the State of Israel. As such, it was three times larger than the branch of the Mossad, with its headquarters in Tel Aviv, that concentrated on hunting down Nazi war-criminals, and particularly members of ODESSA, the group of Nazis still functioning throughout the world but particularly in South America to maintain and promote the Fourth Reich.

The Talbieh office was run by Major Ben Moishe, a second generation *sabra*, whose family had come to Israel from Russia.

Ben had been brought up in the north-eastern hills of the Golan Heights, and had spent much of his youth among Palestinians. He could understand enough of their language to converse with them. Early in life he had learned a hill man's caution, a habit of natural distrust of anything that came from without the closed circle of the village and the family tribe. He knew the Palestinians had a particular attitude towards human life, and recognized that, for them, nothing counted, no one was important, outside of their own close-knit circle. Their attitude towards the Israelis was simple but totally ruthless. Even though the Israelis came and made fertile land that had lain unused for many generations, even though the Israelis built clean villages and progressive communities, they were still raiders who occupied the land, to be repulsed with the same vigour that the hill tribes had always used against marauders of any kind. And, if it was necessary to make forays against them at the dead of night, to kill them on their own soil, then that was the will of Allah.

Often Ben had tried to explain them to other *sabras* by comparing them to a child with a toy. This toy is mine, no one shall have it. And even if the child has no use for the toy, except to destroy it, he will never yield the toy to another. 'It's *my* toy, it's *mine*!' was a heart-felt declaration that could excuse any tantrum, any violence. And what child will not kick and punch and scream, when it sees its toys being taken away?

The Palestinians were kicking, punching, and screaming, but their weapons were not tiny fists and feet. They used knives, and bombs.

In joining the Mossad, Ben was merely following a family tradition. His grandfather had been part of the Secret

Police of the Russian czar; his father had fought with the Irgun against the British in the days before 1948.

Ben was a friend of the Prime Minister and often travelled, incognito, with him on his trips abroad. It was natural, therefore, that the Prime Minister should talk to him when he received the 'invitation' to attend the meeting in London.

Ben looked at the list of other people who were to attend.

His hill man's caution floated to the surface, unbidden.

'I don't like it, Prime Minister,' he said. 'I don't like any part of it.'

He noted that the meeting was not to be publicized, that an arrangement had been made for the Prime Minister to speak to a meeting of Jews in Leeds, Yorkshire, ostensibly on a fund raising visit. 'Samuel has already left for England; he will take care of the security arrangements with the British Special Branch. I have not yet been told exactly when or where the meeting will take place, but Samuel will check that and notify me. You do not look happy, Ben. But, come to think of it, you never look happy. Except when you've just been walking through your native hills.'

'I would like to go to London,' Ben said.

'To sniff around?'

'To talk to some people, listen to some others.'

'You don't think this is yet another big-brother, big-stick attempt to get us to accept the PLO?'

Ben shook his head. 'You forget the nature of the French, and also particularly the Franco-British, Franco-American mistrust. The French Premier would never take part in such a meeting. He'd never sit side by side with them in that kind of role. Even though one can't forget how committed the French are to the Arab oil-producing nations. How dependent they are on Franco-Arab trade. But they wouldn't risk that situation with either the British or the Americans. Remember how they signed their *own* oil-treaty with OPEC? No, this meeting stinks, Prime Minister and I want to go to London to find out why.'

'You don't have much time, Ben!'

'I don't need much time. Don't forget,' he said wrily,

'in the British government and Civil Service, some of my best friends are Jewish.'

The three CIA men were somewhat awed to be alone in the Roosevelt Room of the White House. They had been shown into the room by a Presidential aide and left there. They did not know whether they should sit at the long table and rise when the President came in, or remain standing.

And why had Burkenheimer, their section boss, said: 'No written report. You're to go to the White House, make your report in person. And don't louse it up!' Burkeheimer had obviously been miffed at a situation in which three of his subordinates got to talk directly with the President. But, what the hell! So many kooky things were happening in the CIA these days . . . It was getting so a man couldn't tell his ass from first base any more.

The President came in. They stood to attention, feeling like a squad of rookies. He nodded to them and their chorus of 'Good morning, Mr President.' Beckoned for them to sit in the chairs gathered around the low table in the corner. He sat down, relaxed, his finger-tips together.

'You've talked about this among yourselves?' he said.

'Yes, Mr President.'   .

'Then one of you can be spokesman, right?'

Two of them looked at the third. He shrugged. 'Don Grimwald, Mr President . . .'

'Go ahead, Mr Grimwald . . .'

'Well, like the brief said, we checked out the London situation. And it sure looked like the real thing.'

'Looked like, Mr Grimwald . . . That's not the same thing as "is".'

'It sure isn't, Mr President. That's what I was coming to. It *looked like* the real thing. That was a real live grenade, detonated, fused. It would have exploded if the lever had been allowed to fly. And, if it had exploded, there's no way the Ambassador could have lived through it. Everything was done according to Hoyle. The Special Branch were there, but they couldn't move. We had two men there, one of them with a Colt ·45. The girl picked him clean. You understand, Mr President, it wasn't his fault, and it doesn't reflect in any way on his ability. He was just cold-cocked, that's for sure.'

'And afterwards . . . ?'

'You understand, Mr President, there was a time factor involved. One thing that girl learned – if you have people on the hop, keep 'em that way. Don't let 'em take a deep breath. Don't let 'em get back in balance. She sure had everybody hopping. And there wasn't one little thing they could do about it. Not with that chain around our Ambassador's neck, and the girl's hand on the lever. So, like I said, it *looked like* the real thing. The Prime Minister took direct control of the situation, gave out the orders. And when that girl moved, she sure moved. Out of there like she was a Marine.'

'Again, Mr Grimwald, you said, *looked like!*'

The President had not moved once while Don had been giving his explanation. His fingers were still touching, one knee crossed over the other, a man used to listening, evaluating, probing. A man used to judging by nuance as much as by content. One of the difficulties of being President was that people tried to tell you what *they* thought you wanted to hear. They seldom got it right.

'The whole set-up stinks, Mr President. I'm sorry. It looks like I'm shooting off my mouth. After all, our Ambassador and the British Prime Minister are involved. Our Ambassador's life was in danger for sure. But it still stinks . . .'

'I thought it did,' the President said. He rose to his feet, but beckoned them to remain seated. 'As of this moment,' he said, 'you three are on special assignment. You report only to me, personally. Do you understand?'

They nodded.

'I think, to use your words, that it stinks. I want you to go back in there. And this time, find out exactly *why* it stinks. If someone is playing games with me, I want to know. That means I'm trusting you to find out. And you don't have much time.'

The President pressed a button on the box on the inlaid

deck. A voice came on the line. 'I want three White House Accredited Special Investigator cards made, right now. And I want one off-the-board line kept open at all times,' the President said. 'The men will come down at once for photographs.'

He clicked the switch back and came across the room. The men rose to their feet. He shook each of them warmly by the hand, his mind searching for a suitable message with which to leave them.

'Good luck, gentlemen,' he said. 'And now know this – a heavy burden of responsibility has been placed upon your shoulders. I have every confidence you will carry it faithfully, loyally, and with success and honour.'

That particular closing message never failed. Like the Committee of the Boys Clubs of America, the League of Mothers Clubs of Arkansas and the Society of American Gas Technologists, they left the Roosevelt Room feeling seven feet tall.

Yshtak's headquarters on Crete was one of the many buildings started by the Germans during their occupation of the island and not completed when the partisans swept the foreigners away so that they could fight more easily among themselves.

It nestled on a promontory beneath the towering mountains of Sfakia, the Lefka Ori rising to 2,500 metres between the Libyan Sea and the Sea of Crete.

Marc Chantal's men had been near the place when they investigated the site of ancient Phoenix and modern Loutron. Further along the coast to the west, a promontory jutted into the sea and on the top of it was one small hut such as the shepherds used in winter with their flocks. Beneath the hut the Germans had built a four roomed installation carved into the rock, with steps going down to a submerged cave whose entrance was five metres below sea-level. The cave, a natural one, like the many along this coast, was intended by the Germans for use as a submarine repair pen.

Kostas Aronakis had come across the plans in the last

days of the war when he led a party raiding the German headquarters at Chora Sfakion, a village further east along the coast. Since, at that time, he was the only one of his band of partisans to understand the German language, only he knew what the papers were. He put them away, realizing that, like so much of the plunder of those days, they would be of use later.

He had been twelve years of age when the Germans captured him and sent him as a prisoner-of-war to Germany. In those days, he was not so certain of his loyalties. The time in Essen gave him an opportunity to work in a factory and learn the German language from the guards, and English from a couple of his fellow prisoners. The factory made small diesel engines; soon Kostas could strip one and re-assemble it in the dark. He also learned the method of putting them together in the final assembly so that they would seize up after fifty hours of running. It was inevitable that the rash of troubles in diesel engines should be investigated by the Gestapo; when they came to the factory, Kostas went over the outside wall and never stopped running until he arrived, via Austria, back in his native Greece. Like so many before him, on arrival he bent down and kissed the soil of his native land.

He made the crossing of the sea alone in a boat, by the simple expedient of setting out in a gale that sent every other vessel in the eastern Mediterranean scurrying for harbour and sheltered moorings. To this day, he could remember the mountainous seas, with waves often thirty feet high that threatened to engulf him each time they crashed against his bows. He could remember nursing the little diesel engine of the fisherman's caique, babying it along, knowing that if it failed he could do nothing to hold his bows into the waves. He had had no means of navigation other than the occasional glimpse of stars. When people asked him how he had set his sights on the island, he said, 'I smelled it, there, ahead of me. I smelled the herbs, the orange trees, the lemons. I smelled the carob and the goats that eat it. I smelled the cooking oil of Crete and the vines. But, above all, I smelled Crete herself.'

Despite his keen nose, he nearly missed the island, came to it from the west, had to run, helpless, down the western side and turn into the Libyan sea. Here, the waves pounded against the high rocky shores, smashing a boiling cauldron of foaming spume against the rocks. The fisherman's caique gave up the ghost off Aghia Roumeli, when the diesel fuel petered out. The boat itself was thrown against the rocks, smashed into small pieces. At the last moment, Kostas had jumped overboard. An enormous wave had pounced down on him, picked him up like a baby, carried him along on its dancing crest and deposited him, like a baby, on the shingle beach to the immediate west of the village of Aghia Roumeli itself.

When the storm had died down, an hour later, the women of the village came out, picked up his lacerated body, and carried him, beneath bundles of washing, two kilometres up the track into the mouth of the Gorge of Samaria. They remembered Theseus, and the bull who came from the sea, and treated him as a god, a son of Poseidon.

When the partisans came for him, he was already fully recovered from his ordeal, apart from a few superficial cuts and bruises that oil and wine soon healed.

No one ever asked young Kostas where he obtained the boat he sailed after the war ended, or the twin diesel engine with which it was powered. No one asked him where he obtained the supplies of German Army boots, the woollen greatcoats, the acres of thin cotton, or the food, much of it in new tins. If you needed a rifle and some ammunition for hunting in the mountains – you saw Kostas. If you wanted penicillin, American cigarettes, tins of ham, binoculars with British War Office markings; if your boat needed a new fuel injector, a new feed pipe, a new engine – you saw Kostas. Could you use a few bags of cement to rebuild part of your house? Iron rods to re-inforce the cement? Kostas would supply them. Kostas Aronakis was the universal supplier in those days of scarcity when the war ended. There was nothing Kostas could not obtain.

And all this time, Kostas lived in a small hut below the Lefka Ori on a promontory by the ocean. When Kostas was away on one of his frequent 'voyages', the hut was heavily locked, bolted, and barred. No one but Kostas ever went into that hut. Nobody knew, as Kostas knew, that one day, what it contained would command a price. Every day he was around, Kostas came into the coffee-shop to play tavli with the men, drink ouzo, wine and raki with them. He ate his meals in the corner of the taverna overlooking the bay of Aghia Roumeli. The village women would look at him and say: 'Poor Kostas, he is lonely at night. He lives in a lonely house'. But they also remembered the fearsome time when he arrived among them, the way they had half believed he was some supernatural being from the sea. And did he not prove it, now, by refusing to take any of the local girls to himself? Many had lingered along the path that led to Kostas's hut, picking *horta* where it grew. The path was steep and dangerous, fit only for sheep, goats, kri-kri, or Kostas. No matter how much he had drunk, no matter how much he weaved as he left the village, he managed to find his way somehow along the path to his home. He lived much nearer to Loutron, of course, but seldom if ever chose to go there. It was as if Aghia Roumeli was the place of his re-birth, his timeless home.

What none could know was that Kostas had a dream. One day he would make more money than any man in Aghia Roumeli could dream of. And Kostas would take that money and with it find himself a house in the South of France, perhaps Monaco, and a pretty young American wife. On one of his many 'trips', Kostas had put into the harbour at Monte Carlo. He had been dazzled and bewitched by the splendour he saw about him, and transfixed when suddenly he heard Greek being spoken. He had dwelt upon the unmistakably Greek features of some of the men, with their young, blonde women.

Kostas wanted a young, blonde woman more than anything else in the world.

Then, a number of years ago, the tall, hawk-faced man had come to Aghia Roumeli and anchored his boat off the harbour. It was too big to come further in. Kostas had been waiting when the man was brought ashore in his tender.

Kostas the part-god of Aghia Roumeli and Yshtak, as the man said he was called, from the *Revenge*.

Yshtak had a blonde woman lying along his foredeck. Kostas hugged himself, and that night danced for hours on the bare boards of the coffee-shop when George came with his lyre to entertain the visitors. Then Vasili joined in with his bouzouki and they all drank raki until it seemed it would come out of their ears. Kostas could not take his eyes from the young blonde. Yshtak, once he had seated her with the young boy who served as his engineer, ignored her. Yshtak drank no wine, ate only sparingly, but seemed overjoyed at the goat's meat stew, dipping into the pot with his fingers and picking out pieces of the meat and the bone, sucking hungrily at them as if reviving some childhood memory. Kostas's eyes glittered. Here was a man who had not always known wealth. Here was a man who had been poor when young, who had lived the communal life of the village, squatting round the fire, eating the treasured goat that had grown too old to give milk.

Here was a man who had not always had a blonde to sleep in the crook of his arm.

Kostas's dream grew larger that night, threatening to burst from his body. Because here, he knew, was a man who had trodden the same path he intended, and had made it to the end, the luxurious end. A boat, freedom, money to travel, and a blonde to warm his bed. And Kostas danced, and danced, and danced.

The boat stayed off the harbour for three days. Kostas went aboard after he had listened to the diesel engine they used for charging the batteries. 'That engine, boss, will let you down one of these days. Let Kostas look at it for you.'

Yshtak had been suspicious, but had finally consented when Tony, his engineer, had suggested that the Greek sounded as if he knew what he was talking about. Tony himself had been a little worried and had wanted to suggest, on their return journey, that they put into Genoa to have the engine overhauled.

Kostas took it apart in half a day, spreading the parts carefully, after cleaning each one, on a white cotton so immaculate you could have eaten from it. He showed the worn part to Tony, who showed it to Yshtak. 'We'll need a spare,' Tony said. 'I don't have one on board.'

Kostas disappeared, and they saw his caique leave the harbour. Yshtak eyed the mess of the engine, each part laid out on the cloth spread across the engine-room floor. 'I hope you know how to put it all together again,' he said.

Tony swallowed. He was strictly a maintenance engineer, not a fitter . . .

He need not have worried. Kostas reappeared an hour later with the spare part in his hand. It fitted perfectly. Laughing, he reassembled the engine, his eyes flashing, his hands moving swiftly in a well-known ritual. He seemed to be paying no attention to the work he was doing. The engine room port-hole faced forward and Penny was stretched out on an airbed on the deck, wearing a bikini the size of three large postage stamps.

The engine fired first time when he had reassembled it. The rate of charge had increased, the noise had decreased. It ran sweet as sugar. He wiped his hands on the white cloth, folded it and packed it away with his tools, most of which, Tony had noticed, were stamped with the Wehrmacht or the British W.D. sign, and were well worn.

Yshtak took him into the saloon, poured him a glass of Scotch whisky from a crystal decanter with an enormous flat base. Kostas eyed the decanter. Yshtak explained it was that special shape so that it would not tip over on a boat, and Kostas nearly wept with pleasure.

'One day,' he vowed, 'a boat, a blonde, and a decanter such as this for my ouzo. No, not my ouzo – am I a crazy peasant. For my whisky!'

The tears did actually come to his eyes when Yshtak finally told Kostas what he was looking for. Tears of joy! Had he not known, had he not always sworn by everything sacred that one day, one day, his treasure would find a price. 'Boss,' he said, leaping from his seat, grasping Yshtak's arm, and bursting with joy. 'I have it. I have the place you're looking for. God sent you to Kostas, as sure as he sends the kri-kri to the mountain top. I have it.'

They motored the *Revenge* slowly down the coast that night. There was no moon. Kostas took Yshtak off in the caique, was astonished to find Yshtak could climb the steep rocky paths as fast as he could. Once again the thought came to him, the same thought he had had when he saw Yshtak dip his hand into the pan for the goat's meat. Here was a man who had lived in the mountains, who had loved the mountains. Yshtak was the first man to enter Kostas's hut since he had discovered it, other than Kostas himself.

The hut was clean, with bare, whitewashed walls, a wooden bed on slats, a woven bedspread of wool as soft as that of the llama. A table, a chair, and a cupboard for the few clothes Kostas seemed to possess.

One door against the far wall. 'Wait until you see, boss,' Kostas said, unable to conceal his delight.

He pressed a switch. From beneath their feet Yshtak felt rather than heard a faint rumble. Kostas opened the door and they climbed down a staircase. Inside were four large rooms and two smaller ones, completely fitted out with bunk beds, tables, chairs, cooking and washing facilities. One room contained a diesel generator that was causing the hum, supplying electricity. 'It was a mess,' Kostas said. 'But I took it to pieces.'

Now it was Yshtak's turn to feel a pounding in his heart. He looked all about him. 'Perfect, if only . . .'

'Wait, boss, wait,' Kostas said. He opened another door. Beyond it was a wide-mouthed lift. He went inside, closed the gate behind Yshtak and pressed a button. The lift descended smoothly but slowly. 'I fixed the motor,' Kostas said. 'I suppose they intended this for carrying heavy parts up and down. Probably going to turn one of the upstairs rooms into a precision machine shop.'

Yshtak's eyes glistened when they stopped in a natural cavern. Kostas had strung a couple of lights across it on wires sufficient to illuminate the clear water, the concrete dock on which they stood. He pressed another switch and underwater lights shone from behind glass panels. The pool of the cavern would certainly have been large enough to accommodate two war-time submarines.

A pair of footprints were cast in the concrete at their feet, and a scrawled – 'Hergestellt von Hans Dieter' – 'made by Hans Dieter, No 7 Company, 3 Pioneer Brigade, 1944'.

Iron rails had been set into the rock walls above their heads and a gantry ran between them that was doubtless intended, when the workshop was completed, to carry a crane.

Kostas had been watching Yshtak's face. 'You like it?' he asked.

The answer was obvious.

'You take it,' Kostas said. 'I will sell it all to you for one pound, English.'

'One pound, English?'

'All. But you pay me one million pounds, English, to forget I know anything about it.'

Yshtak laughed, and then held out his hand. Kostas gripped it.

'One million pounds,' Yshtak said. 'In a Swiss bank tomorrow. I give you the number of the account the day my task here is completed. Until then, you work for me. It's a deal, Kostas?'

'It's a deal, Yshtak.'

Since that day, Kostas Aronakis had been a changed man. Now his dream was no longer the foolishness of a man cursed, or some would say blessed, with eternal youth and hope. Now it had become an awesome reality. 'It's there, in the bank, boss?' he would ask, and Yshtak would reassure him. 'Yes, Kostas, it's there, and you shall have it.'

Kostas would think for a while. 'But, boss, what will happen if you die before you tell me the number of the account?'

Yshtak would smile. 'Don't worry, Kostas, all is taken care of. If I die, my people, who have the number in safe keeping, will give it to you.'

'What happens, boss, if they forget the number, eh?'

'Don't worry, Kostas, the number is written down.'

Another time he asked, 'Eh, boss, what happens if these

people of yours don't want to give me the money? What happens if they keep it for themselves?'

And again, Yshtak smiled. 'They will not do that, Kostas. There are laws about these things in England . . .'

'Ah, boss, so the money is in England . . . ?'

'No, Kostas,' Yshtak explained patiently. 'The money is in Switzerland. The man who has the number of the account is in England, most of the time.'

During the years while Yshtak had been planning, Kostas lived in the hut, his life virtually unchanged. True, he went away more often, and was away longer times. Always he returned at night, moored his caique in a tiny sheltered bay below the promontory, and appeared in Aghia Roumeli the next day, to eat and drink and play tavli in the kafenion.

But Kostas no longer danced.

The girls stopped walking along the cliff path to pick *horta* at the hour they knew Kostas would be coming. They knew from the distant look in Kostas's eye that he had other plans, that someone far away would, one day, warm his bed.

Gradually the installations Yshtak had ordered were completed in the rooms below Kostas's hut. Kostas met Andreas Burgler and took an immediate dislike to him. He could not forget the situation he had found in Crete when he returned from Germany, where the people for the most part had been kind to him, to his own island, where the soldiers had behaved with an inhuman cruelty. Already, the first tourists had started to appear on Crete, and many brought rucksacks with them and came to the door of Kostas's hut to ask for water, or cheese, thinking him a shepherd. Kostas, pretending an ignorance of German, had told them brusquely and rudely to go away and leave him in peace. Gradually the word got around among the hippie communities of the south coast. 'Avoid that hut. The man inside is unfriendly, unsympathetic.'

Burgler always arrived at night-fall, walking from the end of the bus-line at Chora Sfakion in the dark when no one was about. Kostas had fixed a room for him, and had completed the air conditioning. As the installations grew more nearly complete, Burgler taught Kostas radio and radio engineering. Though Kostas could never understand the simple principle of being able to pick unheard, unseen signals out of the air and water, he mastered the technical side completely.

When they needed heavier equipment, it was crated in watertight packages and sent to Brindisi. Kostas would go over in his larger fishing caique, with the more powerful engines and crane, and would lower the equipment, at night, into the water. Burgler would be waiting there, and slowly drag the boxes under the overhang of the cave. Kostas had completed the gantry crane. It was a simple matter to hoist the boxes out of the water onto the platform, then run them into the lift, to take them to the floor above. Piece by piece, they successfully installed the computer they would need to operate the Green Dolphin and launch it on its way.

When Joseph Aram and Ahktar arrived, walking down the Samaria Gorge from Omalos, then skirting the base of the Lefka Ori to arrive unseen at Kostas's hut, they found the installation complete.

Kostas took them proudly around it, showed them the improvements he had made on the original German design. Their quarters were sparse but contained everything they needed. Kostas had spread woollen rugs on the floor and on their beds and made shelves for them and even cupboards. There was a hot sweet-water shower, a flushing lavatory system, full cooking facilities. Who could ask for more? Even Yshtak was delighted when he saw what had been done since his last visit three months before. He grasped Kostas's arm and hugged him; Kostas beamed with pleasure.

The Green Dolphin was programmed to arrive exactly at midnight. At five minutes to, they all went down to the cavern and switched on the underwater lights; the pool gleamed blue green, and surprised fishes darted everywhere. Kostas was examining the sides of the pool. Suddenly, he saw what he wanted and, fully clothes, dived down into the water. The ripples hid his body, but when he surfaced again after what seemed to be an impossible time to be submerged without an air supply, he was holding aloft an enormous lobster. 'How's that for supper?' he shouted.

His voice rang round the interior of the cave.

'He always had to act the fool,' Burgler said. 'I think he has the mental age of a child.'

Yshtak stopped him with an angry growl. 'Be silent! What Kostas has done for us, for what we believe in, no other man could or would have done. Including you, Herr Andreas Burgler!'

'He is paid his price, I imagine . . .' Burgler said, sullen as ever.

'And so are you. And part of that price is for you to keep your mouth shut.'

No one argued with Yshtak. His command of their small group was absolute.

Twelve o'clock. Yshtak looked at his watch.

'What time is it, boss?' Kostas asked, sitting on the edge of the dock, soaking wet, but oblivious to the water streaming off him. Kostas was excited by the thought of the Green Dolphin arriving. He had heard little about it except that it was a submarine that looked like a fish. He was thrilled at the thought that his cave would finally be put to some use after all his work. Like a newly-wed wife awaiting her first guests, he could not sit still. Once the Dolphin arrived, he intended to dive down into the water to greet it, to welcome it to its new home.

Twelve fifteen and still it had not arrived. Now everyone was looking at Yshtak.

'We'll try the radio,' he said. 'If Jacques is having difficulty, he will have streamed the aerial.' They went up in the lift, leaving Kostas behind to look for his new charge. In the radio room, Andreas Burgler tuned the large multi-waveband transceiver and operated the key, using the pre-arranged call sign.

There was no reply.

A sonar transponder had been suspended in the deep

ocean outside the mouth of the cave. They activated it, sending a fifty KHz signal that would pick up the Dolphin at a range of fifty thousand metres, provided Jacques had put out the sonar reflector.

Again, there was no reply, save the quiet ping and the hollow echo from the corrugated bed of the ocean.

Jacques had briefed Yshtak and Andreas Burgler at length about the operation of the Dolphin. 'Try the second transponder,' Yshtak commanded. A second transponder had been dropped to a float that would hold it a hundred feet off the bed of the deeps, some distance off the Cretan coast, but in direct, uninterrupted line with the island of Ibiza. They could communicate with the second transponder by sonar, use it to re-transmit a straight signal that would reach Ibiza at those depths.

Andreas Burgler re-plugged the apparatus, then started to signal.

The sound waves sped through the ocean, scattered when they hit the distant Ibicencan coastline, but in part reflected. The returning sound, coded for the computer print-out, appeared on the screen as an ellipse with shaded edges. From the dimensions of the ellipse, the computer could calculate and simultaneously display the distances, identifying the image.

In the centre of the ellipse a bright spot burned.

Andreas refocussed the reader to enlarge this spot so that it covered the whole display screen. The spot was fixed and brighter than the surrounding pattern had been. He frowned. Jacques had not told them anything about this effect.

Jacques had never observed it, had never therefore studied it. The sensing apparatus of the Dolphin, a frequency modulating system, could accommodate a large number of coded signals and commands. It could accept and transmit these signals during identical modulations. Across the ocean, the Dolphin was transmitting in the cave, and accepting replies. The cave was acting like an eye in reverse with its cold water a lens and the back of the cave a reflecting screen, like the mirror of a searchlight. The Dolphin was beaming out a signal that floated through the opening of Dutch George's cave and across the ocean to their transponder.

But Andreas Burgler did not know how to read the message.

'I can't even get a distance from it,' he said. 'It's so large by comparison with the signals we receive from the shoreline that it blows the computer off the edge of the screen. And I don't know how to tune the sensing transponder down far enough to make sense of it.'

'But it is the Green Dolphin?' Yshtak asked anxiously.

'Yes, I'm sure of that. Though according to my estimation it's somewhere in a line between Ibiza and here, and I don't know where . . .'

'Is it moving?'

Andreas caught the note of anxiety in Yshtak's voice, the complete frustration, the feeling that perhaps this part of their planning had gone astray. He looked up from the screen and wiped his eyes.

He pressed a button and the paper in the typewriter began to clatter, jerking forward each second, stopping, jerking forward again, stopping again, as the time division multiplexer cleaned the signal between pulses.

Each column of figures the typewriter printed at the command of the computer was identical.

'No, Yshtak,' he said, his voice flat with despair. 'Wherever the damned thing may be, it's standing still.'

When Hans had dived up and rammed his knife as deep as it would go into the belly of the monster, he felt it slide through the sound absorbent coating, almost like slicing through blubber, then received an enormous shock to his wrist and elbow as the knife point struck the armoured casing that was the actual skin of the Dolphin. The monster did not move, did not bleed. He swam to the front of it cautiously, saw that the snout, the teeth, and the eyes had only been painted on, crudely.

Dutch George dived down to the cave when Hans did not come up at the end of his shift. Usually the two of them worked the face as a team, but today George had had business to attend to. He had found a Spanish mechanic with his own shop at the back of Ibiza who could cut air bottles on a lathe and give them an inner lining of the gold George was bringing up. George had already flown to Holland with three of these bottles and had passed them easily through Customs as the tools of his trade, since his passport named him as a professional diver.

He had just delivered the gold to Manolo for him to make four more bottles.

He roared with laughter, as much as one can roar with laughter wearing diving gear, when he saw the crude painting on the monster. He went over its outside surface carefully, noting the stubby aerial sticking out on top of the snout, the holes beneath its belly, the movable fins. He found the seam of the hatch cover, but made no attempt to open it. At first, he had thought this some toy a home enthusiast had made, remembering the radio controlled 'Jaws' shark an English landowner had operated to keep unwanted tourists off his private beach. But gradually he realized that, despite the crudity of the nose painting, this was a precision instrument.

As he swam past its snout, the lamp he was carrying shone into its eye. The Dolphin turned as if to follow him, but then was attracted back by the more powerful working light as he turned his lamp away. He realized the thing could see.

He beckoned for Hans to switch off the working lights. When the cave was in darkness he switched on his lamp, and sure enough the monster followed him, stopping when it was exactly one metre from him. He swam backwards slowly, deeper into the cave. It followed him again. He saw a dullness in its snout as it came towards him, so he instructed Hans to put the working light back on again. The monster turned neatly and headed back, taking a mean position between the two strong lamps and hovering. George swam to the front of it and ran his hands over the snout. Here, the rubber coating was thinner, and he found that he could gently part it, as if the beast had a mouth. He bent back the rubber lips. Beneath them, he saw a flat

225

black plate that had been let into the creature's under-snout. A number had been inscribed on the plate. He took his slate and crayon and copied it down. H. Ex. WD. 7007. The sevens intrigued him. They had not been crossed, like a continental 7.

British?

Hans was tapping his wrist, and pointing at his own bottles.

It was time for him to go up.

Dutch George beckoned for him to take off. When Hans had gone he pulled a couple of lengths of chain they had brought down for the gold workings, to make a cradle on which they could stand, and wound them round the monster's body, shackling them together so that they would not slip. He took a length of nylon mooring rope they had also brought down with them, tied one end of it to one of the pegs Hans had hammered into the rock face, and the other end to the chain around the monster.

Then he switched off the working lights, and made for the surface.

The Dolphin, left alone in the gloom, waited patiently. Then it *heard* the sonar signal from the distant source. It started to glide towards it. The nylon rope stopped it. The Dolphin pulled at the rope but could not part it. It generated signals of what, in a human or an animal, would have amounted to anguish.

The signals bounced off the inside of the cave, focussed against the almost perfect parabola of the back wall, and were projected outwards through the entry hole.

The transponder in the ocean off Crete heard them and faithfully transmitted them.

The nylon rope, rubbing against the rock face began, slowly, to chafe as the Dolphin strained backwards and forwards, backwards and forwards, in its attempt to escape these unknown bonds.

CHAPTER TWENTY

Sophie finished work at nine o'clock, mentally cursing Jules Lachard. Over and over again, he had run the computer pattern, trying to discover what had gone wrong with the Green Dolphin.

How many times had they all told him? We can find no error. No malfunction. No *logical* reason for the Dolphin's failure. The technicians had fabricated a mock-up of Dolphin Two, and Jules was running it, unceasingly, in the tank, putting it through exactly the same programme they had used on the original. And the damn thing functioned correctly every time, even though it was only a mock-up. 'Give it two more days,' Jean-Luc had complained. 'And then I'm going to tell him, personally, where he can stick his Dolphin Two . . .'

She paid off the taxi, the self-indulgence she always allowed herself when she finished late. She looked up at the tall silhouette of her apartment building, past it to the sky. A half moon shone. The air was warm for the time of the year, still scented with the oleander the management had planted in the apartment gardens. For an instant she thought that on such a beautiful night perhaps she should take a stroll down the hill to the bistro that would still be open, have a plate of soup, chat to the waiters. She felt alone and lonely, on a night like this. But it would be too much of a hassle to walk down the hill and back up again. She had the remains of a pot-au-feu in the refrigerator. She could warm that, open a bottle of wine, which would put her to sleep.

Another taxi drew up and a little fat man got out of it, carrying two large plastic carriers, bulging with groceries. He set one down and it toppled over while he was fumbling for the money to pay the cab driver. Sophie bent and helped him put the purchases back into the carrier. She noticed the tins of prepared meals and pitied him. Their heads banged together as both tried to stuff the carrier. He apologized profusely. She forgave him, glad of the human encounter. He was such a wistful, little man . . . 'Your wife will scold you,' she said, 'if you dirty the shopping on the pavement.'

'No wife, alas,' he said, as if apologizing. He was wearing spectacles which seemed to have misted over. He tried to clean the lens with his thumb and almost dropped the carrier again. She took it from him.

'Come on,' she said. 'I'll see you home . . .'

She used her key to open the outside door. They went into the lobby, brightly lit but deserted. She reached up and thumbed the button for the lift. 'Perhaps I ought to invite him in,' she was thinking. 'He seems such a poor, helpless waif of a man.'

He was still apologizing to her for banging her head. 'I'm so clumsy,' he said, 'things always seem to happen to me for the worst . . .'

'Where do you go?' she said.

'Seven. Where do you go?'

'Six.'

He bumped into her again, and apologized once more. Really, he was such a sweet but ineffectual little man. Sophie's heart went out to him. How terrible life must be, to be alone, as he probably was, and so utterly incapable.

He was looking shyly at her. He took off his glasses again, holding his carrier bag beneath his arm. He broke the end of the baguette while he was rubbing his glasses, no doubt smearing them.

She pressed the button for six. 'I wonder,' he said. 'Would you think me terribly presumptuous? May I ask, if *you* are, er, how can I put it . . .'

'Married? No, I'm not married.'

The news obviously pleased him. He opened his mouth to speak again, and at that moment, the lift stopped and the lights went out.

She heard his voice in the dark. 'Didn't I tell you,' he said, 'that things always happen to me . . . Now we've had a power failure . . .'

She reached for the panel and pressed the emergency bell. 'I'll ring the alarm,' she said, 'Then the porter will come out of his apartment . . .'

'Yes, do that,' he said eagerly. 'Oh dear,' he said. 'I seem to be losing my carrier bag again . . .' She felt the groceries cascade over her. A tin landed on her feet. Then she felt a sharp sensation in her thigh, like a needle piercing her. She felt the waves of unconsciousness send her brain reeling, knew she was falling, collapsing in a heap among the groceries lying on the floor of the lift. Smelling the odour of the garlic bulbs, the parsley, the onions, the sharp tang of the tomato she squashed with her forehead.

The man driving the Rover held up a British passport. The Rover had British licence plates. The French immigration official looked lazily through the windows, saw the little fat man driving and the woman asleep on the seat beside him, and waved him through. The Italian immigration official did not even bother to look inside the vehicle.

The charter jet was waiting at Albenga Airport, down the Autostrada del Sole below the border. The Rover made good time. The fat man saw the jet landing as he turned off the motorway. The quiet airport was asleep apart from the night staff in the improvised tower, the one man nominally on duty in Customs but sitting in his office by the warm stove. He had been told of the plane's landing. An emergency case. Going from the hospital in Savona to the hospital in Rome. No need to trouble him. He saw the car arrive, looked through his window as it drove across to the plane. The patient was carried into the plane by the hospital orderly, wearing his white trousers and white jacket. Nothing to bother *him* about. He watched the car drive away, saw the plane take off, wondered idly why the car had British number plates. But it was damned cold outside, wasn't it?

The jet landed in the small airport by Sternes, on the Akrotiri Peninsula, Crete. Kostas was waiting. He had had a word with the Customs. 'My old mother,' he said. 'Being brought from the airport at Heraklion. The road journey is too much for her.' The customs officer idly checked. 'You have a take-off by private plane, destination Sternes?'

'Yes, a charter. With a sick woman.'

The customs officer helped Kostas bring the lady out of the plane. She was wrapped in black, with most of her face hidden, in the old style. God, she was heavy enough to be dead. He helped her into Kostas's truck with its open, flat bedded back.

'You're sure she's going to be all right in that thing?' he asked. 'You should show more respect to your mother.'

'Respect? Didn't I spend my life's savings to bring her here by aeroplane . . .'

The customs officer was impressed. 'Take it easy over the roads,' he said. 'How far are you going?'

'Only to Xania.'

'Then do as I say, take it easy.'

Kostas drove to the beach of Chora Sfakion over the mountain tops. His 'mother' groaned once, but did not recover consciousness. Once in Chora Sfakion, he bundled her across his shoulder, and waded out into the surf to where the fishing caique was moored. An old man who could not sleep watched him from the window of the house above the Xenia Hotel. But nobody ever questioned the movements of Kostas.

Sophie woke up on a plain but comfortable bed. The room was windowless, but air smelled sweet and fresh. She saw a sprig of a flower she instantly recognized from her girlhood in Provence as wild thyme. She looked at the strange pattern of the bed-spread, the wall-coverings, and the strange shape of the bed itself. She turned her head. A man was sitting by her bedside, looking intently at her.

'I am Kostas Aronakis, Miss Sophie,' he said. 'You have nothing to fear, believe me. Welcome to Crete . . .'

All leave and off-duty time was cancelled for the Special Branch and the Flying Squad in London, and chosen men were brought in from the provincial police forces. For the most part, they moved quietly and unobtrusively in plain clothes through the Arab dominated districts of London, looking, always looking, and listening. The FBI and CIA contingent was the largest London had ever known; the Deuxième Bureau and French Special Force operatives numbered over two hundred. In among them all, Ben Moishe deployed ten of his hand-picked Mossad men, each of whom knew London well and spoke perfect English.

But then, Ben had the inside track. One of the civil servants helping to organize the meeting was also a former Russian Jew who had come to England as a newly born baby. His parents had been friends of Ben's parents by correspondence. Their grand-parents had been intimates in Moscow, Leningrad (as it was now called) and the czar's summer palace.

Through his contact, who was also an intimate of Dick Feather, Ben Moishe learned about the loss of the atomic warhead by the British, and the loss of a submarine by the French.

He was able to guess exactly what the meeting would be about.

Air Force One brought the President into Heathrow exactly on time. The President walked through to the VIP lounge in a wedge of FBI men; every rooftop, every vantage point for a rifle marksman carried a British police officer and an American agent. He held a short conference for the British press; the text had been released as his plane touched down, by teleprinter from the US Embassy to the P.A. and Reuters. The comps of Fleet Street were already setting the type, the editors were grumbling. It had all the key catch phrases; great honour to be invited by your Majestic Queen, Your fine old University, Your City of London whose much respected reputation spans many centuries of progress.

The Press Secretary also elicited groans when he made an announcement. 'These are the ground-rules, gentlemen. The President is here on a purely private visit. He feels it would be a dishonour to your Queen to engage in any political polemics. He will therefore make a prepared statement for the TV cameras and radio, and will answer three questions, submitted to me in advance, about the private nature of his visit. He will not answer any other questions.

At the first sign of any politics, he will leave the press conference. Is that clear?'

It was all too tediously clear.

After the prepared speech, the President left the terminal, was carried by bullet-proof car to the helicopter, and took off with an escort of three helicopters manned by police and FBI, to land on the Palace lawn. Few people, hearing the cavalcade overhead, bothered to look up.

The Frenchman arrived at Victoria Station aboard a special coach which had been clipped to the back of the Golden Arrow, the Flèche d'Or, operated jointly by British and French Railways.

At the end of the platform, he transferred to a Rolls Royce with tinted black windows, and was driven to the Palace.

Prince Charles had been waiting at Victoria to meet him, sitting in the back of the Rolls, which he did not leave. The car carried Prince Charles's personal coat of arms and pennant. Everyone assumed he was meeting a girl friend from France or Monaco but, since no one was allowed within a hundred yards, no one could be certain.

The Israeli Prime Minister landed at Stanstead Airport. He was driven by car to the outskirts of London where he transferred to a two decker bus painted silver in honour of the Queen's Jubilee. The top of the bus was open. Despite the weather, a group of variety artists, supplied by a theatrical agency, were sitting holding musical instruments. When they arrived in Lambeth, they started to play jazz, one of them wearing a bowler hat and an extravagantly striped shirt, and playing a clarinet. Everyone along the street swore he was Acker Bilk. He was the only man not supplied by the agency. Ben Moishe. He played a mean clarinet. The bus drove past Victoria Station, turned up Buckingham Palace Road. A group of German tourists cheered when it eventually turned, at the conclusion of 'When the Saints go Marching Home', into the Royal Mews. The Prime Minister of Israel, sitting in the downstairs part of the bus behind its Jubilee screened windows, had enjoyed the music.

The Prime Minister of England, seeing that it was a pleasant day, put on his deer-stalker hat, took a walking stick, and strode along Whitehall. Several people, recognizing him instantly, said 'How d'ye do, Prime Minister' as he turned into the park. He strolled beneath the trees, raised his hat civilly when greeted by ladies and appeared utterly relaxed. Everyone, he felt, would vote for the party of a Prime Minister they had actually seen. It would emphasize his Common Touch.

The ten Special Branch officers trying to be inconspicuous in a loose ring around him heaved sighs of relief when he entered the safety of the Palace gates.

The meeting had been arranged in a small but elegant drawing room on the ground floor, overlooking the Queen's extensive gardens. An Equerry greeted each one as they arrived, and showed them the Rose Room. A large, round table stood in the centre of the priceless carpet, and six chairs with tapestry seats and backs had been arranged round it. A Louis XV sideboard occupied one wall; on it were four telephones. Another telephone stood on a tambour table near a velvet covered arm-chair. Above the table hung a heavy crystal chandelier with elaborately chased electric 'candles' and crystal glass shades. The pictures on the walls included a Stubbs, two Gainsboroughs, a Millais.

The new Chef de Protocol— Sir Maurice Winfield was in hospital before premature retirement – had arranged for the circular table. He had not thought it expedient to afford the choleric Prime Minister of Israel any suggestion of suppliant seating.

In deference to the Queen, at whose home they were meeting, the Israeli Prime Minister wore a tie. Its effect, however, was spoiled by the fact that his shirt would not button at his throat.

The US President was the last to arrive, after his lunch with the Queen. In view of his subsequent meeting, the Queen had suggested the American might prefer to wear a lounge suit for the meal. Princes Philip and Charles had both worn them.

No one felt like asking him how it went. He felt, however, that he ought to make some appropriate comment.

'Your Queen,' he said to the British Prime Minister, 'puts on a meal fit for a king.'

The Israeli Prime Minister guffawed; even the French Premier permitted himself a smile.

'I'll be sure to tell Her Majesty the next time I see her,' the PM said. 'Now, gentlemen, if we could all be seated. I suggest that you, Mr Prime Minister, sit on my left here, between me and the US President. The President of France could then sit here, on my right, if he so wishes.'

It was a neat diplomatic gesture, to put the Israeli PM on the right hand side of the US President, and the French Premier on his own right hand side. Somehow it emphasized the 'special' nature of the relationship between the two English-speaking countries.

The Israeli seated himself first, waited until the others had taken their places, put his elbows on the table and his head mischievously between his hands, like a young schoolboy who knows he is due for a lecture from a fond uncle.

'What a clown,' the French Premier thought. He had been brought up in a wealthy family and had been involved in politics all his life. Above all things he had cultivated an air of seemly decorum in his public appearances; the sight of this *buffoon* behaving in this way was anathema to him.

The US President was amused. The British PM, like Queen Victoria, was decidedly *not*.

'Let's have it then,' Mueller said. 'This is a private meeting, right? No notes? Just a private talk between heads of government. So, what's it all about? And if you say it's about quitting the Occupied Territories, abandoning 242 in favour of 3236 and the Purple Pamphlet, or about the Holocaust Syndrome, let's start thinking again.'

The French Premier made a gesture, deferring to the Briton. The PM coughed. The US President was sitting back in his chair, relaxed, his finger-tips touching.

'One other man is coming to this meeting,' the PM said.

234

'His name is Frank Elks. He is the managing director of Bonds Merchant Bank in Threadneedle Street . . .'

'Bonds,' Mueller said, 'is owned by a Palestinian Front Organization run by a man called Ishmael Mohamed. He is known throughout the Middle East as Yshtak. Offices in Beirut, where he made his start. We have been on to this Yshtak for a couple of years though, since his break with Arafat, Kaddoumi, Labadi, and the so-called terrorist organization the PLO, he seems to have retired. Why have you brought me all this way to meet a man from Bonds . . . ?'

The Israeli PM was extremely angry, like a man who had stepped into the ring expecting an easy fight, and suddenly been given a jolt in the teeth by his opponent.

'Can you explain, James?' the President asked.

How do you tell a man that an atomic bomb and a submarine have been stolen, and that they could be aimed at his country? For an unspecified purpose. Rolf's face grew more and more grim as he listened to what the British PM had to say. When he had finished, there was silence. Each man considered the enormity of the situation, thinking not only in terms of the damage that could be done to Israel by an atomic bomb, but also the awesome possibility of a full-scale nuclear war.

Involuntarily, they all looked at the door to the adjacent lobby.

Behind that door, a young man waited, in the uniform of a US Marine. In his hands, chained to one wrist, he carried a box.

He was never very far from the President of the United States.

The contents of that box could start World War Three in a matter of seconds. The President looked around the room and saw the telephones on the elegant Louis XV sideboard. He rose from his seat murmuring, 'Excuse me, gentlemen,' then walked across to the telephone which carried the US Seal, picked up the instrument, and said three words into it. The code was received in the US Embassy Communications Centre in shocked silence, and, within seconds, were transmitted to Washington. Within minutes, the War Room, built into the bunker below the White House, was operational, under control of the Vice President, and the Joint Chiefs of Staff.

The signals flashed throughout the world, to atomic submarines lurking beneath the oceans for just such a call, to mountain tops across the USA, where missiles waited only for the final turn of a key to launch themselves at prepared targets.

Red Alert Three.

Three steps to the end of modern civilization.

The President came back to his chair and sat down. The rest of them sat there, stunned.

Big Brother had just shaken his fist.

When a telephone on the side table jangled, each of them leaped from his seat, so intense was the silence. 'That will be the man from Bonds,' the PM said. He went to the telephone. 'Bring the gentleman in,' he commanded crisply.

'Yes, let him come in,' Mueller snarled. 'Let's get the worst over.'

The man who entered was a round faced, Pickwickian character wearing the uniform of the City, a dark Savile Row suit, a white shirt, a Club tie. In his hands he carried a slim briefcase. A gold watch-chain dangled across his ample stomach. He was wearing a wafer-thin gold watch on a gold bracelet, and a gold signet ring on the little finger of his left hand. 'Good afternoon, gentlemen,' he said, as if addressing a selection board for a new flotation. The Prime Minister motioned for him to sit down. No one had left his seat. There was no need for the trappings of courtesy.

'You understand, gentlemen,' he said as he opened his briefcase, 'that I am only a courier in this matter, acting on behalf of a client . . .'

'Balls,' Mueller said. 'Cut out the spiel and come to the point.'

'Very well. I have a number of documents here with me, all in four copies. I shall be distributing them later. The first one, I am instructed to read. It is quite short.' He took a pair of rimless spectacles from his waistcoat pocket,

236

extracted one document from the briefcase which he put on the table by his side. He drew the document towards himself and began to read.

'We are in possession of a submarine vessel, formerly the property of the French Naval Authorities, a photograph of which is attached. I'll be distributing all this material later gentlemen. We are also in possession of an atomic device, formerly the property of the British government. Again a photograph is attached.

'We have joined these two devices together, and have removed the protective shield from within the atomic device, thus enlarging its effect by a considerable but unspecified amount. Not going too fast for you, am I, gentlemen?'

The man from Bonds was enjoying himself. How many men have been privileged to dictate to four heads of government at the same time?

'Get on with it,' Mueller growled. 'You've got the bomb, you've got the submarine, now what do you intend to do with them?'

'Aim them at Israel, naturally, Mister Prime Minister. In fact, they are *already* aimed at Israel.' He continued to read.

'We have aimed these devices at the shores of the state arbitrarily calling itself Israel. We shall start these devices on their path to total destruction, unless every Israeli citizen leaves the State of Israel. All out,' he added, no longer reading. 'All out.'

He sat back in his chair, took off his glasses and polished them. It was apparent he was enjoying himself hugely.

He reached forward and dipped his hands into his briefcase, coming out with a bound document that looked about two hundred pages thick.

'This, gentlemen, is a feasibility study that was done recently by computer. It tells you, if you care to read it, exactly how you can set about withdrawing everyone in the minimum time. It also makes certain suggestions as to where and how they might be relocated. You understand, gentlemen, this is only a *feasibility study*. The method you adopt, of course, is entirely up to you. What is *not* up to you, however, is the date of completion . . .'

'You're giving us five years?' Mueller asked, a cynical glint in his eye.

Mr Elks looked at his watch, as much to emphasize dramatic effect as to know the time. 'It is now 1500 hrs on the 25th. You have exactly one calendar month in which to carry out this total exodus.'

'Nonsense,' the Israeli shouted. '*Absolutely* impossible, even in one calendar year, let alone one month.'

Frank Elks was not perturbed. Still looking at his watch he said, with deadly quietness and composure. 'Unless the last Israeli has left the soil of the country known as Israel, at exactly 1500 hrs on the 25th of next month, a nuclear device will explode on its shores.'

He paused for a moment, looking specifically at each of them in turn. His face betrayed no emotion. He could have been announcing a date for the completion of the most banal company merger. He stood up, adjusted his waistcoat, extracted four envelopes from his briefcase and set them carefully on the table side by side. He then took off his spectacles, replaced them in his waistcoat pocket, and closed his briefcase.

'Just a moment,' the PM said. 'We have a few questions, no doubt . . .'

Frank Elks held up his hand. 'Questions are not necessary,' he said. 'Everything is contained in these envelopes. Acting purely as a courier, you'll understand that I've nothing to add. Personally, *I* don't mind *where* the Jews live! In fact, I might go so far, personally, as to say that some of my keenest business rivals . . .'

'Are Jewish.' Mueller said bitterly.

Frank Elks did, however, pause at the door. 'One thing I should add, gentlemen. The full text of what I have just said to you, plus the contents of the envelope, were released to the P.A. and Reuters at 1500 hrs exactly. In case you should try to embargo the story, it has also been released, at the same time, to *Al Ahram*, the German *Bild Zeitung*, the French *Le Canard Enchainé*, the London *Daily Express*, and the *Washington Post*. One other thing. I am instructed to tell you that if my freedom of movement is hampered in any way, the submarine and the bomb will be launched immediately.'

He gave a mocking half-bow, then turned and left the room.

The Prime Minister picked up the telephone. 'Yes, let him go,' he said. 'But keep him under surveillance.'

Then he joined the others in grabbing his envelope and tearing it open to examine its contents. One letter which seemed to carry the same text as Elks had read to them. And one bound volume, entitled, in gold lettering stamped on its title page, 'A Feasibility Study for the Evacuation of the Land known as Israel'.

'I think, Gentlemen,' he said, 'We should abandon this meeting, you to go to your embassies and me to my office, and meet again early this evening . . .'

'That doesn't give nearly enough time,' Rolf Mueller immediately protested.

'We don't *have* nearly enough time,' the British Prime Minister said.

It was, of course, the news story of the century, and the press made full use of the little they had to go on. Every news editor began making preparations, sending correspondents and teams of cameramen into Israel by the first available planes, chartering jets for the TV and radio networks.

The Israel Prime Minister was besieged when he returned to the Embassy. He gave one direction – to let all the world press come into Israel, as many as possible – before locking himself in the Ambassador's office. Short though the time had been, all the evening papers managed to re-set the front page to carry the ultimatum, and a brief summary of the text of the 'Feasibility Study'. The chief suggestion seemed to be that the United Nations be convened immediately; that countries offer to act as host to as many displaced Israelis as possible; that the World Bank finance the entire movement of people; that no one be allowed to take more than two suitcases full of material possessions; that the cash balances of all Israeli businesses be distributed, via the World Bank, to the shareholders; that each Israeli family be given a cash 'relocation allowance' to be decided by the World Bank, and the United Nations.

The countries most feasible for resettlement, the Study indicated, were Canada, America, Brazil, Peru, Australia, and New Zealand. No mention was made of South Africa, with its abundant territory, nor the vast unpopulated areas of Russia, or Uganda.

Reference was made to the Berlin Air Lift. If the first planes started taking off within four days, the evacuation could be completed within the time. Those who, for health and other reasons, could not fly, should be taken off by troopships of the Israeli and the US Mediterranean Fleets.

Those who could not, for health reasons, travel by *any* means, should simply be put to death.

Any attempt at vandalism, or destruction of remaining properties, installations, services, *could*, the report emphasized, be countered by the premature launching of the nuclear device.

On the question of religion, of access to Jerusalem, and other places considered sacred by the Jews, it was suggested that in the future limited *visas* would be issued, to permit any Jew to visit certain areas. Any attempt to interfere with future occupiers of formerly Jewish premises would be punished by immediate imprisonment and death.

In one particular, however, the world press failed.

Mr Frank Elks of Bonds Merchant Bank was, unaccountably, not available for comment. He was nowhere to be found. The Special Branch leaked the news that he had gone straight from the meeting to the airport at Gatwick where he had boarded a private jet with take-off clearance for Zurich. The plane had left England via the southern air corridor, had turned right, and disappeared somewhere over the Atlantic Ocean, out of reach of British radar. There had been no time to organize a British military jet pursuit.

CHAPTER TWENTY-ONE

'You go along to the restaurant,' Marc said to Phillipe. 'I'll join you later. Order a Ricard for me, eh?'

Phillipe left the office, descended in the lift, and stepped out into the quiet streets of the Croix Rouge. The late night crowds had thinned but he knew the Faisan d'Or would still be open, serving the delicious Lyonnaise cooking for which Ghuibert was justly famous among the connoisseurs, the cabaret artists, the theatrical people. He turned right and walked slowly down towards the crossing of the Boulevard St Germain-des-Prés. How this corner must have sparkled at night during the time of the Grand Epoch, when it was one of the two centres, with Montmartre, of La Vie Parisienne. Now the quarter was sordid, full of tourists trying to recapture the lost images of Hemingway, F. Scott Fitzgerald, Gertrude Stein. Merde, there was even le Drugstore . . .

And the place was full of drunks. One was squatting in a doorway ahead of him, a bundle of rags. A Citroen pulled up and several flics jumped out, crossed the pavement, and lifted the *merde* of an *ivrogne* upright. As Phillipe drew near, suddenly, the police were all about *him*. The drunk stood erect, came in fast and low, and before Phillipe knew what was happening, he had been bundled into the back of the Citroen, which was now being driven wildly down the Boulevard.

He was still fighting, still struggling gamely in the back of the truck. One of the flics grabbed his hair, bent his head forwards, and tapped him expertly with a truncheon below the ear. Phillipe collapsed on the bed of the truck in a heap as disorganized as that of the drunk in the doorway. The flics pulled out cigarettes, put their feet on him, and lit up.

'They said he was a tough bastard . . .' one of them commented. 'They should have been there the night we took

The Bear blind drunk out of Madame Thoreau's whore-house!'

Phillipe woke up with a splitting headache in a cell three metres square with an iron bed bolted to the floor and a plastic bucket without a handle, which nobody had bothered to empty. A warder placed a plastic bowl containing soup on the floor beside him, and a length of bread.

'Where am I?' Phillipe asked.

'Fresnes. Now shut up and eat your supper.'

Bill Harrington watched Sally Price as she frustratedly punched the buttons on her computer terminal. After her short stay in the London Clinic, it would have been difficult to detect anything wrong with her, except for a certain tightening around the eyes, a look of greater awareness. And sometimes she would sit there with tears in the corner of her eyes, and he would know she was remembering. He had not wanted her to come back to work so quickly, of course, but she had insisted. Then he realized it was better for her to be employed in the office with all hell breaking loose about their ears, than to sit back in her flat, brooding.

He walked across to her desk, read the print-out over her shoulders, put his arm across her back and hugged her.

'Oh dear, Bill,' she said from her deep frustration. 'If only we could be *doing* something, instead of punching these damn buttons.'

'We *are* doing something,' he said. 'Somebody has to be here punching the buttons. This is the modern age, Sally. The days of Erroll Flynn, dashing across the desert on a charger, are over. We've sent men to check all Yshtak's residences, with no result so far. Thanks to you and your bravery, we do at least know for sure it is Yshtak we're looking for. Ishmael Mohamed. Obviously he's gone to ground. The place in Ibiza was just another hideaway, from where he could make all his preparations. Among those preparations, eventually, we'll find some reference to another place. It won't be in his name, it'll be in the name, or the pseudonym, of one of his men: Andreas Burgler, Kostas Aronakis, Joseph Aram, Jacques Morel, Henri Dupree, Ahktar . . .'

'Or any other of the many men he seems able to command – like Frank Elks . . .'

'But, thanks to you, Sally, we do have that lead. Look, I can give you something positive to do. Wherever that other place may be, it would need a great deal of sophisticated equipment. If he's going to mastermind this whole Israeli business from there, including the movement of the sub, the Green Dolphin, he's going to need radio receivers, transmitters, computer hardware. With his international arrangements, he would be able to buy that stuff anywhere in the world. But it would need to be shipped to him. Somewhere he must have *received* all this stuff – he has most probably bribed the local Customs people to let it in, or he's established a phoney excuse. Most of the stuff would be paid for by local currency, from one of his Bonds-type organizations. Since these are pseudo-legitimate, they would use shipping agents. The shipping agents would have applied for export licences. Right, you can trace that line. Start with Bonds. Find out which shipping agents, if any, they use. They go through the file of export licences for material going to likely places.'

'Oh God, Bill,' she said. 'That'll take days.'

He tapped her terminal. 'Not with this, it won't,' he said.

He went back to his desk. He, too, felt irked and frustrated by his inability to do something positive, but was trying hard not to show it. He longed to be out there, doing something, but he had meant what he said to Sally. The days of Erroll Flynn were long gone. Anyway, what could he be doing? He had men in the field checking everything, looking for any trace of the wanted men. Not one of them had shown anywhere. He knew Marc Chantal had scoured the Mediterranean, so far as he was able, looking for the Green Dolphin and, by now, presumably, its attached atomic warhead.

This was no fool stunt, dreamed up by a local group of tear-arsed terrorists. This was total war, modern style. Yshtak had obviously planned this coup over a large number of years; his preparations would be complete and thorough. And he was rich enough to carry them out. He had suborned Fairclough, hadn't he? And Fairclough had fled the country before they could lay their hands on him. Frank Elks, the same. Well, they had Phillipe in Fresnes and, when the time was ripe, Marc would surely extract every ounce of information he could from him. Everything Yshtak did was cold, careful, calculated. Except, of course, his quixotic aid to Sally and Khaylia. Bill could even understand that. If a man had so disciplined himself to behave according to a set of rules, it must be tempting sometimes to break them. There had been an outcry, of course, from the press, when Sally came back. She had appeared in the Magistrates' Court at Marylebone, and had been remanded for trial, released on bail.

That had been a neat way of stifling the press. With the case sub-judice, the Law said they could write nothing about it. The Prime Minister had written a stiff, formal letter to the editors, explaining that enquiries were still going on, and excessive publicity would stifle those enquiries. The press alternately blessed and cursed him for the meeting he had held with them. At least, he said, he had tried to warn them *something* was afoot though, obviously, National Security considerations had prevented him taking them further into his confidence.

The case of Sally Price had been dropped quickly, the minute the story of Exodus 2 hit the front pages. Even the women's magazines who had previously hounded her for 'her personal story' had quickly switched to Israel.

Sally was on the telephone to Bonds. Bill turned on his extension and listened in. 'This is the switchboard operator at Phillips. You know, we make radios and TVs, all that sort of stuff. One of my bosses, a right bastard he is, has just told me to get hold of our export agents. I daren't ring back and tell him I've forgotten their names. But I know they're the same ones you use, because we got them from you. You wouldn't be a pal and help me out, would you?'

Switchboard operators the world over operate their own private club. 'We've got a few like that,' the girl at Bonds said. 'Get me this number, get me that. Export Agents. Want to do what I do, love, and keep your own book. Ah, here they are, Taller Hole – funny sort of name. Number – 097-6262.'

'Thanks a lot . . .'

'That's all right. Anytime . . .'

Bill clicked off, made the success sign with his thumb and forefinger. The red light told him his own telephone was ringing.

'Harrington.'

'Stewart, at C7. Got a funny sort of bird in here. A young-ish lad, sounds like a Dutchman. Won't give me any par-ticulars. Apparently, walked up to the commissionaire and asked to see one of the "political officers". I got him even-tually. Says the name he goes under is Dutch George.'

'Why should I be interested in him.'

'He's given me a reference. H.Ex.WD. I can't touch that stuff. And I can't understand how he could get hold of it. H.Ex.WD is your department!'

'Did he give you a number?'

'Matter of fact, he did. Hang on, I've written it down here.'

'Is it in the 7,000 range . . . ?'

'It is. What shall I do with him . . . ?'

'For Christ's sake, hang on to him, Stewart. And don't let anybody else near him.'

'You coming over?'

'I'm already half way there . . .'

They had put Dutch George in a small room off the Cabinet Office. The Sergeant Commissionaire who was sitting with him taught karate to several boys' clubs in the London suburbs. He had been an Army PT instructor before that.

Bill came into the room, nodded to thank him, and the PT instructor left.

Bill looked at the man calling himself Dutch George. The first thing he noticed was the suntan. George lived somewhere a lot further south than Amsterdam. He was a lithe, wiry man in his early thirties. It was a good job the sergeant had not needed to tackle him – George looked to Bill as if he could give an excellent account of himself.

'Bill Harrington,' he said, thrusting out his hand.

Dutch George shook it with a firm grip, looking steadily at Bill without a flinch.

'They all call me Dutch George,' he said. 'I may as well stick with that.'

'You have some means of identification?'

'Yes, I have. Here it is.' Dutch George took a piece of paper out of his tailored blazer pocket, and gave it to Bill who unfolded it. Written boldly across it was the reference H.Ex.WD.7007.

'This is only a number, George,' Bill said. 'A meaningless number.'

'Hardly meaningless. It made your Mr Stewart shit his pants when he saw it. It got you here in two minutes flat. Hardly meaningless. Anyway, to cut the cackle, I'll tell you where I saw that number. On the nose of a submarine . . .'

Bill felt a wave of relief flooding through him. 'You've seen a submarine?'

'I've not only seen it, Mr Harrington. I've got it. Look, I've been reading the papers, listening to the radio. We don't go in much for television where I live, but we're not peasants.'

'And where would that be, George?' Bill asked, with feigned casualness. His heart was pounding with excitement, like a fisherman who's just hooked a big one. Now he must play the line carefully, make damned sure this one didn't get away.

'There are things we have to talk about first.'

'I guessed there might be.'

George reached again inside his blazer pocket and produced a couple of photographs. He passed them to Bill. They were recognizable immediately. The Green Dolphin. This photograph, however, the first one he looked at, showed the Dolphin snout to be much longer than the ones he had seen. At least six inches.

The second photograph, obviously taken with an under-water flash, showed a pair of hands holding open a slit along the Dolphin's snout. In that slit a flat plate could be seen, with the reference H.Ex.WD. 7007 clearly visible.

With the slit held open, the Dolphin appeared to have broken into a horrible grin.

'I took those pictures yesterday,' George said. 'But I thought you might not believe me.' He dug into his pocket and produced a third photograph. It showed the masthead at the top of the front page of the *Daily Telegraph*, held next to the Dolphin's snout. 'We varnished the newspaper,' George explained. 'To keep it dry down there. We're working quite deep.'

'We, George?'

'I have an assistant. His name is Hans. If I don't keep in touch with him he has instructions to release the Dolphin. I reckon it has a mind of its own. And it doesn't take two guesses to know where it will go, if Hans chops the mooring . . .'

'You seem to have thought of everything, George.' Bill said. 'You've come, presumably, with a purpose. Would you care to tell me what that purpose is?'

'If I turn the Dolphin over to you, I lose a great deal of money,' George said. 'I won't tell you how, just yet. But I also leave myself wide open to prosecution. I have a good thing going where I live. It's not strictly legal. I'll need to give all the details for you to recover the Dolphin. Those details are going to cost you a lot of money. The way I figure it is this: the British government made the atomic warhead, so you're the ones most interested in recovering it. If you can get it back intact, you'll be able to paper over the whole affair of Exodus Two. Of course, you'll wind up, internationally, with a black eye, but that's better than a broken head. I reckon what I have to offer must be worth a lot of money to the British government.'

'How much money, George?'

'That's what we have to talk about, Mr Harrington, isn't it?' George said, with an impish smile on his face. 'And for a conversation as heavy as this one is likely to be, I guess we ought to include the Prime Minister, the Chancellor of the Exchequer, and the Chairman of the Bank of England.'

CHAPTER TWENTY-TWO

The wealth of apparatus that confronted Sophie would have been meaningless had she not had her training in Toulon. She studied each aspect of it with a scientist's interest, then turned to Kostas Aronakis. 'Jacques Morel designed that,' she said. 'I recognize his touch.'

Andreas Burgler switched on, waited a moment, and punched up the sonar programme for the Green Dolphin, on long-range. Again he saw the oval he knew represented the coast of Ibiza, with the bright spot in the centre. She looked at the screen, her interest aroused. 'May I?' she asked.

Andreas Burgler moved out of the operator's chair, and beckoned sardonically for her to sit down. She busied herself at the console. The picture on the screen changed to a wave-form. She punched other buttons until the wave-form became a straight horizontal line. Then she operated the buttons to bring back the oval. Now it was perfectly round, but the spot was still in the middle of it, considerably reduced in size, but increased in intensity. 'You weren't tuned correctly,' she said.

She punched buttons again. A number of figures appeared. She printed some of them out, fed others back into the computer.

'How do you access geographic details?' she asked.

Burgler smiled, leaned over her, inhaling her womanhood, and touched a couple of buttons. A geographic outline of the whole of the Mediterranean appeared on the screen.

He put his hand on her shoulder. She reached up her thumb and forefinger, handling his wrist as if it were something quite offensive, and removed it. 'If I want to be fondled,' she said, 'I'll choose someone who's had a bath recently, and brushed his teeth.'

Kostas guffawed. 'That's a smack in the eye for you,

boss!' he said. Burgler would have hit her had Yshtak not come into the control room. She bent over the keyboard, measuring angles and distances on the Mediterranean map, printing out coordinated details. She fed them back into the data base and the computer programme checked them, came up positive. She changed the picture again, back to the circle with the dot in the middle.

'You probably know that's the island of Ibiza in the Balearics,' she said to Yshtak, ignoring Burgler.

'Yes, we know that, Mlle Sophie.'

'What's the spot in the middle?' Burgler growled.

She switched off the apparatus. 'That's the Green Dolphin,' she said simply.

'We know that, too. But where the hell is it?'

'Somewhere, it would seem, between here and Ibiza. On a straight line coordinate. You've estimated its speed?'

'It isn't moving.'

'What?' she said, surprised. She swivelled the chair back again and reactivated the apparatus. When the spot reappeared, she checked its coordinates again. Then she waited exactly ten seconds on the computer digital clock and accessed once more. The coordinates had not changed. She performed the computer calculation again, just to make certain, but the coordinates still had not changed.

The Green Dolphin was immobile.

Then she went into a long series of operations, pulling information to the screen, printing some of it out, feeding some of it back in, cross referencing the print-outs with the figures she had already obtained. 'I can't understand it,' she said finally. 'The Dolphin is fully operational, reacting perfectly. It's on automatic ranger, heat, light and sound orientated. But something is holding it. All I can suppose is that it has found a large heat source, or light, or sound. But I don't see what it could be, at that depth. Whatever it is, the Dolphin is homed in on it and can't move away. Hang on a minute.' She went into an even more elaborate series of calculations. This time, the look of frustration on her face grew deeper and deeper. Finally she turned to them. 'The Dolphin is switched to automatic response,' she said, 'which means it would home in on heat, light or sound. But it isn't receiving any of those stimuli. At least. I can find no trace of them on its reactance mode. The automatic response is a transmission/reception transaction – you understand what I mean?'

'Not me,' Kostas said. 'Not one word!'

Yshtak nodded. 'I think I understand,' he said. 'The Dolphin puts out a signal; that signal goes to a lighted area, a heated area, or into a noise. The signal is received back, augmented, boosted by the energy source. It tries to achieve a maximum by going nearer and nearer to the energy . . .'

'That's it. With a peak, an over-ride at one metre.'

'And the signal is leaving the Dolphin . . .'

'Yes, that's the reason for the bright spot. But when the signal comes back, it has not been amplified. In other words . . .'

'No heat, light, or sound.'

'That's right.'

'Can you tell where the Dolphin is located?'

She switched off the apparatus again, swivelled the chair round, and crossed her arms. 'I could,' she said. 'But first of all, I need an explanation. The last thing I remember, I was going up in the lift of my apartment building. I was helping a little fat man with his parcels when the lights went out and the lift stopped. I felt a gentle stab in my thigh, and woke up here, with Kostas sitting by my bed. This isn't Toulon, unless you've gone to great trouble to disguise everything. The food I've been eating isn't French food. Where am I, Yshtak? And what the hell is happening? How did you come by all this?' She said, beckoning to the apparatus. 'And what are you doing with the Dolphin?'

'Tell us where it is,' Burgler snarled, grasping her shoulder again. 'Tell us where the Dolphin is, you bitch!'

She looked up at him. Her normally mild face had set into a hard mould her friends would have recognized. Sophie may appear easy going on the surface, they used to say, but if she loses her temper, watch out!

Her right hand, behind her, touched the switch of the apparatus and it sprang to life. Without needing to look at

250

the keyboard she punched two digits. A red light flashed. Her finger hovered over a button. 'Take your hand off me, you filthy Kraut,' she said. 'Or I'll wipe this data base cleaner than your stinking face . . .'

Burgler looked at the flashing red light. Yshtak knew what it meant. The data base was a magnetic tape on which millions of digits of information had been recorded. Just as a cassette can be wiped clean by the 'record' button, so could a data base, only much faster. Without that data base, without the information it contained, their entire scheme was lost.

Yshtak slammed the back of his hand across Burgler's mouth.

'Leave her alone, you fool,' he said, his voice a whiplash that cracked through the room. A line of blood trickled from the side of Burgler's lip. 'Mlle Sophie,' Yshtak said. 'I apologize on his behalf. Believe me, we mean you no personal harm. We need you. Your friend, Jacques Morel, needs you. Wherever the Dolphin may be, Jacques is trapped inside it. He may still be alive but until we recover the Dolphin, we shall never know.' His rich, melodious voice was believable and persuasive. 'If you wipe that data base clean, you pass a sentence of death on Jacques Morel. Would you, could you, do that?'

Kostas had told him her first question, when she had seen the apparatus, had been about Jacques Morel. 'I think she was fond of him, boss,' Kostas had said. Kostas knew about human feelings; too often he'd used them in the past to get what he wanted. Unlike Burgler, Kostas never resorted to violence; he was too much of a simple, pragmatic psychologist for that.

'I will do it,' she said. 'But only because of Jacques. Not that I share any of your points of view. I don't know what you want with the Dolphin, but I know it must be something evil. I want Jacques himself to tell me why he let himself become involved in such a mess. But I warn you, if that stinking animal comes anywhere near me, if he lays so much as one finger on me, I'll find a way to make a total mess of this operation. Don't forget, I helped design this baby. I could think of a hundred ways of destroying it, ways you'd never even dream of. So, until we get Jacques here, we have a truce, d'accord? I do what you want, and you do what I want. Keep that monkey off my back.'

'It's a deal,' Yshtak said. He held out his hand. Sophie hesitated and then she took it, clasped it in hers. 'Whatever you're doing, Yshtak,' she said with a woman's intuition, 'I know it's evil and wrong. I beg you to reconsider and to stop.'

Sophie had been incommunicado since her arrival. She had not heard a radio. If she had seen the Greek headlines, she would not have understood them.

'We have already gone too far to stop,' Yshtak said with simple faith and dignity, strong in the primitive belief that had nourished and inspired him since that unforgettable day in his mountain village.

'Where's Jacques Morel, Miss Sophie?' Kostas asked gently, seeing the emotion on Yshtak's face. 'Find Jacques Morel for us, eh?'

She turned and punched the buttons that put out the red light.

Burgler muttered something they did not hear and left the control room, slamming the door behind him. Sophie and the others ignored him. She punched up the circle with the dot in the centre of it. 'I can't estimate the range,' she said, 'while it is transmitting. But I can over-ride the automatic and switch it to another programme. When it comes near enough for our signals to be greater than the automatic responses, we'll be able to estimate the distance. Do you understand me?'

'Yes,' Yshtak said. 'Will you do it, please?'

'I'll need to write an alternative programme. That'll take some concentration. You could help by leaving me alone . . .'

'We have an agreement, Mlle Sophie?'

'Until Jacques Morel gets here, we have our agreement.'

They left her. Sophie sent the coded pulses to over-ride the automatic, programmed a set of coordinates that should start the Dolphin moving.

*

The Dolphin was confused.

It was receiving signals it could understand, weak though they may be. The signals gave it an order to move. But when it tried to move it was stopped almost immediately by something beyond its understanding.

It could not know, of course, because no one had told it, that it could not move because it was attached, by chain and rope, to the inside of that cave.

The cave was dark and no one was working there, so the Dolphin could *see* and *hear* nothing to tell it to stay where it was.

Meanwhile, it was receiving this command to go which its electronic brain and memory told it to obey.

But it could not obey. Every time it moved forward two metres, it was stopped. The current drifted it back two metres, then it started forward again.

Sophie was baffled. She had set up the transmission from the transponder. The transmission was accurate and contained a command to move towards the source of the instructions. The computer reacted momentarily to show that everything was happening, that the Dolphin had received the command to move and was obeying. But then the system instantly reverted to 'fail' and the Dolphin remained static.

She tuned the transponder again, as fine as was possible, ensuring maximum signal strength. Then she sent the signal, the command that was the equivalent of a frustrated and imperious call to a wayward child. Come *here*!

Hans was not a venal man, he kept telling himself, but he had worked the mine with George and surely that meant he had certain rights, didn't it? Now George had instructed him not to work the mine anymore. They were closing down! Jesus! What about the bonus Hans had coming? What about his dream of starting his own school somewhere, living a life of ease? And, let's face it, he deserved a bit of luxury.

George had said, before he left for London, 'Don't worry, Hans, I'll see you're all right.'

'What does all right mean?' Hans had asked, trying to pin him down, but George was a cautious devil, and hated being pushed.

'I don't know *exactly* what it means,' he said. 'And I won't know until I get back. So you'll just have to trust me.'

These devils who trusted nobody were always asking other people to trust *them*. Well, trust was all very well in the right place, food for fools in the wrong. And this was definitely the wrong place, Hans decided.

So, he began to think about insurance.

He took the school dinghy, a pair of bottles and a mask, and dived down into the cave. The Dolphin was still there, moving backwards and forwards towards the entrance, but securely held by the rope.

Hans had a plan. He would take the Dolphin to another cave he knew, about half a mile away, and moor it. Then, when George came back, he would be in a good position to negotiate. He knew George had gone to London to get money in connection with the Dolphin. But getting the money would depend on George having *possession* of the Dolphin.

Hans would sell George his knowledge of where the Dolphin was now hidden. For half of what George obtained in London.

It was only fair, wasn't it? After all, the Dolphin had found Hans, not George. He was only ensuring his rights.

He flippered round behind the Dolphin and was suddenly aghast. Good job he had come down – the nylon rope holding the submarine to the pitons was frayed three quarters of the way through. He would chain it, not rope it, when he got it to the other cave.

He took his knife from its sheath, slashed at the frayed part of the nylon, holding the end attached to the Dolphin in his left hand.

The rope was tough. Thank God, he thought, or it would have frayed through long ago.

He worked at the rope, slicing it strand by strand.

When it parted, the Dolphin pulled him towards the mouth of the cave.

'Steady,' he said, winding the nylon cord round his wrist.

The Dolphin had tasted liberty.

Its systems, thanks to the commands it was receiving from Sophie, across the ocean on Crete, were all set to 'go'.

'Whoa,' Hans said, flippering madly backwards to brake it.

The engines on the Dolphin were capable of developing the equivalent pull of a tractor. It pulled Hans out of the mouth of the cave, selecting the centre of the hole as it went.

Once it was clear of the rock face it started to turn gradually, Hans flippering madly to try to halt it. He glanced at the compass strapped to his wrist. The Dolphin was heading due east. He knew that ahead of him lay nothing but the eastern Mediterranean, limitless miles of deep ocean.

He unwound the cord from his wrist and stopped flippering, treading water. And painfully watched the Dolphin disappear into the opalescent green.

Sophie saw the print-out spewing from the platten and her senses tingled with excitement. She scanned the jumble of numbers, tapped a key to remove the information she no longer needed, leaving only the series of ever decreasing figures. Then she sat back, satisfied.

The Dolphin was obeying her. It was on its way.

She could not know, however, that Jacques Morel, perversely, had not *programmed* the Dolphin for Crete. He had been bringing it to Crete on manual over-ride, to overcome his 'taxi-driver' boredom.

The Dolphin, with its atomic warhead, was programmed direct for Israel.

CHAPTER TWENTY-THREE

At last, Bill Harrington could do something. The meeting with the Prime Minister, the Chancellor of the Exchequer, and the Governor of the Bank of England had yielded immediate results. The final negotiated figure of £20 million had been transferred to the bank in Zurich. Dutch George, with Bill as escort, had travelled to Zurich and received the money in the form of a bank draft. He had taken that draft, again escorted by Bill, to another bank and had deposited it.

The cashier did not even raise an eyebrow.

George had asked for a safety deposit box and into it had put the Certificate of Deposit. Immunity from prosecution had been more difficult to arrange. He had told them about his gold-mining operations. Spanish law said that anything found off the Coast of Spain under the surface of the ocean belonged to the State. Too many people had brought up precious amphorae and archaeological remains now that scuba diving was so extensive. They had suggested that George walk away from the gold mine, forget it ever existed. After all, with £20 million to his credit, he had no need of a mere million. They had agreed that the Spanish authorities would be notified of the mine as soon as the Dolphin had been removed.

Jules Lachard met them at Ibiza Airport. Plus the Director of Technical operations from the Harwell Centre.

A French salvage vessel was on its way from Marseilles, with a full crew. Marc Chantal came, for good measure, postponing his visit to Fresnes Prison.

Bill had diving experience, so had Jules Lachard. The Director of Technical Operations could not even swim, nor could Marc.

George kitted them out with neoprene wet-suits, masks, flippers, and bottles, as if they were students of his diving school. Hans came down with them. Though Bill had not been underwater for a couple of years, the technique quickly came back to him, the shallow surface breathing, the minimum of effort as he flippered his way downwards. George was wearing a light on his head, and had attached Bill to him by a length of thin cord. Jules Lachard and Hans were lashed together as they flippered over the side of George's rubber dinghy, moored off the rocks. Hans, too, wore a light. It was eight o'clock in the evening and the sun had gone down. Bill remembered previous night dives, the startled appearance of the many shoals of fish, whose size increased as they went further down. He remembered the brilliant colours of this exotic underwater world, the curious appearance of the creatures that clung to the rocks, the vivid growths of bright green and purple, pulsing with the motion of the water. Many, he knew, would sting viciously to protect their beauty, if you touched them with a naked hand.

The descent to the mouth of the cave took two minutes, going slowly, giving their bodies time to absorb the increased depth, maintaining the shallow breathing, ears popping as they adjusted to the greater pressure of water above them.

The mouth of the cave was wide, ringed by sharp rocks. The inside was black as pitch.

Bill felt a shiver of fear. He had never gone inside an underwater cave in his diving experience but had heard many stories of vicious creatures who lived there, giant moray eels, savage, enormous octopi that could strangle you with a tentacle as thick as your thigh. The rope between him and Dutch George tightened, but he swallowed his fear and followed him inside.

George's headlight bounced off the naked seam of gold, sending a flash across the vast underwater cavern.

A hugh mero glided past them, brushing Bill's arm as it went. He saw the myriad lobsters on the walls and the roof, the crayfish whose eyes glistened at him. His skin crawled, but he followed the tug of the rope.

George led Bill to the piton that had been hammered into the rock wall. From it hung two metres of nylon rope, the end hopelessly frayed.

George stretched out the rope, showing where the frayed end touched a sharp tooth of rock.

The Dolphin had gone.

The people of Israel had been stunned by the first announcements in the world press. Work in their country had virtually come to a standstill. During those first few hours while the Prime Minister was locked in the Israeli Embassy in London, there had been a radio silence over the whole country. But many people had tuned in to foreign stations, all of which gave the news full coverage. The Arab stations were, without exception, jubilant, and the news poured out of them. The first crowds began to gather in the Dizengoff in Tel Aviv. The Wailing Wall of Jerusalem was thronged with people, all waiting their turn for religious expression.

The Knesset went into immediate session though, without the Prime Minister, there was little that could be said other than to hear denunciations of the activities of the terrorists.

Ben Gurion Airport was immediately jammed with people, trying to get a booking on a plane, anywhere.

Lorries began leaving the remote kibbutzim, heading for Tel Aviv and Jerusalem. People walked along the roads when they became jammed with transports. They moved slowly, without much talking, looking to the far city.

Boats leaving Haifa and Jaffa were full within a couple of hours of the broadcast.

The Deputy Prime Minister went onto the radio at last, and made an announcement. 'My people,' he said. 'We must remain calm. Our Prime Minister, Rolf Mueller, is in England at this moment, and will soon be having a further meeting with the British, the American, and the French leaders. Our United Nations Ambassador has called for an immediate session of the Security Council of the United Nations, to condemn the actions and ultimata of these terrorists. These men, whoever they are, will not, cannot, carry out their threats. They are being hunted by the forces of the civilized world and, wherever they may be, they will be dug out like rats in a nest. Meanwhile, here in Israel we must remain calm. We must remember that the eyes of the world are once again upon us. I urge you all to return to your homes, to switch on your radios, and wait for the news that will be broadcast to you the minute it arrives . . .'

The Israeli War Cabinet met in an atmosphere similar to that which preceded the raid on Entebbe. The Chief of Staff, General Mordecai Rosen, took immediate charge.

'In the absence of the Prime Minister, I think we should take a leaf from the terrorists' book, and work out a feasibility plan of our own. Not for the evacuation of Israel, but for its defence. Normally we know from where the threat comes; we can estimate the size of the problem and work out a counter-offensive. This time, we have a known enemy, but we don't know where they are located. The force arraigned against us is simple to estimate. An atomic warhead on an undetectable sub. The bomb will blast apart everything and everybody within a vast, but unknown, area. We don't have the information to talk about counter-attacks, let alone plan them. The Mossad is working world-wide and under full pressure to try to get that information for us. They have one brief, find the bastards, so that we can annihilate them!'

Mort Backhaus, Chief of Naval Operations, was the first to answer. 'We could lay down a curtain of explosives – depth charges with proximity fuses, stretched all the way along the coast-line.'

'Two objections,' Mordecai Rosen said immediately. 'Firstly, we'd need to put down a net with a mine every few hundred yards, horizontally and vertically. We don't have, and can't manufacture in the time, anything like enough depth charges, or fuses. Secondly, and this is only a guess of course, if this damn thing doesn't react to sonar, how can we expect it to react to a proximity fuse? But don't let me shoot it down out of hand. Have someone in your office prepare a scheme and we'll consider it. Gentlemen, at this moment in time, we'll consider anything.'

'Have we sufficient steel mesh, fishing nets, any kind of

nets, to hang a curtain round Tel Aviv and Haifa?' Moses Chaiman, Commander, Israeli Air Force, suggested. At the moment he saw no way his planes could be used.

'I don't know,' Mordecai said. He turned to Colonel Weitz, his aide. 'That's something you might get Ordnance to check out, Bill.'

Mort Backhaus was shaking his head. 'Won't work, Mordecai. How do you imagine this thing will be exploded? Either by contact, or by proximity, like my fuses. It hits the net, it explodes. The effect would still be felt on shore. I was going to drop my depth charges fifty miles off shore.'

They batted ideas about for three hours. Some were straight out of Wells, *War of the Worlds*, or *Star Trek*. Any that had even the slightest grain of possibility, Mordecai gave to someone to investigate further. At the end of the three hours they were all agreed on one thing; whoever had thought out the scheme had done so with demonic simplicity and ingenuity. As the meeting broke up, each one of them knew, in his heart, that unless the Mossad could find the atomic submarine in its home pen, there was nothing effective that could be done.

A meeting of the Civil Defence Committee took place at the same time. It was chaired by Abraham Sofair, the mayor of Tel Aviv, and convened in the Civil Defence Headquarters in Jerusalem. This meeting was larger; all the mayors of the major towns of Israel had been hurriedly summoned, plus elected representatives of the larger kibbutzim. The Chairman looked out over the hundred strong audience. 'We're going to need some discipline here,' was his opening announcement. 'I'd like to open, then throw the discussion out into the hall for comments. We can't have everybody talking at once, so if you'll raise your hands if you want to speak, I'll signal to you in turn. Okay?'

There was silence. 'Thanks for that,' he said. 'Okay, no warm up, no opening remarks. You've all heard the broadcasts, you know what the score is. Either we do as these bastards tell us, we leave Israel for points unknown, or by everything that's in us, we fight to stay here. That's going to take a lot of planning. But first, let's find out what we're up against. If we decide to go, the method is easy. Why waste our time replanning something that's already been planned for us by our benefactors . . . ? If we stay, what do we do? My immediate thought is that we move everybody out of the danger area, away from the coastline. We can put up camps all along the West Bank of the Jordan – that's a long way from the coast. We can send people down into the Sinai, down to Eilat. Feeding the people when we get them there becomes the immediate problem. One thing is for sure, none of our neighbours is going to volunteer to give us food. We could ask the US Sixth Fleet to anchor out of bomb blast distance and give us a flying shuttle service for essentials. We don't know what the condition of the water is going to be like after the bomb goes off. We'll need to move desalination plants into the areas where we put the people. We're going to need medical facilities, lavatory and toilet arrangements . . .'

He paused for breath. Jacob Fein, Mayor of Nablus, immediately shot up his hand.

'Okay, Jacob, you take over . . .'

'I am not a coward,' Jacob said. The meeting growled its approval. Jacob was six feet tall, a heavily built man with a strong beard and hard eyes, a Reserve Parachute Major, a renowned *fedayeen* stalker and killer in the early days of the kibbutz. Now he was fifty years old, but still a bull of a man. No, whatever he might be, Jacob Fein was not, most assuredly not, a coward.

'Nor am I a fool!' he shouted.

Again they growled approval.

'I am a realist. Once we move away from the coast, we will never come back without fighting our way across every inch of ground. The minute we leave our hectare of coast, the Arabs will occupy it, pillage it, devastate everything we have spent blood and lives to create. All right; place our camps on the West Bank of the Jordan or at Eilat, provide them with sweet water and toilet facilities. But leave our men behind, fully armed, fully supported by the military, to protect what we have built on the coastline . . .'

There was a half-hearted cheer of approval. The terrorists had been specific. Any delay, any sign the Israelis were not complying completely with the instruction to quit, and the bomb would be launched. The men who volunteered to stay would, almost certainly, be volunteering to die a horrible, atom-blasted death.

The representative of the kibbutz at Yentas thrust his hand in the air and was recognized. 'We have our own atomic capability,' he shouted. 'We have the planes, bombers and fighters to support them. Why don't we orbit Damascus, Cairo, Amman, why don't we orbit all the Arab capitals with our fighter protected bombers. And then tell them they must bring these terrorists to us, with their atomic submarine, or we will devastate all their capitals. Must we ignore a thousand years of history, a century of struggle and fighting and suffering, to be put to flight once again by the threat of yet another holocaust. If they want a holocaust, let's give them one the likes of which they've never dreamed.'

That broke up the meeting into individual shouting, wild counter-suggestions, demands, even personal antagonism and the threat of blows. Abraham Sofair had come prepared. By his seat was an Uzzi automatic rifle. He pointed it to the floor of the platform on which he was sitting, and pulled the trigger. The harsh staccato sound of the gun reverberated through the hall and quickly brought them all to silence.

'We'll pass your suggestion,' he said mildly, when they had all quietened down, 'to the military. Though I imagine they have already considered such a project and, so far as we know, may be actively planning it. Our concern, gentlemen, if I may so remind you, is for the *safety* of the *people*.'

He had noticed one group in the front of the hall conferring together in whispers. 'Jaime Costello,' he said. 'If you or your party have anything to say, please say it out loud to the meeting.'

Jaime stood up, though he was not an impressive figure, as Jacob had been. Jaime had been born in the slums of Genoa of a Spanish Jewish mother his Italian father had met on a building contract in Madrid. A youth of slum living had left its mark on him. He was barely five feet four, with thin, wasted shoulders. Time in Israel had put some flesh on his emaciated frame, but not enough to eradicate his past.

'We say go!' he said. 'Not from fear, not from cowardice. But from the certain knowledge of the inevitable. Here, we cannot survive. Israel has been a dream. Now we must waken to reality. What has recently happened in Germany should have taught us a lesson. If an established society such as the Germans cannot successfully oppose the modern wave of terrorism, how can we hope to do so? We have been given an opportunity to start life in new lands. Israel will be carried with us wherever we go. Instead of one Israel, we will found a hundred, in America, in Canada, in Brazil. There we shall be safe. There, we can begin to live again!' He spoke without rhetoric, without raising his voice, yet everyone heard him clearly, and possibly because of the lack of artifice or drama in the way he spoke, everyone fell silent, listening to him, taking in his words and their meaning.

It had been a dream, hadn't it? The Promised Land for the Chosen People.

The atomic submarine was the reality.

Abraham Sofair was silent with the rest of them. 'If we shall forget thee, O Jerusalem,' he whispered to himself, into that silence . . .

He felt the hot tears spring unbidden to his eyes.

To go into a strange land. To become, once again, an alien in a foreign world, a minority. He was not worried about the task of starting life over again. He was strong, he had a skill with mathematics and with figures. He could always earn a living, support his wife and his three children.

But, never to see Jerusalem again, except with a visa in his pocket and permission granted by the occupiers of his country to stay for a day, an hour. Never to walk again through the sand-dunes of Natanya with his children, to travel the crazy little train to Jerusalem, to visit Bethlehem, to show his kids where Solomon had his mines. Never to walk down the Dizengoff again on the eve of Shabbat, or eat on a terrace in Jaffa.

He brushed the tears from his eyes. 'We can make no decisions here. To stay or to go will be a matter for each one of us. Our sole concern is for the safety of the people. Can we please concentrate our minds on that one, single principle? What can we do to save the lives of those who decide to remain . . . ?'

The door of Phillipe's cell opened slowly and the man who stood there wore the white coat of a doctor, and glasses.

The guard stood behind him, trying to look past. 'I wish you'd let me go in first, Doctor,' he said. 'He has a reputation for violence.'

'No need. If he ate his supper he won't know anything for six hours at least.'

He walked to the side of the bed on which Phillipe lay beneath one rough blanket. He had not undressed. Nor, from the smell of him, had he washed for a few days. The doctor's nose wrinkled as he turned Phillipe over on his chest, putting his head sideways so that his breathing would not be hindered. 'Something wrong with the ones who don't wash,' he thought. Every day when he himself had been a prisoner-of-war, taken in 1940 when a young pre-medical student, he had sought out even a cupful of water with which to cleanse himself. Somehow, it had seemed to give him renewed hope each time he felt himself clean.

He pulled off Phillipe's shirt, exposing his muscular back. He pinched a handful of the thick skin and grunted with satisfaction. He used Phillipe's arms to estimate the extent of his reach; there's always one tiny area between the shoulders a man cannot scratch for himself, either from above or below. He washed it with alcohol.

He sat on the bed beside Phillipe, and opened his instrument case. From it he took a clamp with which he puckered a portion of Phillipe's flesh and skin. Using a razor sharp scalpel, he made an insertion in the skin and the fatty tissue beneath. He inserted the scalpel into this slit and used it to expand the size of the pocket he'd cut in the flesh. He took an envelope from his case and from it extracted a glassine packet. Inside it, floating in liquid, was a pink disc a quarter of an inch round, and an eighth of an inch thick. He slipped the disc from the glassine packet, using tweezers, held it in the air and allowed it to dry. Then he rinsed it in the small amount of blood that had come from his incision, and slipped it into the hole in Phillipe's back. He dried the incision he had made, washed it again with a sterilizing liquid, then sprayed it with liquid skin. When he took off the clamp, nothing could be seen.

Throughout the world, government and non-government groups were meeting in emergency session. The Jewish Aid and Relief Societies, the Friends of Israel Groups, talked with each other by telephone. All agreed that the most urgent demand was for transportation. They immediately chartered every plane, British Airways, British Caledonian, Dan Air, and Laker could spare. Lufthansa, Condor, Air France, Sabena, SAS, KLM, all provided a quota, all, by agreement, cutting their charges to operating costs only.

The Italian Parliament, meeting in emergency session at the Quirinale, offered to take as many Israelis as wanted to come to the south of Italy, abandoned largely by the Italian people themselves in favour of the industrial cities, Milan, Turin, in the north. Alitalia would fly them all, without any charge. They pointed to the many abandoned villages which could rapidly be brought back into occupation by a nation as industrious as the Israelis had proved themselves to be. Even the Italian Communists voted for the Resolution.

Members of the European Parliament, meeting in Strasbourg, passed a resolution of their own, and then adjourned briefly to give members time to communicate with National Governments. The Resolution said that Israelis arriving in any country should be given a 6-months resident status provided they could produce one sponsor. Others should be given a renewable visa of one month before moving on to the resettlement areas as soon as they could be designated and prepared.

The United Nations went into Assembly. The pro-Arab faction proposed a motion demanding that the PLO be recognized and included. With the aid of the Third World countries and the Eastern bloc, though Russia abstained, the motion was tabled for immediate debate. The Secretary-General peremptorily suspended the meeting, adjourned *sine die*. He then arranged another meeting, this time in the ballroom of the Waldorf Astoria, by invitation only. It excluded the Arab and Third World countries, and the Eastern bloc, with Russia. The ballroom was set up for a 100-dollar plate dinner in support of Jake Monaby for Mayor. The members agreed to leave the place settings undisturbed, and not to smoke. All member nations offered support for the Israelis, pledging money and facilities to fly them from Israel and house them in temporary accommodation. A national levy was agreed, based on the country's contribution to the support of the United Nations. A short Resolution was passed, condemning the actions of the terrorists, whatever nationality they may be. The resolution was paper-hanging; it would do nothing to strengthen the walls of that tottering edifice, the United Nations itself.

The Secretary General and Mike Hapgood, the US Ambassador, walked out of the meeting together. 'We can lick this one,' Mike said. 'Not for publication, you understand, but it would be darn good not to have a Middle-East problem any more . . .'

'We still have one major problem,' the Secretary General said. 'How on earth do we persuade the Israelis to leave?'

The Prime Minister of Israel was in the strongest fighting mood of his life when the meeting re-convened at half past six that evening.

'I can't speak for my people,' he said, 'but one thing I can say for sure. We're not going to leave. Not all of us. It won't be the first time the Jews have chosen to stay and die, rather than be shuffled about the face of the earth. A lot of them could have come out of the ghettoes if they'd chosen. But they preferred to remain and face the Germans, the Polish, the Russian butchers. Well, we know what happened to them. So maybe it's going to happen again. But this time, instead of the slow murder by starvation and torture, with the quicker ending in the gas chamber, this time, it's going to be one damn quick bang, all together. This much I can tell you. When that bang comes, when those of us who remain see that mushroom-shaped cloud over our sky, rolling across the fields we have cultivated, planted, and made fertile, when we smell that poisonous atomic vapour we know will rot our bones and dry our blood, we shall turn our eyes to Jerusalem and we shall sing. And that song will be an echo in the hearts and minds of men for thousands of years to come.'

Even in the face of his determination, none of them could offer anything positive. Only urgings and recommendations.

'They will look to you, Rolf,' the US President said. 'They will look to you for leadership and guidance out of this wilderness. Think carefully before you lead them all into death, and destruction. It is in the nature of man to be strong or weak. You are strong, Rolf. Sometimes, the strong can lend their strength to the weak and lead them. Sometimes, they must. But don't use your strength, I urge you, to lead the weak to an unwanted death. Let each man choose for himself, freely and without fear of contumely. Let no man in your country castigate any other for his decisions. Some may choose death, some may choose life. From fear, from cowardice, from weakness. Do not make them suffer additionally because of that. Death contains its own solutions to all problems, all heart-ache, all misery. Those who live on, must also live with their own consciences. Don't make that life unbearably burdensome to them. I beg of you.'

What the President had said cut across everything Rolf Mueller believed. Why was a man given strength if not to use it to support the weak, if not to fight for the weak, to crush opposition and, when that failed, to go to death with head high?

'I'll try, Mr President,' he said. 'But I cannot promise I will succeed.'

'You *can* succeed, Rolf,' the President said. 'You have the strength to succeed. For that, you must use it, not to lead men blindly to death. Let me tell you this. Any of your people who choose to come to my country, will immediately be granted full rights of citizenship. I pledge myself to that. Your people can be happy in the United States of America. We will find employment for them all. All the aid we give your country each year will continue, but now it will be used for their resettlement into happy, free, and useful lives, removed from the fears of constant war, of death at the hands of the Arabs, of mutilation. Come with them; lead them here, Rolf. *This* can and will be their Promised Land. Your Promised Land.'

'And, if I forget thee, O Jerusalem . . . ?'

'Build a new Jerusalem, here. Build it with care and love, with effort and industry, with freedom from war and the cries of happy children.'

Rolf Mueller knew he could never make any non-Jew realize even one small part of the pull of the Holy Land for all Jews, everywhere. No need to dip into the Torah, to wear a yarmulka, to light the candles on the eve of Shabbat. No need to train your hair to fall round your ears in ringlets because you had taken a vow never to touch it with metal of scissors or razor. No need to stand at the Western Wall, and to beat your breast in anguish. It was as if the heart of a Jew contained a magnetized needle that pulled him, always, to the pole of Jerusalem, wherever he may be. It was as if the blood of a Jew were thin, without salt, except in the Holy Land. It was as if the souls of all Jews, wherever they may be, were in Jerusalem, waiting only for the arrival of the body from the distant land to join with it, and make the man whole.

'I'll try, Mr President,' he said. 'Believe me, by all that I believe in, I *will* try.'

A British military jet flew the Israeli Prime Minister home at 1200 miles per hour, and even then it seemed to him they dawdled through the sky. The airport gave them a stacking time of at least two hours; the skies above Lod were thick with planes at all altitudes, one landing, one taking off, at two minute intervals. When the radio operator told airport control who was on board, they gave the military jet an immediate landing pattern.

'Bring him in safe,' the tower operator said. 'But bring him in fast. We need him down here.'

'Sorry I couldn't give you advance notice,' the skipper said, 'but you never know who's listening these days.'

They landed on the eastern runway, parachute streaming behind them to brake their forward dash. As the plane turned at the end of the runway, an armoured car came across the field towards them, with Mordecai Rosen at the controls. 'Did you ask for a taxi, Rolf?' he asked. Neither laughed at the joke.

'War Cabinet first,' Mueller said. 'Then the Knesset.'

Mordecai was looking sideways at him as he drove. 'What's your decision?' he asked softly. 'Do we stay, or do we go?'

Rolf had had time to think during the plane ride. 'It's an individual choice, Mordecai,' he said. 'From the look of this airport, some of them have already chosen for themselves.'

Mordecai dismissed the airport crowds with a wave of his hands. 'Whenever water comes to the boil, you'll find some kind of scum on the top of it,' he said.

'Call it steam, call it froth, Mordecai, eh? It's bad for them, too, don't forget. No man can have self-respect after he's tucked his tail between his legs and run. Have a little understanding and charity, Mordecai!'

'What happened to Rolf Mueller, man of iron, back there in London? Don't tell me you've joined the runners?'

'I don't know, Mordecai, I truly don't know. Yes, in a way, I do know part of it. I haven't sympathized with the rabbits who are running without knowing where the footfall comes from. No, I haven't joined them. But there's sense and logic in it; I think it is perhaps time we listened to some of that logic. That's why I want to hear the War Cabinet tell me there's nothing we can do . . .'

'I can tell you that. The only thing we could do is to take our own nuclear bomb and hang it in the air over the Arab capitals . . .'

'You've thought of that one, eh?'

'Everybody immediately thought of that one. It's part of our Israeli training. If anyone threatens you, threaten them with something bigger. But it won't work. You know how the Arabs are armed. Air to air, ground to air, they could knock us out of the sky before we crossed the borders. We've already been inundated with reports from our people in the field – every damned missile the Arabs own is ready to go, the minute they get a target. Where's Ben Moishe? I personally put more faith in him than in nuclear threats.'

'You don't expect me to know where Ben is?' Rolf said with the first trace of a smile. 'You won't believe this, but the last time I saw Ben, he was standing on the top of a London bus, with a clarinet in his mouth.'

The door of Phillipe's cell opened and the warder stood there. Not the old one, who worked days, but the younger one who brought his supper of soup and bread, and his breakfast of coffee and bread. Phillipe stroked the growth of beard on his chin, sitting back on his bolted bed.

'Hello, Sunshine,' he said. 'Come to make sure I'm still alive? That I haven't hanged myself with the sheets?'

'Save us all a lot of trouble if you'd do us that favour,' the warder said. 'Get up and follow me.'

'Where are we going?'

'Don't ask questions. And behave yourself. Or I'll break your arm. They told me you'd trained and you were tough. Nothing I'd like better than to take you on . . .'

He went out of the cell, stood with his back to the door opening in the corridor. Phillipe moved quickly but the second warder moved faster. He was standing beside the door, out of sight. The stick in his hand crashed across Phillipe's spine, as the first warder moved to the side, propelling him face forward into the wall.

When he got to his feet, both warders were grinning at him.

'See what I mean, pederast?' the first warder said. 'Behave yourself.'

One behind, one in front, they took him down the corridor past closed steel doors. Up the flight of stairs at the end. The grille at the top was locked, and the first warder rattled it with his stick. Another warder came to open it, without speaking.

Along another corridor, through two more grille doors.

When they emerged into the court-yard, the autumn sunshine dazzled Phillipe's eyes. The warder behind pushed him, sprawling, into the back of a parked grey Citroen wagon, then climbed in beside him. He took a handcuff, snapped it round Phillipe's wrist, and clipped the other cuff to a wooden pole that went from the floor to the roof of the van, held in metal sockets, like the end of a curtain rod.

Phillipe could neither stand, nor sit, nor squat comfortably. So he lay down on the floor.

The van started; the guard took out a Gauloise and lit it. He made no attempt to offer one to Phillipe, and Phillipe had no intention of risking a kick by asking for one. The grille that led from the back of the cab to the driver's cabin was open. After a half an hour of driving, Phillipe saw they were passing through trees in some sort of forest.

Lying on the floor, he felt the truck begin to swerve from side to side even before the driver did. Soon, however, the driver could hold the wheel no longer. He braked the truck and stopped at the side of the asphalt road through the forest.

'Damn,' he said to the other guard, sitting beside him. 'I think we've got a puncture . . . Merde!'

He climbed out of the driving seat and went round checking the tyres. One of the front ones was flat.

The driver and the warder in the front took out the jack and the spare and started working on it. The warder with Phillipe looked at him, then dropped out of the back of the truck, leaving the door open, and stood chatting, watching them. 'Don't just stand there,' the driver said after a few minutes. 'Give me a hand with this spare.'

Phillipe had climbed slowly to his feet, and was crouching around the wooden pole. An inch and a quarter thick. Seemed to be made of some sort of oak. He lifted it; half an inch of play in the bottom socket. He looked up at the roof. The wooden pole was not secured to the sockets, only standing in them. He lay back on the floor, lifted his legs up in the air, touched his feet on the roof of the truck. Then he pressed his shoulders down and his feet upwards, slowly. The roof of the truck buckled. One hand held the rod, and pushed upwards as the roof went further and further. He was sweating profusely; the driver seemed to have put the wheel on and was now beginning to tighten the nuts. The pole slipped suddenly clear of the lower socket. Phillipe pulled it to one side, brought his feet down again. Quickly, he slipped the cuff down the pole, tucked its end under the link round his wrist. He heard the warder coming back, and crouched on the floor facing the back, holding the pole upright. The warder appeared round the door, and as he was off guard, climbing into the back of the truck, Phillipe brought the pole down on the top of his head, drew it back then rammed it forward against the warder's throat. The man fell backwards, gasping, tripping over his own legs. Phillipe jumped, saw him reaching for his gun, but ran zig-zagging towards the trees at the side of the road. He heard the driver shout; seconds later the bullets were zipping round his head. He kept on zig-zagging and running, bent almost double, coursing like a hare for the shelter and protection of the trees. Once inside them, he knew he would be safe.

He leaped the last few metres and rolled, coming up behind the trunk of a thick chestnut, amazed to find the stick still in his hands. He held on to it and struck into the wood at a narrow angle with the road, guessing they would expect him to make an immediate deep penetration. When he had gone a hundred yards or so, he burrowed into a bush. Sure enough, he could hear them behind him and to his left, going deeper into the woods.

They had left the truck with the key in. Three minutes

later he was driving it along the road, humming softly to himself.

The 'Think Tank', official name: The President's Committee for Research into Possibilities, had for once been given a simple brief before going into benzedrine-aided night and day sessions. They had researched the effect of the drug on a man's concentration, his ability to 'think deep', and had found both unimpaired for durations of up to 72 hours. After that, the mind suffered a rapid and disastrous deterioration. They did not believe this problem would take 72 hours. The brief was as follows:

    (a) What happens in general if the Israelis leave Israel?
    (b) What happens in general if the Israelis do not leave Israel?
    (c) From a point of view of world political stability, is (a) to be preferred to (b)?
    (d) What is deemed preferable?

Antal Kreiter, former Professor of Applied Logic at the University of Texas at Austin, took the answers, after only 60 hours, direct to the President.

'The full text is being typed and mimeographed right now, Mr President,' he said. 'You know, one of these days we're just going to have to sit down and work out a way of typing by speech. You'll have the full text very shortly but, in view of the urgency, I thought you'd better have a summary in advance.'

The President liked summaries; he also liked to see all the documentation, too. But the summary was something he could work on to clarify his thoughts on issues, before getting down to factual matters in detail.

'Right, Antal, let me have it.'

He put his fingers together and closed his eyes, settling back in his deep swivel chair. In that posture, he looked as if he were taking a nap. His favourite 'committee' technique, it permitted him to close his mind to extraneous matter and concentrate on essentials – the detail in the report, the nuances in the spoken word.

'Since some documentation was involved,' Antal said in

his eager scientist's voice, 'we checked that out first. I don't know who composed this feasibility study, though I would guess it was an American company. Certainly, whoever did it made a good job of it. I might go so far as to say it's impeccable. We've put it through our computer forwards and backwards, and it will work. That leaves me able to answer immediately, question (d) part one. If your original premise, (a), is preferred in question (c), then this feasibility study shows the best method of achieving it.

'If the Israelis leave Israel, that study tells us how to set it up, right?'

'Right, Mr President. Now, a summary of (a). If the Israelis leave Israel, they disperse throughout the world, conferring great benefits on some of the communities they join, like the southern Italian or the Brazilian. And creating small community problems which time will solve, in others, such as the USA and Canada. The PLO *and* the Arabs occupy Israel. They do not agree on points of detail, and, within a predicted ten years, we will have a mini-Middle East war in which the Syrians massacre the Palestinians and annexe the country. They will also annexe a considerable portion of Jordan, and Hussein – deposed, most probably murdered. Sadat will have disappeared from the Egyptian scene within a couple of years, anyway, and the Syrians will occupy the whole of Sinai. They will annexe the Suez Canal and Egypt will not be able to resist them. Thus, for a considerable number of years, there will be border disputes between Egypt and Syria, similar to those between Somalia and Ethiopia.'

'In other words, the Middle East will still be a crucible of Arab/Arab rivalries, but the possibilities of world war, provoked by the presence in their midst of the Israelis, will be removed.'

'That's about it, Mr President.'

'And what happens if they don't leave?'

'Cataclysm, Mr President. Holocaust. The Israelis will make all sorts of moves to buy time; the Mossad will look for this sub fruitlessly. Taking into account the French estimate of the success of this Dolphin device, we do not believe the Israelis will find it in time. What they will do, however, is make a desperate last-ditch assault on one or more Arab nations using their nuclear strike capability. In their desperation, it is our belief they will make part of that strike against the Soviet Union, as the chief supplier of nuclear weapons to the Arabs. They will also make a strike against the British, as the originators of this nuclear warhead, and the French as the manufacturers of the submarine. We envisage a situation, Mr President, in which reason will have been replaced by hatred and despair, and the strikes they will make will be those of a desperate, dying person. When the Russians have been hit by the Israeli device, they will react against America, to prevent our taking advantage of the weakened Russian position. When Russia reacts against us, we will be obliged to double react against them . . . I need go no further on that blue-print, Mr President. That ground we have covered several times.'

The President was silent. Yes, they had covered that several times. It was his one and only nightmare.

'Now your question, (d),' Antal said, his scientific manner unchanged by the dour picture he had just painted. 'It seems to us that (a) is preferable to (b). The Israelis should go. As regards how to achieve it: we suggest by political and economic means. The USA should immediately cancel all its aid programmes to Israel, but should offer to double them in quantity, to assist the resettlement of the Israelis in other lands. The USA should bring this matter vigorously before the United Nations.'

For the first time, Antal ceased to look and sound totally detached.

'Just one more thing, Mr President. You remember the study we carried out for you before Dayan came here, when we recommended you bring the Russians back into the Geneva issue? That document expressed our feelings about the reaction you would get from the American Jewish Community. This time, you'd expose yourself to even greater political danger. We think, therefore, that after you have announced the double aid, and been to the United Nations, you yourself, Mr President, should make one appearance

275

on nationwide TV stressing your intention to secure World Peace, and then step down from the Presidency.'

'Step down . . . ?' The President reacted to the suggestion immediately, jumped up from his chair, walked about the office, his stride agitated.

'Yes. Step down, Mr President.'

'And throw away everything I've worked for, everything I've achieved, both personally and politically? Are you out of your mind, Antal?'

Antal watched the President. He had expected a more violent reaction to his suggestion. The President was said to be doing a wonderful job; his ratings in the polls, not that any true scientist took any account of polls, had never been higher. He had taken all the lame-duck legislation of his predecessor and made political sense of it, had sorted out the energy situation, made peace with the big business factions, successfully wooed the Unions. Both Congress and the Senate were solidly behind him – a situation no President had achieved within living memory. There was even optimism that he would get through his amended Medicare legislation. And now Antal was suggesting he leave the Office at his personal pinnacle of success . . .

'Damn it, Antal,' he said. 'I thought you'd come up with some rational reasoning, not this half-baked idea that would throw me on the ex-Presidential scrap heap. What in God's name am I supposed to do? Start writing my memoirs? Endorse ball-point pens to make a buck or two? Become a tired old university hack nobody ever listens to any more? If I resign now, surely that would be the end of my political career, the end of me as a political force . . . ?'

Antal Kreiter occupied a special position in the Presidential hierarchy. Other people, these days, had gurus to advise them where once they had bishops. Washington was peopled with elder statesmen, each of whom could claim familiarity with a handful of Presidents. They liked to think of themselves as an exclusive club, like the Pilots of the Pool of London, the Gondoliers of Venice, the Charter Skipper/Owners of Bermuda, the Sherpas of the Himalayas. Antal Kreiter did not belong to that club because he had not even applied for membership in the three-martini lunch temples.

'You don't need me to advise you politically, Mr President,' he said. 'You can get that sort of information in a fortune cookie. But, since I'm sticking my neck out – no, it wouldn't be the end of your political career. I believe the majority of people are so *bored* by this Middle-East long-runner, they'd be so pleased to see an end of it, that they'd draft you for a second term before the TVs were switched off on your broadcast. Nobody cares if Arab eats Arab. But when the Jews are involved – there's a whole heap of identification there. New York has the largest Jewish population in the world. The whole Jewish bit is emotive. Get them out of Israel, and it's like turning off the tap on that never ending stream. Don't bother calling me anti-semitic. I'm anti anything sectarian. I'm anti-protestant, anti-catholic, anti anything that lets one group fight another group because they don't happen to worship the same God at the same shape of altar. Don't forget one thing, Mr President. This country, some say, was founded by one group running away from another group. So, what happens? They immediately start a little persecution of their own. What do I care if a guy says Shalom or Hail Mary? He's a citizen of this country, and more than that, he's a citizen of this planet . . .'

'And so, Antal, we let the terrorists tell us how to run our lives? We sit back and let them dictate terms? They'd love that in Moscow, and a few other places . . .'

'No, Mr President, we don't sit back. We tackle this whole terrorist bit the way it should be tackled – from the inside out, not from the outside in. We find out *why* the kids are turning to bomb throwing terrorism and anarchy. And that's where we apply our efforts. We use our money and our knowledge, our strength, to understand the *origins* of terrorism, not to patch up the outward manifestations of it. I don't want to know *what* Baader-Meinhoff did – I want to find out *why* they started doing it in the first place. Okay, this time they've caught us with a big one. But in a way they've offered us, incidentally, the solution to what since the days of Lord Balfour and Ernest Bevin has been an insuperable problem. If Bevin had honoured the Balfour Declaration, if the State of Israel had been set up legally with the proper provisions for the Palestinians, instead of being "declared" by Ben Gurion and immediately recognized by the USA without any legal territorial limits, we wouldn't have had the mess we have now. Look, Mr President, you don't need a lesson in political history from me, either. In summary, our opinion is that you should encourage the Israelis to leave by every means at your disposal, that you should explain to the American people why you are doing it, and then resign . . . You'll get the full report just as soon as it can be typed and xeroxed. Okay?'

The President smiled. 'Okay, Antal,' he said. 'As usual you talk too much; but you give me a great deal to think about!'

'We've all got a great deal to think about, Mr President.'

CHAPTER TWENTY-FOUR

Wherever Phillipe went, three cars were able to track him through the 'bleeper' installed under the skin of his back. The round direction-finding antenna on the roofs of their cars could home in on him; the coordinates they called over the radio to Marc Chantal's car were plotted on a map. Where they crossed, Phillipe could be located, any time Marc wanted him picked up.

Phillipe drove the Citroen for about ten kilometres along the back roads, then parked it in the space behind a Routier's café.

He waited beside the road for five minutes and then the bleeper showed him to be travelling along the trunk road into Paris, at the speed of a lorry.

Marc talked into his microphone. 'Release the news to RTF and the newspapers,' he said. 'But get them to keep it low-key. If that lorry has a radio, and his escape isn't on the news, he'll suspect a phoney deal.' He switched on his commercial radio to hear the next newscast:

'Phillipe Leduc, a prisoner of the State Prison at Fresnes, escaped from the custody of two warders today, slightly injuring one. Leduc is wanted in connection with an investigation the authorities today described as politically sensitive. Leduc, twenty-eight years old, wearing grey corduroy trousers and a green jacket, six feet tall with black hair brushed back from his forehead, is believed to be heading for the South of France. Anyone seeing a man answering that description should immediately communicate with the nearest police station. Leduc is not believed to be armed, but has been trained in modern forms of combat. No attempt should be made to tackle him.'

The lorry continued along the road, undisturbed by the radio broadcast. It halted briefly on the outskirts of Paris, and the bleeper led through back streets, coming to rest in the Rue des Strapontins.

'Cheeky bugger!' Marc said. Phillipe was using one of their own 'safe houses'. It contained food, changes of clothing, weapons, even a 'safe' telephone. And passport blanks . . .

After half an hour, Phillipe left the house, and went to the air terminal.

Forty minutes later he returned to the safe house, waited five hours and was driven by taxi to the airport.

The Air France flight to Rome took off one hour afterwards with Phillipe Leluch on board. Leluch had a fat perspiring face and a pot belly, a straggly moustache and blond cropped hair, stooped shoulders. He looked forty-five, though his much used passport said forty. The occupation given in his passport was *accountant*. He looked the part.

Three of Marc's men from out of Paris, also on the flight, carried transistor radios with directional aerials.

From Rome, Phillipe Leluch flew to Athens on PIA.

From Athens, he took the Olympic Flight to Souda.

From Souda he took a taxi to Xania where he stayed overnight in a B-class hotel in the Old Port. He ate mousaka and dolmas for supper, paying with American dollars and asking for the change in drachmae.

The following morning he took the bus from behind the Xania market to Chora Sfakion, on the south coast of Crete.

From the end of the bus-line he walked along the cliff path, deserted at that time of year, to the hut of Kostas Aronakis.

Two rubber dinghies, apparently carrying fishermen, tracked him along the coast. They confirmed his final location as the tiny shepherd's hut on top of the cliff.

Thanks to the French Air Force and a Mystère jet, Marc Chantal was in one of the rubber dinghies, though it would have been impossible to recognize him wearing his wetsuit hood.

The telephone came late to the island of Crete, but the installation there was among the most modern in the Mediterranean. In almost any bar it was possible to pick up the phone and dial an international call. Marc Chantal dialled London and spoke to Bill Harrington.

'They tell me your man escaped,' Bill said.

'You don't want to believe everything they tell you, Bill. We've located him.'

'Let me guess where,' Bill said. 'When I received your call, I was just about to head out of the door. You know we've had people all round the Mediterranean, reporting having seen Yshtak?'

'So have we . . .'

'We've had lots of sighting in Ibiza, Paris, London, Lausanne.'

'So have we . . .'

'And one from Chora Sfakion, a small fishing village on the south coast of Crete. Apparently, Yshtak took his boat, the *Revenge*, there a couple of times.'

'That's where I'm ringing from. PL is holed up along the coastline from here.'

'In a shepherd's hut belonging, by acquisition, to a local called Kostas Aronakis, who was very big in the black market after the war . . .'

'And who was in the meeting in Dupree's apartment . . . ?'

'The same. It's a long haul from a shepherd's hut to a Paris flat, don't you think?'

'Too long for an innocent man. I just received a call from my office. They'd been checking the German Naval Records Office in Hamburg. Turned up copies of the war-time "Master Plan" for Crete. Pencilled in, but apparently never completed, is a small submarine repair workshop, on this coast-line . . . Kostas, apparently, was a partisan hereabouts towards the end of the war. Non-communist. There's some mystery about where he actually spent the earlier war years. I've been talking with a man who owns a restaurant here, a keen diver. He was swimming along that coastline one-time and saw a large cave mouth. Apparently there are many, just below the water-line, but this is bigger than most. And, he thinks, directly below Kostas's hut. He's never bothered to go back. We have the *Chameleon* in the Eastern Mediterranean, part of our NATO contribution. On board is a detachment of French Marines. I'm going to bring it close inshore tonight. At first light, we'll go in and take that hut apart.'

'With Greek permission? NATO permission?'

'Did you get Spanish permission for your jaunt on Ibiza? Bill, you know how things are. The fewer people who know in advance what we are going to do, the better. I'm sick of committees. The *Chameleon* has a team of divers. When we make our assault overland, they can block the mouth of that underwater cave . . .'

'Marc, think what you're saying, for God's sake. If Yshtak launches the Dolphin through there, and your block stops it, with its atomic war-head . . .'

'Where would you prefer it to explode, Bill? Along a deserted coastline where there are at most a thousand people, or in a crowded Israeli harbour?'

The question was unanswerable. 'You'll be there, Marc. One of those "thousand people".'

'I know, Bill. I used to think I'd care, but somehow I don't think I do any more. Now you understand why we couldn't notify the Greek authorities. Please may we have permission, possibly to explode an atom bomb on your territory . . . ? I don't think they would have said yes very easily. Or very quickly.'

'Where are you actually located, Marc?'

'Above a restaurant, run by a Sfakian with a young American wife. They have rooms, and a telephone.'

'I'll see you there as soon as I can . . .'

'No you won't, you silly bastard. The days of the English milord, riding in on his white charger, are over, Bill.'

'Marc, I'll be there. That warhead is *my* responsibility. And, so is that butcher Yshtak . . .'

Bill was in luck. An RA-6C Vigilante reconnaissance aircraft was refuelling in Northolt, prior to being reassigned to the US 6th Fleet in the Mediterranean. It put him down on the flight deck of the attack aircraft carrier USS *Independence* (CVA-62). From there, a helicopter landed him, that clear, cool moonlit night, on the plain below Komitades. Flying without lights, the chopper was on the ground only thirty seconds before whirling away again, out to sea.

Bill arrived at the restaurant shortly after midnight, keyed up for action.

Marc was in the room above, smoking his inevitable Gauloise. He looked appreciatively at Bill, dressed in a jumping jacket over Army woollen trousers, cleat-soled boots, with a khaki woollen balaclava rolled into a neat hat.

Marc was wearing dark trousers and a dark leather jacket. His concession to the night's action was a beret, and a pair of fell-walking boots with rubber soles.

'Merde,' he said. 'I hoped you'd change your mind.'

Bill shook his head. 'Don't get me wrong,' he said. 'Somebody might get an opportunity to defuse that damned thing. It was easier for me to come to do it, than try to explain it over the telephone to you.'

'You've seen that merde of a moon?'

'Yes.'

'We went over the terrain today. All the paths to the hut are under electronic surveillance.'

'So it *is* the place?'

'You wouldn't put your sheep under the magic eye, would you?'

'So what happens if a sheep blunders across the beam?'

'Infra-red scopes are mounted under the roof. I guess the sheep turn on the infra red beam, and they check from inside.'

'Joseph Aram was a security expert.'

'Andreas Burgler is also an explosives expert. It's my guess the approaches are also mined, set to be fired from inside.'

'What is their way out?'

'My guess is that they have something like a battery-driven underwater sledge. Or perhaps they all just put on the bottles and swim. Kostas Aronakis has a boat moored about five hundred metres along the coast-line.'

'That looks too obvious . . .'

'Look, Bill, they've had a long time to plan this thing. And no one has been disturbing them, because no one has suspected anything. Kostas had a brilliant cover. He was known as a smuggler, a fixer. Anything he cared to bring ashore – well, it would just be yet another piece of stolen goods for somebody, without any questions asked by the locals because, who knows, you might be the next one to want something. Dammit, he came ashore one time with a 12 kilowatt generating set for a man in Aghia Roumeli. Refrigerators even, and, would you believe it, a washing machine. He was Mr Anything-you-need.'

'You haven't seen any of the others? Yshtak himself? Aram? Jacques Morel? Khaylia Patin? Burgler? Dupree?'

'I don't think they're all here. My guess is that the ones they don't need are in a safe place somewhere. Probably collating information from Israel, from the vast network of people I suspect Yshtak employs – people we know nothing about.'

'Men like Fairclough. We nailed him . . .'

'And, damn their eyes, my Phillipe. Right in front of my nose, and I never suspected . . .'

'And Sophie?'

'No, I don't believe Sophie was one of theirs. My guess would be that they figured Sophie perhaps knew too much about the sub's programme and might be able to work out a way to bitch them. She specialized in navigation techniques, don't forget. We'll find her in one of two places. Either at the bottom of the Toulon basin, with a lead-weight belt round her middle, or here . . .'

'In Jacques Morel's bed . . .'

'Toujours l'amour, and cherchez la femme? Yes, damn it, in his bed. Though, if they did have a love affair going, it was and still is the best kept secret of that whole merde of an establishment.'

Sophie was sitting at the console of the apparatus, rubbing her eyes. All day long she had been staring at the video screen as the Dolphin drew agonizingly nearer and nearer to them. Every so often, the computer, acting on the instructions she had given it, read off a set of figures and printed them out on a tear-off sheet. It told her signal-received strength, signal-transmitted strength, but maddeningly, not the distance. A long time ago, the halo circle that denoted the cliffs of the island of Ibiza had faded to obscurity. To obtain a distance using sonar, a signal was transmitted to the object under surveillance. Part of that signal was bounced back from the object. The speed of the signal was known, and therefore the distance of time between the signal leaving the transponder and returning to it could be used to measure the distance the signal had travelled. But the Dolphin itself was transmitting signals on that 55KHz band, and these signals, of unknown strength, interfered with the return signal. Sophie knew no way she could separate the two. All day long she had tried various methods, but none had worked.

And now, she had the added problem that the Dolphin *seemed* to be travelling at an angle to the island. Of course, she consoled herself, that might not be important. Jacques may have his own reasons for choosing that path. The bed of the Mediterranean is not very smooth; there are several continental shelves and even one deep fissure he might want to avoid.

Perhaps he was just trying out the navigation system on a vector. She punched up a logical path pattern based on probability, assuming she could estimate the Dolphin's present position on a calculation of its known speed.

And then she discovered it could be headed for Israel. To hit the coast just south of Tel Aviv.

Kostas was sitting in the control room with her, watching her with care in his eyes. 'You must be tired, Miss Sophie?' he said. 'And you didn't eat the supper I cooked for you. I went out and caught those sardellas today, specially for you . . .'

He had taken out his fishing boat as an excuse to keep an eye on Agonistes's rubber dinghies that appeared suddenly, hovering a half a kilometre off the rocks of the headland. Agonistes seemed to have one of his 'suckers' on board. They'd been down, and caught a few kilos of fish. Kostas did not like the buggers who used a spear gun underwater. Agonistes had stood up in the rubber dinghy and showed him the fish on a large hook. Kostas opened his buttons and urinated over the side, to demonstrate his opinion.

He had fried the tiny sardellas in oil after first dusting them with lemon, flour and herbs, but Sophie had hardly touched them, even though he had shown her how to eat them whole.

Joseph Aram came through the control room. 'Have you checked everything,' he said, fussing as ever.

'Yes, boss,' Kostas said. 'Everything's ready for the Dolphin when Miss Sophie brings her home, safe and sound. I've checked the top. The door's locked, the cat's eyes are working . . .' He had marvelled when he had seen the effects of the beams with which Aram had ringed the hut, the 'cat's eyes' as he called them, that could see in the darkness when one of the beams was broken. And the lines of high fragmentation shrapnel explosive they had dug into the ground, wired to be fired from inside if they did not welcome their visitors.

Yshtak came in. The control room had become the focus of all their attention, like the kitchen in a farm-house. Sophie had seen the Frenchman; she had not been told his name, but knew he was French the moment she saw him. She noticed the dark roots of his hair – somebody had done a quick clip job on him and dyed him blond in a hurry.

Andreas Burgler had looked into the control room once, but had not entered.

'Anything you can tell me, Mademoiselle?' Yshtak asked courteously.

She shook her head. 'It's moving,' she said. 'But I can't tell you where it is yet. It shouldn't be too long now. Every print-out shows our signal is being received stronger and stronger. Soon, it will be strong enough to overcome the transmission effect, and then we can begin to sort the two out.'

She did not mention her fear that the Dolphin might not be headed on a straight line to Crete. Jacques, she hoped, would explain that, when he arrived.

She looked at Kostas. 'I could drink another cup of that herb tea you made, Kostas,' she said.

He leaped to his feet, happy to be of service again . . .

Agonistes and his wife, Emma, had been told that Marc Chantal and his men were on a NATO exercise, from Souda Bay. He was used to men of all the NATO nationalities. Agonistes's father had been a guerilla fighter during the war, killed by the Germans during their retreat. He thought of the French, the English, and the Americans as enemies of the Germans, and therefore friends of the Cretans, so was happy to comply with Marc's strange requests. He closed the restaurant shortly after one o'clock; returned about three and knocked on the door of the room Marc occupied. The sight of Bill in his Army clothes reinforced Marc's story. 'All ready, Mr Marc,' he said.

Marc nodded. 'You couldn't arrange a few clouds for us, Agonistes?' he said hopefully, looking out of the window.

Agonistes smiled. 'Don't worry, Mr Marc,' he said. 'Tomorrow will come one big storm . . .'

'Tomorrow is no good, Agonistes . . .'

'Ah, Mr Marc. Always before one big storm is coming some little clouds. Already, is coming . . .'

Marc went to the window and looked out. 'I don't see any clouds, Agonistes.'

'From the north, from the mountains. I see when I go look for Ioannis.'

They went to the back window, looked out over the rooftops of Chora Sfakion, to the high mountains beyond. Sure enough, small clouds were beginning to form on the mountain top. And the wind was getting up from the north.

'We'll move at four o'clock,' Marc said.

Bill nodded. Marc pressed the switch on the microphone on the table. 'Rouge vert to blanc noir.'

The reply came back immediately, strength five. 'Blanc Noir.'

'HC 0400.'

'Blanc Noir. D'accord. HC 0400.'

'Rouge Vert. I am told there will be less moon.'

'Blanc Noir. Very good. Start signal?'

'You'll hear it.'

'D'accord. Bonne chance!'

'Bonne chance. Out.'

The Navy Lieutenant in the French motor torpedo boat from the *Chameleon* checked his log and his chart. He looked at the six men grouped around him in the well of the boat.

'We have a start-time,' he said. '0400 hrs. Apparently there will be less moon. We'll hug the coastline as far as the promontory. I have an exact bearing, below a hut. We should be able to see the hut against the mountains unless the moon is completely obscured. If it is, there'll be a blinking light on the rocks. We go straight overboard and down. You all know what the Dolphin looks like. It's our job to see it stays in there, assuming it is there already.'

Six men and himself. A team of seven volunteers. 'It's still not too late to back out,' he said gravely. 'You know what the risks are, not only from the men there, but from the Dolphin. Any man who wants to can stay aboard when the rest of us flip over. There'll be no recriminations.' He turned to the rating behind the wheel. 'Once we go,' he said, 'you get out of there as fast as you can, understand.'

'I understand, Lieutenant.'

He also understood he would have a one percent chance, if the bomb went off, of getting away alive.

A large nylon net was rolled up on the deck of the MTB. Two corners had lead weights on them; the opposite two had cork floats. The mesh of the net was marginally smaller than the width of the Dolphin. They were going to try to catch it, like a fish. Two of them had volunteered to man the net, attached to which was a string of buoys and flares. They would hang on to the net, travel with the Dolphin through the water, attach the net more firmly as they went along, and periodically fire the buoys and flares to mark their position. Meanwhile they carried extra air bottles with which they would try to inflate a rubber belt they would wind round the Dolphin, to bring it to the surface. It was a desperate, last-ditch endeavour, a nightmare ride through the ocean's depths, struggling to hang on and achieve the various tasks before their own air supply ran out.

'Okay,' the lieutenant said, glancing at his watch. 'Let's go.'

The rating behind the wheel pressed the throttle forward; the twin 1000 hp diesels opened up, and the boat leaped forward, planing before it had gone a hundred metres through the silver, moonlit sea.

It was four thirty in the morning when the red lights above each door in Kostas's complex began to flash. Kostas, in the control room with Sophie, who had refused to go to bed, punched the button that would activate the infra-red cameras built under the eaves of the roof. The monitor screen glowed with light.

The door opened and Joseph Aram came in, tousled from sleep. The red lights could be replaced by a soft buzzer, which had woken him instantly.

'Look at that,' Kostas said. 'No wonder that fool Ioannis

never has any money. All his sheep, loose on the hill-side. I've told him he should pen them at night, if he wants to milk the ewes for cheese.'

The infra-red cameras clearly picked out the sheep wandering across the ground outside the hut. There was no sign of Ioannis, the shepherd. Joseph Aram cursed, and was going to return to bed when one of the sheep turned and he saw the dark outline riding along its side. No wonder the sheep were moving nervously. 'Look at that,' he said. Kostas peered at the screen, and saw the figure of a man clinging to the sheep's belly, his hand round its neck, his foot cocked over its back. Other sheep had turned, and they could make out nine such clinging men.

Burgler burst into the room, followed by Yshtak.

'Sheep,' Joseph explained quickly. 'But there are men clinging to the sides of them.'

Yshtak turned immediately to Sophie. 'Do you have the Dolphin for us?' he asked. It had been too much to hope they could keep their hiding place secret indefinitely. They had all known they could be discovered. But, by now, the Dolphin should have been there, in the cave below. They could still have made use of it. If all else failed, they could have launched it so that their efforts would not have been in vain. 'Do you have the Dolphin, Miss Sophie,' he asked desperately.

She had to shake her head. 'It's on its way,' she said. 'That's all I can tell you . . .'

'Stupid bitch,' Burgler said. 'Let me have a look.'

She had already punched up the sonar, the confused sounds of reception and transmission the computer was turning into pictures on the video screen. 'Try to make sense of that,' she said, getting up from the chair and stretching herself. Yshtak looked at the infra-red pictures and clearly saw the figures of the men crouching against the sheep's sides.

Joseph Aram was looking at him for a command. He passed his hand wearily across his face, then nodded.

Joseph pressed the button that would fire the high fragmentation charges concealed just below the surface of the ground.

The explosion threw gouts of yellow and orange flame in all directions, with whirring deadly projectiles of flesh-tearing metal. The screens went black as the infra-red cameras were shattered.

'Get the Dolphin here quickly, Mlle Sophie,' Yshtak pleaded, his voice an outburst of passionate French. 'Get it here quickly. I beg of you . . .'

CHAPTER TWENTY-FIVE

Every network in the world was represented at the United Nations General Assembly. Those who could not be allotted space for a live television camera in the galleries over-looking the vast hall had been promised an immediate print of the videotape the United Nations staff team were making. Every delegation was there, in full strength, sitting with feigned casualness behind their country name plaques.

The atmosphere was quiet, but charged with an almost palpable tension as the Secretary General came in and took his place on the rostrum, behind his microphone.

All night the Steering Committee had fought to formulate a workable agenda for the meeting, in the face of the Arab and Third World insistence that a PLO representative team should be seated. The Secretary General was conscious, during this fierce argument, of his own invidious position as a salaried employee of the United Nations, not its leader, its master. In his mind he likened it to driving a car, or trying to, without your feet on the accelerator or the brake.

Finally, he won agreement by disclosing to the Steering Committee a portion of the text of the first speaker he wanted to introduce.

There was a sporadic round of applause, quickly stilled, when the US President walked into the hall.

No one rose to his feet.

The President had not expected anyone to.

He walked to the microphone stands below the imposing seat of the Secretary-General. The picture he made there was transmitted, by television and satellite, throughout the world.

The interpreters, wearing headphones, each in his small booth, looked at each other as he began, automatically translating his formal salutations.

Cameramen made last minute adjustments to framing the picture, knowing the technicians behind them in the chain would be fine-tuning focus, contrast, colour, on this formal introduction.

The President paused. Not one rustle could be heard in the Assembly as he looked straight out past the microphones, ignoring his notes.

'What I have to say today comes at the conclusion of many agonizing hours of consultation, of information gathering, and finally, of personal contemplation.

'The world is on the brink of a cataclysm such as mankind has not known since the Great Flood.

'The facts are known to all of you; I need not reiterate them here. I have come here today to state, categorically, the attitude of the United States government, confirmed by special meetings of Congress and the Senate, to the events taking place in the land of Israel.' He paused significantly.

'It is our belief that the people of Israel should leave the country they have chosen as their own.'

The pandemonium was immediate. The Arabs, without exception, began to yell and to cheer, to slap each other on the back, to whoop out loud.

The Israeli delegation rose as one, and walked out of the Assembly, followed by the lenses of the cameras, by the boos and cat-calls of many of the more excitable delegates. Its leader, the Ambassador, Menachem Shorem, made no attempt to wipe away the tears that streamed from his eyes. He had been informed in advance of what the President intended to say; it was by his own decision that the delegation had sat stoically in its allotted seats to make the only gesture left to them, a walk-out.

The voice of the Secretary General slowly made itself heard above the ear-shattering noise. It took six minutes to quieten the delegates, while the US President silently stood to attention. When silence reigned he continued to speak as if there had been no interruption.

'The United States will immediately withdraw its aid to Israel, but will double it in monetary value and place it at the disposal of the displaced peoples. To this we pledge ourselves.'

This time the President himself stilled the noise which arose, by raising his hand.

'I would like to close by informing this Assembly, and anyone who is watching on television or listening on radio, that before I entered this building, I announced to Congress and to the Senate my intention of resigning from office just as soon as the appropriate arrangements can be made.'

Now there was no noise, only puzzled stares as delegates looked at each other to try to understand the meaning behind the President's resignation.

'I thank you all,' the President said, 'for permitting me this opportunity to speak to you.'

He made a half bow towards the delegates, turned, inclined his head symbolically towards the Secretary General, then quickly left the Assembly, surrounded by his personal guard.

Minutes later, a helicopter carried him away from the United Nations Plaza. As it whirred across the river, he looked back at the box-shaped building, and slowly, without speaking, he shook his head.

The Navy lieutenant had checked his watch before the explosions. Exactly on 4 o'clock, he heard the blasts, muffled by the height but echoed back by the mountains. He saw the stabbing glare of the flames briefly against the sky. And then all was dark, all was silent. As promised, the clouds had obscured the last of the moon; the light was flickering on the rock above them.

'Right, go!' he said.

Every one of his men followed him over the side, except the two who stayed to see the net uncurl itself. When the last folds streamed overboard, they took a double grip on the loops holding the cork floats, and went over with it, dropping straight down.

The Lieutenant and his men were already floating at the mouth of the big cave, revealed in the light from their head-band lamps. The two men on the net speedily manoeuvred it into position, and then the head-band lights clicked off.

The Lieutenant's arm had moved in the last of the light.

Forward, into the cave.

Bill and Marc were crouched beside Ioannis in a fold in the ground. Tears were streaming down his face. 'I gave them all a name,' he said. 'I knew each one of them. Now gone, all gone.'

Bill and Marc rose, crouched and ran for the door of Kostas's hut, dodging the blasted sheep and the human effigies Agonistes had made from sacks filled with straw to resemble human beings, that had been tied to their sides.

The force Marc had assembled converged rapidly on the hut, carrying the short-barrelled Belgian FLN rifles issued to NATO troops, set on automatic.

A heavily built Norman, a Navy bosun, did not stop there, but crashed his shoulder against the door, which burst open under the impact.

Phillipe was emerging through the inside door, the back of which had been camouflaged with plaster to match the wall.

The bosun had no orders to take anyone alive. His job was to get down to the submarine cave as quickly as possible. He pressed the trigger of the FLN and Phillipe was hurled backwards by the impact, a red gash across his chest, tumbling slowly down the staircase. The bosun continued onwards. For a moment it seemed as if he would be entangled by Phillipe's flailing limbs but he put his foot on the man's back and vaulted the last four stairs over his body. Open area in front, sort of lobby. Door open to the right, leading to what looked like a bedroom. To the right of that, another open door. A room with a table, chairs – dining room possibly, kitchen beyond.

He jerked his hand right, waited only long enough to see Simon go that way. A door ahead, open. Inside, people. Man near the door with a gun coming up from where he had been holding it on his knee. The bosun fired a burst into the room, leaped forward and kicked the door further open. One, two, three men in there, and a girl. He had been told to watch out for a girl, a French girl. Told also to watch out for a Palestinian, sallow features. Shoot the Palestinian; try, if possible, not to shoot the French girl. This one was clearly French. He fired again. The man beside the desk took the burst in his chest and up to his throat, bowled over backwards, down, dead.

One man, one woman. The woman's face started to turn in horror. Don't worry, cherie, it would all be over soon at this rate. Then his FLN jammed.

He threw it, drew his revolver. Too late. The tall man with the hawk face had been holding a gun in his pocket and pulled the trigger without taking it out. The bosun felt the impact in his chest, looked down, saw the hole where he had always thought his heart was. And then the long slow fall. Before he hit the ground he had time to see the man grab the girl, open a steel door, and go through it.

Laurence, Bosun's Mate 1st Class, saw his chief take the bullet and start to go down, blocking the doorway. He pushed him forwards. Saw the man at the side of the console, screaming, pushing buttons, and shot him. First through the arm, then, more carefully, through the head. The man's brains spattered over the console.

The large picture on the television screen in front of him had changed when the man hit the buttons. The loudspeaker beside it, which formerly had been sounding a ping, then a silence, then a prolonged pinging, suddenly burst into a hysterical shriek.

The picture had assumed the form of a wave, with crests on it.

When the note changed, the picture went dead.

The loudspeaker went dead too, except for a deep, mocking, hiss.

Bill and Marc came into the control room. Looked around. Marc straddled the body of the bosun, lying sprawled across the floor. The bosun was trying to speak. Flecks of blood were coming to the side of his mouth. 'Two of them,' he said, 'went through that steel door!' Bill heard what he said and rushed to the door to open it. The handle came away in his hand.

'One was the French girl,' the bosun said. There was a rattle in his voice as it forced its way out of his throat, and then he fell backwards, his head crashing against the floor.

They heard a shout from Simon and ran into the lobby.

He had found the top of the lift shaft.

The lift was coming upwards.

Marc beckoned them all back, into hiding, one in the doorway of what looked like a mechanic's work-room, another in the doorway of the bedroom, he and Bill in the dining room.

Suddenly he realized that whoever was in the lift would see the body of Phillipe sprawled on the floor. He and Bill dragged it out of sight.

The top of the lift shaft was guarded only by a low mesh gate, not a full door. They could hear the lift coming nearer.

They saw the mechanism at the top of the lift cage itself, the wheels through which the rope was threaded.

Two men in black were crouched on the roof.

The lift itself was empty.

When the men realized the lift top did not have a conventional door, they leaped off it, back to back.

Both were wearing rubber wet-suits, and carrying FLN rifles.

'Okay,' Marc called out without showing himself. 'We've dealt with them all up here.'

The two men straightened up as Marc and Bill came from their hiding places.

'We got two of them down there,' he said. 'A Cretan, by the look of him, and an Englishman. Our lot are all right.'

'Alive? The Cretan and the Englishman?'

'The Cretan's okay. The Englishman wanted to play. He may survive.'

'The Dolphin?' Bill asked.

The man who had been speaking shook his head. 'No trace of it,' he said. 'A vast cavern with all mod cons, lights, cranes, a dry-docking area. But no Dolphin.'

The disappointment hit Bill like a physical blow. Twice he had been so near the damned thing. Twice he had been keyed up to find it. And both times, this shock of disappointment. He went into the workshop, brought out a pair of thin nosed pliers and a screwdriver. 'Fetch the Cretan up here,' he said. He shone his torch into the hole in the door where the handle had been. The handle must have been removed, with its opening rod, from the other side. To delay pursuit. Well, Yshtak had had plenty of time to plan the small details.

He put the thin-nosed pliers into the hole, felt them grip the sides, and turned. The lock would not move.

Marc heard a moan from behind him, and went quickly into the dining room, to where Phillipe was sprawled on the floor. His eyes had opened though they had that glazed look of imminent death.

Marc bent down beside him, gently touched his face.

Phillipe felt his hand and turned his head.

'It's me, Phillipe,' Marc said.

Phillipe managed the ghost of a smile. 'You put a plant in me,' he said, painfully slowly. 'Where is it, in one of my teeth?'

'No. In the small of your back . . .'

'I've had an itch . . .'

'. . . where you couldn't scratch it. Why, Phillipe? Why?' Marc asked. 'Was it for money?'

Phillipe gulped, fighting for air. 'No, not money . . . You see, it's in the blood, Marc,' Phillipe said. 'Blood is thicker even than that wine we used to drink together, at the Faisan d'Or. Remember?' His body was racked by sudden pain. He reared up, trying to fight it, but could not. Marc put his arm beneath Phillipe's head. Phillipe sank back, his face drained pale by the exertion. His eyes closed, and he died quietly, without saying any more. Marc held him until he heard the lift come up again, then lowered Phillipe gently to the ground, covered his face with his own beret, and left the room.

The man coming from the lift was certainly Cretan. He had a smile of defiance on his face. 'Kostas Aronakis, boss,' he said with his quick instinct for spotting the top man. 'And who do I have the honour of addressing . . . ?'

'This door,' Bill said. 'How does it open, and where does it lead?'

Kostas walked across and looked at it. 'Oh damn,' he said. 'If I had had time to fix it, the handle would not have come off again, would it?'

'Where does it lead?'

'To a store-room.'

'What's in there?'

'Cables, wires, a couple of barrels of a very friendly grassi, a few bottles of ouzo and raki, a sack of potatoes . . .'

'Can you open it?'

'Yes, boss.'

'Then get it open.'

Kostas bent down, picked up the handle from which the spigot had disappeared. 'Ah, boss, that's not going to be so easy if the metal rod is on the other side, now is it?'

It took ten minutes to open the door. They finally blew it off its hinges using the grenades Marc's men had brought with them but not needed.

It did lead to a store-room, containing wine, potatoes. But it also led to a tunnel cut in the rock, going upwards. They raced along it. At the far end was a flight of steps. Sophie was sitting on the bottom step. 'Yshtak told me to wait here,' she said. 'That way, no one would shoot me. I hate being shot at . . .'

She went back along the corridor while Bill investigated the rest of the passage. It led to a cave in the rock face, only four metres below the top of the cliff and an easy climb, up or down.

By now, Yshtak could be anywhere in the vast mountains of Sfakia. Or below them, on the ocean.

Suddenly, Bill heard shouts from the end of the tunnel and raced back inside. Sophie was standing before the console, looking at the weird picture the video screen offered, like a series of the letter D. The loudspeaker was emitting a hollow note which peaked, died rapidly away, peaked again, died away once more.

She pointed to the print-out on the platten of the terminal, a look of horror on her face. 'That madman, Burgler,' she said. 'It can only have been him.'

Bill looked at the typing. It did not mean a thing to him.

Sophie ran a hand through her thick hair, and sat down, looking awestruck at the video image.

She punched a combination of buttons, removed the picture and the sound. Then she pressed others, but no new picture appeared, no sound.

'What's happened?' Bill asked.

Sophie swivelled round in her chair. 'So far as I can judge from the print-out I found here,' she said, 'Andreas Burgler has armed the nuclear device in the Dolphin, has set the Dolphin on its final course, severed connection with it, and wiped the data base. Now, there's no way we can get it, hold it, redirect it. It's gone . . . And Jacques Morel has gone with it.'

'Alive? Perhaps steering it?'

'Dead. He must be dead. The life support systems have also been switched off . . .' She buried her face in her hands and wept. Bill went across the room and put his arm round her shoulders. He knew there was nothing he could say to comfort her other than to offer her the warmth of his presence, and hold her while she cried. Each of them revealed his inner pain in a different way. He remembered how he had felt at the sight of Sally's tortured body, telling himself over and over again that she could have been dead, knowing he would have been responsible, reproaching himself. Sophie was perhaps reproaching herself for not having been able to prevent what Burgler had done, for not having taken steps to make it impossible.

'I should have copied that data base,' she said between

sobs. 'Then, at least, we could have gone on trying to make contact.'

Marc was interrogating Kostas Aronakis, seated at the dining room table, and not getting very far.

'I met Yshtak a number of years ago,' Kostas had said. 'He was looking for a place. I offered him mine. He seemed a nice guy. He told me he had a marine exploration company – you know, looking for oil and minerals on the bed of the ocean. He said that there were big meetings going on about it, but he didn't want to let anybody know until after these meetings just what he was finding. He told me they were building an exploration vessel, like the bathyscaphe that Frenchman Cousteau built. And they'd want somewhere safe, out of sight, to store it. I'd found this cave, and these rooms, and offered them to him. Look, boss, me, I'm just a simple Cretan peasant. You know what they say – one Englishman a boat, two Englishmen a navy, three Englishmen an empire. One German a soldier, two Germans an army, three Germans a war? Well, one Cretan a peasant, two Cretans two peasants, three Cretans, four peasants . . . And me, I'm the fourth peasant. I worked for Yshtak, and that's all.'

'You went to a meeting in Paris . . . ?'

'That's right, boss. Wonderful apartment overlooking a forest. Those guys really know how to live, eh?'

'What was the meeting about?'

'How would I know, boss? I wasn't in the meeting. Yshtak asked me to go, tell them about this place, and then I left. I wish I'd never gone to Paris, even though it was all expenses paid.'

'Why not?'

'After the meeting, I went up to Montmartre. Caught a case of the – what do you call 'em – the crabs. Itched like a bastard until I could get back here and treat them with raki . . .'

'And all this . . . ? All this apparatus . . . ?'

'Look, boss, like I said. I don't know anything about such things. A man asks me to fix wires, I fix them.'

'And the explosive outside?'

'I didn't know what they were putting in the trenches, did I? They told me to dig the trenches – I dug them. They told me to fix wires, I fixed them. They told me to cook meals, I cooked them.'

Bill was doing no better with Joseph Aram, in the bedroom. What could you say when a man simply would not speak? Aram had not uttered one word since Bill came into the room after leaving Sophie. Silence was the best answer to the techniques of interrogation. If you uttered even one word, the dam was opened. Few men could maintain silence for ever in the face of provocation, taunts, repeated questions, fatigue, lack of orientation.

Bill did not have the time to try any of these.

And Joseph Aram did not utter one single word.

Rolf Mueller had to throw the whole affair open to a full debate of the Knesset, which quickly divided into three factions. The first was in favour of an immediate strike against an Arab country. A full scale war. Jordan was the country most favoured for attack, though there was a considerable lobby in support of another attack on Egypt. 'Only this time, no pulling back after six days. We'll take Cairo, and occupy it. We'll take the East Bank of the Jordan, expel all the Palestinians from Israel. A total Jewish State.'

The religious leaders were in favour of evacuating the shoreline as far as the Bethlehem – Jerusalem – Ramullah line. They had never really approved of the state within a state, Tel Aviv, with its lack of belief, its hedonism, its secularism and worship of Mammon. 'No Palestinian would explode a device to devastate Jerusalem,' they said. 'Jerusalem means too much to them.'

The third party, and by far the largest in voice, if not in number, was formed by people who had come to the end of their patience, who saw the possibility of new life in new countries and an end to the constant erosion of war with the Arabs and the Palestinians. They objected to the burdensome nature of taxes spent on the defence budget, the state of military preparation they had to, most of them reluctantly, maintain. But when members of the first faction, ignoring protocol in the heat of the debate, began to shout and call them cowards, Rolf Mueller remembered the words of the US President, and stood up, demanding silence.

'Let no member here be vilified for his beliefs,' he said. 'Let us maintain the right of free speech and the expression of our convictions. Let no man who is quick to seize a sword pour scorn on he who reaches for the Torah, the olive branch, or the crutch to help him along the road to his own vision of peace and freedom. To seek that vision is the birth right of every one of us, without fear of ridicule, without disapprobation . . .'

His speech was interrupted by his clerk, who hurried in bearing an ominous crimson-coloured folder. Rolf reached down and took it, knowing that only a signal of the gravest importance would have been brought to him at that moment.

He opened the folder and read the message it contained.

The Chamber was quite still, every man and woman watching him.

He seated himself, still staring at the piece of paper. He closed the folder and rested his hand on it. When he looked out into the Chamber, his face was grey, as if carved in stone.

'I have to inform you,' he said slowly, 'that the nightmare we have been living through has become reality. The submarine, armed with its monstrous warhead, is heading for our shores, to strike at a point estimated as ten miles south of Tel Aviv. The moment of impact is not known, but it is believed to be any time after the next twenty hours. I suggest that those of you who wish to spend that twenty hours with your families should leave at once.'

CHAPTER TWENTY-SIX

Ben Gurion Airport was a scene of pandemonium. Desperate people fought their way to the runways, to get onto planes being loaded for take-off as fast as possible.

A great horde thronged the airport buildings, the roads outside, the approaches to the airport. The Army had been called out long ago to help man the entrances to the landing area. Now the crowds pushed against the improvised barriers, which had no hope of resisting. When the steel and wire shutters to the right of the departure building parted, the soldiers standing there saw the deluge of people racing towards them like the wave of a broken dam. They pointed their Uzis in the air and pulled the triggers. The barrage of shots above the refugees' heads momentarily slowed them, but the rear ranks, unable to see the soldiers, the machine guns, or to hear the firing above the impassioned screams of those about them, pushed inexorably on. The flood-tide was in motion; nothing could stop it. The people in the front rank tried to stop but were immediately bowled over and went down with screams of helpless agony. The mass surged over them, trampling them to bloody death. The second rank fell, and were trampled too under the crowd's pounding, remorseless onrush.

The Captain commanding the soldiers had never been so sick at heart as when he signalled the men to aim lower and lower, until their shots were narrowly missing the heads of those out in front, hitting some of those at the back of the crowd.

Now that people heard the shots and realized where they came from, they began to slow, to swerve, to fall back. Many of the unfortunates caught in the centre of the mass went down; the old ones, the ones with children, the cripples.

The Captain saw only the sweating, fear-crazed faces, the open mouths shouting, screaming, yelling. He was long past hearing individual words, or seeing individual features. To him they were a congealed mass of waving faces and limbs, a fused homogenuity of writhing flesh that, somehow, he had to stop.

He lowered his hand. His men began to shoot at waist height. The first wave of people, shocked immobile, formed a solid dead-weight barrier as they fell, and now the thrusting force of panic was held. The crowd drew slowly to a halt, and then, like the tide, began to recede.

The Captain stopped counting the dead bodies when he came to a hundred, stopped looking at the streams of blood that ran along the hot concrete, turned his head away as he saw the hatred and anger, the unanswerable accusation, in the eyes of those who had survived. Relatives began falling to the ground beside their killed or wounded loved ones, and a mourning wail hovered like a pall over the scene. The rumble of angry voices began, the shouts. 'Assassins. Murderers. Arab-lovers!'

A line of military ambulances came into sight, moving slowly. Where would they take them? What would they do with them for the next twenty hours?

Three of the soldiers threw down their Uzis, tore off their belts, turned, and walked slowly away from the scene. One of them was being sick as he walked along, the vomit jerking from him with each step, dripping down his khakis.

A couple of Army scout-cars came hurtling along the runway road, their mounted machine guns panning round to face the crowd. A lorry arrived, and from it a squad of men dropped a roll of canvas, two metres high. They held the canvas upright, and unwound it rapidly, pushing the front people with their staring eyes back behind it. The canvas carried lathes every couple of metres and stayed upright as a temporary screen, blocking the space between the two buildings. Before the block was complete, an armoured car went through the remaining gap and parked there, its gun continually weaving. The other joined it. A stone was hurled from the centre of the crowd and rattled against its armour. Then another, and another. Soon, the anger of the crowd was being vented by throwing anything, everything they could lay hands on. The armoured cars took it all, mute, waiting. Gradually the energies of the throwers were dissipated as they left, making for other possible routes onto the planes.

All pretence of ticketing had been abandoned. People were being herded through the building and out onto the tarmac in a continuous stream, first come, first aboard, with no luggage allowed.

All the off-duty air controllers had come back on duty to cope with the impossible rush of traffic. No planes were being refuelled on the ground or serviced. People were being packed on board, in seats, squatting along the aisles between the seats. The planes carried only one hostess to make even that much more room. They were operating a fast round trip to Nicosia airport, Heraklion, Athens, Souda. From those airports people were being airlifted as quickly as possible to the next stage. Rome, Nice, Genoa, even Ibiza and Palma de Mallorca or Barcelona.

Planes were landing at Lod within a minute of each other, the pilots seeing the long snake of passengers straddling the road to the airport, with a line of soldiers on each side keeping them in an ever flowing stream, containing any individual attempts to jump the queue. Every so often, the stream was narrowed by armoured cars, jeeps, tanks, rolls of barbed wire, and chopped into blocks of fifty, an armed soldier walking between each block. Gradually the people outside the line were marshalled into the main stream, and the airport itself was ringed by troops with short bayonets on the ends of their rifles, and orders to stick anyone who did not immediately obey their commands.

The wild rumour of the shooting incident, which quickly escalated the number of dead into the thousands, did as much as the bayonets to enforce discipline.

An hour after the shooting had taken place, Mordecai Rosen received a telephone call in his office from Colonel Levy.

'The situation here has been contained,' the Colonel said.

Mordecai Rosen had received similar reports from the

other airfields that had been opened up round the country, airfields operating from any piece of ground large enough for a plane to land and take-off. The ports were under control; the sea off the coast-line was said to be filled with all manner of floating craft. Inevitably, there were stories of fishermen taking people on board only for a cash payment, sometimes up to the value of five thousand dollars, in any currency, or in watches, rings, personal jewels.

Every pleasure-cruise boat, cargo vessel, even tanker, within range of Israel had either arrived or was arriving, prepared to take as many people as could hang on to the decks and superstructure.

They came from everywhere. Everywhere, that is, except Arabia . . .

The PLO's de facto officers were at a meeting in Damascus with the Syrians. The Egyptians, the Jordanians and the Saudi Arabians had not been invited.

Yassir Arafat was reported to be somewhere near the east bank of the Jordan, with a token force ready to strike for Jerusalem when the country had been abandoned. Or atom blasted.

The meeting was chaired by General al Mahmoud el Aziz, of the Syrian Force Commander's Staff. On the wall was a map of Israel and its surrounding borders. Al Mahmoud used his leather-covered walking cane, a present from the British over thirty years ago when he passed through Sandhurst, to emphasize the locations of Syrian Units in the Lebanon, in Syria, in Jordan.

'In addition to the forces you see represented here, gentlemen, we shall land units of the Syrian Parachute Regiment here, here, and here.' He stabbed the map each time he spoke. 'These units will be supplied, via airborne transport, with armour and guns. Our intelligence shows us that the Israeli Air Force is not being used to ferry civilians out of Israel, but has been concentrated at two single airfields, here and here.' Again, the stick tapped the map. 'Other military airfields are, however, being opened for the use of foreign air forces and lines, to speed the exodus. We shall not, of course, interfere with these planes. Our informant in the Knesset tells us that a last minute attempt is being made to rally some remnants of an Israeli Army which will be held along the Hebron – Jenin line. It seems that the pocket behind them is the only territory the Israelis consider to be, in the circumstances, defensible. We shall show them, of course, that not even that premise is valid.'

The PLO officers were less interested in the military plans than in political matters.

'We are prepared to set up a government immediately,' they said. 'But we shall need an injection of technicians to man the essential services, and of course, assistance from the military to maintain security. But we repeat that we are ready to set up a full working government *immediately*.'

'Under Yassir Arafat?'

'Yes.'

The General was silent. Like a good military man, he knew not to stray from secured and defensible positions. 'You understand,' he said, 'that I have no authority to speak of political matters. I was asked to chair this meeting to outline to you our *military* intentions. Political matters I leave to the larger arena of the politicians. I can, however, assure you that within twenty-four hours of the bomb's explosion, any part of Israel fit for human survival will be held by the Syrians . . .'

'I hope you mean, by our joint forces,' the Palestinian spokesman said, chillingly.

'A mere slip of the tongue,' the General said. 'Of course I mean by *our joint forces*, ready and willing, as ever, to place their strength unreservedly at the disposal of the politicians.'

With nothing to add, he rose to his feet to indicate the end of the meeting.

'Someone must get to Yassir immediately,' the spokesman whispered to the man next to him, under the noise of the scraping chairs. 'I think we're being deceived . . .'

The General halted at the door. 'Just one more thing,' he said. 'In view of the delicate nature of the disclosures

I have made to you as regards our military plans, I'm
certain you will agree to remain inside this building for a
short time?'

'You mean we're to consider ourselves under house
arrest?'

'Not *arrest*. Merely, shall we say, protective custody.'

'And how long is – a short time?'

'Thát, I'm afraid, is another matter that must depend
on the politicians,' the General said, as he turned and left.

The former inhabitants of Kibbutz Givona had, somehow
miraculously, managed to stay together, getting onto the
same aeroplane at Lod, flying to Heraklion, transferring
to Alitalia, arriving in Naples Airport, being loaded onto
a convoy of ten trucks after a hasty meal, and driven south.

To Aona Vecchia.

It stood on the summit of a hill with magnificent views
over the arid countryside, neglected for decades. The houses
were forlorn, abandoned, many with roofs caved in, broken
walls, doors and window frames long ago cracked by the
blistering heat.

The lorries dropped them at the base of the hill with
sacks of flour, tins of sardines, cans of water, barrels of
olive oil, and two crates of live chickens.

'Someone will come,' the drivers said. 'Soon. There is a
committee in Rome. Already they have promises of one
billion lire.'

They trudged slowly up the hillside to the houses above.
Already, Abraham was seeing the slopes covered with vine-
yards, citrus fruits and tomato vines. Already he could see
the derelict houses repaired, cleaned and whitewashed,
with red tiled roofs. There was even a church, a large awe-
inspiring edifice with a tower containing three bells.

Abraham led the way through the ruins. 'Here,' he said,
'we will build our synagogue. Here we shall have our meeting hall, here, our dining room, here the kitchen and the
laundry. The school will be here, the dormitory for the
children here, in this large house. It is a miracle,' he said.

Others saw the long-tailed rats slinking around the ruins,

the dryness, the broken walls and the dead trees, and lamented.

'You Joseph, and you, Aaron, will travel across the plain to the north, to find the nearest village still alive. Find where we can obtain seeds, food, until we can grow our own, and medicines.'

They gathered about him like sheep. None had his courage, his strength, his resilience in the face of adversity. But slowly, one by one, he brought them to his way. 'You, Simon, take charge of the food. Make out a daily portion to last two weeks . . .'

'But they will come with food! The committee in Rome . . .'

'Bah! The committee in Rome! They have one billion lire. First, they must hold out their hands and have a meeting to decide how much we get, how much they get. Since when did we rely on any committee.' He held wide his arms. 'We are our own *Committee*,' he said. 'With God's Blessing we have come out together. We will stay together, work together, as we have always done!' He bent down and, in a dramatic gesture, picked up a handful of the sterile dirt at his feet. 'We will make this into soil, we will make it fertile. Yes, though it is not the soil of Israel, we will make it grow. And Aona Vecchia will become Givona Nova! The New Givona, shining like a star on this barren plain. Rachel, don't stand there! Take a team of women and make us a camp for this night. We will huddle together and sleep beneath the stars. Ben, go again and inspect every house. Mark those which can be saved, mark those which we will pull down to use the stone. Matthew, you are the architect. Go with Ben and lay out a plan for us. Rebecca, go with Simon and work out what you can cook. Emmaline the Gracious One, take a horde with you and scour the fields of the plain for anything, any tiny plant whose leaves will nourish us. And, when you find it, bring it carefully, with its ball of soil about it, and plant it lovingly into the ground near to those trees. If they can find water beneath the soil, so can our little plant. And you, Archimedes, for the love of God, find us water!'

Water! On this arid plain? It was like asking for gold.

But without it, each one of them knew they could not survive.

They gathered together, eyes that had been dull now shining with the light Abraham reflected into them, the hope and the strength. They knelt on the ground, facing the land they had left. Abraham reached into his pocket, took out his handkerchief and opened it. The handkerchief contained a handful of melon seeds he had grabbed at the start of their flight. They turned and faced the land from which they had fled. And slowly, above them, rose the chants of prayers of hope, faith, and a courage that burned with unextinguishable fire.

The planes arriving at Gatwick Airport discharged their bewildered passengers onto buses that took them to the terminal. There, the WVS from the nearby town had arranged a continuous buffet in the large dining room. Each passenger, given a tray, walked along the line of beaming ladies, each standing behind a prepared dish of roast beef in gravy, toad-in-the-hole, thin sliced bread and butter, boiled potatoes, cabbage, peas. For those who preferred, a glass of milk was available, or a cup of milky sweetened coffee.

The first refugees, as the WVS ladies called them, took the trays heaped with food and sat at the tables provided. They looked at each other. Few ventured to eat. A few nibbled the boiled cabbage.

The newly-appointed President of the Committee for Israeli Refugee Aid, himself a Jew, arrived late but dashed to the dining room where, he was informed, the first refugees were being served their first 'British' meal. He frowned with alarm as he climbed the steps to the restaurant. When he arrived, his worst fears were confirmed. He saw the meat served with milk, the pork sausages in their milky batter . . .

'We know about the eating habits of our friends,' the lady from the WVS told him with pride. 'So you'll see we haven't offered them any ham, though personally, I see nothing wrong with a good ham and egg salad.'

He looked round at the men sitting at the tables with their black hats, their ringlets, others wearing the yarmulka, a glazed expression of incomprehension on their faces.

'Madame,' he said heavily. 'I'm afraid I have a lot of explaining to do. Both to them, and to you . . .'

The USS *Cambridge* was part of Task Force 63, the service force of ships providing fuel, supplies, ammunition, and repairs to all units of the Sixth Fleet.

The *Cambridge* was a salvage and repair vessel, virtually a floating workshop with the ability to effect major repairs to fleet vessels while still at sea. It had engineering rooms, welding equipment, wood-working, even a forge with induction furnaces for casting stainless steel. The laboratories could repair optical lens systems, radio, radar, and sonar.

The deck carried two 100-ton cranes and a full diving facility.

The sonar room, located below the Fighting Bridge, itself behind the Duty Bridge and separated from it by heavy armour, operated not only as part of the *Cambridge*'s normal navigation system but also as an ear for the location of submerged and possibly crippled vessels.

Chief Petty Officer Margerisson was sitting at his desk, filling in duty return forms, when Petty Officer Third Class Vrajek called him over. Vrajek took off his head-phones and handed them to the Chief. 'Want to take a listen, Chief?' he said.

The Chief held one of the phones to his ear, heard the customary ping, pause, ping, looked at the setting of the sonar console. 'What've you got, Vrajek?' he asked.

Vrajek scratched his head. 'I've been onto it, now, for ten minutes I've plotted a course for it, and a depth . . .'

'So . . . ?'

'It's headed for the coast of Israel, about five miles south of Tel Aviv, by my plot.'

'Jesus . . .'

'Steady speed of five knots. Funny thing, Chief. Seems to be following a programme . . .'

'How come?'

'It's keeping a fixed height off the sea bed. When the sea bed rises, that damn thing comes up. When the sea bed goes down, that mother follows it. You couldn't get such an accurate reaction from a human navigator. It's uncanny.'

'So, what the hell is it?'

'It's my guess we've found what they're all looking for. The untraceable French Submarine. That Green Dolphin baby.'

CHAPTER TWENTY-SEVEN

They winched Bill Harrington onto the deck of the *Cambridge* from a helicopter of the USS *Independence*. Marc followed him two minutes later, looking distinctly green.

An ensign, distinguishable by the half inch ring round his sleeve, led them down to the sonar room where both listened to the echo. The Chief showed them to the chart table in the centre of the room. A light shone from below, illuminating the chart, covered with plexi-glass. 'You understand,' the Chief said, 'that it's difficult to get a route from just a few plots, close together. We've connected them as best we can, and whatever it is, it seems to be headed on a very well controlled compass bearing. Extrapolating that line leads to the coast of Israel. We estimate – well, I'll be frank, it's a "guesstimate" – that it will hit ten miles south of Tel Aviv, give or take five to six miles, either way, around ten hours from now.'

'I don't get it,' Marc said, bewildered. 'How can you get a reaction from a vessel that's not supposed to give one? How is it that Sophie couldn't get a reading, with all the sophisticated equipment at her disposal?'

'She did get a reaction,' Bill reminded him. 'But she couldn't separate it from the transmission of the Dolphin itself . . .'

The Chief had been following their dialogue. 'If I might suggest something, gentlemen?' he asked deferentially. 'Look, I'm just a working technician. This girl, Sophie, was presumably working with specialist equipment designed for one purpose, the detection and control of one piece of apparatus?'

'That's right.'

'I thought so. I was on the Wood's Hole project. Spent a lot of time working underwater equipment by sonar transmission on a deep core alignment project. Look, that equipment is designed for one specific purpose. The best way I can explain it is this. Give a guy a pair of very strong binoculars, right? So strong that every movement of his hands registers as a shift of fifty or sixty yards on the terrain he's surveying. Useless, huh? Properly mounted on a tripod, with a means of delicate adjustment, and the binoculars will tell you the sex of a fly at a thousand yards, know what I mean? But give a guy a pair of normal, say eight or ten power glasses, and he'll find what he's looking for. The apparatus your gal Sophie was using is probably like the ultra-high power binocs; what we have here is like the eight power. We work coarse, tune in fine. That's our job . . .'

'D'accord,' Marc said. 'I accept your very good illustration of why Sophie couldn't find it, but that doesn't explain how you *could*. That submarine was designed, Chief Petty Officer . . .'

'The guys have a warped sense of humour. They call me Marge . . .'

'D'accord. Marge. It doesn't explain how you *could* find it. It was designed so that one *couldn't* – or, rather the *Russians* couldn't – locate it.'

Marge walked to the headphones. 'I don't swear categorically that it is your Green Dolphin,' he said. 'But sure as hell, there's something down there, and it's headed for Israel. There's only one way to find out . . .'

'And that is?'

'Go down and take a look.'

They kitted Bill in the diving room on the aft deck. Three

petty officers, second class, put on wetsuits to come with him. The other members of the diving crew stood by, for rescue work if required.

'That baby will be doing five knots when you get there,' Marge said. 'From what you say, it'll have an impact or a proximity fuse on the warhead. So, for chrissake, stay away from the nose.'

Bill had spoken to Jules Lachard on the radio telephone from the *Cambridge*. 'If is it the Dolphin,' Jules said, 'the propulsion mechanism is underneath. You'll see a forward facing and a rear facing hole. The forward facing hole contains a self-clearing grille, two plates which rotate on each other, like the blades of a mincer. Ça va sans dire, you don't put your fingers in there. If you can take down with you a circle of half inch thick sheet plexiglass, or even aluminium, you should be able to block the intake. The plexiglass or metal will be sucked back against the skin of the Dolphin with enormous force, so be careful. The circle should be 30 cms diameter. Once you have blocked the engine intake, the engine will overheat and trip the electric supply. But be extremely careful. The Dolphin has a negative weight in water of 10 degrees centigrade. Once you have stopped the motor, the Dolphin should slowly come to the surface. If you get it to the surface, don't, whatever you do, attempt to touch it. I'm leaving Toulon now, and hope to be with you as soon as possible.'

The Chief Engineering Artificer on board came into the diving room with two sheets of plastic, from which two elastic toggles were hanging. The plastic had been bent in the shape of a U, with one side very much longer than the other. 'Look, Bill,' he explained. 'That monkey down there has to have some kind of navigation apparatus. My guess is a couple of stubby side fins. Maybe you can hook these round the fins, and they'll act like ailerons, lift the damn thing up through the water. It'll be a lot easier to work on if you can get it to the surface.

'We could even pick it out of the drink, and swing it inboard . . .'

The computer had worked out a time-and-place schedule, taking into account the direction and speed of the Dolphin, the time it would take for them to descend to its depth. A helicopter came over the *Independence* and, one by one, the three CPOs were winched aboard. The Commander of the *Cambridge*, Captain James Nelson, Jnr, had come to the deck to see them off; he clasped Bill's hand in his. 'Good luck, Mr Harrington,' he said. 'The eyes of the whole US Sixth Fleet are upon you . . .'

'And England expects that every man will do his duty, eh Captain?' Bill said, his smile removing any suggestion of malice from his words.

'I'll do as my predecessor did, and turn a blind eye on that remark,' Captain Nelson said. 'Good luck, successful mission, and a safe return!'

But as Bill turned away, the Captain's jovial smile receded. His face drained suddenly of colour. Harrington, he thought, was a very brave man indeed.

The ship's radio guided the helicopter on a computed bearing until it estimated they were exactly above the path of the Dolphin. Bill had strapped his chronometer next to the depth gauge on his wrist; by reading both together he hoped to be able to achieve a controlled rate of descent.

The helicopter pilot was now hovering a few feet above the surface. The water below was choppy, with six foot rollers moving down from the north, but no white caps. A brilliant late autumn sun shone and would penetrate well for the first hundred feet of depth. Sonar had the Dolphin steady at a depth of twenty-five fathoms, one hundred and fifty feet. They had scanned forward, predicting a path. The sea-bed was flat for the next twenty miles or so.

They sat side by side in the open door of the helicopter, ankles braced together. The skipper of the helicopter signalled a one-minute warning to the despatcher. He tapped Bill's shoulder once. Bill turned so that he was hanging from the sill of the doorway by his stomach, his bottle pack clear, his mask around his throat but the demand valve already in his mouth. The other three flipped over, to hang in the same position. There had been no time to check

Bill's buoyancy before leaving. He was wearing three lead-weighted belts, two of which he could jettison if he were too heavy and sank too rapidly through the water. He was wearing a triple pack in a plastic housing; the three bottles should give him a maximum of forty-five minutes working time at that depth, plus decompression time.

In case of accident, the hospital aboard the *Cambridge* contained a full manned decompression unit.

'Go!' Three rapid taps. Bill pushed with both hands, lifted himself well clear of the sill, and dropped.

As soon as he was in the water, he rubbed his mask and put it on his face. He held it tight across his forehead and blew out of his nose. The blowing cleared the trapped water downwards out of the mask, and he could see perfectly. He bent up his foot, put on one flipper, lifted the other and put that one on too.

He checked his watch and depth gauge. Hard to tell accurately, but he seemed to be sinking too fast. He held the watch close to his mask and checked the seconds; yes, definitely fast. He looked about him and saw no sign of Peter, Mack, and Don, the three POs. He looked upwards. Christ, he was too far below them. He assumed that they, with knowledge of their equipment, were closer to the designed rate of fall. But, lacking experience, he was reluctant to jettison his first lead-weight belt. Peter, recognizable by the large P painted on his bottle holder, came level with him, flippering himself head downwards. He gestured to Bill's belt; Bill unbuckled and dropped it, and immediately felt his descent checked. Peter stopped flippering and both fell naturally under their calculated negative buoyancy. Peter gave him a thumbs up sign, unwound the loop of cord at his waist and handed the clip to Bill. Bill attached it to his belt, and Peter flippered away to the south, on a compass bearing. Don came down, handed Bill another cord which Bill clipped on, then Don headed to the north, still visible in the water at the end of his cord. Finally, Mack attached a third, and swam behind and below Bill, covering visually as much of the ocean as they could.

Bill heard a rumble slowly approaching when they had

reached twenty fathoms, one hundred and twenty feet. The rumble died down a little, but remained on the surface of the ocean in front of them. The *Cambridge* was hovering; picking them up on its sonar just as a trawler skipper can pick up the mouth of his trawl and the location of a shoal of fish.

Bill watched his depth gauge. He was approaching twenty-five fathoms. He strained his eyes ahead towards the compass bearing west. The Dolphin, if that's what it was, would approach them at five knots.

They would only get one chance at it.

If they missed, they would have to go up and dive in its path again.

Then Bill heard the percussion signal from the *Cambridge* above them. One. Okay for depth. One more. Okay for lateral position.

It was coming straight at them.

Another signal, from the *Cambridge*. A thousand feet from them.

Bill flippered gently, keeping height, scissoring slowly to counteract any tendency to fall deeper. He slowly adjusted his position so that he was lying at forty-five degrees on the water, ready to make his lightning flipper dash.

One percussion signal from the Dolphin, then a second almost immediately afterwards. Five hundred feet away.

'Watch the nose,' the Chief Engineering Artificer had said. 'It's bound to be an impact fuse, and probably a proximity.'

Down below them. Jesus. At least fifty feet below them. Sudden quick flash. Two pulls on the line attached to his back. a fish, Jesus, what a fish. A whole school of large mullet came past, flashing pink. A fish four feet long, black and grey, with an enormous ugly head and a comb of bristling spines. It headed towards Bill, its eyes gazing fixedly at him, its mouth working like that of an idiot. He reached down, unfastened the buckle on the knife sheath attached to his right leg. 'Piss Off!' he thought, unable to shout with the demand valve in his mouth.

For some reason, his mask began to mist. He removed

it, rubbed it with his finger, put it back on, and had blown half the air out of it, when he saw the Dolphin. Ten feet below him, fifty feet or so away to his side. The others had seen it and he felt the initial tugs on his cords, which then went slack as they all converged on it. It was driving through the water at what seemed to them to be a fantastic speed. Bill turned and flipped sideways and down, working out a course that would bring him level with the Dolphin and slightly in front. It was like working out the angle for a rugby tackle, when real time vanishes and all you can do is project yourself, hoping your mental arithmetic, performed by pure instinct, is correct. And on a rugby field, the only penalty for an error is a black eye, a busted nose, a broken collar-bone . . .

Flipper fast, using ankles, legs to the knee, with economy. Hands outstretched.

Now he knew why they had been able to hear the *untraceable* Dolphin by sonar from the *Cambridge*. She was wearing a girdle – festooned with the iron anchor chain Dutch George had looped around her. They had not heard the Dolphin. They had heard the chain.

Going down and across fast. Seeing the painted eye from above. The damn thing looked almost real.

Going too fast, he thought. I'll overshoot.

He bent his waist and jack-knifed, reaching out, grasping for the chain, slimy to his hands. He grabbed again, caught a finger in a loop, two fingers, three, then his hand around a whole section. The Dolphin was pulling him along, his body streamlining alongside her, flippers touching her. He pushed his hand through a twist of chain and out again, grasping it from the inside, holding on with the other hand. The slipstream swept along the sleek, spongy skin, snapping his mask from his eyes, down alongside his throat, but he held on. He held on. Other arms beside his clasped the chain, a knee kicked him in the face, on the bone beside his eye. He fumbled with his free hand for the goggles, brought them up over his eyes and blew the water from them. Now they seemed more secure.

A sudden jerk in the small of his back. Damn it, Mack

had missed and now was being towed through the water on the end of Bill's line. Bill knew he could not hold on much longer one-handed, towing a twelve-stone man behind him. He tapped Peter's shoulder quickly and repeatedly. Peter turned and Bill pointed to the line, streaming out behind. Each put a hand on it and pulled. Together they managed to take up four or five feet of slack. Peter wound the cord round his wrist; Bill unclipped it from his belt and re-clipped it around a link of the chain. They felt the throb of the engine increase as the Dolphin maintained speed with its added weight.

Bill had a two-metre line secured to his shoulders, coming round in front of him and ending in a snap-hook. He clipped it round the chain as far forward as it would stretch. Then he unwound his hand from the chain. The cord took the strain of his body and he was able to ease himself, hand over hand, around the Dolphin's belly, heading beneath it. The skin was slimy and horrible to the touch. Worse still, the chain had bitten into its softness and the links were buried. Bill had to dig in his fingers to maintain a grip as he went round; it was like dipping his hands into raw meat.

Now he was lying beneath the Dolphin, the back of his neck facing the direction of travel, his legs, apart, on each side of its underbelly. The intake hole for the engine was ahead of him, the hot water stream from the rear of the turbine blades about six feet behind him.

He let go with one hand. The cord was taking most of the forward pull, though, with only one hand holding, he had a tendency to whip sideways. Don came round the side of the Dolphin, grabbed Bill's waist, and dragged him further forward. He clipped one end of the cord that had been attached to his waist through a shackle of the chain. By pulling it, he could bring Bill slowly forward.

Bill could hear the rushing water entering the forward intake about twelve inches above his head. He made a thumbs up sign to Don, who lashed the end of the cord securely.

Bill now let go with his second hand, hanging from both

cords. The pressure of water past his streamlined bottle case pushed him, not too strongly, against the underside of the Dolphin. He opened the bag he carried on his chest and from it slowly drew the aluminium plate they had made according to Jules' specifications. He worked it against the skin of the Dolphin, his hands bitterly cold in the rushing water. He pressed his knees up against the underside. By bringing them up towards his chest he found he could arch his body into a shallow crouch that gave him more room to use his hands and arms to convey the aluminium plate forwards towards the water intake. Now that he was nearer, he could feel the tug of water being drawn into the turbine, through those rapidly revolving mincing blades. He wondered how many fish had been drawn in there, minced, and spewed out the back as effluence, like a living animal will pass food through its intestines.

The plate was at the tip of the mouth of the hole. He braced his hands against it. Slid it further forward, straight in line. He suddenly felt the tremendous pressure on his hands as the force of the intake tried to tilt the plate against him. He knew he couldn't hold the strain too long. He tried to ram the plate forward, but the entry force was too much and tipped it across the edges of the hole, threatening to pull it completely forward. He held on and braced himself backwards, but he had no leverage, no pull. Don had been watching what he was doing and saw his dilemma. He wound one arm round a chain, offered Bill his other arm, bent, for him to hang on to, to steady himself. Then they both pulled and slowly the lower edge of the plate was brought backwards, against the pull of the intake.

Bill glanced back along the Dolphin. Mack had made it, pulling himself against the drag along the cord they had clipped to the chain.

Peter had wound his half of the flotation belt around the belly of the Dolphin. Mack handed him the other half he had been carrying and worked his way across Bill's legs to the other side, out of view. If Bill could stop the engine, they would inflate that collar and bring the Dolphin to the surface.

The plate snapped home. They heard the inner throb of the engine build to a crescendo.

The motor stopped.

The Dolphin shuddered.

Then it slowly began to sink. It should have had positive buoyancy, as designed. But now it was carrying a girdle comprising several hundredweight of iron chain.

Mack took the spare hose from his air supply and clipped the end to the valve on the collar. Using the hoses's trigger, he started to inflate the collar with air from his bottle. Slowly the Dolphin stopped its downwards plunge and came to rest, hanging nose down.

In that posture it would be hell to lift on board the *Cambridge*. They tried dragging the collar along the Dolphin's sides, with cords pulled around it, but the pressure of air inside the collar forced it tight against the Dolphin, as had been intended. The collar could not be moved. Mack checked his bottle pressure. He had insufficient left to deflate the collar and reinflate it.

And they dared not deflate the collar too far, lest the Dolphin slip out of it and plunge nose down, to the bed of the ocean.

Bill swam along the Dolphin's side, examining it. He found the stubby directional fins. One each side, one above. In the rush to stop the engine, he had not thought of using the fins the Engineer Artificer had supplied. But they would not have fitted anyway.

He knew the sonar room of the *Cambridge* would understand what had happened, would see the two reflections had coincided and were now stationary.

The procedure should be that having inflated the collar, Mack would make for the surface, spooling with him the thin nylon line Peter was carrying on the outside of his bottle case. At the top, that thin line would be attached to a net which would be lowered by one of the 100-ton cranes at the end of a hawser. They would wrap the net around the Dolphin, and it could be hoisted to the surface. That was the theory.

He beckoned for the others to join him on the Dolphin's

tail. They tried exerting all their leverage downwards but, with nothing to grip, and no weight in the water, they could not force it down. He swam slowly to the front of the Dolphin, still hanging downwards in the water. How the hell did proximity fuses work? Obviously there would need to be a minimum mass requirement or every fish in the ocean could explode them. Did his body, with its attached bottles, constitute a *minimum mass*? He did not go close enough to find out.

Suddenly, the flaw in the whole technical plan they had devised on board the *Cambridge* hit him. They could not possibly hoist the Dolphin up there. He was damn sure the *Cambridge* would be well over minimum mass, the deck, the wheel-houses. Even if they could get it into the net safely, and hoist it through the water laying flat, the minute it came near the deck . . .

He beckoned to Mack, took the slate from his pocket and wrote on it with the underwater pen. 'No net. I defuse here.'

Mack looked at him, surprise in his eyes showing through the glass of his face mask. He wrote: 'Why?'

'Explain topside. All go.'

Mack shrugged, showed the slate to Pete and Don, both of whom shook their heads to indicate they would stay.

Bill thought for a moment, but then realized that if he made a mistake it would not matter where they were, with him, or with the *Cambridge*, overhead, at the fountain head of the massive atomic blast that would split the ship with one giant belly punch. He took Mack's slate again and wrote. 'You go. Tell ship move fast away. Okay.'

Mack nodded. He had glanced at his air pressure gauge in the meantime and knew he had only enough air to reach the surface if he left now. He clapped each of them on the shoulder, patted the Dolphin, made a thumbs up sign, and obviously reluctant to go, flippered upwards following the trail of his own air bubbles.

Bill had located the Dolphin's entry door, fortunately unhampered by the chain girdle and the compressed air collar. It was a rounded rectangle, about five feet long and three feet wide, near the tail on the top. He pushed his cold hands into the squidgy rubber, and located two indented catches. He beckoned to Peter and Don to swim away to some distance, not knowing what would happen when he opened the door. Jules Lachard had said that blocking the water intake to the engine would cause the electrics to overload and trip. He had not implied it would stop the Dolphin's power source.

Fingers into the first catch, he slid it sideways. It moved easily, obviously precision built and well lubricated still, despite its immersion in corrosive sea water.

Second catch. Bill hesitated. Would the interior of the Dolphin be under pressure from the air that must be inside it? Was Jacques Morel still there? Alive? If so, opening that hatch must surely condemn him to an immediate drowning death.

Could he have heard them working on the outside, through the rubber skin? Might he, in fact, be waiting inside the door, wearing bottles and a mask, with a knife or an underwater gun in his hand?

Bill reached down and took his own knife from the sheath on his leg, holding it in the palm of his right hand with the blade pointing forwards.

He slid the second catch all the way.

The door banged open, came off its slip hinges and went clattering away down the side of the Dolphin, narrowly missing the nose as it whirled past.

A monstrous bubble of air ballooned from the inside of the Dolphin. Bill was caught in it, gulped automatically as the water blew out of his nostril ends, and then smelled the terrible foetid stench, sickeningly rotten, of unoxydized sulphides.

He was immediately sick, the vomit pushing the demand valve from his mouth as it burst from him. Instinctively he grabbed for it and swished it through the water before wiping his mouth with the back of his hand, and clamping the demand valve back in.

He breathed the clean air it gave deeply, turned back to look inside the Dolphin.

The rotten, hideously bloated face of Jacques Morel floated six inches from his own.

He pushed himself backwards, gagging again.

The body slowly slid itself free of the hatch, its belly grossly inflated by gas, and began to float upwards through the ocean. Bill, his head bowed down, racked by spasms of nausea that griped his stomach, let it go.

Other air bubbles foamed from the Dolphin as water flooded it. Bill flipped himself out of reach, and hovered until what seemed to be the last one escaped.

The mouth of the hatch was filled with floating detritus; plastic bags containing food solids, papers, two seat cushions, a hank of nylon rope. He went forward again, dragged the hatch clear of obstructions, and poked his head inside.

Three lights behind glass panels still gleamed inside the Dolphin, illuminating its interior. It would be logical, he thought, to make everything water-proof in such a vessel. The power source was obviously still working. Maintaining the detonator and fuse system of the atomic warhead.

He reached for the inside of the Dolphin, using corners to pull himself, face forward, down along its interior.

He braced himself against the back of the seat where Jacques had been sitting. The computer was still operational, to judge from the pattern on the rubber sealed screen in front of him. He pushed away the piece of paper that partly obscured it but could not make anything of the pattern.

To the left of the screen a small red light gleamed. He went close to read the Dymo-type tape that had been fixed below it.

It said, simply, ARMED.

Bill's worst fears were confirmed.

Below the light was a digital timer. As Bill watched, the timer clicked from 00002 to 00001. He glanced at his watch, noting the time.

The propulsion engine must be housed below this console, to judge from the locations of the inlet and outlet tubes. To the right of the console, was a box about three feet square, taking up most of the right hand side. As he listened, he could hear a quiet throb. That would be the isotope decay engine, which provided power both for propulsion, and for the instrumentation. Beneath it would be a bank of cadmium cell batteries, constantly recharging themselves. Somewhere would be a relay so that the power would automatically switch from the batteries when they were fully charged. The wiring would be beneath the flooring panels.

The digital timer changed from 00001 to 00000.

The red light began to flicker.

The human mind is its own computer, pulsing thoughts through the brain faster than any electronic data base.

At that instant in time, Bill realized how he had been caught. Obviously, they would not just rely on an impact or a proximity fuse to detonate the warhead. If, for any reason, the Dolphin were held at the entrance to a harbour, temporarily stalled, it would lie there, useless, for ever.

Once the Dolphin were stalled, the clock would come into operation, turning the Dolphin into a self-motivated time bomb.

The flashing light would indicate that the atomic warhead was now on its countdown.

But how many hours, minutes, even seconds, would elapse before it exploded?

Bill's instinct was to scrabble backwards as fast as he could, even though he would have no hope of getting out of the range of that monstrous explosion.

They say all your life flashes before your inner eye when you know you are going to die. A last, split-micro-second of chance to acknowledge your sins and ask forgiveness.

Bill could only think how stupid he had been not to think this thing through. But how could he have known, until he had seen the light and the digital timer in operation? This anger at his own stupidity propelled him forwards, down into the nose of the Dolphin. A flat black metal plate, stamped with the code letters H.Ex.WD.7007.

Three wires coming out of the floor gully and going inside a rubber-grommeted hole.

Think, Bill, in the micro-seconds that are probably all

you have left. Why *three*? A contact can be made with *two* wires, a contact of electricity strong enough to make a spark to ignite a detonator.

One wire – an additional safety device, perhaps? Two of the wires would not work unless the third is also connected, like the input to a solenoid coil.

Three wires. Yes, they could be a fail-safe device, but just two wires would work, the third containing an alternative supply. If one wire breaks, is severed, the other ones function. Like some types of burglar alarm.

But, which were the two, which was the one? All were grey. He spun them gently in his fingers, now no longer cold. Sometimes wires carried a colour code down their length, in the form of dots.

Nothing distinguished any one of these three.

Do something, Bill, his mind screamed. *Do* something! Yes, but what?

Sheer necessity took over. He grabbed all three wires, bunched them in his hand and yanked them towards him.

There was a flash from within the black plate that illuminated the side of the rubber grommet.

He pulled the wires towards himself, towards his face, through the rubber grommet, and left them dangling as he worked his way backwards.

The red light had gone out.

The isotope decay engine had ceased to throb.

The three lights illuminating the inside of the Dolphin slowly faded in intensity as they drained the unrecharged batteries.

He dragged himself backwards and out through the hatch.

The Dolphin was dead.

He felt no exhilaration, though, no triumph. Only an immense fatigue, a marrow-bone-cold tiredness that drained him of all energy, all thoughts, all expectations.

He beckoned Pete to come near, took the end of the thin nylon line from the spool, signalled for them to stay to handle the net.

Then he flippered slowly through the tranquil waters above him.

At the same time, one of the officers on board the *Cambridge* went for'ard to the wood-working shop where Artificer Class Three Lemuel Rosen was spindle-turning a piece of African walnut to make a furniture repair for the ward room. The officer handed Lemuel a piece of paper without speaking. Lemuel switched off the lathe and went down to the mess-deck, where he gave the paper to one of the radio operators. He glanced at it and nodded.

It was a telegram addressed to a small hotel in Athens.

For the attention of a guest called Benjamin Moishe.

The radio operator went back on duty, but only after he had eaten his chicken Maryland and piece of pecan pie with ice-cream.

CHAPTER TWENTY-EIGHT

There were scenes of jubilation aboard the USS *Cambridge* as the news was flashed to the Flagship, *Albany*, and thence to Gaeta, Italy, and Washington.

'The Dolphin has been located, and disarmed.'

Washington/London.

Washington/Paris.

Washington/Jerusalem.

The President himself made the brief telephone call to Rolf Mueller, who listened without speaking and then sat back in his chair, and cried.

General Rosen ordered all units of the Israeli Air Force into the skies to make a highly visible tour of the border territories.

He also ordered a commando force to head for Tebratha, where Yassir Arafat had last been sighted by Mossad agents.

General al Mahmoud ordered the release of the Palestinians, and closed the Exodus Two file on his desk before dropping it into the waste-paper basket for shredding.

The White House press corps besieged the President's Press Secretary, Will Wentz. 'Does the President now withdraw his resignation?' Will went through to the President's office and put the question to him.

'No, Will, I do not.'

'Any reason I can give, Mr President?'

'Do you really want to know, Will? Not for publication. I just do not think, any more, that any one man should have to take such decisions. I do not think any *one* man *can* decide the fate of a whole nation. I no longer want to be the President because I no longer believe that any country should *have* a *President*. Unless it's an honorary title, like that of the Queen of England . . . But you can tell the boys from the press – no comment.'

The Prime Minister of England addressed a crowded House of Commons. There were such loud shouts of 'Resign, Resign,' from the Opposition Bench that the Speaker of the House broke the centuries' old gavel trying to secure order. When, at last, the tumult subsided, the PM bowed towards the Speaker. 'It's rather depressing to see the Honourable Gentlemen of the Opposition reminding us so vocally of their juvenile approach to the conduct of the affairs of this country,' he said. 'Perhaps they would be better employed watching football matches. I merely wished to inform them that the Dolphin has been located and defused but, since that matter is of no interest, perhaps we should pass back to the matter of debating the amendments to the Bill for the provision of more public utilities in remote areas, a subject I am sure will be more dear to their hearts . . .'

His last words were drowned in cheers.

The refugees, located in a disused Army camp in Froston, Surrey, queued silently for the buses that would take them back to Gatwick Airport. Each of them carried a bag containing apples, the only available food they could guarantee was kosher.

Abraham drew his people around him in the cleared square of Aona Vecchia. 'There is no need for talk,' he said. 'Each of us knows what is in his heart. We will vote. Will all those who are in favour please raise one hand?'

The hands were unanimous.

'Very well. We stay. Isaac, you will carve the name Givona Nova on the board, and we will hang it for all to see.'

The US Sixth Fleet sailed east as rapidly as possible. Soon, they were lined alongside the coast of Israel, a clearly visible display of strength.

The queue of people stretching for a mile from Lod Airport turned and began to walk back the ways they had come.

Bill was standing on the aft deck of the *Cambridge*, dog-tired, while the crew produced cameras and took pictures of him, with Don, Pete, and Mack, standing beside the Dolphin. Its eye seemed to leer at him, its gaping mouth ready to snap. In the crowd of ratings thronging around, suddenly he saw a face he recognized. 'Come here, Vrajek,' he said. 'If any man deserves to have his picture taken, it's you. And you, too, Marge. Get in here.'

When he tried to bring Marc Chantal into the pictures, to take some of the embarrassing pressure off himself, Marc smiled at him with good humour and shook his head.

He knew, they all knew, the moment belonged to Bill.

The desk clerk at the Hotel Lukia finished writing the cable that had been telephoned from the post office. He tore the page from the pad. 'Look after the desk,' he told Sylvia and took the lift to the fifth floor, then walked rapidly along the corridor to room 507.

The air in the room was thick with cigarette smoke and the odour of a Greek cigar.

'I have a telegram,' the clerk said.

'And I have a belly-ache from all this lousy Greek food,' Ben Moishe said, holding out his hand.

The clerk looked around the room. Eight men, two girls, all with the hard faces, the lean muscular frames, of *sabras*. All wearing jeans, patch-pocket shirts. A map of the Mediterranean had been pinned to the wall, next to the wardrobe.

He handed the telegram to Ben, who glanced at it, seeming to take in its contents with a flick of his eyes.

All were watching him. 'We're moving out,' he said.

He grabbed the desk clerk's arm. 'Get on to Aaron for me, at Olympic. We'll need tickets . . .'

The desk clerk's face beamed. 'Am I coming with you . . . ? Back to active duty? Honest, my wound's healed. I don't even feel any pain in that shoulder any more . . .'

Ben shook his head. 'No, Joseph,' he said. 'We need you here in Athens . . .'

'Oh, shit, Ben. Bring me back in, for God's sake.'

'Joseph, the Mossad needs you *here*. It needs all the undercover men it has, spread all over the globe. You're our eyes, our ears, Joseph. Without you, we'd be blind, and deaf.

'And, one day, this will happen again . . .'

CHAPTER TWENTY-NINE

By direct appeal to the Prime Minister, Sally Price got herself aboard an RAF jet, and was waiting by the dock when Bill arrived at Chora Sfakion. He could not bear the thought of returning at this moment. He had asked for, and been granted, a few days of leave. Chora Sfakion was as near and as good a place as any; he intended to spend those days sitting on the shingle below the walk around the harbour, doing nothing more energetic than watching the autumn breakers come rolling in. And, in the evenings, he would drink an ouzo while he decided what he would have for dinner, eaten, long and slow, on the terrace by the sea.

Marc had returned to Paris, with Sophie and the body of Phillipe. The body of Jacques Morel had not been found.

Joseph Aram had been airlifted to London. Held in maximum security, he still had not said a single word.

Akhtar was dead, Burgler was dead, and Henri Dupree had not been found.

Kostas Aronakis had disappeared when the Greek policemen who had come for him were leading him down the goat-track. He had simply dived into the sea over the edge of the sheer rock face, and had not been seen since.

Ioannis had been given a cash compensation for the loss of his sheep, and had now taken possession of Aronakis's place. The Greek military had blocked up the entrance to the downstairs rooms and the cave with steel doors, before closing the file.

These last thoughts flashed through Bill's mind as the cutter from the *Cambridge* brought him alongside the dock. He leaped onto the concrete, seized Sally in his arms, and held her. Neither of them spoke for a while. The Ensign who had escorted him ashore gave a salute, then offered his hand. Bill shook it.

'It's been a great honour to meet you, Sir,' the ensign said, then leaped back aboard the cutter which moved off, and headed back out to sea.

'I didn't catch Yshtak, Sally,' he said. 'Or that she-devil, Khaylia Patin.'

'Don't think about that, Bill,' Sally said, taking his arm to walk around the short harbour road.

'We *must* think about it, Sally. We must all think about terrorism in more positive ways. So far, the terrorists have been held back only by the limitations of the weapons they could steal, to use as a means of frightening people. Ordinary people, Sally. The German beauty queens aboard that flight from Mallorca – I can't think they had an ounce of political thinking among them. The pilot of that plane – a hero, who died a pointless, useless, death in Aden.'

'He was a brave man. Look what he risked to let people know about the hijackers . . .'

'We need brave men to *live*, Sally, not to *die*. And now the terrorist cause can escalate. If, as Yshtak did, they can get hold of nuclear weapons, they can hold cities, even countries, to ransom, and there's nothing we can do about it. This time, Sally, we had a stroke of ridiculous luck. If that Dolphin had not chanced to go into the cave while Dutch George was working his illegal gold-mine, if Dutch George hadn't just *happened* to have a metal anchor chain down there, if he hadn't just *happened* to lock that anchor chain securely round the Dolphin's middle . . .'

'Surely, luck plays its part in everything that happens, Bill. If we hadn't just *happened* to have a man watching Dupree's apartment we wouldn't have connected the team together . . .'

'Sally, we've got to try to organize things so that luck plays *no part* in what we do. We can't depend on having good luck. The new Commando units are good, but are they enough? What could a Commando unit have done, here, that we didn't achieve by sheer chance?'

'And your bravery and skill, Bill!'

'That didn't prevent you being tortured by that bitch, Khaylia Patin, Sally, and Andreas Burgler. They could have killed you . . .'

His arm tightened about her; his eyes were full of remorse. 'I'll never rest, Sally, until we nail that bitch, Khaylia.'

'Khaylia Patin is dead, Bill,' she said quietly. 'The Mossad caught her in New York.'

'And Frank Elks?'

'He's in Switzerland. They've put him in protective custody while everybody works out what, if anything, can be done with him. They're saying in the office that they don't have anything to charge him with. He was acting as agent. Some people are saying release him. The Mossad will get to him, as surely as they got to Khaylia Patin. And presumably, they will eventually find Yshtak, and get to him.'

'So, there's nothing left to do. Except take a few days holiday, then get back to work and tidy up the loose ends before going on to the next print-out, the next computerized search and analysis.'

'It would seem so, Bill. You might find the strength to take me to see Knossos. I've never been to Knossos.'

'Nor have I,' Bill said, without apparent enthusiasm.

Agonistes was waiting at the door of the restaurant. 'Welcome, Mr Bill, welcome,' he said. 'We listen all, on the radio, look all, on the television.'

Emma saw them arrive and ran out from the kitchen. Bill introduced her to Sally Price.

'We've already met,' Emma said smiling. 'Sally has fixed up the front room for you, overlooking the ocean. It's yours, as long as you want it. On the house.'

God, he was tired! He looked at his watch, astounded to discover it was only nine thirty in the evening, although of a day, admittedly, that had started long before the 0400 hrs assault.

Sally had looked in the kitchen. 'Bill, they have marvellous big red mullet, and a lentil soup, and a salad, and feta cheese . . .'

He suddenly realized he was also hungry. 'I'll go upstairs and wash,' he said.

Sally had pushed the two single beds together, arranged two night tables beside them, each with a pot in which she had put fresh smelling herbs. She must have been to his Crawford Street flat; she had brought one of his small suitcases, with several changes of underwear for him, a pair of slacks, a woollen roll-neck sweater.

He sat on the bed and took off his cleat-soled boots, to exchange them for the loafers she had brought.

He rolled back, one boot on, one boot off, already fast asleep when his head hit the pillow.

He did not even feel Sally, when she came up an hour later to see what could have happened to him, took off his other boot and tucked him under the blankets.

Yshtak was woken by the clink of a stone upon a stone. He was sleeping in the entrance to the cave, on a ledge overlooking the gorge, wrapped in the wool of a sheep he had killed. The sheep was hanging in the back of the cave; its meat would keep him going for many, many days. Together with the greens he could pick everywhere on the rock-side, the prickly pears he could take from the opuntia below. It all came back, nothing forgotten. Here, in the rocks of the lower mountain, he was at home again, as if in his own village so long ago. Here he could survive until things became quieter in the world outside. And then, slowly, he could decide what he wanted to do, where he wanted to go. In truth, his heart ached to be back in his own mountain village.

That had been his plan, to return to that village once the Allah-cursed Israelis had left. He wanted no part of Palestine, other than his own village. Let Arafat and all the others squabble over it, just so long as he could live out the rest of his life up there in his own mountains, with his own people gathered again around him. Or as many of them as he could find. Joseph Aram had wanted to build an army; Jacques Morel a scientific university. What was it they had said – that they wanted to jerk Palestine forward into the twentieth century? Kostas Aronakis, simple soul like he, Yshtak, had wanted no part of Palestine. Only his blonde, his boat, and his apartment in Monaco. Burgler, more complex. Burgler thought he wanted money, but in reality, he wanted power and an outlet for his inner cruelty, his sadistic urges. And Dupree had wanted – how very strange are the minds of man – an observatory. Fairclough had wanted a stable government, and Frank Elks a satisfactory financial system.

He, Yshtak, must be honest with himself. He had wanted revenge, the most powerful motive of all. The death of a country for the death of a village, and then the chance to live and die in peace. In the village where he was born, his homeland.

His eyes were tuned again to the darkness. A man on the path below him. Leading a goat, or rather pulling a goat along. The goat was reluctant, but the man was skilled, as Yshtak himself had been. The man had the goat by its ear, and was twisting it. He had lashed a loop round its jaws so that the animal could make no noise.

Yshtak smiled to himself. A goat-stealer. In Palestine, in the old times, he had chopped off a man's hands for that. He brought the sheepskin more tightly around his chest. Tomorrow, he would take another, and then make himself a coat.

Now the night had fallen, he could smell the herbs, perspiring after the day's sun, giving out their essential oils. How long it was since he had just sat, on a hill-side at night, drinking in the sweet essences of sage and thyme. He would stay here for six or seven nights within sight of the sea, and then go further up, into these Sfakian mountains. Somewhere up there he would find a hut, or a shelter for sheep, he could make his home. For as long as he needed, he would show them that Yshtak was a patient man.

He climbed swiftly but silently back into the cave, found a small piece of raw sheep's liver, popped it into his mouth, and chewed, feeling the nourishment course through him.

Yes, he would show them.

The man waited until Agonistes had risen, until he had seen the shutters of the restaurant opened. Then he climbed the steps behind the block and tapped on the bedroom window.

After a minute, the curtain opened and Ruth was standing there, wearing only a thin wrap. She held her fingers to her lips to tell him to be silent, then unlocked the window and opened it. He climbed over the sill.

'One day, someone is going to see me coming into your bedroom and they're going to tell Agonistes. When that happens, watch out. He'll have my balls in a vendetta. My grandfather always said to me, "when you return to Crete, as I hope you will one day, watch out for the Sfakians . . . !" Now you've married one.'

He called her by her American name of Ruth, and stroked the side of her face. He was old enough to be her grandfather. He had known her grandfather long long ago, when they lived in the same broken block in the Bronx.

'It's him all right,' he said.

'You're certain?'

'Yes. That Kostas – he never fooled me. All those times, I sat in the corner and watched him and listened to him. But, I tell you this, he can dance . . .'

'And you can play . . .'

'But not, as we'd better tell Agonistes one of these days, with a married woman. You've talked to the Major?'

'Yes, I called him in Athens. He's only waiting for a telegram, from Lemuel.'

'When he arrives, you can confirm, Ruth. I know where he can find that Palestinian polecat . . .'

Ioannis came to the restaurant the following morning at six o'clock. Agonistes had been up half an hour, and was raking the charcoal grill on which he would be cooking later. He saw Ioannis, went and drew him a glass of grassi from the barrel, put it on the counter with a hunk of bread and a few olives.

'Efkaristo,' Ioannis said.

Agonistes did not speak. Ioannis would tell him what he wanted, when he was ready.

Ioannis finished the bread and the olives, drank the wine, wiped his mouth with the back of his hand, took a toothpick from the glass and plied it.

Agonistes got his broom and began to sweep the floor of the restaurant. He liked to have the floor swept before he had his first coffee of the day.

'You know the cave under the two Madonnas?'

'Yes, I know it.'

'Well, I bet you don't know there's another cave, above it, almost at the feet of one of the Madonnas.'

'No, I didn't know that.'

Ioannis always had to tell you something his own way. There was no point in asking him any questions. He must be at least sixty-five, seventy years old, but his eyes were as keen as an eagle's, his ears as sharp as a rat's. All day long in summer he wandered the slopes of the mountains above them. Some said he had been conceived in the mountains – the unkind ones added, with a ewe for a mother – and was restless when winter came, and the mountains were covered in snow. Often he could be seen as a black speck against the snow's mantle, unable to keep away even in the worst weather. Many were the tales of his exploits. How he had carried a sheep on his back all the way down from the peaks above Pachnes, one of the highest points of the Lefka Ori. How he had once raced another Sfakian who had declared his intention of going to see 'the widow', all the way down the Lefka Ori and, so the tale was told, had satisfied the voracious woman four times before the other man staggered into the village.

'Someone is living in that cave,' Ioannis said, as he wandered out of the restaurant.

Agonistes called him back. 'What did you say?'

'Shouldn't have to repeat myself all the time. Someone is living in that cave below the Madonnas, and it isn't Kostas Aronakis.'

'Wait here,' Agonistes said, as he made for the bedroom stairs.

'Why should I wait, if there's no wine?'

'Help yourself. Take one raki. One, do you understand. I want you sober!'

He shook Bill's shoulder gently. Bill came quickly awake and saw Agonistes bending over him, his finger on his lips. He leaped swiftly but silently from the bed and followed Agonistes out of the room. Downstairs Agonistes started to make him a cup of coffee. 'Ioannis has come with a tale about somebody living in a cave above the Gorge of Samaria. He says it isn't Kostas Aronakis.'

'How do you know that?' Bill asked him.

'Kostas has wide shoulders. This man is taller and more meagre in the chest. Like a grape and a raisin, if you know what I mean.'

Bill did know. Yshtak carried no surplus flesh, according to Sally. And ate sparingly. Kostas had a gargantuan appetite, as Sophie had reported.

'But this man, also, is a mountain man. He sits in the angle of the mouth of the cave from where he can see all,

336

and thinks not to be seen himself. I have tracked kri-kri from six kilometres in the mountain. Nothing escapes my eye.' It was not a boast – merely a peasant's simple statement of fact. 'And he wears a sheep skin, scraped on a rock in the mountain way. I could smell it.'

'Can you take me to where I can look at this cave? Without being seen?'

'That depends on you, man of long trousers,' Ioannis said. He was over six feet tall, wearing the outfit of a Sfakian. High black boots and jodphur-like *vrakes*, covered by the *foufoula* of softer cloth that hung in baggy folds from his waist. A vest wrapped around his chest carried a number of buttons and cords for decoration. On his head he wore a black fringed *sariki* tilted jauntily towards one eye. Of immense bulk, Ioannis, as Bill had already seen, could move silently, with speed and grace bred into him by generations of mountain living.

Such men despised all plainsmen as *macropantalonades*, wearers of long trousers.

'I can move quietly, so that only a Sfakian would hear me,' Bill said diplomatically.

'And would not sell me seaweed for a silk ribbon?' Ioannis asked, teasing him. The allusion was too much for Bill's rusty knowledge of classical Greek. Agonistes laughed, and translated it for him. They ate bread, yogurt and honey, drank coffee and raki, 'to keep out the chill', Ioannis explained, his hand on the bottle. 'Better take this with us,' he said, his eyes twinkling mischievously. 'Today, there is much cold.'

Agonistes started his Toyota truck, and drove them over the track to Anapolis, Ioannis sitting dour and uncomfortable in the back, hating the noise of the engine, the bumping, the dust and smell of exhaust.

From Anapolis, he and Bill struck out alone, using tracks Bill could never have found and could hardly see. Ioannis covered the ground with a long shambling stride that seemed to float him along. The morning was warm and the early sun had heat in it. Ioannis seemed to feel neither heat nor cold; Bill had to remind himself that this was the second

337

time the Sfakian had done this journey. They skirted Agh-
ios Ioannis, the village of St John, to the north. 'My name
Saint', Ioannis said. 'Though he's never done anything for
me . . .'

'Perhaps you haven't offered him enough candles . . . ?'
Bill said, thinking the Sfakian too much of a wild man to
be influenced by religion. But he was wrong.

'A man could make a thousand pairs of wings with the
wax I've lavished on that indifferent fellow,' Ioannis said
with deep feeling.

Down the steep cliffs to the river bed below. Up the other
side, every muscle in Bill's legs beginning to pull. The
storm Agonistes had predicted had not come, though the
waves were freshening and, looking out from their height
over the deep blue of the sea, he could find many small
white-caps. Up another steep slope to the top, gasping for
breath, then down again to a second smaller river below.

The Sfakian leaped lightly across it without stopping.
Bill would dearly have loved to sit down, bathe his feet,
wash his forehead, dribble a little of the crystal clear water
around his lips and mouth, but resisted the temptation.
Ioannis looked back approvingly at him. 'Water is good
for sheep and goats,' he said, and offered Bill the bottle of
raki. The raw spirit was more than Bill could take at that
time of morning, but Ioannis put the neck to his mouth
after wiping it delicately, and took a deep pull. He pointed
to the top of the mountain, towering above them. Bill
estimated from the position of the sun that the time was
just after noon. 'Over there,' he said, 'we'll find the two
Madonnas, looking down into the Gorge of Samaria. And
we'll find the raisin man. Go quietly now, *macropantalonades*.
Sound in the mountains soars like an eagle.'

Bill could believe that of the vast stillness around them.
Earlier he had heard the sound of clinking stones and had
been amazed to locate the source half a mile away.

They climbed steadily, following an ancient goat and
sheep path that wound its way inexplicably among the
rocks, always upwards, taking advantage of every twist and
bend to gain a little more height. Every so often, they

338

passed clumps of wild herbs that emitted a pungent odour, one in particular seeming to clear Bill's nose and lungs whenever they came upon it. Now he had his second wind and the climb came easier. Now he was less clumsy, less likely to trip over loose stones and cause them to fall, jingling, down the path. The false summit arrived, revealing another summit half a metre further, across a flat but sloping plain. On one side of the plain was a small hut, built almost into the side of the rock, roofed with stones. The hut had a door of wood, nailed together in separate pieces, the salvage of boxes, crates, driftwood. As they walked across the plain, Bill felt uncomfortable with Ioannis's eyes constantly upon him, an expression of interrogation in them. As if Ioannis were trying to solve some problem.

'This girl who shares your bed, English,' he said. 'I think she is much a woman . . .'

Bill, not offended by his curiosity, couldn't begin to guess how the Sfakian had learned about Sally in such a short time. Though secrets travel like the plague in villages.

'Yes,' he said. 'She is much woman.'

Ioannis stopped. 'Much woman,' he said, pointing back the way they had come.

Bill turned in time to see Sally top the slope behind them.

'You shouldn't have left me behind, Bill,' she said reproachfully. 'Yshtak belongs to me as much as to you.'

'Another *macropantalonades*', Ioannis said, grinning across his face like a split melon. 'Welcome!'

'Welcome,' Bill said, belatedly.

'It is my good fortune to have met you,' Sally said to Ioannis in the elaborate old Cretan courtesy.

He grinned, delighted. 'Come,' he said. 'No more talk!'

He led them into the hut. Inside, one wall had been built out to form a fireplace. The hut was spotlessly clean and even had clean bamboo leaves on the floor. A truckle bed had been built across one side, of bamboo poles.

He held out his hand, palm down. 'You and me, English, together?'

Bill knew it was Ioannis's way of asking for a pledge.

'Yes, Ioannis, together.' He reached out and laid his

hand, palm down, on the Sfakian's wrist. Ioannis twisted his hand, palm upwards, and clasped Bill's wrist from below. It was a bond of fidelity and friendship.

Ioannis unclasped his hand and went to the side of the fireplace. Slowly he worked out one of the stones, and put his hand inside the hole he had revealed. From inside, he drew his old British Army Lee-Enfield rifles, wrapped in the oiled silk the navy used during the last world war. He unwrapped them. Both rifles were in pristine condition. Both had magazines already attached to them; the bolts were even shiny beneath a thin smear of oil. 'If the Turks or the Germans come back,' he said, 'Ioannis is ready for them.'

Bill looked at him admiringly. 'It seems to me,' he said, 'that Ioannis is ready for anything, and anybody!'

Sally had taken one of the rifles, unclipped the magazine, and worked the bolt to eject the round in the breech. She picked up the round and examined it. Then she took the rifle towards the door, reversed it, and put her thumb nail in the breech at an angle, looking through the barrel. 'Clean as a whistle,' she said. She put the round back into the breech, closed the bolt, checked the safety, and clipped the magazine back on.

Ioannis had been watching her. 'Yes, much woman,' he said.

CHAPTER THIRTY

Yshtak had cat-napped during the night, taking time to adjust to the many remembered, but still strange sounds about him, each of which shook him instantly awake. He knew that soon he would learn again to separate the sounds into those with danger, those without. Fully awake by dawn, he squatted again in the entrance to his cave, content to stay without moving, contemplating, waiting. He could see the curling sweep of the gorge to each side of him. Beyond the gorge, to the left, he could see the ocean. On this side, he was sheltered from the direct light of the morning sun, sitting in shadow until the sun came round the shoulder of the rocks. He drew back slightly in his cave, his eyes continually searching the terrain around him. By noon, he knew the position of every sheep and goat within eye-sight, could close his eyes and locate them by hearing only. He could tell, for example, that one sheep on the other side of the gorge, about half a kilometre distant, had somehow caught itself in its rope hobble, and could not move surely without stumbling. The ewes had all been taken to pasture lower down; he heard them being milked shortly after dawn, saw the shepherd with his donkey, leading another carrying a burden of tins containing the ewe's milk. They would be heading for the 'factory', where several shepherds would gather to spend the morning starting the ewe's milk cheese. He could remember the taste of the cheese they had made in his own village.

Another shepherd came down the edge of the mountain above him, with a small herd, moving down to lower pasture. The winter would soon come. Already, an experienced mountain man such as he was once, and soon would be again, could smell the cold tang in the air. Though the sun was still warm to grateful, ageing bones .... He huddled the sheep's skin more closely about him, his fingers endlessly working in the leather, keeping it soft and supple. He felt neither hunger nor thirst; he had never permitted himself to acquire the bad eating and drinking habits of non-mountain men who lined their bodies with useless fat.

He heard the first shot at about one o'clock.

His eyes swivelled in the direction of the source of the sound as it rolled around the hills, and caught the flash of a rifle barrel, saw the wreck of the bird fluttering out of the sky. Why not? Partridge makes good eating.

Another shot two minutes later, and then silence.

The hunter was away on the other side of the gorge, to the north. After ten minutes, Yshtak saw him working his way downwards across the rocks and the pine tree scrub, the carobs, the olives growing too high for fruit.

Yshtak settled back, relaxed again.

341

A clink on the rocks above the curiously shaped natural formation. Sheep or goat? Stone on stone, anyway.

He moved slowly to the other side of the cave mouth, from where he could see the almost imperceptible path that led down from above.

A slight noise in the cave behind him? How was that possible? He turned, saw a ray of light against the back wall of the cave where a stone had moved. He moved rapidly into the cave like a cat and stood behind the moving stone. A figure, dressed in black, came through the opening. Carrying a large knife.

Yshtak glanced back at the mouth of the cave. The sheepskin still lay where he had thrown it off; from here, it could seem as if a man were inside it. The man in black, whose clothing Yshtak recognized as that of the mountain men, the Sfakians, moved like a panther across the floor of the cave.

Yshtak followed him.

The Sfakian leaped from four yards away, knife held back, and swung a blow inwards and upwards. The knife pierced the sheepskin and moved with it, clogging the movement of his hand. Thrown off balance by the lack of resistance to his stabbing blow, he staggered forward; Yshtak moved quickly behind him, his foot lifted, and pushed violently and with all his strength. Already off balance, Ioannis could not help himself. The heave threw him forward, staggering on short steps, trying desperately to regain his balance but then, with a long, agonized moan, he fell sheer over the edge of the rock face.

The rifle bullet whipped past Yshtak's cheek, drawing blood. He turned right, and ran three paces; a rifle bullet from somewhere in front of him pulled at his shoulder.

He went quickly back round a bend of rock, rested for a moment to think. He touched his cheek, and his hand came away wet with blood.

'We have you trapped,' Sally Price said. 'We have you, Yshtak. Come out with your hands behind your neck and, with luck, we'll let you stay alive. Though feeling the way I do, I can't make any promises.'

Yshtak barely listened to her. He was studying the ground with his experienced mountain eye, knowing they would be no match for him, once he got away from this short stretch of path where they had pinned him down.

He heard the man's voice. 'Come out, Yshtak, or we'll come in.' As if to reinforce his words, the man fired his rifle. The bullet ricocheted among the rocks, whining away down the mountainside like an angry bee. 'Keep away,' he growled. 'I, too, have a gun.' They could only be two or they would not have fired, but stormed his position, with other people giving them covering fire. He lay down and crawled to the end of the path, just before the rock around which the shot had whipped so near his shoulder. His keen eyes had seen the start of a path, going upwards, in a shallow gully. He looked up and studied it. Zig-zag all the way. There was a small stand of pines about fifty metres along it. If he could make the pines . . .

'Go in, Bill,' Sally's voice said. 'I'll keep you covered.'

Yshtak took a breath, deep, then sprang upwards like a cougar, landing with his feet straddling the small stone-strewn path on two thyme bushes he knew would deaden the sound. He continued upwards silently, placing his feet with infinite cunning where they would start no stone slides.

He heard the man below advancing along the track he had left, at right angles to his one. He could not see him; the man, wisely, was hugging the side of the rocks, moving well.

Yshtak went further upwards, leaned inwards, paused. The final leg towards the pine stand was over rock carved by the sun and rain of ages. The stones were smooth but he, Yshtak, would find footholds easily up the steep slope. He rested his fingers lightly on the first almost invisible ledge for his foot, braced, and lifted.

Here on this blind rock face he was in greatest danger, exposed should the two below move to the edge of the path, looking over the top edge of the rocks there. He swung, found another foothold, lifted, swung again, the technique coming back to him as if it were only yesterday he had gone up Tatouli, which had risen sheer from his village. He was bleeding still, copiously, his blood dripping from him, but that was no matter. A man could lose much blood and still survive. And then, when the shadows lengthened, he would turn the tables on them, go back down and hunt them, as they, with the Sfakian, had hunted him. In the last second, before the tall man went over the edge, he had recognized him as the goat-stealer of the previous night. So, on his first night out, Yshtak had made some small error, permitting himself to be seen and identified. The goat-stealer must have gone to the village and brought these two with him, doubtless seeking a bounty on Yshtak's head. Well, the goat-stealer had gone the way of all thieves, and he, Yshtak, would deal with these two when darkness began to fall, and lengthening shadows played tricks with the imagination.

One more stride, to the top, one more footstep, and then, safety. He pressed upwards with his knee.

His head rose level with the top of the rock.

A man was lying there, with a pistol in his hand.

The pistol was pointing directly at Yshtak's mouth.

Sally and Bill met outside the cave. Quick check inside. No Yshtak. 'He couldn't have come my way,' Bill said. 'It was solid rock.'

'He didn't come past me,' Sally replied.

They started to go back the way Sally had come looking for an escape track. Bill suddenly held up his hands. Both of them heard the sound of scrabbling over the edge. They bent down and cautiously looked over. Two feet below them, Ioannis, his face covered in blood, his clothing torn, one arm hanging useless at his side, was inching his terrible way upwards, pain etched in every line of his grey face. He was muttering silently to himself, seemed unaware of them. They each put an arm down, grasped him beneath his shoulders and lifted him.

'I fell into a tree,' he said, resting his head back, looking upwards. Then he struggled upright. 'Give me your rifle,' he said to Sally, almost wrenching it from her. They looked

where he had looked, and saw the outline of Yshtak against
the rock slope above. He appeared to be just standing there.
Sally gave Ioannis the rifle. He limped and hobbled to the
rock, threw his rifle across it with his one good arm, and
took aim along the sights.

'You don't know me, Yshtak,' the man with the pistol said.
'My name is Moishe. Ben Moishe. That's right. I am a
Jew. An Israeli Jew. A *sabra*. I bring you a gift from all
the *sabras*, Yshtak. The gift of a quick and easy death.'

The pistol and the rifle shot sounded simultaneously.
The pistol shot jerked Yshtak's body from the rock face.
The rifle shot slammed him back again. Yshtak began to
slide. One after the other, Ioannis put three bullets into
the tumbling figure, working the bolt each time with his
one useful hand, before taking rapid aim again.

Yshtak's body tumbled down, sliding face against the
rock, leaving a bloody trail behind it. Then, at the very lip,
his feet caught against the shallow outcrop. His body arched
backwards, and he did an almost perfect swallow dive into
the gorge below, where there was no tree to break his fall,
no sound, no requiem but the echo of the shots around the
mountain-side of the Lefka Ori, and the age old Gorge of
Samaria.

Bill put his arm round Sally's waist briefly, then they
went to tend the Sfakian. His arm had been broken by
his fall into the tree. The lacerations and scratches were
superficial. He would live. He used his good hand to
open his pack and from it took the broken neck of the
bottle of raki.

'That devil,' he said. 'He made me break my bottle.
Now we'll have to go all the way down to Chora Sfakion
to get another. But you,' he said to Sally, 'you, who are
much woman, may have to hold my hand a little before
we get there. *Macropantalonades*, here, can lead the way . . .'

Bill laughed. 'And while we are going down, Ioannis,
you can keep us awake by telling us what you were stealing,
here in the Lefka Ori, at the dead of night. Was it a sheep,
a goat, or another man's wife . . . ?'

345